CW01497903

Copyright © 2021 by J.D.L. Rosell

Illustration © 2021 by René Aigner
Book design by J.D.L. Rosell
Maps by Kaitlyn Clark

Published by Rune & Requiem Press
runeandrequiempress.com

ECHOES OF CHAOS

THE FAMINE CYCLE: BOOK TWO

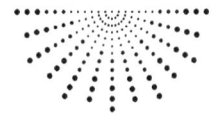

J.D.L. ROSELL

RUNE & REQUIEM PRESS

CONTENTS

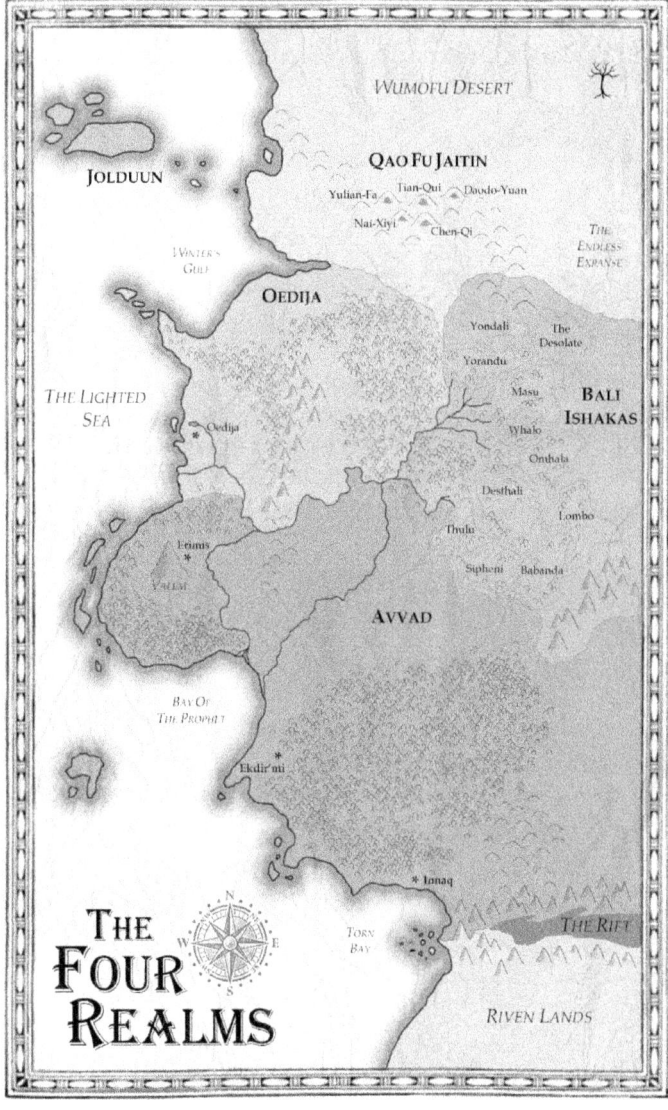

WUMOFU DESERT

JOLDUUN

QAO FU JAITIN

Yulian-Fa   Tian-Qui   Daodo-Yuan

Nai-Xiyi   Chen-Qi

WINTER'S GULF

THE ENDLESS EXPANSE

OEDIJA

Yondali   The Desolate

Yorandu

THE LIGHTED SEA

Masu   BALI ISHAKAS

Oedija

Whalo

Onthala

Desthali

Lombo

Eramis

Thulu

VALLAT

Sipheni   Babanda

AVVAD

BAY OF THE PROPHET

Ekdir'nti

Innaq

THE FOUR FOUR REALMS

N
W   E
S

TORN BAY

THE RIFT

RIVEN LANDS

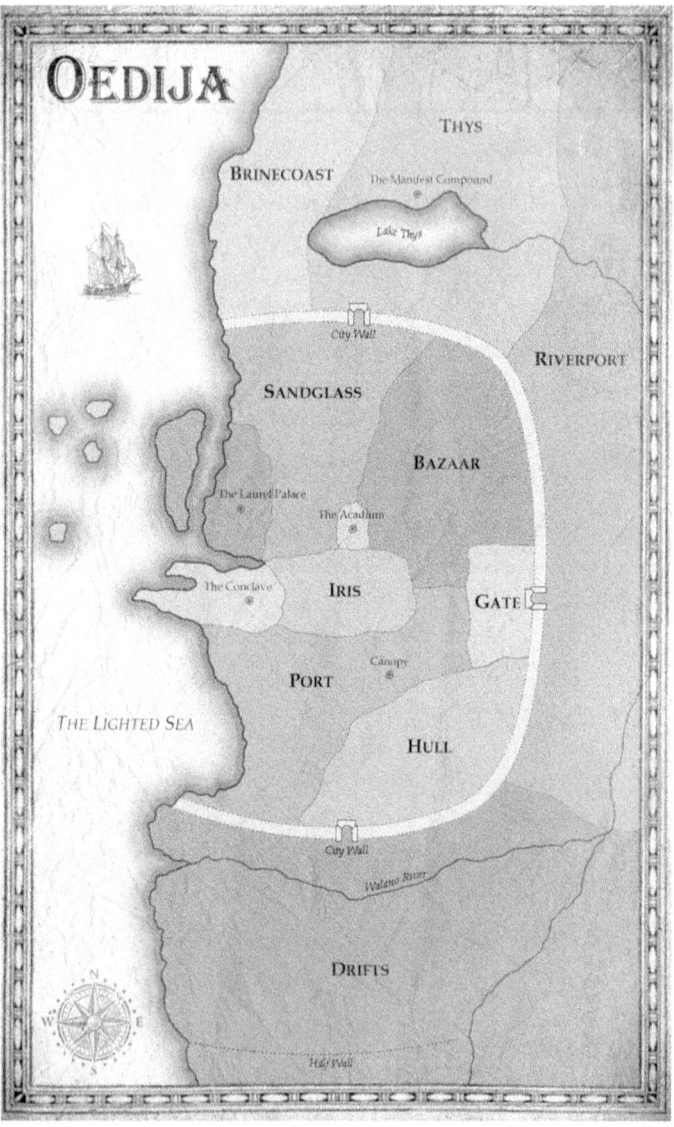

PROLOGUE

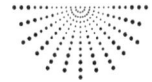

He watched the great serpent coil tighter around the ailing man.

Azhi had long grown used to waiting. Perhaps he'd been a boy when he died, but two centuries had turned his mind ancient beyond any elder. Patience was the measure of his existence, more constant than the flow of time, more persistent than a cancer.

But the time for waiting was coming to an end.

The serpent twitched for a moment, then turned toward him. Azhi kept miles between them, but as the beast's eye turned on him, fear carved into his core. The leviathan was black as a moonless midnight, black as an endless chasm. Black as a hunger that could never be sated.

He shivered and turned away. The Corrupted couldn't reach him, not while he was still bound. But his bonds were fraying. Taozu had never been contained for so long by a man — nor could he have been, if not by his own choice. When the moment came for him to break free, Azhi had no doubt it would also be of his choosing.

Changing his form into force, Azhi flew back over the city. Oedija was mirrored above and below him, the towers of the Laurel Palace stretching toward each other. Only the Pillars touched, and these melded together, crossing the boundaries of the higher, lower, and material planes.

As Taozu reemerged, these cities would shift, changing to suit the great serpent. But only if he remained uncontested.

Azhi had learned many lessons in the Wumofu during his childhood long, long ago. *When the serpent coils,* his father had said, *back away. It has claimed that sand for itself.*

So Azhi would move far away, and leave Oedija's defenses to the last god to claim it. But only so he could bring back that which could seal Taozu once more.

Azhi flew up into the city hanging above, keeping within Oedija's walls. He swept through the streets, searching amid the shadowed forms for the spark that he had started. For the man who had grown to trust him through his constant guidance and companionship.

He found him curled up in the churned mud of an alley, head bowed, hiding his tears and shame. His headwrap had unwound slightly, letting loose thin, brown hair in tufts. His body was spare, but lithe. A man still in possession of his strength, even if he did not know it. A man far from his end.

Ascending again and leaving the man behind, Azhi broke through the illusion of the city and arced through the cloudy emptiness above it. When he descended, he found himself in a tower. Birds flew below him in the rafters, and a woman, bent with age but still moving with vigor, fed one from her hand.

As he entered, her keen, golden eyes found him. The smile she'd shared with the finch transformed into a scowl.

"You need her again?" she scoffed. She spoke, but it was the reverberations of her thoughts that sounded clear in his mind.

Yes.

"Fine. But mind you take care of her."

Azhi drifted down to where the bird waited. She watched

him approach, her blue crest seeming to glow brighter as he neared.

Then, as gently as the woman held her own bird, Azhi coaxed the whisper finch to admit him.

The world lurched, then righted itself. Abruptly, Azhi found himself clutching wood with clawed feet. He twitched a wing, then the other, cocked his head, and blinked.

"You'd think you'd be used to it," the woman called from below.

Azhi flapped his wings experimentally, then threw himself off and glided down. He flew once around the woman, then settled on a window sill. The window was boarded up but had a gap just large enough for a small bird to pass through.

"He's breaking free," Azhi said, his voice coming out as a boy's. Always, it was startling to hear it unchanged from the twelve years he had been when he died.

"We always knew he would."

"I shall have to leave soon. Now you must be the watcher."

"So I have always been. Where do you go?"

Azhi turned his bird's head out the window and glimpsed gray sky outside. "To where hope rests."

The woman snorted and released the finch. "Hope. Does it still exist? But never mind. Dead or not, we'll still try." She waved a hand. "Go. But bring my bird back whole."

Azhi just cocked his avian head, then turned and leaped from the window.

As he flew over the city, the wind lifted his light body, sending it far aloft. Chill as it was with the coming monsoons, the whisper finch wasn't bothered. This was what it had been made for.

As he neared the wall, he turned and dove, heading for the familiar alley. Breaking his dive short as he drew close, he flapped his wings and settled on the roof above the man.

He'd stopped sobbing now and rested his head against the wall behind him.

His eyes turned up, then widened as he saw the whisper finch's glowing crest. "You again," he whispered.

"Hello, Eazal. My friend."

The man didn't smile, but only bowed his head again. "Why don't you leave me alone? I want to be alone."

Azhi considered him for a long moment. Perhaps he was wrong. Perhaps he was too broken for this task. But he had to make use of what tools he had.

"But did you think Valem Branded you for nothing?" he suggested softly. "Did you think he held no purpose for you?"

Eazal threw his head back and laughed, the sound sharp and devoid of mirth. "Oh, I know Valem's purpose for me, or at least those who claim him. I failed in that as well."

"You have not served it yet," Azhi soothed. "But first, we must keep you alive. Come; follow me. I will lead you from the city. Then I will show you what you were meant to do."

The man turned his head back to Azhi, eyes narrowed, mouth drawn. "Why should I care?" he asked, the words choked. "I've failed them. Over and over, I've failed them. How could I ever do enough?"

Azhi knew to whom he referred. "You could save them, and this city, and the whole of the Four Realms. But you must trust me. I saved you once, on the cliff. Do you remember?"

"Yes. And I've lived to regret it."

"But you lived, and you have time to right those regrets. Come, Eazal. Your purpose doesn't end here. You're destined for something greater."

Though his connection to the Pyrthae was tenuous, Azhi felt a glimmer of a sensation at his words, as if someone had smiled in approval. He ignored it, and ignored, too, the shiver that ran through his bird's body.

Eazal slowly rose to his feet and looked at him. "I don't

believe you. I don't think I'm meant for anything. But... I don't know what else to do."

Azhi flew forward and alighted on his shoulder. "Then come," he whispered in the man's ear. "I will show you the path."

1
TRUTH IN DREAMS

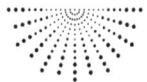

From the Lower Realm of the world beyond ours, a Seed rose. It was a small thing, no larger than a pebble, and none noticed its passing as it lifted higher and higher, until it reached the Higher Realm where our gods, the Eidola, reign.

Tyurn Sky-Sea, Ruler of All Realms, Lord of All, was strong in arm and limb. He was master of the stormy sea and the violent sky and could be harmed by neither. But his quintessence was fallible, the fabric of his mind loosely woven, and his actions had ever been erratic.

The Seed, upon arriving in the Higher Realm, sensed this weakness in the Foremost of Gods and sought to exploit it. Creeping in as Tyurn Sky-Sea slept, it fed him dreams of glory and plenty and filled him with pride, slowly whittling his mind to its own purpose.

- The Seeds of Famine, a translation from the Lighted-tongue; by Oracle Kalene of deme Hull; 881 SLP

I drifted between dreams.

From one scene to another, I was swept along, each

image as devoid of meaning as the next. I watched, unable to do anything, unwilling to even if I could.

A man, broad in stature, with thick gray hair just beginning to bald, sat hunched in a cell, knees drawn up to his chest. Fallen from grace, he seemed, a different person than the one he was supposed to be.

A gust of wind whipped the man into sand, and another took his place. This man was clad in a tattered robe that looked to have once been white. He swayed as he walked into a shadowed room, then sunk to his knees on a worn reed mat. His eyes, dark as the heart of a monsoon storm, told of pain. Yet though the shaft of a quarrel was lodged in his side, it didn't seem the source of his torment.

Another turn — now a gray woman, eyes preternaturally wide, smile twisted and bitter, gazed down on me as she floated above the ruins of a city.

Another turn — now the face of a boy, still as snow on a distant mountain peak, stared up from a bed. Phantoms moved in a haze around him, but he didn't notice. He had eyes for nothing but what he saw above. I felt I must lay next to him, and as I did, I lifted my gaze to see what he saw.

The great maw, an endless abyss lined with long, sharp teeth, descended. It didn't come quickly, yet I couldn't move to escape. I grasped the boy's hand as slowly, inexorably, the jaws closed over us—

I sat up, gasping. Darkness blinded me. For a moment, still caught halfway in the dream, I thought myself in the terrible beast's mouth. Then I felt a bed beneath me, and the thick covers that had fallen away as I sat up. My skin, sticky with sweat, grew rough with chills as the cool air washed over me.

Night. I was in a bed, unclothed, and it was night. No beast had hold of me. I was safe.

Wasn't I?

"Airene?" An accented voice, drowsy with sleep, spoke from the darkness next to me.

I flinched, as much from recognition as surprise. "Corin?"

In the darkness, barely lifted by the faint light from the windows across the room, I heard her movements rather than saw them: the rustling of clothes, the creaking of a chair. "Yes," she said. "I am here."

"Here?"

"The Laurel Palace."

I clutched the blankets closer. Memories from what seemed a long time ago assaulted me, one after another. Despite the covers, the chill seeped in deeper. My teeth began to chatter.

"Are you well?" Another creak of the chair as she rose.

"Yes," I said quickly. "I'm fine. Just caught a chill, nothing more."

Corin made a sound that might have been agreement or doubt, then the chair creaked as she sat. I stared at her outlined figure until I was sure she was settled, then eased myself back down.

"What happened?" I asked quietly.

Another protest from the chair as she shifted. But Corin gave no answer.

My heart thumped harder at her silence. "Did you... see me? See what I did?"

"Yes."

I thought it must have been a dream. What I imagined that I remembered was impossible. Or if not impossible, then so unlikely and rare that it could only be called that.

"Are you sure? Perhaps a candle spilled. Perhaps it was something that Eazal did—"

"No. It was you, Airene. I saw."

I shrank away from her words. The cold struck deep through me once again. *It can't be*, I told myself again. *It can't be true.*

I couldn't have channeled.

But I didn't challenge Corin. Though the events afterward were hazy, I recalled all too clearly the moment it had happened. It had felt like a completion, a sating of a desire I'd never known I had. A warming of cold parts of me I hadn't known were frozen. I remembered the opening to it, the drawing of it, and the expulsion, all occurring so naturally that it had seemed impossible for it to be the first time.

But I recalled, too, the fire burning and scorching as it swept over me. Yet as I ran my hands over myself, I didn't feel raw flesh or angry boils but smooth, unbroken skin. I sat back again. If I'd imagined that part, how much of the rest did I misremember?

"The Archon visited you," Corin spoke again. "While you slept."

I couldn't think about Jaxas at the moment. Not with everything else I had on my mind. "What about Xaron and Nomusa? And Talan?"

"Yes. They have come often, though the Guilder only once."

I took a steadying breath. If my memories didn't lie, and if I were found out, everything I had worked for, everything I strived to do, would be compromised. My very life could be forfeit.

So why did I feel giddy with anticipation?

I'm a warden.

I held the words in my mind. It was too strange a thought to believe. For Xaron and Talan, it was natural to call them wardens — it was who they were. But me? It couldn't possibly apply to me.

I'm a warden.

I'd channeled fire and force. Radiance and kinesis. I'd nearly burned a building down. Unless it was the most vivid dream I'd yet had, it was true. And Corin claimed to have seen it as well. Burns or no, it was true.

I was a warden.

A sudden vertigo swept over me. I felt as if I couldn't take a proper breath. But with Corin present, I fought back for control. With each breath, I slowed my pulse. Yet other memories from before I'd channeled intruded, quickening it again.

Corin had betrayed me. She'd lied to lure me into a house in Sandglass. She'd served me up to the whims of the Valemish. True, she'd confessed at the last moment, and warned me of what waited within. But it didn't change that I'd been forced to enter and face down my would-be assassin. Even with her warning, even with Eazal's obvious reluctance for his task, I'd have died if my attunement hadn't manifested at that moment.

Caustic words burned on my tongue, but I held them back. She'd done it for her sister. Even if she'd been a daemon-struck fool to put her sister's life in the hands of the Valemish, I understood why Corin had acted as she had. But understanding didn't fix what had broken. Trust couldn't mend in a day. If it ever could.

I broke the long silence. "Where are they now, Xaron and Nomusa?"

"Xaron is Hilarion." Corin shrugged, barely visible in the darkness. "He follows the Archon and the Despoina."

"I'm sure he's pleased about that." I smiled at the thought of Xaron in the jester's sackcloth clothes. It didn't seem every Hilarion wore them, but I hoped Xaron would be forced to put them on. His sensibilities of fashion would be driven mad. But more importantly, Xaron being Hilarion meant he was safe from the Shepherds. Though I wasn't sure how many Shepherds remained within Tribunal control now.

"And Nomusa?"

"We… do not speak."

A wry grin found my lips. At least that much hadn't changed. "She's visited though?"

"Everyday."

Everyday. Only then did I realize I'd overlooked a critical fact. "This isn't the same night as Despoina Asileia's trial, is it?"

"No. It's the third night."

I lay still. *Three days.* I'd lost three days. Who knew what changes had come over Oedija. How much Vusu had recovered his strength.

How much Famine had gained in power.

I sat up again. "I need clothes."

"Why?" Corin sounded alarmed. "It is night. Time for rest."

"There's no time to lie around. Where are my clothes, Corin?"

"Airene." Corin had stood, but hadn't moved toward me. "You've lain as if dead for three days. You've had little more than broth. You need rest."

Ignoring her, I swung my legs out from under the covers. A fire had lit inside me. Weakness wasn't going to put me off, nor any shame of nakedness. "If you won't bring me clothes, I'll get them myself."

I stood, or tried to. The ground lurched, sending me tumbling, and I fell hard on my hands and knees. As I tried to rise, something wrenched in my gut. I found myself heaving, little more than a dribble coming up.

Corin was helping me up a moment later, and I didn't resist as she settled me back into the bed. "You need to rest," she said again, reprimand in her voice.

I was suddenly too weary to respond. My seizing gut had woken a terrible ache that made me want to curl up into myself. "Is there more broth?" I asked, stopping just short of mewling. "I'm starving."

"I'll see if there is some in the kitchens. But only if you stay here."

I nodded against the pillow. "Yes. I will."

Corin paused a moment longer, not seeming to trust my word. But she left the room all the same. The door creaked as she pulled it closed, then there was a small clatter as she turned a key. I pressed my lips together, considering. Whether she'd locked it to ensure that I stayed or to protect me from those without, I couldn't say.

The thoughts that had wracked me now seemed too vast to consider. Sleep crept up at the edges of my mind. I didn't resist. Before Corin had returned, I fell free from the world once more.

I woke a second time to sunlight creeping in through the windows. Groaning and stretching, I gazed blearily around the room. Corin didn't stir from the chair where she sat, head lolling against the wall. She couldn't be comfortable, yet I saw no signs that she'd sought to make the situation more bearable. On a table beside the bed sat a bowl of broth, fat congealed over the surface.

Hunger suddenly assaulted me so that my hands shook as I seized the bowl and began to quickly spoon the cool broth down.

My noisy eating woke Corin. She said nothing as she cracked open an eye and saw me bent over the bowl. A faint smile crossed her face. "You're awake."

"Mhm." I didn't pause eating but carved out the fat by the spoonful. It filmed my throat as it went down, but starved as I was, I didn't mind.

She rose and stretched with a yawn. "Your visitors will likely come soon. You wish to dress?"

I nodded and set the bowl aside as I finished. "And maybe have some more food," I said hopefully. "Something solid. I think I can hold it down now."

Corin complied, moving lethargically across the room to

bring me a chiton and underwraps from the dressing closet. As I took the clothes, she turned to the door and unlocked it.

"Corin," I said to her back. "Thanks."

She turned around and gave me a weak smile. I returned it as best as I could. Perhaps things between us couldn't return to being the same. But I hoped they would. Corin had always been the steady rock in Canopy. I felt slightly unmoored without being able to rely on her.

Corin left, and I stood to dress. My body still felt tired and trembling, but when I eased onto my legs, they held. I marveled at the weakness that made standing an accomplishment.

Corin hadn't returned by the time I finished dressing, nor anyone else arrived. My mind began to wander. I checked my skin for burns and confirmed what I'd suspected: not a blemish marked my body. I shook my head in disbelief and resolved to ask Corin if I'd had any wounds when she'd taken me from the house. I could wonder more over the mystery once I knew more.

I lowered myself back onto the bed and examined my fingertips. The skin seemed as it had before. No matter how I searched, I didn't see any sign of movement on the prints there.

I lowered my hands and tried to keep the panic at bay. Perhaps one's shifts didn't appear immediately. Perhaps it took channeling at least twice before they showed. But now, I couldn't help but wonder if Corin and I hadn't both imagined it. Maybe I wasn't attuned.

Maybe I wasn't a warden.

No. I wouldn't accept that. I would prove what I knew myself to be. Because, though I'd rarely allowed myself to admit it, I'd always wished to understand what Xaron and Talan felt when they channeled. I wanted the power of the Pyrthae at my fingertips, achingly so.

Unwilling to give in, I closed my eyes and tried to channel. I dredged up the vague memories of that first occasion four days before, and even dimmer remembrances from how Xaron and wardens in my books had described the experience. The locus, located at the center of the body around the navel, was where the link was supposed to form. But no matter how I concentrated on the spot, no matter how I clenched my gut or gritted my teeth, I couldn't open any such connection.

Relaxing my muscles, I sagged forward. When I'd channeled the first time, the energy had pushed out without any effort on my part. Why were things different now?

I left off the attempts and lay back down on my bed. My head hurt, and the queasiness had returned with a vengeance. I sighed and let myself go limp. Sleep edged against my awareness.

Three soft knocks came at the door.

I bolted back upright and stared toward the entryway. My heart thundered in my chest, and fear made chicken-flesh of my skin. I hadn't realized how badly recent events had shaken me. In that moment of mute terror, I'd expected that knock to signal Shepherds calling at the door.

The knock came again. "Airene?" a muffled voice spoke through. "Corin said you were awake. We thought we'd come check on you."

Xaron. I exhaled in relief as I recognized his voice. "Come in," I called, hating the way my words warbled.

A key turned in the lock, and the door swung slowly open. Xaron entered first, tiptoeing as if fearing to intrude. He looked much the same as before, with sharp, handsome features and narrow, brown eyes that darted about nervously. But there was one significant change. Gone were the colorful coats and trousers he'd always worn, replaced now by a long, drab tunic of coarse sackcloth, belted together by a short length of rope. His sandals, too, were lashed to his feet with rope that must chafe, and his dark, silken hair was bound back by a piece of twine thread with dried corn husk, a crown fit for a jester. He donned a grin at my smile, though no doubt he knew what made me laugh.

"It's good to see you up," he said as he approached.

Before I could answer, another familiar figure entered behind him. Jaxas Wreath was as thin as before, his face hollowed, and his dark eyes nearly lost in shadows. The Archon's spare frame shrunk into the opulent robes and heavy stoles that hung about his neck. Of the two of us, he looked the likelier candidate to have barely eaten in the last three days. Yet I knew that hidden within him was a strength of mind as I'd never seen before.

"First Verifier Airene." A ghost of a smile lightened the formal words. "Are you feeling better?"

I bowed my head, the most respectful acknowledgment I could manage. "I can stand for a minute or two and am hungry enough for a feast." I cocked a smile. "I'd say I'm on the mend."

The Archon returned a wan smile of his own as he entered further into the room. He kept his distance, as if fearing I might pass ill humors to him. "The hunger is to be expected. You've been unconscious for several days."

I met Jaxas's sharp gaze and wondered uncomfortably how much he knew about my bout of illness. I remembered all too well how he'd turned Talan aside for being a warden. Xaron had been forced to become the new Hilarion in order to stay around. If I were in the same situation, I doubted he could devise a similar arrangement. I certainly couldn't be kept as First Verifier.

Xaron, who had kneeled by my bedside, took my hands in his. "I would have been here," he said gravely. "But a certain taskmaster has kept me very busy."

"I've asked you to tumble once," Jaxas said with an amused twist to his lips. "But I'm afraid I must ask another favor. If you could give us the room for a moment, I would have a private word with Airene."

Xaron's expression spasmed, but he nodded sharply and rose. "Of course. I'll be right outside."

With a perfunctory bow to the Archon, he turned out of the door and closed it behind.

Jaxas moved no closer. "It must be quite the malady to have rendered you unconscious for nearly three full days. Do you remember what happened?"

I studied his face, which had creased with seeming concern. Did he honestly believe me sick? Or was he giving me a convenient excuse? Or was it the terrible third possibility: that he knew the truth, and handed me the rope to hang myself? Why I felt Jaxas might wish to trap me, I couldn't say. I had plotted with him to take down Vusu. But even so, I'd only known the man for a handful of days. Anything might have happened in the days I'd lain unconscious.

But as long as he didn't speak of my channeling, I had no intentions of mentioning it.

"Not much," I said. "Everything is a bit blurry. But Corin has been able to help fill things in."

One thin eyebrow raised high. "Indeed. And yet she was so forgetful when I asked her of it."

I repressed the need to swallow. This wasn't what I wanted to be doing right now. My stomach felt as if it ate itself with my hunger. Had he come to interrogate me now because he knew I was vulnerable? No matter how I wished to see the best of Jaxas, ruthlessness was bred into him. He had acted as my benefactor, but even still, he was a Wreath through and through.

"It was a confusing time for us all," I said carefully. "And she didn't have the complete picture."

Jaxas inclined his head. "Of course. Perhaps you can fill in the gaps for me as well."

I considered refusing. After all, even though he boarded

me in the Laurel Palace, I didn't have to report to him anymore. It was to the Conclave that Nomusa and I now owed our allegiance, so long as they reinstated the Order of Verifiers. But Jaxas had given us Finches a chance when few others would. Even if it had been Vusu's machinations that first brought us to his employ, I owed Jaxas much.

So I spoke what I could: a lie laced with truth. I said that Corin had brought me to help Maesos, who had been robbed and injured. I said that Maesos wasn't there when I arrived, and instead, someone who meant to kill me lay waiting. Of Corin's betrayal, I mentioned nothing, nor of what happened after the encounter with Eazal.

Jaxas barely blinked through the telling. "I see," he said as I finished. "And what of the fire?"

My mouth went dry. "Fire?"

"It must have been a deep slumber you fell into. For you had burns up and down your body not three days ago."

It had become hard to breathe. I wondered if I should admit the truth now. But as the words formed on my lips, an idea came to mind. I jumped at it, no matter how unbelievable it seemed.

"Yes, I've been puzzled by that since Corin told me," I said, wrinkling my brow. "The only thing I can think of was my trip into the Pyrthae. With so few people having gone there, it makes sense we wouldn't know what happens when they do visit. Maybe it healed me."

"Ah." His even tone betrayed no sign of what he thought of my theory.

"But if something strange had to happen to me," I hurried on, "I'm glad it was healing. I have a feeling that a lot of work lies ahead."

"Yes. I think the Council will keep you busy."

Something in his tone struck me as curious. Before I could speculate, Jaxas suddenly slumped into a chair. I watched in surprise as the Archon put his head in his hands and rubbed at his eyes.

"This is too exhausting," he said, his words muffled by his hands. "I'm sorry, Airene. I didn't come here to pitch barbed questions. These past three days… I almost envy you being able to sleep them away."

Guilt flickered in me. "Regardless of what happened, you should take care of yourself. You look even thinner than before."

He looked up with a smile twisted on his lips. "An accurate observation, if lacking your usual tactfulness. But your concerns should not lie with me. I fear we've only slowed Vusu and his Seekers. And if you can believe it, the Manifest is the least of my worries." He held my gaze. "Avvad marches north."

Only then did I remember the horns. They'd called as if in a dream, two long blows from the shell horns mounted atop the Laurel Palace. One signaled a fire spreading in the city; three the death of the reigning Wreath.

Two were called for war.

"Avvad marches north," I repeated. Many variations of those words had been uttered before, but always as an eventuality. Not something that would ever happen in our lifetimes. It was like a boulder positioned above that we'd said would never fall, but now barreled down upon us.

"Birds arrived the day of the trial, telling of the gathering of their troops from the southern provinces and the marshaling of their resources. The object of their conquest is all too clear from our spies' reports. They are still several spans from even setting march toward us, but I convinced Low Consul Daelya that we should sound the horns as soon as possible, to prepare the people for what is to come."

Several spans to gather and prepare, then several more to march. I had little experience with armies, but I knew it took time and resources to move that many soldiers. "They'll be here by the first of the monsoons," I guessed.

Jaxas smiled wryly. "And I hope their troops feel the brunt of what the rains have to offer. So long as drought doesn't steal them away."

We sat quietly, contemplating all that this meant. One thing hung between us unsaid. Even if the Manifest did not threaten us from the north, Oedija couldn't withstand the might of the Avvadin Imperium.

"Why?" I muttered, almost to myself. "Why now?"

"You know as well as I do." He sank back against his elbows. "We are vulnerable. Our trade is weak and unprofitable. And Leia has insulted the Kahin-Shah on numerous occasions. But truthfully, it is mostly because Burak Aasjuqal is a conqueror. Ever since he took the imperial reins twelve years ago, he has cast a greedy eye north, seeking to claim the Pearl of the Four Realms."

But my thoughts had turned in another direction. "But the Kahin-Shah isn't our primary concern. He can't be. Don't tell me you've forgotten."

Jaxas stared at his hands for a long moment. "I haven't forgotten," he murmured. "Nor will I. But what can I do, Airene? What can any of us do against such a force? Against… a god, or whatever he is?"

His despair only served to strengthen my resolve. "Whatever is in our power. Famine must be stopped. No cost will be too great, no price higher than the one he'll extract."

"No cost too great." The Archon shook his head. "You say that now. But will you still believe it when the time comes for the sacrifice?"

Before I could respond, Jaxas rose. "I'm afraid I have many things to be about. But I'm sure I'll see you up and walking soon."

With his imminent departure, a nagging thought became urgent. "Jaxas, my family — do you know if anything has happened to them? Vusu threatened them before the trial. I think he might retaliate."

"You need not fear that. I sent them to one of the provincial Wreath estates as soon after the trial as I could. Your mother didn't go easily, but wine, good food, and care for your father convinced her in the end."

I couldn't help a bemused smile. "That sounds like my mother. Thank you. It's far more generous than I deserve."

Jaxas didn't return the smile. "I cannot pretend I did it only for your peace of mind. To have you compromised by threats against your family would be... untenable."

My smile slipped. I should have expected nothing less of a Wreath. "I understand. Whatever the reason, I'm glad they're safe."

The Archon nodded and turned away. "Come see me when you're up. Though once you talk with Nomusa, I'm sure you'll have even less occasion to than before."

I wondered at that. "I know we won't report to you anymore, Jaxas. But I hope we'll continue to work together."

"With so few eyes on the true enemy, we'd be fools not to."

Unsmiling, he turned and swept from the room.

A moment later, Xaron slipped back in. He wore a happy grin that, paired with his clothes, should have made me laugh. But my thoughts were so heavy that not even the sight of him as Hilarion could lift them.

"Oh, cheer up," he said as he sat on the bed next to me. "He's gone now. No need for the long face."

I tried for levity. "That's not what has me down. I was just thinking how sorry I am that you're a fool now."

His grin redoubled. "Fitting, isn't it? You'd never believe the freedom it affords me! I can channel nearly whenever I want, so long as I'm not making people nervous."

Knowing well how often he'd yearned for that liberation, I smiled. "Like a dream come true."

"But you," he continued, his brow furrowing. "What

21

happened to you, Airene? Corin just kept saying that you should tell us yourself. Her story to Jaxas doesn't add up. What were you doing in Sandglass searching for Maesos?"

I hesitated. I wanted to tell Xaron the truth, but I wasn't sure he'd see Corin's betrayal the same way I had. Part of me wondered if it would be better to lie.

But no. We couldn't start keeping secrets from each other again. We'd already seen how well that played out when this whole hunt began.

So I told him. Of Corin's betrayal, and Eazal's attempted assassination, and my channeling — or my dream of it. Holding up my hands, I showed him how no shifts moved.

"Can I have imagined the whole thing?" I asked tentatively. "Am I that desperate to be a warden?"

Despite all I'd told him, he looked pleased. "I never knew you wished for it so badly. But no, I don't think you imagined it. Corin saw the flames coming from you, didn't she? And after what she did, I doubt she'd lie again. Besides, I saw your burns when she brought you back, and now look! They're healed, and it's only been three days." He shook his head. "I have no idea how you did that. Though you're not the first — that Acadian, Kallias the Sculptor, is said to heal as well. As for your shifts, back when I was living in the wardens' commune, a woman who went by Hel came by her attunement late in life, the same as you. It took her a long while to be able to channel on command, or even for her shifts to show up."

It was almost too much to hope for. Yet hope I did. "You believe me?" I asked tentatively.

"Of course! Did you think I wouldn't?"

I pulled him into an embrace. "Thank you," I murmured. "You don't know how much that means to me."

His lips curled into a smile as he pulled back. "Oh, I think I do."

A knock came at the door. I immediately stiffened and

pulled away. *You're safe,* I chastised myself. *No one is coming for you.* But my heart continued to pound all the same.

Xaron cast a worried glance at me, yet he only called, "Who is it?"

"I brought food," Corin responded from without.

Xaron's expression blackened as the key turned in the lock. I put a hand on his arm. "Don't say anything," I warned him.

He gave me a mutinous look but remained quiet as Corin entered, a huge platter of food balanced in one hand. I stared in astonishment at the array of dishes. Fresh bread, both flat and in loaves; skewered and spiced goat, fish, and mutton; golden grapes, mangoes, and nectarines; and in the center, a generous bowl of soup.

"Who are we feeding, a taxos?" I said over the grumbling of my stomach.

Corin started to smile, but a glance at Xaron wiped it away. She set the platter on the waiting table near the wardrobe. "I can bring dishes to you," she offered quietly.

"No, I'll come over there." I pulled Xaron with me. His arm was tense beneath my grip, but I settled him in a chair next to me and gestured for Corin to do the same. "Eat with me. There's no way I can finish all of this."

She hesitated, then shook her head. Her eyes darted toward Xaron again. "No, thank you. But I'll return later."

"Not too soon," Xaron called snidely as she slipped out the door.

"Stop that," I chastised him half-heartedly as I dove into the meal.

Xaron spoke around a mouthful of bread. "Stop what?"

"Treating her like that."

He stared at me, his mouth falling open to reveal half-chewed food. "She could have gotten you killed, Airene. She lied to you and intentionally led you into a trap. How can you expect me to be civil?" He shook his head. "She can't stay in the room with you."

"What will you do? Throw her out?" I gave him a wry smile. "You're forgetting something, Xaron. She saved me after her betrayal. And she only betrayed me because the Valemish hold her sister captive."

"The Valemish *still* hold her sister captive. You can't trust her, Airene."

"But I do, Xaron. Even if it's broken somewhat, I still trust her. She was torn between two loyalties and slipped up. I don't think she'll do it again."

Until I'd spoken, I hadn't fully realized how I felt. But the words rang true.

He threw up his hands. "There's no reason to believe that! Besides, why take the risk? You can be friends from afar. Just don't let her stay near you."

"I know you're just trying to protect me. But I have to give her another chance. If others don't deserve second chances, why do I?"

His expression softened, and he squeezed my hand, though the gesture was spoiled by the grease filming his hand. I laughed and pulled my hand away to wipe it on a cloth.

"You did your best, Airene," he said seriously. "No one could have done anything more, considering what we're up against. Linos will be fine — you'll see."

I pretended to be absorbed in my meal so I wouldn't have to meet his eyes.

Xaron rose, looking longingly at the rest of our feast. "Much as I hate to, I should return to my duties."

I raised an eyebrow, hoping it hid my disappointment. "What? Taking a tumble for the Despoina?"

"Ha-ha. Actually…" It was his turn to hesitate. "It's not my Hilarion responsibilities exactly."

"You have my attention, if that's what you were after."

He ran a hand through his hair, untucking a tuft from his corn-husk crown. "No secrets," he mumbled. "I'm not even sure why I'm so awkward saying it. May as well get it over with. You remember that group of Acadians? The one Kyros had been training?"

My eyes narrowed. "Yes."

"Well. I've joined them."

I hesitated, sorting through the rush of feelings. "Do you think that's a good idea? You're sailing uncertain tides as it is."

"It's our only option, Airene. With Vusu having taken most of the Shepherds and commanding who knows how many other wardens, the only place to find reliable wardens is at the Acadium."

I shrugged, not finding an adequate response. Training to use his channeling to fight certainly wasn't what Hilarion was supposed to do, and I didn't like the idea of him violating the rules of his position. But he was right. In times like these, we couldn't let what was expected stop us from doing what was necessary.

"I wish I could join you." The words were out of my mouth before I considered them.

He raised an eyebrow. "You?"

I glanced sharply at him. "Why not? If I'm a warden—" I cut off abruptly, realizing how loud I'd been speaking. "If I'm a warden," I continued softer, "then I should use my gift to fight Vusu directly, not hide behind the rest of you."

Xaron looked stricken. "But Airene, you're early in your attunement. Your shifts aren't even appearing. This isn't something that can be rushed. You have no idea how dangerous it is. If you try to channel before you can control it—"

"I'll just have to manage." I waved wearily to the door. "I don't want to keep you from what you need to do."

He suddenly seemed reluctant to leave. "Airene, promise you won't bite off more than you can chew."

"Will you train me then?"

His swallow was visible. "I suppose," he muttered. "Though you should go to Eltris for that."

"Eltris?" I laughed low and bitter. "I doubt she would give me the time of day. Even if my shifts do show up, there's no way I'll be a ten-shift. What's the word for that again?"

"*Shur.*"

"You were a special case. From her manner, I don't think she often teaches."

He donned a small smile. "You're probably right about that."

I rose and pulled him up as well. "Thanks for visiting. But we both have things to do."

"The only thing you should be doing is resting," he said seriously. "Airene, I know the world is ending. But you should take it easy."

I rolled my eyes. "A compelling argument. Can you be in your quarters later this evening? I want to see what luxuries Hilarion is afforded."

"I'm probably the best-rewarded jester in the whole of the Four Realms." He pulled me into a tight embrace and spoke in my ear. "Please. Give yourself the time you need to recover."

"I will."

We both knew it was a lie.

As soon as Xaron left, I hastily finished my meal, putting away two more skewers, a loaf of bread, and two mangoes. Then, groaning from my distended belly, I pulled on my sandals, which someone had stored in the closet. I didn't have a mirror, though from the way everyone reacted to me, I doubted I wanted to see how I looked. My one concession to decorum was to run a hand through my tangled hair, hoping the greasiness wouldn't be too noticeable.

Though exhaustion assaulted me all the more with a full belly, I resolutely walked to the door. But before I could leave, I suddenly noticed something. A familiar weight was missing from around my neck. I touched my chest, even though I knew I wouldn't find it there.

My Verifier medallion was missing.

I thought furiously. Had my channeling somehow affected it? But the medallion hung on a chain — it would have taken a powerful fire to burn it off. The likelier option was someone had removed it. But who had done it, and where had they taken it? Without it, I wasn't sure that I could wander the Laurel Palace, or go anywhere else for that matter.

But I couldn't stay in my room. There was too much to do. Though my stomach protested, my legs wobbled, and my head felt stuffed full of wool, I yanked open the door. Everyone else seemed to have a key to my quarters, yet no one had thought to leave me one, so I left it unlocked. I didn't own anything of value anyway.

I looked to either side down the halls, striving to remain upright. At every moment, exhaustion assailed my weary body. Three days of sleep had never been so tiring. It took me far too long to recognize the hall as the same that I'd stayed in before, my current room two doors down from my former.

I started walking, then stumbled to a halt. Where was I heading? I knew I had duties. As one of the First Verifiers of a recently established order, the Conclave would no doubt expect things of me. But until I spoke with Nomusa, what my duties were wasn't clear.

But I knew I had an even more critical task. The greatest of our enemies was still largely undetected, and I knew far too little about him. I had to understand what Famine was to know how to fight him. And to fight Vusu as well.

Eltris was the obvious choice for such information. I

doubted she would tell me any more than she wished, but it was a start. I nodded to myself and set off down the hallway again. To Eltris's tower then.

"First Verifier Airene?"

I spun, hand going to the small of my back where my knife used to be. The unbalanced turn almost sent me sprawling. As I righted myself, I saw a female honor watching me with evident sympathy.

I was disoriented by more than surprise. My first reaction had been to reach for my missing knife. When had violence leaped to the forefront of my instincts? But I shook away my alarm and tried on a smile. "Yes?"

The honor smiled uncertainly back. "I am sorry I surprised you, First Verifier."

"Not at all." My smile was swiftly transforming into a grimace. "Were you seeking something?"

She bowed quickly. She was younger than me, I saw then, and had pretty green eyes. "Yes, First Verifier Airene. First Verifier Nomusa has been sending me to see if you were awake."

"Has she?" I knew how busy she must be, but I couldn't help a stab of annoyance that she wasn't coming to check in on me herself.

The honor nodded. "Yes, mistress First Verifier, every two turns. If I found you up, I was to give you a message."

I crossed my arms. "I'd better hear it then."

"You are to meet her in the gardens. So long as you are able." From the honor's expression, she felt doubtful of that.

"I'll manage," I said drily. "She's there now?"

"Yes. Would you like me to accompany you?"

"No need. I'm sure you have other responsibilities to be about."

She bowed again and parted with another wary smile. I turned in the opposite direction and, like a soldier after a long march, began to make my way to the gardens.

2

THE ORDER OF VERIFIERS

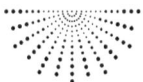

It began with a hunger.

Tyurn Sky-Sea stared over his dominion. He loved his worlds — the Higher and Lower Realms of the Pyrthae as well as the material world of Telae. But that day, instead of feeling pride, he felt an emptier feeling.

The Lord of All longed for more.

He saw starvation. He saw the craven overcoming the brave, the petty disdaining the proud. Tyurn Sky-Sea looked and knew there must be more he could give.

'There can be,' a whisper sounded in his ear. 'If you but listen to me.'

The Ruler of All Realms knew himself impervious to charms and glamours, and thus he believed this voice came of himself. Intrigued, he asked it, 'What do you mean?'

'You wish for more than you have,' the whisper said. 'You crave it. Your dominion is flawed, and you wish to perfect it. Yet you, King of Many, do not know the way.'

'No, I do not,' said Tyurn Sky-Sea, troubled, for there was little he did not know.

'Am I not Lord of All?' he questioned the voice. Had the doubt

come from anyone but himself, he would have thundered his denial.

'If you were Lord of All, how could you and your subjects ever lack for anything? But I, born of your desire, know how you may live up to that name, King of Many. It is simple, what you must do. Then all the lands will grow rich and bountiful.'

It rankled the pride of Tyurn Sky-Sea to be less than the master of everything. Thus, he said at once, 'And what is it I must do?'

Thus the Seed spoke to Tyurn Sky-Sea, and the Ruler of All Realms went forth and did as it said.

- The Seeds of Famine, a translation from the Lighted-tongue; by Oracle Kalene of deme Hull; 881 SLP

I walked the gardens for a long, painful time. Plodding along one winding path after another in the mile-long courtyard, sheltered under rows of columns on either side, I forced my leaden legs forward and managed to remain upright.

As I passed a willow tree, I suddenly stopped. My ear always keen for whispered words, the hushed conversation alerted me to someone on the other side of the tree, secreted within the foliage. I peered through the gently swaying branches. Two figures stood on the other side, their features hidden beyond the red and pale yellow of their robes. Quieting my breath, I stepped through the willow branches, trying to come near enough to make out their words.

But no sooner had I stepped under the tree than my foot found a branch and cracked it. The figure wearing pale yellow whirled around, and I recognized Nomusa even before she spoke. She was dressed as I hadn't often seen her, with her chiton plain and no jewelry adorning her neck or wrists. Her hair was in simple plaits against her head, though still executed with her usual tidiness. Humility seemed to be what she sought to present to the world, and she captured it perfectly.

Her surprise faded as she recognized me in turn, only to be replaced by an expression I couldn't read. "Airene!" she said too loudly to be natural. "You're awake! How are you feeling?"

I stepped through the sweeping leaves. The figure in red was already quickly walking away, a hood masking his or her face. Before I could say anything, Nomusa stepped up and embraced me. I returned it, curiosity biting deep.

As we pulled apart, I wore a smile. Considering everything else we had to discuss, Nomusa could keep her secret for the moment. "I'm fine now, though my belly is still trying to eat itself," I said truthfully.

She laughed heartily and pulled me into another hug. "I'm glad to see you up. We've all been so worried." She abruptly pulled me away again. "What happened? What Corin said made no sense."

I studied her. While I'd been asleep, Nomusa had undergone a metamorphosis. Instead of the reluctant, skeptical partner, she once again seemed alive and invested. It was like having her back from our early days of Finching, the friend I had long missed.

"I'll have to tell you later," I said. "I can't have anyone overhearing."

"If they do as poor a job spying on us as you did earlier, I think we'll be fine."

A wry grin worked its way onto my face. "I'm far from my best right now."

She looped her arm in mine. "I suppose your tale can wait. I have plenty to catch you up on."

She began walking us back through the gardens the way we'd come — the opposite of the direction the figure in red had taken, I noticed. But I said nothing of it, wondering if

Nomusa would speak of the hooded stranger herself. And if she didn't, what that might mean.

"How about we sit while we talk?" I suggested.

"I would, but... Since you're up, you really should go before the Council. They've been asking for you every time I see them, and my usual meeting with them is in just over a turn."

I groaned. "I should have stayed in bed."

Nomusa looked me up and down and pursed her lips. "Yes, you should have."

"Come on. I'm not that bad off."

She snorted lightly and continued to pull me along. "I suppose I'll begin with what's most pertinent. It's official, Airene."

I looked sharply at her, guessing what she meant. "They actually went for it?"

"They did. The Council approved the mandate two days ago. The Order of Verifiers is once again an official branch of the Oedijan demotism."

I had thought I was over that particular victory, particularly as I knew it came with strings attached. But despite my apprehension, a glow of pride warmed my chest, and I had to hold back a grin.

"But though we're Verifiers now, you still have to be confirmed as my fellow First Verifier," Nomusa quickly followed up.

The warmth dissipated. "By the Council?" Half of the Low Consuls were Preservists under Orhan's thumb. Considering their close alignment with the Valemish and their ancestral home in Avvad, it seemed a safe bet that they were privy to Eazal's attempted assassination of me. Probably they were the orchestrators of it. I doubted any of them would support me gaining power. I'd need the full support of the other five Low Consuls to pass. If I could manage that, I at least could count on Jaxas casting the deciding vote in my favor.

"Did any of the Preservists confirm you?" I queried.

Nomusa's brow furrowed. "Actually, yes. All of them did."

I stared. "And you don't suspect this is a trap?"

"I know it is." She gave me a nervous smile. "I haven't told you of the agreement binding us."

"Best tear off the bandage."

She raised a finger. "First, we must make a full account of our activities and the coin we spend. We have a clerk to help with that portion, at least, to whom we'll report each day for the Aviary ledgers."

"The Aviary? It's ready to reside in then?"

"Of sorts." Nomusa grimaced. "It still reeks of finch droppings — they'd been using the whole place to keep birds, you know, not just the tower. And the furniture is minimal. Still, there are some comforts — we have a cook and an honor who comes by daily to tidy up."

I wondered if the honor would also take the time to rifle through our belongings and report anything of interest to the Council. "I can live in most conditions. After all, I've stayed one night with Talan. Not like that," I hastily amended.

Nomusa smiled coyly. "I'm sure it wasn't."

"You're hopeless." I abruptly switched the topic. "Do we have a collective allowance, or is it individual?"

"Both. Fifteen silvers a day for the whole Order, though we'll raise eyebrows if we individually spend more than five."

I felt even weaker in the knees than I had before. Fifteen silvers had been half our collective savings before the shell horns had blown. To be afforded that amount in a single day was staggering. "We could buy off Nikias every day," I marveled.

Nomusa's frown told me she hadn't forgotten my earlier contentious bribe. "We could. But once we bring on more Finches, it will spent quickly."

"More Finches?" I was baffled. "But we can't initiate Xaron and Talan."

"I wouldn't want to hire those lazy sops anyway. But of course we'll gather more, Airene. With a war coming, and the Manifest stirring trouble, and corruption in our own government, we're going to need more than the two of us to keep tabs on it all."

"But who could we trust?"

She watched me carefully. "Things are going to be different, Airene. We'll likely have to give people responsibilities even if we don't fully trust them. You need to be ready for that, because that day is coming soon."

I turned my gaze away. After all the treachery we had recently undergone, I was far from sure I was ready. But all I said was, "Very well."

We exited the palace. With the monsoons soon arriving, the sky was thick with clouds, yet the muggy heat of summer still clung on. Given the state I was in, I dreaded the walk down to the Conclave and looked longingly at a carriage waiting on the marble road below the stairs. Instead of turning our path to avoid it, however, Nomusa pulled me toward it.

"What are you doing?" I hissed.

"Catching our ride down." She glanced at me, amusement glinting in her eyes. "Who did you suppose this carriage was waiting for?"

Without stopping for an answer, Nomusa greeted the driver familiarly and took his hand to step up into it. As the driver turned to me, I mutely accepted his aid as well and entered. It was a relief to sit again, especially on cushioned seats, though the cramped quarters were stuffy and hot.

"Do you regularly use a carriage now?" I asked Nomusa.

She smiled faintly. "Another of our privileges. Though our special treatment from the Laurel Palace may end if things continue the way they do."

"Tension between the Council and the Despoina?"

"Between the Council and the Archon. Jaxas has been

vocal about confronting our foes now that we know who they are. He's drawn the ire of Orhan and his lackeys for it."

Anger stirred in my gut, more insistent than hunger for the moment. "Of course," I muttered furiously. "You'd think that having lived here as long as they have, they'd feel more loyalty."

"You never forget your homeland." Her eyes had a distant look, and I knew she was thinking of her own home ishaka a thousand miles away.

"What do they want us to do anyway? The Council, I mean."

Nomusa drew away from her contemplation. "Ah, now we're at the crux of it. We're to investigate corruption."

"Corruption?"

She nodded. "They — the Preservists and Verchlesa, as it is — are interested in understanding what led to the Despot being taken and the rise of the Manifest unimpeded, and who was behind it."

I stretched my cramped legs. "Ironic, isn't it?"

"Of course. But what better way to keep ahead of charges of corruption than pointing the finger at others?"

"Maybe they hope we'll go after Jaxas. Since he was affiliated with Vusu and all."

"Or maybe that we'll try and take down the Tribunal." Nomusa snorted. "As if we would be that much of fools."

Despair clawed at my chest. "Is nothing being done then?"

"Some things are. They can't completely ignore an oncoming army, so the Council has put out an order for the taxoi to be raised again. When Avvad marches, we'll have the semblance of an army... though if they'll fight for Avvad or Oedija remains to be seen. Particularly when we may not be able to feed them."

"Have the droughts become that bad?"

"They're only the beginning. The more immediate problem is bringing what little harvest there has been into the city. The Council is negotiating with the Underguild for passage, but Kalindi's demands have been untenable, to say the least."

I winced. "The Council is negotiating with the Underguild for food now? That's more desperate than I'd hoped for."

Nomusa shook her head. "Since Kalindi overtook the Underguild, he has used far more aggressive tactics than we've yet seen from the syndicate. Crime has increased on the streets for many reasons, but most of the murders seem to be traced back to him. His most significant attempt at control has been to seize many of the shipments of grains and other foods before they pass through the city gates and hold them ransom."

The Underguild was extorting the demotism itself. I'd missed more in three days than I could have imagined possible. Yet still, I knew I hadn't heard the heart of what I needed to. "But what of the real danger? What are they doing about Famine?"

Nomusa pushed the curtain aside from the window to peer out. "Nothing," she said softly. "Nothing at all."

"They know, don't they? That Famine is real and rising again?"

She didn't meet my gaze. "Jaxas told them what you'd seen and implored that they remember what they saw at the trial, the Pyrthaen serpent swallowing Vusu and Linos and all. But the Low Consuls weren't convinced. They said it was an illusion, that it must be a simple conjuring for a warden of Vusu's strength."

I trembled, hot anger coursing through me. "But you corroborated him at least, right? You told them what I saw?"

Her hesitation spoke volumes. "The Order is still in its infancy—"

"You know he's real! I saw him! I went into the Pyrthae and saw him, Nomusa!" I noticed my voice was loud enough for the driver to hear, but I found it hard to care. Why should I hide the truth from anyone? They would all know far too soon.

"I know," Nomusa said hurriedly. "I know what you saw. But that doesn't change the fact that we need to seem credible as an organization right now. And no matter how true it is, claiming that a daemon god has risen from the legends is not a good way to establish our name."

I reined in my anger. It wasn't fair to put the blame on Nomusa. Even if she should have done more. "Then target Vusu," I suggested. "They saw what he is capable of. Surely that at least can stir them to action."

"You'd think. But he hasn't been seen since Asileia's trial, and you know what they say: When the pyr doesn't appear—"

"—It isn't here, I know," I finished the saying with irritation. "But he's had three days to recover now. If he can heal like Kallias the Sculptor, then he's already at work again."

Nomusa gave me an odd look. "I never took you for a believer in that sort of thing."

I flushed despite myself. "Vusu has the power of a daemon god behind him. I don't think regeneration is outside the realm of possibility."

She shrugged. "But maybe he won't recover. Maybe that quarrel you put in him will kill him. After all, even wardens aren't immune to corruption of the flesh."

"You don't know that," I pointed out heavily. Her words were tempting, and I wanted to believe them. But I felt the wrongness of them in my gut. Vusu still loomed large, and as long as he was a danger, Famine would be as well.

Standing before the god in the Pyrthae, I'd sensed far more than what my material senses could tell me. I'd felt the hunger that drove him, endless and ever-sharp, cutting at him every moment that he couldn't sate it. It was a craving far greater than what any addicted asher felt while waiting for his next hit of silvertongue. And his hunger wasn't for flesh. More I couldn't understand, but remembering that feeling of a predator casually studying me as prey struck icy fear through me anew.

The carriage rolled up before the Conclave. For a moment, it was all I could do to stare at the changes wrought over it. The broad dome of bronze and white marble was broken like an egg's shell, half of it torn away during our struggle with Vusu. Everywhere it had cracked and crumbled, time was catching up with the grand edifice, green and gray patina spreading out from the rents.

As Nomusa exited, I tore my eyes away and followed. As I lowered myself, my legs nearly collapsed under me. I bitterly wondered if my hunger was yet the depth of Famine's. A smile twisted onto my lips as I took Nomusa's offered arm, and we walked toward the tall double doors, now riddled with wide fractures.

It was only as the Conclave guards studied us that I realized I'd forgotten to mention something. "Nomusa," I muttered, "I don't have my Verifier medallion. Someone must have taken it while I slept."

"I took it," she responded briskly. "At the behest of the Council. Until you're confirmed, they didn't want you flashing it about."

"I never flashed it about," I protested, but was relieved nonetheless. If it was missing, best that there was a chance of getting it back. Even if it came at a cost.

The guards barely delayed us as they greeted Nomusa warmly. I kept my face carefully composed. It didn't surprise me that Nomusa had already made friends with the guards, particularly since one of the pair hadn't been hard on the eyes.

As the handsome guard cracked open the door, we slipped inside. Amusement was replaced by silent awe. Much of the great chamber had been swept of debris, yet the signs of the fight were still written on the walls. A thick layer of dust began a dozen cubits up where it seemed the cleaners couldn't reach. All but the most massive blocks had been cleared away. Now that I thought about it, I was astounded that the Servants and Low Consuls were continuing to use the building at all. It didn't look stable with the many crevices in its pillars, walls, and floors, not to mention the cracked dome above.

Yet I followed Nomusa around the edge toward the Archon's platform. The giant bell that had been mounted there to call everyone to attention had split up the middle, and the offending rock, twice my size, lay nearby. Banishing silly thoughts of omens, I focused my attention on the small door behind the platform as we stopped ten paces short of it.

Nomusa paused. "You're sure you want to do this now?"

"We're already here," I said wearily. "And you said it was a shoo-in, didn't you?"

"We'll see," she answered, with less confidence than I'd hoped for.

Nomusa turned to the guards waiting on either side of the door. "I am First Verifier Nomusa. Will you admit me and my companion, Airene of Port, so that she may become First Verifier alongside me?"

A male honor appeared from the shadows of a nearby column. "They are in conference at the moment and requested that they remained undisturbed. If you will wait, they should be done within the turn."

Nomusa's nostrils flared, but she only turned on her heel and marched for the dais. I followed and gratefully sat next to her on the edge, resting my protesting legs and leaning back on my arms.

We waited in silence. Both of us knew the things we had to tell each other must be spoken in secret. Yet now that we paused, I felt the pressure of my news once more. I wriggled my fingers on the stone, wondering if my shifts had appeared yet, wondering if I'd be able to channel if I attempted it. But I didn't dare try. Though I hoped I would be able to control it, my memories of the first instance inspired little confidence.

My gaze wandered over to the Archon's bell again — but for a moment, my eyes saw not what was, but what had been. Asileia Wreath stood upon the dais, her chin uplifted. She scattered into mist as a hole ripped through the fabric of the world. Teeth, iridescently white, erupted from nowhere. And from between them stepped a shadow. The shadow paused, then turned its head toward me, revealing Vusu's face. *"After all this,"* he said slowly, *"and it is you who have doomed us."*

A touch on the arm startled me out of the reverie.

"Airene?" Nomusa asked, concern plain in her voice. "Are you alright?"

"Fine," I said faintly. I stared at where I'd seen the vision, but it had become only ruined stones again. I shook my head. No amount of sleep could cure madness, but I had to hope that was the only remedy I needed.

The Council's small door finally cracked open. "Is she here yet?" an irritable man's voice called out. *Berker*, I recognized with a twist of disgust; Orhan's righthand man, and as staunch a Preservist as they came.

The male honor hurried forth from the shadows. "Yes, Low Consul. First Verifier Nomusa has come, and she has brought the other you wished to see."

"That's putting it strongly," Berker growled. He revealed his pockmarked face as he opened the door further. "Well?" he barked. "Are you coming or not?"

"She has only just risen from her sickbed," Nomusa rebuked him as we rose and walked to the door. "Have some patience for once, Berker."

"Have care, Finch." The large man didn't move from the doorway. "You serve at our leisure."

"We serve the people and the demotism," Nomusa said smoothly. "Now, I'm sure your fellow members of the

Council would appreciate if you didn't waste any more of their time with juvenile antics."

The man's heavy jowls became yet more pronounced as he scowled, but he relented, turning and stalking back inside. Sharing an amused look with me, Nomusa led the way in.

The Council's meeting chamber was much as I remembered it, and I couldn't detect any changes from the battle that had waged outside its doors. It still seemed more a cave than a room, with the unshaped walls and ceiling melding into each other, and small, uncovered windows opened toward the shore. The winds were strong off the sea today, as they tended to become in the spans before the monsoons arrived, and the scent of salt was heavy in the air.

In the middle of the room, seated around the glass-smooth slab of gray stone that served as a table, were the nine other Low Consuls. As before, the Preservists sat on one side, while the Equalists and the two independent Low Consuls sat opposite. I did my best not to look at Feiyan, but I couldn't help but notice her small smirk as she studied me. Jaxas, too, was present, though he stood by the windows apart from the rest.

"Airene of Port," Orhan greeted me warmly. As usual, he was immaculately groomed and decorated, his remaining gray hair finely curled, and he wore a robe of crimson lined with gold. "I am glad to see you up and walking. I heard you took frightfully ill after the events following the Despoina's trial." He didn't stand, nor did any of the others, but it was hardly surprising. As they were Low Consuls and I was presently little more than a plebeian in their eyes, decorum didn't call for it.

I, on the other hand, was obligated to bow. "Low Consuls. I apologize for my earlier absence. As you said, I had taken ill and have only just risen."

"You need not have rushed," Orhan said pleasantly.

I studied him, wondering how much he meant by that.

Zehaar of the Equalists took a turn next. "We have many matters to attend to, so I suggest we quickly resolve this quaint formality," she said briskly. "Airene was elected as First Verifier by Jaxas before her illness, and was, as we have discussed at length, behind the counterplot to Vusumuzi's plans. Her accomplishments speak for themselves."

Berker snorted, but it was Orhan who spoke. "Indeed, they do. Which is why I am quite skeptical of her appointment."

I looked sharply at the portly Avvadin man, but at a warning glance from Nomusa, held my tongue.

"After all," he continued, "she was, as you say, responsible for that whole bloody debacle. If not for her, Photina would still be alive, as would many Servants and other stewards of the demotism. Your First of the laurel guard, Jaxas, would also be alive. The rabble that wanders our streets every evening, these so-called 'dusk mobs,' would not terrorize our streets and markets. And if you failed to notice, we do not even know the location of our Despot, nor have we received any demands for ransom — if, indeed, he is alive. Only First Verifier Nomusa's report causes us to believe so, and she claims to know this secondhand by Airene's account."

Jaxas turned toward the Low Consuls and stood over them. The gray light behind him limned his robes and cast his face in shadow.

"It is dangerous to assume you know how things might have gone otherwise, Orhan," he said quietly. "Vusu is set on power. With or without Airene's intervention, it would have come to blood."

"You say one thing and contradict yourself in the same breath," Orhan noted with a smile.

Daelya, head of the Equalist faction, leaned forward, her dark brow drawn. "Enough. Speak plainly your position, Orhan, as well as the rest of you who seem to take issue. What's your complaint?"

Esen, the only woman among the Preservist Low Consuls, spoke now, wearing her usual severe expression. "We know too little of her, and what we do know is contentious."

"I can vouch for her," Jaxas offered. "It was enough for Nomusa's appointment."

"Except she had Feiyan's backing as well," Esen countered.

Despite my earlier resolution, I looked in amazement first at Nomusa, then Feiyan. The Qao Fu woman wore an even smugger expression than before, while Nomusa shifted with discomfort.

"I'm afraid I can't speak as well for Airene as I could for her companion," Feiyan said in a tone so full of sorrow a playwright would have applauded her performance. "She has been troublesome and tiresome in all my dealings with her. True, she has some talent for sniffing out trouble. But I cannot see her in a leadership position in the Order of Verifiers."

"Feiyan," Daelya said with undisguised exasperation, "I know you have some personal vendetta against the woman. But try to prevent it from coloring your professional opinion."

Feiyan looked so affronted I had to fight back a smile. At least one of the Low Consuls appeared to lean in my favor. Still, as I needed at least five to win the appointment, my odds were not looking good.

"Low Consuls," Nomusa spoke up. "If you need someone to attest to her competency, you need look no further. As I told you before, she and I have worked together for the last nine years. In all that time, never once has she been less than trustworthy and dependable, and has often been the primary investigator in our cases."

"If that's so, why are you presently the First?" Berker smirked through his scraggly beard.

Nomusa ignored him. "Airene is entirely capable of acting

as First Verifier beside me. It would be a grave mistake not to appoint her so."

"This is taking far too long," Zehaar snapped. "It is past time we put this to a vote."

But Orhan leaned forward, wearing an expression that filled me with foreboding. "But what of what Vusumuzi said?" he asked softly. "He all but named you his accomplice, Airene. I would like to hear an adequate explanation if one can be provided."

I stared at him. I'd forgotten that brief interaction, forgotten even the words Vusu had said to me. Had they actually been incriminating, or just allusive enough to arouse suspicion? Forming a defense without knowing seemed all but impossible.

So I told the truth, or as much as I could. "He insinuated that we worked together because he believed it to be so. I allowed Vusu to think that he and I were accomplices in discrediting the Despoina so that we might ambush him."

"Vusu, she calls him," Berker sneers. "She implicates herself through her familiarity!"

I flushed, but before I could speak, Jaxas stepped forward. "Vote as you must. Just don't maintain this mummery any longer."

Orhan smiled, the mockery in it plain to see. "Very well, Jaxas. There's no need to be testy. If you wouldn't mind?"

Jaxas's eyes flickered to me for a second, then looked down. "All in favor of appointing Airene of Port to be First Verifier alongside Nomusa in the new Order of Verifiers?"

Daelya raised her hand, then Zehaar. Verchlesa and Tychon, to my relief, followed suit. But though I scanned the assembled members of the Demos Council, no more hands rose. Feiyan sat back with arms crossed, a small smile playing on her lips. Fury and frustration clashed so that my vision blurred and my head grew light. I reached out for the wall to steady my balance and set my jaw. I wouldn't collapse in front of that spiteful woman.

Jaxas's disappointment laced his words as he said, "All opposed?"

As expected, all five of the Preservists' hands shot up. I glared at Feiyan, expecting hers to rise as well. But still, she sat unmoving.

Jaxas's frown deepened. "Abstain?"

Feiyan shifted, but only to rest her hands on the table. "You know," she said slowly, her eyes still on me, "I'm still quite uncertain."

"Then abstain," Orhan advised pleasantly. "After all, that is what the option is for. And you seemed more than willing to practice it when you didn't attend the Despoina's trial."

Feiyan ignored the gibe but continued to look at me with a small smile. "But for such an important vote, I feel it is my duty to choose one way or the other. If only I knew the proper course."

My eyes challenged her, daring her to be so petty as to ruin me over our rocky past. She was more than capable of it, I knew well enough. Yet I couldn't pull my gaze away.

"Stop this at once!" Berker barked. "Which way will it be, Feiyan?"

She moistened her lips, raptor eyes still on me. "I vote in favor. Let us leave it to the Archon to decide."

Berker's face went red, while Orhan's smile slipped a bit. I didn't know how to react. Why had she suddenly acquiesced? I doubted she'd found a conscience. It was just as hard to believe she was not as petty as I'd thought. Which could only mean my appointment somehow played to her hand.

"I vote in favor," Jaxas said at once. "So it's decided. Congratulations, First Verifier Airene, on your new appointment."

Nomusa put an arm across my shoulders and pulled me close. I let my gaze drift from Feiyan to my fellow First Verifier and shared a smile with her. At Nomusa's whispered prompting, I murmured a thank you, then was ushered from the room. I only glimpsed Jaxas's broadening smile before Nomusa pulled me from the Council room and out into the main chamber of the Conclave.

"Airene!" She seized my hands as soon as the door closed, heedless of the honor and guards standing nearby. "You managed it!"

"Barely." My head felt woozy again, and my legs threatened to give way. "I thought you said it would be simple."

"I thought it would be. But you know Feiyan — she loves getting a rise out of you."

I shook my head. "That was more than enough excitement for one day. I need a large meal and a long nap."

"Very well, my fellow First Verifier. But there's something else you should accept first." She reached inside her neckline and drew out not one chain, but two, hidden beneath her dress. I was surprised at the eagerness with which I reached for the medallion hanging from her hand.

Grinning, Nomusa handed me one of the Verifier medallions. I immediately slipped it on. As it settled on my neck, the solid weight of the iron was reassuring. I didn't hide it under my robes, though. Even if it had first been given to me by Vusu, I would now wear it openly and proudly.

"That's better," she said approvingly as she led me out of the Conclave. "Now, time to enjoy the fine, new quarters our position affords."

3
VISITORS IN THE DARK

...But though Tyurn Sky-Sea sought to assuage his kin, Clepsam-mia, Goddess of Fate, stepped forward and announced in a quiet, carrying voice:

'Ruin will this Seed of Bounty bring. The fields, now abundant and green, will turn fallow and yellow. The rivers will dry into desert canyons. Your people will starve and curse your name, Father. Famine, this kin of daemons will bring, and famine will be the harvest you reap.'

But Tyurn Sky-Sea would not listen. Though his daughter had never spoken an untrue word, his hope for the Seed was too great, its whispers of power and plenty too intoxicating to deny...

- The Seeds of Famine, a translation from the Lighted-tongue; by Oracle Kalene of deme Hull; 881 SLP

I had missed the Aviary on the carriage ride. Now, as we crossed the Conclave grounds, our new home came into sharper focus. It was a misshapen thing, three stories high at its tallest point, that clung to the slippery stones along the top of the cliff like an ancient lizard. Its sloped roof was covered in dark green moss and the cracks in its walls were lined with black mold. It didn't promise the rest and retreat I'd hoped for.

Yet I caught glimpses of its former grandeur as well. Fluted columns adorned the front of the atrium, and its pediments had once been etched with great care, even if the carvings were now worn and obscured by moss and vines. From its right side rose the tower where, Nomusa informed me, some of the Conclave's many finches were kept, which were now at our disposal.

The neglected building was starting to grow on me by the time we reached it, all the more from my exhaustion. My energy waned with each passing moment; I felt I could sleep on a bed of stone. But Nomusa, full of enthusiasm, insisted that she give me the tour immediately.

"Here's the atrium, which doubles as a feast hall," she said as we entered. Two long tables that each seated ten were in similar condition as the rest of the building. Pointing to the back corner, Nomusa continued, "Off that hallway are the kitchens. Never fear, those have been thoroughly scrubbed out."

"What a relief."

"Through here," Nomusa said as she led us off to the right down a narrow hallway, "are the bedchambers. Ten on this floor, twelve on the second."

"Where are the stairs up?"

"Off the finch tower."

I shook my head. "That doesn't make sense."

"I didn't design it, did I? Come on — you still haven't seen the tower."

The tower was much as I'd expected: tall and filled with small birds of every color and pattern. The stench of droppings was so strong my eyes watered. No doubt the place hadn't seen much cleaning since its abandonment. I spotted nearly forty finches at a glance. Nets draped at regular intervals throughout the tower, allowing a swift hand to capture birds at any level from the stairs that wound around the edges.

"I've seen the tower. Now can I see my room?"

"Of course." Nomusa smirked and started up the stairs.

I didn't follow. "Why up there? I saw plenty of room down here."

"The ones further up have more air flow and less mold. So, unless you want to be breathing that stuff in all night…"

With a heavy sigh, I followed her up.

She spared me at least by turning into the first room. "This one will do, if you don't mind the smell of bird dung."

"Let's see how it is at the end of the hall."

"You'll be right across from me then. I can't wait to shout conversations across the hall."

"I can't wait to hear one of those Conclave guards who will no doubt visit," I muttered.

Nomusa only smiled coyly.

We turned into the last room on the left, and I finally saw the state of my new room. There was nothing in the way of furniture, only a rotted frame that seemed unlikely to support a mattress. It was hard to believe there was less mold up here than the chambers below, for it spread across every surface. The open windows, with no glass or shutters to keep out the coming cold of the monsoons, had only worsened the situation, bringing in the wet winds from the sea.

"I know where our first fifteen silvers are going to," I observed.

Nomusa laughed. "It's not so bad, really. I didn't know which one you'd want, so I was having Hyrol — he's the honor who comes by — clean the main areas first. But we can have him attend to your room first." She gestured behind her. "I've got a bed and a relatively clean room if you want a nap. Just don't sleep there all night."

I wrapped her in a hug. "You have no idea how much this means to me."

"From the look of you, I think I do. Now go ahead. When you wake, you'll have food and a bed. And I hope you'll be in a more talkative mood. I won't wait for your secret forever."

Nodding, I swayed into Nomusa's room and collapsed onto her bed. Almost as soon as I closed my eyes, I fell into a heavy sleep.

~

My eyelids fluttered open. The dim light told of evening fast falling, yet my exhaustion had barely lessened. My hunger was sharp enough, however, that I rose and slowly descended to the atrium. To my relief, Nomusa had been true to her word, and the pleasant aromas of fresh food greeted me upon entering the room. Recently baked flatbread, ripe mango and soft cheese, a long, smoked fish — all waited on a covered platter on one of the long tables. I set to clearing the platter out in a manner that would have made Xaron proud.

I groaned as I thought of Xaron and my promise to find him this evening. The hunger dulled as I set into my third portion, but little energy came with its retreat. Even sitting up and eating was a chore. My Hilarion would have to wait for another night for me to visit.

Besides, if I could move about, I had more important tasks. If I were to retain my position, I had to show the Council I took being First Verifier seriously and make headway on their investigation of corruption, as much as that was possible. And even though Vusu hadn't been sighted, the Manifest remained a constant threat. Most of all, I needed to learn more about the true enemy lurking behind all the others. A visit to the Acadium seemed in order come morning.

When I couldn't manage another bite, I returned upstairs. In my haste to find food, I'd barely glanced at my room, and so hadn't noticed the scrubbed walls, ceiling, and floors, as well as the mattress and night table, complete with a pot of yellow pyrkin, that now decorated it. The mattress sagged in the middle and the blankets looked well used, but clean. I resolved to thank Hyrol at the first opportunity as I settled into it. Though I still needed to do something about the open windows. Even wrapped in the two blankets the honor had provided, a faint chill seeped through.

But though the sun had fallen and light faded from the sky, sleep eluded me. In its place whirled thoughts my exhaustion had kept at bay. Slowly, tentatively, I focused on my navel, on the spot where I'd felt the Pyrthae's power flow into me, and imagined it opening. First as a flower; then a fountain spilling forth; then a shaft of light through a window in a dusty room. Nothing worked. I remained as closed off to the Pyrthae as if I'd never become a warden.

If I even was one now.

For the first time since waking from my long slumber, I wondered how I'd have become attuned. I thought I'd channeled when Eazal attacked me. But it was said a god had to open you to the Pyrthae, and I was sure I would have remembered if one had come calling. Could this fluke have resulted from my journey into the Pyrthae, a parody of the theory I'd suggested to Jaxas? I didn't want to consider it, but the possibility suddenly seemed likely. No one traveled through the realm of spirits that I knew of — no one save Vusu and Eltris. But they were both wardens, and I—

I was not.

I breathed out heavily. That was all this had been: the rare effect of a strange experience. I wasn't a warden after all.

Something scuffled across the room. I sat bolt upright and stared at the dark corner. Likely it was a rat, or perhaps an escaped finch from the tower. But after what I'd done to Vusu, it was as likely knives in the dark sent to finish the job Eazal had started. Unarmed and exhausted, I stood little chance against them.

A patch of faintly glowing blue emerged from the darkness.

I guessed what I was at once. *A whisper finch.* The rare bird had perched on the foot of my bed. I stared mutely at it, my fading terror having driven all thoughts from mind.

"They will come for him," it said, the familiar, boyish voice strangely contrasting the avian body. "You must warn him before they do. They fear the knowledge he'll bring to Oedija."

Cold struck through me. "Who?" I asked urgently. "Who comes for whom? Why do you speak in riddles? If you mean to help me, speak plainly."

"I cannot," the whisper finch murmured. "They hear all that passes through these tongues."

"Who hears?" I demanded. "Vusu? Famine? How can you help if I don't know what you mean?"

The bird fluttered into the air to land on the nightstand, its small body limned in the faint light of the pyrkin pot. With an incline of its head, it seemed to beckon me closer. Apprehensive, I set my ear next to it. The whisper was so soft I could barely detect it.

"They will come for him the night he arrives."

The whisper finch suddenly moved, and I jerked back. But rather than lunging forward, it had toppled backward from the night table and hit the floor with a soft thud.

I stared at it for a long moment, unmoving, as the blue patch of light slowly began to fade. As the shock of the moment faded, I slowly brought my will to bear and reached out toward it. A finger brushed the soft feathers that made up the blue spot on its breast. It didn't move, and I felt no stirring of life.

Slowly, I withdrew my hand. Questions rose in my mind, driving away all hope for sleep. Why had it died? At the very least, it confirmed a suspicion I'd long held: that this bird was a messenger for someone else, not the speaker itself. But who was behind it? I'd had too much assistance from the boy who spoke through the birds to believe he meant me ill, even if his counsel had always been shrouded in enigma. But what form did my helper take? A patrician boy with far too much knowledge? A pyr? A god?

I sighed and leaned my head back against the wall. Of his message, I could divine little more. *They will come for him the night he arrives.* It was too little information to know whom he meant. "They" could refer to the Manifest, Avvad, or the Underguild, or perhaps another unknown party altogether. But who would they come for? The Underguild might go after Talan. Or perhaps it meant Shepherds hunting Xaron. But those were both more important to me than they would be to some random boy. More likely it meant someone more public — Myron perhaps, or Jaxas. There were too many players for me to know for certain.

They fear the knowledge he brings to Oedija. What knowledge could be feared? And who feared it? Who could bring such knowledge? At the very least, they sounded like someone not of Oedija. Was it someone coming from Avvad? Or perhaps an immigrant from the Bali or Qao Fu?

Some of his words at least seemed clear. The last "they" it had spoken of, the one who heard what came from whisper finch tongues — it had to be Vusu and Famine; such power must be beyond anyone else. I pulled the worn blankets tighter about me. How much could the daemon god and his follower hear? Just what whisper finches spoke? Or far more?

So deep was I in my thoughts that I only noticed the scraping outside my window a moment before a figure peered in. I shouted and grabbed the pot of pyrkin from my night table, holding it aloft. The intruder's face was shadowed in the fading light, but I recognized the chuckle as he folded the rest of the way in.

"You ought to shutter your windows. Vagrants could

climb in at all turns of the night." The man glanced around the room, then down, quickly finding the fading glow of the dead whisper finch. "Or invaluable birds can die."

"Talan." I set down the pot and rose from the bed to wrap him in an embrace.

Talan pulled me close and rested his chin on my head. He smelled of smoke and sour wine, but also the earthy smell that was solely his own. "Hello, little Finch," he murmured in my hair. "You might wish to bathe."

I pushed him away, unable to keep my scandalized expression completely hidden. It only provoked another laugh.

I couldn't help smiling back. "Speak for yourself. Where have you been?"

"Busy," he said with his usual half-smirk. "I'm sorry I couldn't visit you more often, but Kalindi is tightening his grip. His spies are everywhere around the Conclave and palace. I had to—" He cut off abruptly. "But never mind that. How are you? Are you feeling better? And what of this dead whisper finch at my feet?"

"I'm alive — it's about all I can ask for. As for the bird, I'll tell you in a bit. If you wouldn't mind us sitting…"

He immediately settled me onto the bed and sat next to me. We leaned against the wall and, at my insistence, he pulled the blankets over both of us. I was distinctly aware of his warmth nestled against me.

"I have something to tell you."

He cast a quizzical look at me. "I think you have a great many things to tell me. Like why Corin has been allowed to remain by your side after she betrayed you."

My stomach sank. "How'd you figure that out?"

"It wasn't difficult to reason. She summoned you in a rush, lured you from the palace to an undisclosed location on an excuse that proved to be false, where you were almost murdered."

His eyes flashed with such anger I had to stop myself from flinching.

"She betrayed me," I admitted. "But she had very good reason to."

"What? Her sister being held by the Valemish?"

I shook my head. "It's unsettling how much you know."

"It's my job to know, and your job to act on that knowledge. So. What will you do about her?"

"I don't know. But that's not what I wanted to tell you."

His eyebrows shot up. "No? You have my attention now."

"There's one thing you can't have already guessed." I drew in a deep breath and let it out slowly. "When Eazal attacked me, I… channeled."

He stiffened. "Is this a jape?" he asked quietly.

"I'm serious, Talan. I channeled. I felt myself open, then fire and pure force came out from my feet and hands—"

"You weren't touched by one of the Buyujinn," he interrupted. "You weren't a warden before. How can you be now?"

"I don't know!" I was starting to grow annoyed. "But I know what I experienced. Do you believe me?"

For a moment, he looked away and said nothing. Nearly a minute passed before he sighed. "Yes. I believe you. Though I don't understand."

Considering all we'd encountered, I marveled that this was what baffled him. "I'm not the first to have become a warden late in life."

"No," he agreed. "There are two of us in this room that have had that pleasure."

I'd almost forgotten his own origins as a warden. He'd been able to channel all the three years I'd known him, so I'd never thought of Talan as anything other than a warden. "A Buyujinn, isn't that what you called her? The one who opened you to the Pyrthae?"

He nodded. "She was one of the many faces of the Lost Mother. I distinctly remember what it was like when she opened me." He looked askance at me. "Did you feel a presence when you channeled? Did anyone speak to you?"

"No one but the apothecary."

Talan was silent again. "Perhaps there are more ways of becoming a warden than I knew."

I didn't want to say my next words, but I was tired of doubting. "What if... what if it was a fluke? From visiting the Pyrthae?"

He slowly met my eyes, but I turned my gaze aside. I didn't want him to see the depth of my longing.

"I don't know," he said at length. "It's possible. I know much, but of the plane of pyr and gods, I'm as ignorant as a child."

It had been too much to hope that he'd know more. "What of Pyrthaen-blessed birds?"

He cocked his head. "I suppose you're referring to the dead whisper finch on your floor."

"It passed me a message, one I can't understand. Someone is coming for a man the night that he arrives in Oedija, someone who fears some knowledge the man has. And I'm supposed to warn him."

Talan studied me for a moment. His eyes were hooded from the way the thin light hit his face. When he spoke, his tone was measured, but I could feel something pressing behind the words. "You don't know who sent the bird?"

I hesitated. "It was a boy's voice, as it has been before."

"Before?"

I told him of the two occasions the whisper finch had visited me in my room in the Laurel Palace, and how they had seemed more like conversations than messages, though that wasn't supposed to be possible through whisper finches.

"I don't know who the boy is," I confessed. "But he's been helpful."

"Riddles aren't of much help," Talan noted drily. "And that seems to be all he gives you. Airene, this is a dangerous game

4
THE ACADIUM

For eleven seasons, the lands of Telae saw bounty like had never been known before. The harvests were abundant; the wells and springs were full of clean water; the plagues and wars that had pestered the lands retreated into memory. All was well, and the people thanked the Lord of All for it, praying that it would continue for another eleven seasons to come.

Tyurn Sky-Sea looked down upon his people and listened to their praise and was satisfied. Here he had wrought something truly worthy of his name.

In the turning of the seasons, the Seed had taken root in his ear and sprouted a single tendril trailing down his back like a snake from the trunk of a tree. Again, it implored, 'More. You want more.'

And Tyurn Sky-Sea, Ruler of All Realms, found that he did.

- The Seeds of Famine, a translation from the Lighted-tongue; by Oracle Kalene of deme Hull; 881 SLP

W hen I awoke the next morning, I felt almost myself again. Though it was an overcast day, an omen for the coming storms, my mood remained buoyant. Finally, I could move without feeling as if my bones were made of iron and my stomach an empty pit I couldn't fill.

I'd neglected to take off my chiton the night before, but lacking any other clothes, I smoothed it out as best I could. With any luck, I'd be able to send Hyrol over to the Laurel Palace and retrieve the clothes that had been stored there, though I wasn't sure they were mine to claim. Perhaps he could find me some trousers and tunics as well. It felt strange going so long without them underneath my robes.

Going downstairs to the atrium, I found a surprise waiting for me. Corin stood as I entered. Despite myself, I couldn't help uneasiness rising in me. Talan's words stirred in my mind, as did Xaron's reprimand. Ignoring them, I approached my old loftmate.

"Sorry I didn't tell you where I was yesterday," I began. "Everything's been a blur."

The large woman shook her head. "I knew where you'd go."

"Where are you sleeping now? Did they keep you up at the Laurel Palace last night?"

Another shake of her head. "Here," she said simply.

I wondered what Nomusa thought about that. "We'll get you a proper room tonight. As soon as I find Hyrol, that is." I glanced around the room. "Has anything come for breakfast?"

"No."

I sighed and went back into the kitchens. As Nomusa had said, they'd been scrubbed and looked well-kept. Our cook, Sizani, was a Bali woman from a different ishaka than Nomusa. She reminded me of Zipho with her brisk, business-like manner, though she had a warmer smile than the cafe owner. We chatted about small things as she served hot flatbread with some fruit and cheese from the dark pantry. Corin and I ate in silence in the kitchens while she worked, then left.

"What will you be doing today?" I asked Corin as we exited the Aviary. There was a spring in my step. It felt good to have strength in my legs again.

Corin shrugged, not looking at me. "I don't know."

Suddenly, I remembered her mission. "Gods, Corin. I can't believe I haven't asked. Have you heard anything more about your sister?"

Misery softened her stony countenance. "No."

"We'll find where she is. Then we'll get her back." Baseless promises, but I couldn't help uttering them. I doubted I'd have time to find her sister. I hadn't even visited Linos yet. Though that, at least, would be amended soon.

When Corin didn't answer, I continued. "I'm going to the Acadium today. You're welcome to join me, but I understand if you have other things to do."

"I'll come with," she said at once. "It's not safe to wander alone."

I frowned. "Is it so bad out there?"

Her dark look told me all I needed to know.

As we approached the Conclave gates, a noise like stormy waves crashing against cliffs rose louder and louder. We left another of the many groves spread throughout the Conclave grounds, and it suddenly washed over us, stunning me for a moment. A mass of humanity crowded against the walls and gates, shouting and protesting and screaming. Dirty faces, ragged clothes, haunted expressions — to a one, they looked every bit as much the rabble that Orhan claimed they were. Yet I knew what drove them. Fear and hunger, the blights of civilization, had seized hold of Oedija.

I turned my gaze aside and tried pushing down the guilt. Here I was, pampered with good food whenever I requested it and kept apart from the terrors that befell the rest of the city. Yet I was just another of the common people who'd had a stroke of good luck. Why did I deserve to eat when they couldn't?

Corin drew me away. "There's another exit," she said as we left the main gates behind. "They don't know of it yet."

The sounds of protest dimmed behind us, and I felt my guilt ebb. I didn't try to cling to it. Guilt, I'd discovered before, would ill serve anyone. All I could do was my part.

The side gate was guarded by two Conclave soldiers from the inside and was as devoid of protestors as Corin had promised.

"You sure you two want to go out there?" one of them asked at our request to leave, a grizzled veteran with a scar running along his forehead.

"Yes, we're sure," I replied.

"Have a care then. Women like yourselves are easy prey for those dusk mobs."

I ignored the unintended slight, focusing on the unfamiliar term, which I'd heard Orhan use earlier. "Dusk mobs?"

The man stared at me with even more concern. "You don't even know of them? 'Thae above, woman, where have you been? Yes, the dusk mobs — with all those dirty plebs mopping up any bystander unfortunate enough to be in their way. The ones that have been breaking into shops, tearing down stands, terrorizing any markets still foolish enough to open. The mobs have all but put a standstill to honest work in Oedija."

"Is it so bad?"

The guard's companion snorted. "Let's just say it's not good. You at least have some protection on you?"

I was starting to regret not hunting out a kitchen knife in Sizani's kitchen. But Corin nodded. "Plenty," she asserted.

The two men looked up at her, both of them shorter than the big outlander woman.

"Maybe they'll be alright," the veteran muttered. "Well, on with you then." His eye finally caught my medallion, which had been partially obscured in the folds of my chiton, and they widened slightly. "Ah, my apologies, Verifier. I had only seen your superior coming and going here."

"First Verifier," I corrected him. A warmth of pride flushed my chest at the sudden respect. "First Verifier Nomusa is my accomplice, not my superior. Now, if you'll open the gates…"

Any superiority I felt quickly vanished out on the streets. With the guards' warnings heavy on my mind, Corin and I walked quickly along the cobblestones toward the Acadium. It wasn't terribly far from the Conclave, but with tension pounding in my temples and hungry eyes watching us from the shadows, the journey seemed much longer.

"Should we keep to the main roads or back alleys?" I looked up and down the promenade. Few folk walked it at the moment. I didn't want to find out why.

Corin shrugged. I might have thought her unconcerned but for the occasional glance she cast around us. "I haven't been out much."

I chewed my lip. "Let's take the backways. I don't trust being seen out in the open when the road's empty."

I didn't know this part of Oedija well, but by glimpsing the high points of the Pillars between buildings, we progressed slowly toward the Acadium. But when twice we were forced to turn around in dead-end alleys, frustration and fear began to mount. Though we passed many people crouched in the alleys who watched us, and more than a few begged for money, we hadn't come across any who seemed to mean us harm.

As we ran into a third dead end, I cursed under my breath and began to turn around. But a voice came from behind us. "That's far enough, hanims. We'll be having whatever's on you now."

Heart in my throat, I whirled to see five young men stalking toward us. They were ragged and dirty and had a sharper hunger in their eyes than those we'd passed in the alleys. In their hands were makeshift weapons: knives of varying shapes, a club with long nails sticking out haphazardly, a mop handle with a knife bound to the end of it. Yet poorly armed as they were, they severely outnumbered us.

Fury fueled by fear flared up in me. If only I knew how to channel, if only I was a warden, these men wouldn't pose a problem. As it was, there was only one solution.

I unthreaded my coin purse slowly. The five silvers inside clinked softly together, even padded with cloth as they were. Each clink shot rage through me. Here I was once again, helpless. I'd stood down the most powerful warden of our age. Yet soon after, I'd been nearly killed by a middle-aged apothecary, and now I was being robbed by five common youths. Only then did I realize it wasn't me who had stood up to Vusu. It was my allies surrounding me that had been my strength. Without them, I was nothing.

"Don't take all day," the one with the club snapped, his bloodshot eyes bulging. As I saw his white fingertips, fear shot through me. This one was an asher, one who indulged in silvertongue, a drug smuggled up from Avvad. When ingested, the stimulant often made its user manic and unpredictable.

I quickly tossed my purse to the youth who had spoken first, who adeptly caught it. He looked like he'd have been handsome in other circumstances and possessed a calm authority. Hopefully he would keep the asher in line. Corin followed a moment later with her own purse, not bothering to hide her scowl.

The boy peered inside mine, and a delighted grin spread across his face. "What a find! Thank you, hanims." He gave a mocking bow. "Now we'll take our leave. But what's that hanging from your neck?"

My hand went protectively to the Verifier medallion. "You don't want this."

"No? But I think I'll be the judge of that." The youth sauntered over and, despite my attempt to dodge, he hooked the chain with a finger and drew me closer. Against my better judgement, I held on for a moment longer. But I was still too weak to resist as he wrenched it from my grasp and yanked it off my neck.

I seethed with fury as he studied it, a thoughtful expression on his dirty features. "Iron, or I don't know my weights," he said with evident disappointment. "And a crude carving. What's it for?"

"Something you'll be hunted for having," I said, threat creeping into my voice.

The youth tossed it back to me suddenly, and I only just managed to snag the chain before it could hit the dust. "It looks too similar to the Tribunal circle for my liking," he dismissed it. "You a Tribune?"

"No." He deserved no more explanation, and I gave him none.

The amusement had faded from the boy's expression. Behind him, the asher glared at us, the muscles of his face spasming. A rabid dog barely restrained, that one. Fear dampened my outrage.

"Hide it next time," the boy advised. "That way no one will be tempted. And I would cool your anger, hanim. With some other thief, it might get you killed."

Without another word, he turned and walked away. The asher watched us from over his shoulder, but he and the others followed their leader away. I kept my expression stony until they disappeared around the corner.

When they were gone, I let out a breath. I could always find more coin. And having frequented the streets of Oedija my whole life, it wasn't my first mugging. That we'd survived without harm should have been a relief. But it was a poor salve for the helplessness burning inside me.

I started up the alley. "Best not wait for that asher to return. It's time we were inside the Acadium's walls."

A moment later, I noticed Corin hadn't followed. Turning back, I found her rooted in the same spot. "Corin? You coming?"

"Every time." Her voice was tight and strained as a taut rope. "Every time I save coins, they are stolen from me."

Guilt welled up in me. I knew what she was saving her coins for. And I'd been responsible for the first time she'd lost all her savings as well. "I'll find a way to help you, Corin. I swear it."

She cast me a bitter look, then came down the alley and slid past me. Repressing a sigh, I followed.

We kept a warier eye out now. Having no coin to steal put us in a more dangerous position than before, not less. After all, anyone who went to the trouble of robbing us wouldn't be pleased to come away with nothing but an iron medallion. And there were men with thirsts for uglier things than silver. Pushing the thought from my mind, I kept a watch out for the Pillars and pressed on.

Finally, we emerged from an alley to see the walls of the Acadium rising before us. I hurried toward the compound, Corin on my heels. Pulling the medallion out from the folds of my chiton, I let it fall between my breasts as we approached the guards.

But even as their eyes skirted over the medallion, they didn't immediately let us in. "One of the new Verifiers, are you?" one of the guards asked, a woman with braided hair the color of autumn blushing vines. With hair that red, she had to be an outlander like Corin. "Wondered when you lot would come by."

"To come steal Acadium secrets," her companion muttered, a gaunt-faced man.

Though it struck me as strange, I thought it best not to ask. "Your secrets are safe, never fear. But if you would admit us, we're in a bit of a hurry."

"Would love to," the woman said sarcastically. "But I should warn you: I can't guarantee you coming out."

At my narrowed eyes, the man rolled his eyes. "She means the mobs. They come by the gates every few turns to yell about daemons and such."

The woman snorted. "Like these Acadians would hurt anyone. They're sheep for our Shepherds, just the way it should be."

"Thanks for the warning." I couldn't completely hide my exasperation. "Now, the gate…"

As they cranked it open and we started up the hill within, I mulled over their words. I'd heard all of these attitudes about wardens before, but it took on a different feel now. After all, *I* might be a warden. All those ridiculous beliefs could apply to me as well.

"So that's what people think of wardens?" I whispered to Corin. "That they're daemons or sheep?"

She shrugged. "Many believe my people savages. That we do not know which end of a spoon to use. People believe honors to be little more than livestock, not really people. This is not so different."

I opened my mouth, then closed it. Put like that, it was hard to complain, even if it still didn't sit well.

Ascending the initial rise into the Acadium's campus, we navigated our way through its varied buildings. I considered altering our course to seek out Linos, but quickly dismissed the thought. Much as I wished to see my brother, this errand was more pressing. There would be time enough later for him once this was all over. Besides, as much as I might wish otherwise, there was nothing I could do to help him.

Moving along the cobbled road that cut through the center of the Acadium, I made my way toward the place where an old, decrepit tower squatted. As Eltris's home came into view, it once again struck me as the ugly cousin among a homely family. In front of its dingy door, an Acadian apprentice waited, identifiable by his plain brown robes.

"Greetings," he said in a bored voice. "Do you seek Eltris as well?"

I cocked an eyebrow. "We're not the first?"

"Hardly. The Master Augur is very popular lately. But you won't want to wait around. She hasn't graced her tower in three days." The pupil, little older than Linos, sighed and leaned against the mossy tower. "And guess who's left with lookout duty?"

I frowned. I didn't know where else I'd find the augur. As usual, Eltris thought of no one but herself.

Muttering a farewell, I led Corin back down the alley to the main thoroughfare that ran through the Acadium. Reaching the cobblestones, I hesitated for a moment and looked to my right, where a black tower rose from the far end of the campus. Setting my jaw, I headed toward it.

Corin fell in beside me. "Where do we go?"

"To find someone who might know where Eltris is."

As she fell silent again, I studied our destination. The tower wasn't as tall as the Pillar that rose just before it, but it soared far above the rest of the city. Made of seamless black stone, its construction reminded me of the Conclave. Another of the magic-forged buildings from our ancestors, perhaps, or from the people they'd conquered a thousand years ago. As was tradition, the Archmaster of the Acadian had claimed as his own.

As we neared the tower, more Acadians appeared around us. They wore robes of the cheapest dyes, dark blues and cloud grays and clay browns. Acadians had always shown a sense of frugality, though whether it was forced on them or if they adopted it themselves, I didn't know. Despite the meanness of their clothes, the streets smelled cleaner than elsewhere in Oedija, and the passersby wore kindlier expressions. Considering our earlier encounter, friendliness was a welcome change.

Yet a sense of unease crept up on me. My palms grew clammy,and my mouth dry. It took me a moment to understand why. If I were a warden, would the Acadians around me be able to tell? Eltris had seemed to know who could channel, as did Vusu. Kyros was said to be able to detect traces of channeling. What if other wardens possessed similar abilities? Innocuous glances suddenly seemed suspicious. I avoided their eyes, finally understanding the hunted feeling Xaron and Talan always carried with them.

It only intensified as we reached the base of Kyros's tower. Two Acadians and two guards stood by the tower door. One of the guards, a woman of middling years, stared at us as we approached.

"Name and business?" she barked.

"Airene — First Verifier Airene," I corrected myself. "Here to speak with Archmaster Kyros."

"Verifier, you say?" one of the Acadians spoke. He wore a more genial expression than the guard. "How intriguing! But the Order of Verifiers has not existed for over a century."

"Actually, Master Nikanor, it was just re-established a few days ago," the second guard said, a young man who wore an obliging smile. "We were warned you might show up, First Verifier."

His words sent a thrill of alarm through me, but I kept my voice calm. "You make it sound quite ominous."

The guard's grin widened. "That depends. Do 'digging up old bones' and 'stirring up a pot of trouble' sound ominous to you?"

I bowed mockingly. "It seems my reputation proceeds me."

"Fortunately for you, the Archmaster didn't prohibit your entrance. We can escort you up if you're willing."

The second Acadian, who had been watching the

exchange with an irritated expression, suddenly outburst, "They get to go right in? But I've been waiting here for ages!"

"And you'll continue to wait!" the female guard snapped. "As for you, Verifier, I won't hold this door forever. Best get yourself inside."

I glanced at Corin. "My companion ought to come as well."

The woman's face took on an alarming shade of red. "Don't have orders for that, do we? Just you inside, no one else!"

The young man shook his head and hauled the door open to the tower. "I apologize, First Verifier. This way, if you please."

"You don't have to wait for me," I told Corin.

The former cartwoman shook her head. "I'll wait."

I gave her a grateful smile before following the young guard in. A dark, squat atrium waited beyond, lit by faintly glowing pyr lamps whose cultures seemed about to die out. The guard led me to a staircase that spiraled up the middle of the room.

"The Archmaster waits in his quarters at the top. Unfortunately, I cannot guarantee he'll grant you an audience until we knock. His health has been erratic." There was apology in the guard's voice.

It was a good thing I hadn't tried to come here yesterday as I'd intended. From the height of the tower, I doubted I'd have managed it. I was skeptical of even doing so today. "Nothing for it, I suppose."

And so we climbed. After the eighth circle, my feet were dragging. After the fourteenth, my legs were leaden. When we reached the twentieth, I finally begged for a break and sat panting on the landing just by the stairs. The guard looked away politely, but I detected a small smile on his lips.

The one recompense for my labors was a series of fascinating sights. One level hosted an apothecary's laboratory, every surface glowing in iridescent hues. Another was full of nothing but mirrors of every shape and size, some so large they stretched to the ceiling. The floor where I rested was on one of the more ordinary floors, with little more than a kitchenette that looked cold and disused, and wood piled in the corner.

"The Archmaster's chambers are two circles further." The guard spoke in a soft tone now, as if afraid of being overheard. "Whenever you are rested, we can proceed."

Twenty-two circles in total. Our ancestors had always had a fondness for multiples of eleven. The derelict tower where our abandoned Canopy was located had risen eleven itself.

"I'm ready," I said, not eager to be thought weak by the handsome young man.

Rising on jittery legs, we ascended the last few stairs. The final flight rose to a door, the room beyond walled off. An honor waited for us, a woman a decade older than myself by the faint lines on her face.

"First Verifier Airene comes to beg an audience of the Archmaster," the guard told the honor. "Is he taking visitors?"

The honor shook her head. "I regret to say the Archmaster is still taking his rest. He sustained many wounds and needs time to recover."

My stomach sank. All this way for nothing. But no sooner had disappointment set in than a voice boomed from within, "Admit her!"

The honor looked embarrassed. "Pardon me, First Verifier. It seems I was mistaken. Please, come in."

Skeptical but relieved, I left my escort in the stairwell and entered. Kyros's quarters were not as lavish as I had expected, though they were by no means austere. Books were messily arranged on bookshelves lining the walls, alternating with ancient-looking tapestries. Thick carpets layered the floor. A few oddities were present as well. The room was lit by levitating pyr lamps, the same as I'd seen at Asileia's Ascension, that were somehow maintained through magnesis. And along one wall, a series of items were encased in glass that didn't seem to warrant such a display, like a glass orb that contained nothing within it, and a dagger of white wood that looked fit for little more than play between children.

The Archmaster himself lay prone on a four-poster bed in the middle of the room, tucked under a sea of thick comforters. The room was cold enough that my skin rose in chills, but under those heavy blankets, it had to be hot and uncomfortable. I wondered if Kyros Brighteyed had taken some strange ill from channeling too much. After all, he'd contended with Vusu and lost.

"Leave us," Kyros said firmly to the honor. "And bring Isidora."

I wondered who she was and worried that he already looked forward to his next appointment. I set my jaw and stood still with forced patience.

As soon as the woman had left, the Archmaster studied me. "So. You survived your trip into the Pyrthae."

His eyes didn't glow as they usually did, but were a dun dark brown. Still, they carried all the sharp temper he'd displayed before. I shifted uncomfortably under that gaze. If there was an Acadian capable of knowing wardens at a glance, it was Kyros.

"Yes." I offered nothing further.

"Well?" he prompted testily. "Has anything strange happened to you?"

"What qualifies as strange after one has visited the Pyrthae?"

Kyros suddenly slammed a hand on the frame of the bed with a resounding crack. "Damned depths, woman! Now is not the time to tiptoe around the truth like you're afraid of shattering the crockery! You've been abed for three days. Why?"

I held my tongue. Before, I had intended merely to pry what information I could from the man and leave him to his recovery. But now that he'd forced a confrontation, I wondered if I should aim higher. After all, Kyros had held Vusu at bay for a time. And he'd trained some Acadians to fight, two of whom I'd seen in action at the battle within the Conclave. He could prove to be a valuable ally.

And he could teach me to channel. To fight against Vusu and Famine myself, and not expect my allies to do all the work.

But he could also ruin me. I didn't know him, and I certainly didn't trust him. He might have fought Vusu, but that didn't necessarily put us on the same side. I needed my position as First Verifier more than I needed to learn to be a warden right now. Much as it pained me to admit it, Xaron was right. I couldn't progress fast enough for it to make much of a difference. If I was to fight against the daemon god and his servant, it would have be as I'd always done before: plots and lies, webs and whispers.

"Well?" the Archmaster demanded. "Out with it!"

"I've been ill. I was unconscious most of that time, and weak when I was awake. When I could finally rise, I was ravenous." I shrugged. "That's all."

"And what did you see there? Did you see what Eltris claims?" His scowl twisted into a mocking grin. "Did you see Famine?"

A scowl hardened my own features. "I did."

He snorted. "So you're as much a fool as she is. If that's all you have to say to me, leave me be. I, unlike you, have suffered serious wounds and need my rest. Onala!"

I didn't move, even as I heard the door open behind me. "I'm not finished yet, Archmaster. I have questions to ask you in return."

"Do you?" A vein pulsed in his forehead. "Very well, *Verifier*. Put me to your questions."

"What do you know of the daemon god Famine?"

He responded as I thought he would, spluttering a harsh laugh. "It was a trick, girl! An illusion by Vusumuzi! You cannot imagine the things a warden as powerful as him can do. The things he could make *you* do." His eyes glimmered with a maliciousness it was hard to imagine.

I tried not to let it faze me. "Where might I discover more about Famine? Is there a library that might have texts on him?"

The Archmaster suddenly fell into a bout of coughs. "A library!" he exclaimed as soon as he could speak. "Oh, yes, we have a library *full* of legends and myths. In fact, try Tomes — I'm sure you'll find all kinds of useless bilge there to keep you happy."

I took his jest as permission. "Who should I see to find these tomes?"

"Tomes is a section of the library, foolish girl! Go there and tell them I sent you." The Archmaster's lips found a sickly grin. "That ought to give that ancient hag the shock to finally keel her over."

His bitter humor grated on my nerves, but I managed to hold my temper in check. "I doubt she'll take me at my word. I'll need a token of approval. Your seal would do, I assume."

"My seal? Do you think me a king? You need no seal. When you reach her, she'll allow you in."

I was just about to protest further when something gave me pause. It was like a thought unbidden, something half-remembered slipping across my mind. Only I recognized the thought was not my own.

Suddenly gripped by curiosity, I reached after whatever had touched my mind, only to recoil. Pain flared in my head as I attempted to follow. I winced and put a hand to my temple.

As the pain ebbed, I found Kyros watching me with sudden interest. A smirk slowly spread across his face. My heart pounded in my chest, and I pulled my hand away from my temple.

"So," he said at length. "That's how it is. I wonder how."

"Thank you for your aid," I rushed to say. "There is one other thing I wished to ask you about."

"There is one other thing you *should* ask me about." Kyros grinned openly now, his eyes laughing.

I pretended not to notice. "Before the Despoina's trial, you were training wardens. Training them to use their magic to fight as Shepherds do."

The humor swiftly drained from the Archmaster's face. "I don't know what you heard," he snapped, his foul temper suddenly returned. "But I would never do such a thing."

"Of course not," I said smoothly. "After all, such a crime would certainly condemn you to death. It might dismantle the Acadium as we know it. If the head suffers corruption, the rest of the body likely holds it as well. I merely wished to verify it. That's what I do, isn't it?"

"Get out." He spoke the command softly, then repeated it louder. "Get out! Damned if I know why I let you in."

"Thank you, Archmaster." I turned smoothly and left the room, passing by the stricken honor Onala to descend the stairs.

Two circles down, I paused and caught my breath. My heart raced, and regret coursed through me. I'd prodded Kyros where he was vulnerable, picking at his flagrant disobedience of the law, which could ruin him and the Acadium if exposed. But *why* had I done it? Had it been to claim back some measure of control as he smirked and guessed at my secrets? I suspected he hadn't been bluffing; Kyros didn't seem fond of subtleties, nor one to put on a false face. If he smiled the way he had, he knew something that I wished he didn't. And at the moment, there was only one secret I desperately wanted to guard.

Despite myself, a private elation sparked to life. If Kyros believed me a warden, then I couldn't have imagined it. And that wasn't the only proof. When he'd spoken of not needing a seal or message from him, I'd felt something strange passing through my mind. It must have been channeling; how else could my sensing it tip Kyros off? But if it were channeling, it was nothing like the magic I'd experienced thus far.

My thoughts were interrupted by the sound of footsteps coming up the stairs. I quickly moved to the next circle down and stepped aside just in time to see someone rise from the stairwell. I was surprised to find that I recognized her: the Acadian woman who had fought against Vusu and his Shepherds at Asileia's trial. One of Kyros's trained wardens. The very ones I'd implied I'd rat out if the Archmaster revealed my secret.

The woman smiled as she recognized me. "First Verifier Airene. How good to see you." Despite the speed with which she'd ascended, she didn't pant or shine with perspiration. She wasn't a great beauty, yet there was something undeniably attractive to her, a surety and natural grace in the way she moved that couldn't be falsified.

"Yes, I am she," I said. "And you must be Isidora."

The Acadian made a face. "I'll bet you heard that from Kyros. He loves to irk me by using my full name. Please, call me Isi."

"Very well, Isi."

There was an awkward pause as I tried to think of a way to excuse myself. But my mind was too full to make smooth conversation. For the Acadian's part, she seemed to sense something was off.

"I think I understand," she said after a moment. "He's already told you."

I blinked. "Who has told me what?"

It was Isi's turn to be confused. "But why would you—? Ah. Of course. You were at the Despoina's trial."

"Yes, I was."

The air grew yet more uncomfortable between us. Now we both knew I could ruin her with that secret. But who had she thought would have told me? Kyros? It didn't seem likely, but I couldn't imagine who else she'd be talking about.

Isi smiled, and it was tinged with something I couldn't understand. Sympathy?

"I know it can be a shock, Airene, wardens using their channeling for more than tricks or tools. But what Kyros and I did, what our fallen brother did, was what our gifts were meant for. The initial wardens were called to defend and protect, as I'm sure you know. We were only doing our best by Oedija, just as you continue to do. And I would think that with—" She paused. "But if he has not discussed it with you, I shouldn't intrude."

Amid my confusion, I couldn't find a response. At length, the Acadian nodded to me and continued her ascent up, seeming as self-possessed as before. She thought she had my measure, and that their secret was safe. That grated on me more than anything.

Stewing silently, I made my long way down, feeling as if I only understood half of what I'd heard in this damned tower.

5
TOMES

In the twelfth season, the world's fortunes began to turn.

The pyr changed first. Spirits of harvest and benevolent ancestors, who had always been helpers to humans, suddenly played mean-spirited tricks. Tools went missing. Crops spoiled. Calves sickened and died. As the holy men and women were called upon to placate them, the pyr ignored their pleas and continued their mischief.

Then worse things began to occur. Trees that had borne bountiful fruit the seasons before wilted with blight. The breath of frail babes faltered and ceased. Wine became vinegar in as it was drunk. All that had been given began to be taken away twofold, and the name of Tyurn Sky-Sea became a curse on his people's lips.

The Lord of All stared down in horror and rage. 'What have you done?' he cried to the Seed.

'What have I done?' the Seed replied. 'Was it not you who gave all this to your people? Then is it not you who is turning it to ash?'

'What do I do?' the Lord of All begged of the Seed.

'Do not fear. I will help,' the Seed soothed him. 'All you must do is lend me your power, and I will put all aright.'

Tyurn Sky-Sea had lost much in eleven seasons. He did not feel the Seed pressing his roots deeper inside him.

78

'Set things right,' he said to the Seed, and gave yet more of himself away.

- The Seeds of Famine, a translation from the Lighted-tongue; by Oracle Kalene of deme Hull; 881 SLP

As promised, Corin waited for me outside of Kyros's tower. I marveled at her patience. No doubt long hours of waiting for the next person needing a cart had developed it, but it came so naturally to Corin that it had to be in her blood.

Despite my sour mood, I flashed her a small smile as I came down the tower stairs. "If you wouldn't mind, there's a couple more things I'd like to do here."

Her face as impassive as before, she nodded. "It's not safe to return on your own. I'll stay with you."

And I'll help you recover your sister, I promised her silently, hoping I could.

Corin scanned the grounds. "Where to first?"

I hesitated. I knew what I ought to do. My brother had lain here in the Acadium for four days without seeing anyone he knew. To go to him would be the right thing to do. But I couldn't force myself to say the words. A wall of guilt held them back. Guilt at having failed him. Guilt that I didn't want to witness what I'd let him become.

"The library," I finally said. "I guess we'll have to ask directions."

The friendlier of the two Acadians, both of whom still lingered nearby, looked over with a smile. "I can help you with that..."

The old man pointed us in the library's direction, and Corin and I thanked him before making our way across the Acadium once more. The nonsensical winding paths between the eclectic buildings were almost beginning to grow familiar. Following the directions, we wove between edifices and around Acadians leisurely carrying on with their business. In contrast to the city outside, there seemed almost a lightness to the air. The Acadium was not yet starving. I wondered how things would change when they were.

Nearing the library, the crowds started to thin. It brought a small smile to my lips. Acadians were supposed to be studious by nature. But when the only thing they had in common was their attunement to the Pyrthae, it didn't surprise me to see so few interested in the art of reading. With ancient texts, reading became a tedious chore, and one I little looked forward to.

I almost didn't believe when we'd arrived at the library. Had the Acadian not warned us it rose only a story high, I would have passed it by for one of the grander buildings on campus. Still, it had a certain stateliness to it, with two fountains set in long, rectangular mirror pools extending toward the entrance stairs, and squat, stolid columns that were more functional than beautiful. Though I thought it couldn't be more straightforward, etched along the pediment were letters announcing 'library' in the Lighted-tongue of Oedija's ancestors.

We entered through the weathered front doors into a dark, tall-ceilinged foyer. The air was chill and smelled of stale parchment and dust. The room was gently lit by a chandelier of pyr lamps and sconces mounted on walls. All around us, orderly lines of shelves ran to the surrounding walls, blocking from view what I assumed were yet more shelves. Every available space was filled with books.

My earlier derision evaporated as I stared around me. Never before had I seen the promise of so much knowledge. It seemed unimaginable that so many books could have been written in the world, much less collected here in one place. My mouth hung open until I caught myself.

Footsteps echoed through the airy room as a portly boy

hurried toward us. "Hello!" he huffed as he stopped a few paces away. "May I help you?"

For a moment, I forgot what I'd come for. "Ah, yes. I'm looking for books on old Eidolan legends. I was told Tomes might hold the ones I'd want."

"Tomes?" The boy, who I assumed was an apprentice of some kind, seemed surprised. "Hardly anyone but the Master Historian goes down there now. And I'm afraid you'll need permission from the Master Librarian."

"I believe I already have it."

The boy seemed even more confused. "Yes, if you say so, Mistress...?"

"Airene." I didn't correct him on my title. Somehow, it seemed petty to lord it over a child.

"Mistress Airene," the boy repeated, then turned to Corin. "And if you could tell me your name?"

Corin looked startled at being addressed. The woman was remarkably skilled at going uncommented for long periods of time, particularly for a woman of her size.

"Corin," she muttered.

"Mistress Airene and Mistress Corin — a pleasure meeting both of you." He bowed deeply. "I am Pupil Platon."

"Pleasure to meet you as well, Platon." I bowed politely in return.

Platon beamed. "If you'll please wait here, I'll just confirm with Master Hagne that everything is in order." The apprentice grinned at us again before turning and jogging back the way he'd come.

As he left, Corin muttered, "Mistress Corin..."

I hid a smile.

The boy returned a short time later. "She wasn't pleased," he said cheerily, "but she said you were permitted, so long as you followed the rules."

"The rules?"

"I'll tell you as we go, if you please. Now if you're ready, mistresses…"

Walking now instead of running, Platon chattered as he led the way. I found his words washing over me while I marveled at the sights around us. As we approached the chandelier, the ground fell away, revealing floor upon floor faintly lit by pyr lamps below. My eyes widened as I counted five floors before the light became too faint to make out any further. If each level had as many books as this one did, the sheer amount of knowledge contained in these walls was astounding.

It was also intimidating. What I needed to know about Famine was not likely to be common knowledge, if it existed at all. Not to mention I didn't know what kind of text would be most helpful. Ancient histories, mythic stories, religious texts, perhaps even merchant ledgers might hold the secrets I needed. I was searching for a needle in a granary. My stomach sank at the prospect of the turns of work that lay before me, particularly when we had less than six spans before Avvad's armies began sieging the city.

My mood soured as we descended, my already sore legs protesting the many stairs. Platon apologized over and over, explaining that ancient texts were kept as far from the elements as possible to aid in their preservation. I nodded distractedly as I debated whether I should bother going through with this or not. Perhaps all I needed was to track down Eltris. It could be that the augur held the answers to all the mysteries surrounding Famine.

Though, when I thought of it further, I wondered if she did. For all she seemed to know, Eltris hadn't been able to stop Vusu or Famine. She couldn't save Linos. The Master Augur knew much, but she wasn't omniscient. And I couldn't rely on an unreliable woman in times like these.

We descended five floors before the pupil stopped. "Here they are, mistresses!" Platon announced cheerily, spreading his arms at the shelves before us. "The most ancient Eidolan legends from the quills of the finest historians and story-tellers the Four Realms has known."

I stepped forward, leaning in close to the books to squint at their titles. Many were so layered with dust they were impossible to make out. I reached out to clean the spine.

Platon danced forward, smiling nervously. "Ah, Mistress, do be careful. Remember Master Hagne's rules, which I just told you?"

I hadn't listened to his rules, but I didn't want the young Acadian pupil to know that. Smiling apologetically, I withdrew my hand and kept studying the spines, looking for promising titles in legible print. Most of the words were in the Oedijan sea-tongue, but of such an old dialect they might as well have been in the Lighted-tongue. The education my mother and father had given me at home hadn't touched on ancient languages, and the five years I'd attended a public scholarium were scarcely sufficient to read in the older forms of the sea-tongue. This wouldn't be an easy search.

"May I help?" Platon asked after a time. He seemed eager for our task to be over, no doubt anxious we might break another of his mistress's rules.

"Look for titles on the Lighted Passage. Or anything relating to Famine."

The boy bobbed his head and hurried down the aisle. "Go slow, Platon," he muttered to himself as he searched. "Pretend like you're swimming to the book. Slow and even, handling them gentle as lambs."

I tried to block out his words as I squinted at the swimming letters. In such dim light, the ancient script was all but impossible to read. At my prompting, Platon fetched a pyr lamp, but it only helped marginally, particularly as the pyr lamps were kept dim as a rule. Platon explained that the cultures were pruned to reduce risk of light damage to the books. Corin stood at the end of the aisle waiting for us.

Unable to read even the modern sea-tongue, a library was probably the last place she wanted to be. I tried to ignore the squirming in my stomach and kept searching.

By the end of two turns, Platon and I had gathered between us three books: *The Legend of the Lighted Passage; Daemonic Tales: Encounters with Malevolent Pyr;* and *The Seeds of Famine.* Of the three, the last sounded the most promising. Not only was it the oldest, but it was also a translation of a much older text, one the author claimed to be written in 18 SLP, not two decades after the Lighted Passage.

Though my eyes ached and my neck was stiff, I opened *The Seeds of Famine* onto one of the book stands near the end of the shelves which, as Platon explained, kept the book from opening flat and ruining the spine. Then I started to read.

From the Lower Realm of the world beyond ours, a Seed rose. It was a small thing, no larger than a pebble, and none noticed its passing as it lifted higher and higher, until it reached—

"Is it helpful?" Platon appeared at my shoulder and looked curiously at the yellowed pages before me. "Remember, keep it on the book stand and turn it slowly. Like handling—"

"—A lamb, I remember." I tried shutting out the pupil and continued scanning the cramped script.

...Until it reached the Higher Realm where our gods, the Eidola, reign. Tyurn Sky-Sea, Ruler of All Realms, Lord of All, was strong—

"This is probably the oldest book I've ever handled," the boy mused.

"You're not handling it, I am. Now please, will you be quiet?"

Though his interruptions were worsening my headache, I

immediately regretted the sharp words. Turning back, I winced at the pupil's expression.

"I'm sorry, Platon," I said softly. "I didn't mean to snap at you. I just need to concentrate."

The hurt vanished immediately. "It's alright. You're probably uncomfortable down here. I was pretty uncomfortable the first few times I came down here. It's dark and musty, and you have to move so slowly…"

I sighed and leaned my head against my hands, kneading my eyes with my palms. I'd get no peace with the boy here. And somehow, being around him brought Linos to mind. "We'd better go. I'm assuming I can't take these with me?"

The pupil looked scandalized. "Of course not! You'd ruin them! Meaning no offense, Mistress Airene, but any kind of exposure at their age would be bad for them. Particularly moisture. But I can reserve them for you here!"

I pushed away from the table. "Do that. Then we'll get out of here. I've had enough of squinting at squirming lines in the dark for one day."

Once Platon had secured my three finds in a cubby at the end of a shelf, we made our way back up to the ground floor. My legs, already sore from my long ascent up Kyros's tower, protested with every step, but all I could do was grimace and carry on. There was no way I was complaining about getting tired in front of Corin, not to mention the boy, who practically skipped up the stairs with boundless energy.

When we reached the main doors again, the boy turned. "I'll see you soon? When you come back to read those books?"

"I imagine you will."

Platon beamed. He had a way of smiling that made him seem much younger than the thirteen years I'd initially thought him. "I'll see you then, Mistress Airene!"

"Just one thing before we go. Do you knowing where the healing ward is?"

~

After the pupil's directions got us lost, Corin and I eventually received adequate instruction to find our destination. The healing ward — called the Ward, appropriately enough — was on the opposite side of the campus in a long building built of gray stone. It easily stretched five hundred cubits in either direction and rose three stories high. From the look of it, the Ward could house hundreds of the ill, perhaps even a thousand, if not very comfortably.

Nervously, I led Corin through the front door. A clerk waited at a small desk before us, watching unsmiling as we stopped and looked around. From the hall beyond the desk, I heard the murmur of voices, punctuated by screams.

Wincing as another shriek pierced the air, I approached the clerk. "I'm looking for Linos of Port."

"Are you? And what's your interest in Linos of Port?" The clerk studied me with an arched brow.

"I'm his sister. Airene of Port."

The clerk nodded and began to flip through a book splotched with ink, chewing absentmindedly on the end of her pen as she did. Finally, she jabbed a finger at a scribbled line. "Here he is. Ward three, bed sixty-four."

Muttering the clerk's directions to myself, I led Corin through hallway after hallway, every one of them lined with doors. I wondered if this building had been built with this intention, for it seemed to suit the needs of a healing ward perfectly. Most patients occupied their own rooms. All spoke of the healers of the Acadium and how crucial they were in times of plague. But for regular use, with access to the Acadium restricted, I wondered who was actually able to seek assistance. Perhaps only patricians and the other notables of Oedija could secure access.

It wasn't clear from those I saw. Some of their robes were cleaner and of finer material, but the fineness of a garment's weave didn't matter much when a person was in the thrall of foul humors. I turned my gaze aside from angry red boils and chest-wracking coughs. Though healers were every-where, it seemed unlikely that some of those around us would make it out alive.

We passed through another archway, then '64' was on a door ahead of us, engraved in a wooden plaque. The door was shut. Nervously, I approached it and laid a hand on the plaque. It was cool to the touch. I hesitated a moment longer, conscious of Corin watching and waiting behind me, then knocked softly on the door. When I didn't hear a response, I slowly opened it.

Linos lay on a bed within, staring up at the ceiling with wide, unshifting eyes. He didn't look over as we entered and shut the door quietly behind us. Barely two spans had passed since his last visit to Canopy, but as I looked down on him, I felt my little brother had aged far more. The first growth of blonde stubble had appeared over his lip. Someone had washed his face and arms, which lay over the unadorned blankets covering him. He wore a rough brown robe different from the gray one I'd last seen him in. He looked thin, but not much more than since his transformation at Vusu's hands.

As my chest grew tight, I searched for distractions. Opening the drapes to allow in more light, I tucked the blan-kets under him as I had when he'd been a child. Anxious to know he'd been treated well, I sent Corin for a healer. A heal-er's assistant came instead with a long-suffering look, but upon hearing I was kin, he patiently recounted Linos's care. There was not much to speak of. Kallias the Sculptor had visited twice, but neither session had shown progress. Beyond that, Linos had barely stirred, though he took care of his needs when prompted. "It's as if he needs reminding how to live," the assistant mused.

I dismissed him, unable to hide my sour expression.

Once he'd left, I spoke to Corin without looking at her. "Could you give us a moment?"

Without a word, she left the room, pulling the door closed behind her.

I turned back to Linos. His expression hadn't shifted. But for his chest steadily moving up and down, I might have thought him dead. I stepped closer and reached toward him. My hand shook as it settled on the exposed skin of his arm.

Pain split through my skull and brought me to my knees. I was barely aware I'd fallen. I felt myself flayed open, layer by layer exposed like a body under a knife, each spike of pain precise and efficient.

Something was doing this cutting, something foreign and daemonic. Suddenly, I became aware of it, the thing that was pulling apart the deepest parts of myself and laying them bare.

Defiant rage filled me. I gathered the shreds of myself and pushed against the invading presence. At first, my resistance accomplished little. Then, measure by measure, I began to force it out. I became aware of my body again and wrenched my hand away from my brother's skin. As soon as contact was broken, the looming presence fell away, leaving my head aching and my body shivering.

I clutched my arms tightly around myself and rose shakily to my feet. My head felt stuffed full of fleece, my thoughts sluggish as molasses. But I forced myself to see beyond the pain and look down on my brother.

He stared up at me, grinning.

A small, startled noise rose in my throat before I could stop it. "Linos?" I managed to gasp.

"So you are another of his seeds." It was my brother speaking, yet somehow, I knew the words were not his. They came out harsh, biting. My brother had taken pride in his rich baritone since his voice had dropped a year before. He'd never spoken in this way before.

I forced myself to keep his gaze. "What do you mean?"

A mocking grin twisted his face. "You know what I mean. Are you not a First Verifier now? Surely you can figure this out."

I clenched my jaw and forced myself to face the truth. This was not Linos I spoke with, but the one who had taken his place. *Vessel.*

"What have you done to my brother?" My words shook with repressed emotion.

"I *am* your brother. Now, at least." Linos's eyes glimmered. "He has his claws in you, Airene. He wishes to know you further."

"Who do you speak of? Vusu? Famine?"

"You seek answers, to understand what has happened, what *is* happening. He can help you. You must go to him. No one else can tell you all you need to know."

I wanted to shake my brother, to drive out whatever daemon possessed him. I wanted to unhear his words that wormed their way into my head. But, once again, I could do nothing.

"I'm going now, Linos," I said in as steady a voice as I could. "I'll come see you later when you're feeling better."

Finally, those bright blue eyes closed, and his head fell back against the pillow. For a moment, I dared to hope he was returning to his rest, unmarred by daemons.

Then slow laughter rasped from his throat, wave after wave spasming his body.

Clenching my fists so tightly my nails drew blood, I fumbled for the door's latch and fled the room.

6

QUINTESSENCE

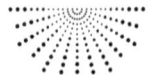

The Seed, engorged with the power of Tyurn Sky-Sea, swept over the land. But where it went, things only worsened. Crops ready for reaping fell as dust in their fields. Lakes and rivers dried up to their sources. The ill lost the will to live, and plague once more claimed the lands.

Clepsammia appeared before her father and saw what he had become. Tyurn Sky-Sea, once as large as a mountain and as strong as a giant, had shrunk to a starved, sickly man. He could not lift his head to greet his daughter, nor even recognize her as she neared.

The Goddess of Fate clasped her father's hands, kneeling by his bed. But her voice was iron, forged hard in grief's fires, as she spoke. 'Father! You must rise from your bed! Come see what your pride has brought to those you swore to protect. Did I not warn you that this would come to pass? This Seed that grows is not of harvest, but famine. You have brought an end to all realms, oh Lord of All!'

Tyurn Sky-Sea roused at her words. But even as his anger and pride stirred, he looked over Telae and found his daughter had spoken true. All that his dreams of plenty had brought was ruin.

'What can I do, Daughter?' he asked, all hope dead in his breast. 'I have doomed us all!'

But Clepsammia, Maiden of the Sands, wore a sad, knowing smile, for all knowledge of what was and is to come was hers. 'Not yet, Father. For there is yet one thing you can still do...'

- The Seeds of Famine, a translation from the Lighted-tongue; by Oracle Kalene of deme Hull; 881 SLP

W e walked the Acadium campus in silence as my mind buzzed. Now more than ever, I needed answers. Linos's words — *Or Vessel's*, I thought bitterly — had made my questions burn brighter. What did they mean? And could the figure he referred to be anyone other than Vusu or Famine?

And then there was what had happened when I'd touched him. I gingerly rubbed at my temples as we exited the Acadium gates. The pain had dulled to an ache, but my mind still felt raw and vandalized. Who or what that had been, I still didn't know. It bore an echo of the ravenous hunger I'd felt radiating from Famine when I'd stood before him in the Pyrthae, but it hadn't possessed the same depth or vastness. And I'd contended with its will and broken free. Whatever that daemon was, it wasn't Famine himself. A dark part of me wondered if it actually was Linos who had attacked me. But I had another theory. And until I consulted Talan about it, I'd cling to it and believe my brother still held on somewhere inside his body.

Corin stopped in the street just out of earshot of the Acadium guards. "Be wary," she cautioned in a low voice. "We are still in danger."

"I know that," I said, rousing from my thoughts. "I'd be hard-pressed to forget our mugging."

She gave me an expressionless look, then turned and left down a side road.

I bit back my words and followed. She didn't deserve my irony, not after she'd waited patiently with me all day. Even if much of it was done from guilt, it didn't change that she'd been a steady friend to me when Nomusa, Xaron, and Talan couldn't be.

"Look, Corin—" I began.

"You've had a long day," she interrupted without turning around. "We've not eaten since morning. And you were recently ill. I'm not offended."

I hesitated, more convinced than before that she was. "Still, I'm sorry. I appreciate you being here today."

She didn't turn, but nodded once. I would have to be content with that, it seemed.

"We should pass through the Laurel Palace," she said after traveling a while along the road. "It's a shorter path out in the open."

I nodded my agreement. "As long as my medallion still opens the way, I'll take any shortcuts."

$\sim$

The laurel guards let us through the gates at a flash of my medallion. Three-quarters of a turn after, we finished crossing the bridge and stood before the Aviary.

"I suppose we need to get a room outfitted for you," I mused as we approached the building. I went a few steps further before I noticed Corin had stopped. I turned back, trepidation rising in me. "Corin?"

"I'm leaving." Her gaze traveled over my head.

I sighed. "I wasn't lying when I said I'd try to find your sister."

"I know."

We were both still for a moment. "Where will you go?" I asked softly. "What will you do?"

The big woman shook her head. "I'll find her."

Corin had come on her own to Oedija, so I knew she didn't have any relations here, nor other friends that I knew of. She had no place to go. Even with her iron will, she needed a place to sleep. And no matter what had happened between us, she was still my friend.

"Seek out Maesos," I said. "He'll give you a place to stay as long as you need one. Though he may have you cart his wares around a bit."

She considered this for a long moment before nodding. "It is a good plan. Thank you."

"It's the least I can do."

By impulse, I stepped forward and pulled Corin into a tight hug. "You'll find her," I muttered into her rough tunic. "Just take care of yourself until you do."

The former cartwoman hesitated, then loosely put an arm around me until I stepped away. Without another word, she nodded, then turned in the direction of the Conclave gate. I watched her go. Not a coin to her name, but she boldly moved forward. If only I could be so decisive in my actions. I delayed even visiting my sick brother. Shaking my head, I turned and entered back into the Aviary.

But I'd only just stepped into my room when restlessness seized me. Now that I had a moment to myself, I wondered what I was doing, returning to the Aviary before the day was done. There was still a turn or two of light left. Yet here I was, back in my room. Was I so afraid of wandering the streets now? Did I think I would be mugged again or worse? Or had it been my encounters with Linos, Isidora, and Kyros that drove me to take shelter?

None of it was an excuse. Though I was tired and sore, I couldn't rest. Not until I'd done all I could. Groaning, I rose and went to seek Nomusa. Surely she would have some Finch task for me.

But the cook didn't know where she was, though she did point with exasperation to the feast she'd made for just me and Nomusa that lay untouched on the foyer tables. I relented and gorged myself on the fine foods. Guilty or not, I still needed to eat.

Full and sleepy, I wandered out of the Aviary, but stopped from indecision at the stoop. Nomusa could be at the Conclave. Or perhaps she was up at the Laurel Palace meeting another mysterious contact. Or a dozen other places that she now frequented but I didn't know about. I rubbed my aching head. Hunting her down would be nigh impossible. She and I would have to start consulting each other if we were to coordinate as First Verifiers.

My headache reminded me of another person I ought to seek out. Rising with a groan, I set off for the Laurel Palace. If I ran into Nomusa along the way, all the better.

I made the long trip back up the hill atop which the Laurel Palace sprawled, then asked the first honor I passed where Hilarion's quarters lay. At her directions, my eyebrows rose. Xaron had not jested when he said Hilarion was afforded fine rooms. But joy for my friend was hard in coming as I mounted yet another spiral staircase to ascend Hilarion's tower. My legs burned and air wheezed in my lungs as I mounted the last of the steps to reach the door at the top. Too tired even to knock, I was startled as the door swung open to reveal my friend's grinning face framed by a black cloud of unkempt hair.

"How did you know?" I said between pants.

"How could I not? I heard your huffing and puffing the whole way up!" He treated me to another teasing grin as he motioned me inside.

I gratefully sank into a chair and accepted the glass of wine he poured me, then examined the rooms he'd been afforded. Hilarion's quarters were composed of multiple chambers. The one we sat in had no bed, and two other doors led off to either side. It was a waiting room like no other I'd seen. The implements of decades of Hilarions decorated the walls and tables, awaiting their next opportunity to entertain. Marionettes hung from hooks. A strange wheel contraption leaned in one corner. What looked to be an unactivated magnetic pyr lamp was tucked against the doorframe. Silk streamers in every different color flowed down another wall. All was situated to remind the guest that the person who occupied these chambers was a fool, and all he possessed was for enjoyment alone.

Xaron settled himself into the chair next to me, sipping on a glass of wine as well, though he'd poured from a different bottle than mine. I discovered why as I sipped my own. A smoky port — Xaron drank lighter wines with tones of fruit, not the strong stuff I preferred. I smiled in satisfaction.

"The decorations are a bit tawdry, but they'll do for now," Xaron said amicably. "Glad you were able to make it up here."

I gave him a wry grin. "If I hadn't already ascended another tower today, perhaps it wouldn't have been so difficult."

He raised an eyebrow. "Not many towers around here. Which one did you go up?"

I told him of my visit to the Archmaster. Xaron's brow furrowed further with each sentence.

"Then he seemed to send her a message," I continued, "though he did nothing but lie in his bed. I think he channeled. After he said I wouldn't need his seal of approval, I felt… something. In my mind."

Xaron stared at me, a wild look in his eyes, before composing himself. "Right," he muttered. "I almost forgot you were a warden now."

A flush of pride warmed my chest. I tried to ignore it as I pressed, "But what was it? Was it channeling? And if so, what kind? All I know are the three energetic elements — radiance, kinesis, and magnesis. But are there more?"

Xaron hesitated. "Possibly. My mother has a way of channeling completely different from anything I know. Had," he corrected himself with a sour expression. "I suppose she doesn't use her gifts anymore."

"What way of channeling?"

"She was an apothecary, if you remember. But she wouldn't just concoct alchemical solutions. She studied their reactions, then mimicked them. She discovered how to channel the energy from those reactions, something she called 'catalysm.'"

He ran a hand through his loose hair. "I was so young when she had her accident, it's hard to piece together what I saw. You know how when you combine two opposing solutions, they might have a reaction? Like... like yeast with honey. If you leave them in warm water, they foam, or when combined with flour, cause bread to rise."

"Of course."

"That reaction has an energy of its own. Yeast doesn't have a strong one, but there are plenty stronger. And my mother discovered all of them." He grimaced. "Hence, her accident."

I still wasn't sure I understood. "So catalysm might be a fourth energetic element. But even if it is, it doesn't explain what Kyros did to pass that message to the Master Librarian. I doubt it had to do with leavening bread."

Xaron grinned. "Humor me a little longer. As I was getting to, the energetic elements are thought to all be found in our bodies."

I frowned. "Radiance and kinesis I can understand. But magnesis?"

"Wouldn't you like to think lightning flows through our veins? But think for a moment. Did you ever rub your clothes against a rug when you were young, then touch something metal, or another person?"

"Of course. I used to tickle Linos on Mother's carpets,

then force him to touch the faux silver vase in the foyer. He'd yelp like a hurt puppy." I smiled sadly at the memory.

Xaron smiled sympathetically. "And when he touched the metal, you saw the spark that formed? Or have you ever felt the shock that goes through you? Well, that feeling is not far from the buzzing feeling of magnesis when you channel it."

"Alright. Say I buy all that. What are you getting at?"

"If it's true, if all the elements are present within us, then perhaps the mind has an energy as well. The soul, or spirit — or quintessence, as oracles would call it."

"An energy of the mind." The thought didn't perplex me as much as it once had. With both Kyros and Linos, there had been another presence touching my mind. And I'd interacted with them using my own. But that didn't mean it was an energy. Did it?

"You've got me questioning everything I thought I knew," I confessed.

He shook his head. "You're telling me. Eltris says I don't know half of what wardens are capable of. And seeing what Vusu could do — traveling into the Pyrthae, summoning Famine — I know it must be true."

"And there's always more to learn."

My thoughts having turned to it, I told him of my visit to the Acadium library. Xaron wrinkled his nose. "I don't suppose you've met the Master Librarian yet."

"No, I haven't." I squinted at him. "Why?"

"Oh, I'll just let you find out for yourself."

I let the cryptic answer slide and told him of Linos and our encounter.

"You're proving quintessence exists in one day." Xaron looked impressed. "But I'm sorry to hear of your brother."

"It's nothing more than I expected," I said dully. I wondered how I'd break the news to my family, whenever I saw them next. I rubbed my eyes. A problem for another time.

Another thought came to me. "Oh, I forgot to mention. I ran into Kyros's Acadian battle warden on his tower's stairs. A woman named Isidora."

Xaron spasmed and spilled his wine. "Did you?" he commented, his causal manner ruined as he jumped up and fetched a rag to mop up the wine.

I narrowed my eyes. "Are you hiding something?"

For a moment, he pretended to be absorbed in his cleaning. Then he sighed, threw aside the stained rag, and settled back in his chair. "Not exactly. Just that the group of Acadians who have been learning battle magic... We've been training under Isi."

Isi. So he was familiar with her enough to call her by her shortname. Just as he called me by mine. "I see."

He looked ready to say more when the door burst open. I rose with fists clenched, but it was Nomusa standing in the doorway. She looked as ready to attack someone as I.

"There you are!" She strode up to us with a scowl on her face. "Good thing you asked an honor for directions or I never would have found you. Had you heard?"

I took a breath to loosen my chest. "'Thae above, Nomusa. Don't barge in like that."

"Had you heard?" she demanded again. "Either of you. Do you know who's coming here?"

"Just tell us already," Xaron said, his bewilderment matching my own.

"Charatta Yorandu Komo." She spoke the name like a curse.

Only one part of it had any meaning to me. "Yorandu. They're from your ishaka."

"Not just from my ishaka. Komo is that usurper's son." Nomusa spat on the floor, heedless that it now belonged to Xaron. "The *Shaka's* son."

The significance finally dawned on me. The son of the

man who killed her parents, who exiled her from her homeland and birthright — he was coming to Oedija.

"Nomusa, I hadn't heard anything," I said honestly. "I'd have told you if I had."

But Xaron flushed pink. "I… may have heard of this. One of Komo's emissaries arrived a couple of days ago telling us he was coming."

I winced as Nomusa rounded on him. "You heard," she said in a low voice, "that the son of the man who killed my parents was coming here and didn't think to tell me?"

"I was barely paying attention!" Xaron protested, but Nomusa just hissed, stalked over to a chair, and slumped down.

Willing my sore legs into motion, I walked over and sat next to her, gently placing a hand on her shoulder. She was shaking with emotion — rage, no doubt, but I suspected grief as well. Nomusa had never really gotten over losing her homeland and family in one stroke, even a decade later.

"Tell me about his coming," I implored her softly. I hoped a report might draw her from her misery.

She drew in a shuddering breath. "He's to arrive here four days from now, come at the behest of the Despoina. Apparently Oedija and Yorandu have been in communication since well before the Night of the Three Horns. The urgency of Oedija's situation has accelerated the schedule for their plans."

"Which are?"

A bitter smile curled her lips. "What else can we offer that false prince but the Despoina's hand?"

I considered this. I'd never heard Nomusa plotting to take back her ishaka, but such significant ties to Oedija would certainly complicate ever making such a plan. By joining our royal family with their rulers, we obligated ourselves to come to their aid in war, just as they did for us.

I was torn. I knew what I should say to Nomusa as a

friend. But Oedija needed every ally we could get. Unable to deny one over the other, I held my tongue.

Nomusa turned her gaze on me, eyes glistening. "Don't think for a moment that I don't know we need allies. I've been attending the Council meetings. I know just how ill-prepared we are to face the threats before us. The Stratechons might be gathering the taxoi, but did you know they still have no definitive plans for dealing with the Manifest or Avvad?" She shook her head. "We need warriors. I just... Why did it have to be *them?*"

"I know." There was nothing else I could say. I intertwined my arm with hers and leaned into her side.

Xaron settled down on her other side and silently wrapped his arm around her, his hand resting on my shoulder. For a moment, it was almost as if we were all back in Canopy, scraping by as unconfirmed Finches. Aching nostalgia filled me to my bones.

But a thought turned the feeling cold. If I could return things back to the way they were, would I? It would take away all the pain and death and uncertainty closing in on us. But with it would go the achievements and dreams of a lifetime. Becoming a Verifier. Becoming a warden.

I was glad I didn't have to make that choice.

Nomusa straightened and gently pried us off. "You never mentioned what you had to tell me before," she said to me. "It seemed important."

I shared a look with Xaron.

Nomusa wasn't oblivious. "What? Does he already know?"

"I told him as soon as I awoke," I confessed. "But you'll understand why."

The telling came easier now that I was more certain. When I finished, Nomusa didn't seem shocked or fearful, but studied me with a narrowed gaze. "You're sure?" she asked softly. "Your fingerprints shift?"

"Fairly sure. Encounters today make me more so. And no

shifts have appeared yet, but as Xaron explained to me, they may take some time to show."

"A span, a season." Xaron shrugged. "If Airene channeled, she must be a warden."

But Nomusa didn't look convinced. "You went into the Pyrthae. Maybe what you experienced was a strange result from it. Like an afterimage from looking too closely at the sun."

"Channeling isn't the same thing as staring at the sun," I noted drily. "But I have other reasons to believe it's not just in my head." I recounted for her the instance in Kyros's bedchambers.

When I finished, Nomusa observed, "So you're not sure it was channeling, what you felt?"

My tongue was growing harder to restrain. "No. I'm not sure."

She looked as if she wanted to say more, but shook her head and rose. "Keep an eye on matters, I suppose. The last thing we need is for you to catch fire. In the meantime, I have plenty to keep you busy. Speaking of which…"

I rose, trying to master myself. Now was not the time to be bickering among ourselves. Even if Nomusa *was* being obstinate and skeptical. Masking my annoyance, I wrapped Xaron in a hug and murmured in his ear, "Maybe we can both pay Isi a visit soon."

The shrug he gave could have been agreement or refusal. I let it slide, and after Nomusa had said her own farewells, I followed her out the door.

As we walked down the Laurel grounds and across the bridge back to the Aviary, I kept the conversation far from Komo by prying information from Nomusa. Speaking in hushed tones and keeping a watchful eye out for those who drew too near, I tried to catch up on everything she knew of the Manifest, Avvad, and the Valemish.

Of Vusu and the Manifest, little deviated from the hasty summary she'd given me before. The Seekers continued to reinforce their compound and maintained a steady flow of food for their followers. Shadows had been seen flitting about rooftops at night in the northern inner demes. Seeker wardens, Nomusa guessed, and not very skilled ones for so many to be seen — unless they wished to be seen. Still, it was another danger to fear at night. *If only shutters could keep out assassins*, I thought drily.

Of Avvad, she had even less to say. They marshaled their forces from the provinces and gathered their supplies into wagons. All seemed on schedule for six spans, as before. One additional thing had been noted, however: they'd sent birds to the Bali ishakas, reportedly to request aid. Nomusa and I both knew Kahin-Shah Burak's real message: stand with Avvad, or be the next to fall. We'd see if the ploy worked.

The Valemish were said to have largely been contained within their temples. Posting the city guard before them was a bigger concession than had been expected of the Council, yet it did little to impede the flow of people in and out of the temples.

The worst of the news concerned food. The public granaries had been giving out the little grain they'd managed to properly store, but the estimates Nomusa had heard at Council meetings reported only enough for two spans more, three if the food was rationed severely. But even those estimates were generous, as they assumed that the foodstuff the Underguild held hostage would somehow be negotiated back.

"A poor time for a drought," I noted sourly over the wind billowing over the bridge.

"You think it is coincidental timing?" Nomusa shook her head. "I don't believe everything that augur Eltris says. But I do think she might have a point about the disasters throughout our history. Perhaps... perhaps the Serpent God is behind this as well."

I was surprised I hadn't seen it, and even more so that Nomusa had. "I wasn't sure you believed me. About Famine, and his return."

"I didn't want to. And I don't like thinking about it." She shook her head. "What can we do against a god? It seems futile to even think about it. We have enough problems without daemons and legends coming to life."

I thought of Linos at that, wondering if I could muster the energy to recount the incident again.

"Airene?"

I sighed. "I know what you mean. But I saw him. Maybe that's why I can't help but worry about him and little else."

"Maybe."

We fell into silence, listening to the sea crashing against the cliffs below us and the wind whistling in our ears. The evening was gloomy and blue, fitting for our somber mood.

Only as we stepped off the bridge did Nomusa speak again. "I suppose we should discuss your responsibilities."

I raised an eyebrow. "Don't you mean *our* responsibilities?"

"I'm already established in certain arenas. The Council knows and trusts me far more than you. You have the Preservists and Feiyan against you. If you try interceding in their politics, they might vote against what you support just out of spite."

It wasn't a responsibility I envied, yet I couldn't help but feel put off. After all, no matter how quarrelsome the Low Consuls might be, it was within the Council chamber that nearly every important decision for the realm was made. To be excluded was a sore blow.

"I'm also growing more familiar with the Conclave every

day," Nomusa continued. "It would be best if I head up that arena as well."

"Considering our responsibilities are to rout out corruption in the demotism, that seems to leave little for me to do."

She smiled thinly. "Not by a long stretch. What I was thinking is that you'd be responsible for calling at patrician homes. After all, corruption takes many forms, and we've scarcely begun to consider them all. Financial backing is what I wonder about now. The Seekers are getting significant money reserves from somewhere. Who's giving it to them, and why? We've barely even considered the question until now."

Before the night of Myron's disappearance, it would have been an opportunity I looked forward to. Now, I just thought of all the time it would take away from my true aims. But I was a First Verifier. Futile though this task might seem, I had to help Nomusa preserve our position for the time when we would most need it.

"Then I'll track their investors down," I answered gamely.

Nomusa glanced at me. "There's another task you could take on."

My enthusiasm proved to be short-lived. I sighed. "Out with it."

"Hiring other Verifiers to pick up your inevitable slack."

I smiled sheepishly. "You see right through me."

She smiled in return, but only briefly. "But do remember to take this seriously. Being Verifiers for the Conclave is different than it was for Jaxas. The Council needs to see progress on their directive, and soon, or they'll disband the Order as quickly as they resurrected it. But this is what we always wanted, isn't it? To be at the heart of thing, cutting to the secrets that matter most? To change the course of Oedija?"

Her resolve inflamed my own. "Yes," I said quietly. "That's what we wanted."

She exhaled like she'd been holding her breath. "Good. Now maybe we'd better rest before yet another long day."

We'd arrived at the Aviary and, after a hasty meal, we both went to our rooms. I briefly debated sending a finch to my family and decided it could wait until tomorrow. I'd already faced that issue once today and couldn't force myself to revisit it. Besides, I wasn't exactly sure which estate Jaxas had sent them to, or if I had the scents needed to direct a finch there. I sighed and put it from my mind as I undressed and settled into bed.

As I drifted off, I thought of another message I'd have liked to send. Talan's visit the night before had been far too brief, and I wanted to see him again. But he'd refused to say where he stayed, and I doubted a finch would be able to safely reach him anyway. I'd pry his location from him the next time he came, along with the answer to my question about Linos.

Sleepily, I imagined reaching out to him, grasping after his shadow as it flitted across the city. I followed it through the courtyard of the Conclave and onto the streets, but always it kept ahead of me. Still, I felt I could find its source, if I could only gain a proper vantage point.

I looked up, and only then saw that Oedija loomed above me as well as around. The world had doubled, half of it hanging precariously overhead. But I was seeking Talan. I drew my gaze away and continued my search, first running, then soaring as I gained speed. My feet left the ground.

I swept through Iris; when I didn't find him there, I sought him in the demes beyond. As I quested further, focusing on my task became harder, and I had to thrust more of myself into my search. I felt stretched, thinned, but I didn't dare slow. If I slowed, I might never find him.

Then I felt him: a warmth in the cold night. Nearing, I saw his bright flame appear amidst the dun bodies that filled the city. Not recognizing the place in Hull where he was, I approached, curious as a moth.

But as I neared, I saw Talan did not burn alone. Another flame, curiously detached, like it burned at the end of a long wick, hovered next to him. This second flame rose into the mirror world above. An impulse to sever the long flame seized me, and I felt the edges of myself sharpening. The anger came so suddenly and strongly that I barely had the strength to hold it at bay.

Then I felt another gaze upon me. I turned from the two flames and was near blinded by the inferno rising silently behind me. It swept forward, a wildfire in full bloom, and closed in around me. It drank from the fury that oozed from me, and from my fear as well, as I comprehended the vastness of this entity.

I gathered myself close and searched for an opening, but any escape was fast closing. All around was a sphere of writhing flames, each tendril yearning to burn me into itself. I stiffened my resolve and dared them to try.

The walls of fire began to close.

"Stop!"

The word reverberated through me, though the voice that had called it sounded weak. The inferno faltered, then retreated to form a gap, as if fearing the voice. In the center of the gap, a small black figure floated, unbothered by the flames that licked its feet. I stared in wonder at this being who could not be burned.

"You are mine still," the figure said, the same booming resonance in its reedy voice. *"Your seed does not yet lie fallow."*

The flames pulsed, as if daring the newcomer to try.

"Return to me!" the black figure hissed, spreading its arms.

But the conflagration didn't obey. Instead, it surged toward me, flames reaching its blistering arms forward.

Another figure, gray with streaming shadows about it, suddenly appeared between me and the great fire. It seemed the flames would consume it as well as me, but at the last moment, the fire surged to a halt.

"Return to me!" the black figure commanded again, voice stronger yet.

Caught between the figures of gray and black, the inferno gathered into itself. Then slowly, reluctantly, the great fire began to retreat. It flowed along itself toward the dark figure, then slithered inside it in glowing streams. The rivulets streamed over its arms like the retreating waves of the Lighted Sea over a rocky shore. The figure's pain washed over me, one wave after another, until the inferno was a glowing sphere inside its middle.

Then the shadowed figure turned its gaze upon me. *"You would doom us all,"* it said. Then it disappeared.

The gray figure, still floating before me, slowly turned around. I stared in mute wonder at its strangeness. She resembled a woman, but her features were so strangely disproportionate I knew she couldn't be human. Her eyes were angled sharply and opened wide, with irises black and silver. Her hair streamed about her head, silver against the gray of her body, moving as if they were a thousand tiny adders. Her robes hung in tatters, revealing gray skin beneath, and streamed in eleven long tails below her.

The strange woman drifted closer, then opened her hands. In one, I saw she held a sandglass, small and without a frame, little more than two glass bulbs fused together. Sand dripped down in it, the stream unnaturally slow to fall. Her other hand was empty.

This empty hand she extended toward me as she stopped before me. Her gesture was unmistakeable. I hesitated only a moment. She had saved me. She couldn't mean me harm.

I took her hand.

Suddenly, I was thrown swiftly down. The ground rushed toward me, closer and closer, then the blinding crush—

I sat up, gasping for air. Sweat beaded my skin, and a

feverish heat radiated from me. All I could do was pant and let the memory of the dream stir in my mind. *A dream.* Surely that was all it had been.

I pulled the blankets off, needing my hot skin to be exposed to the cool air, when I heard a strange crackle. Something flaked beneath my fingers. For a moment, I stood statue-still; then I reached one shaking hand over to the pyrkin pot on my bedside table and lifted the lid. Yellow light flooded the room, revealing two black marks upon my blankets. My hand rested in one. The other, I was sure, was where my other hand had been lying.

I stared for a moment, breath caught in my throat. *Radiance* — the word echoed in my mind. I had channeled radiance.

Relief washed over me.

I should have worried that I might have burned down the room, and perhaps the whole Aviary. But the doubts that had gnawed at me for the last two days were finally dispelled. Shifts or not, I knew I was a warden.

I'd channeled radiance.

And I could have killed Nomusa. The thought chilled my excitement. If I couldn't control my channeling, how could I keep my friends safe? I clenched my fists around the ashy blankets, feeling the black flakes crumble against my palms. I had to learn to control this. I'd endangered my friends far too often already. How could I put them at risk from myself?

Then, out of nowhere, words crashed into my mind, splitting it wide open.

COME TO ME!

The thought burst in uninvited, chopping through me like an axe. Vaguely, I was aware of falling back against my bed, arms flailing out to either side, limp as a corpse. I felt the parts of myself scatter all around me, and it was beyond me to put them back together.

Fragmented, I sank into darkness.

7
THE GOOD PUPIL

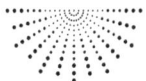

Tyurn Sky-Sea listened to his daughter's words and knew them for wisdom.

'Very well,' he agreed with a heavy heart. 'If the fault is mine, the price is also mine to pay. Thank you, Daughter, most true to my heart.'

Clepsammia, the Hand of Destiny, said nothing, but only smiled a sad smile.

Tyurn Sky-Sea looked at the world below, the world he so loved, and made his decision. He would give of all his remaining strength to grant those he had failed the power to protect themselves.

From among humans, he chose eleven of the noblest, bravest, cleverest, and wisest. Foremost among these was Agmon who would become known as Brandheart, already a famed general in his own right.

To the eleven, the Ruler of All Realms said:

'I, Tyurn Sky-Sea, Lord of All that walks, swims, or soars, do admit to you, my lost children, that I have committed a grave sin. And so I will repay you with power only a god has before wielded, that you might defend yourselves against my error.'

And so he made these eleven humans the First Wardens, and the First Wardens awoke to their newborn divinity.

- The Seeds of Famine, a translation from the Lighted-tongue; by Oracle Kalene of deme Hull; 881 SLP

Pain like nothing I'd felt before greeted me when I awoke. I gingerly touched my temples, opening my eyes to slits. Even that small amount of light evoked a fresh round of agony. My mother had sometimes complained of migraines as if there were no greater pain. Now I understood why.

Groaning, I forced myself to sit up. My stomach roiled, queasy and unsettled. For a moment, I thought I wouldn't hold down whatever remained of last night's dinner. I felt miserably sorry for myself as I put my legs off the side of the bed. Why today, of all days, did my mother have to be proven right?

Then the memory of last night rushed back in.

Come to me.

I would have sprang to my feet if I could have. As it was, I hunched against the misery and slowly began dressing. Somehow, I now recognized who had spoken the command. Even though I couldn't explain it, I had no doubt it was Eltris who had reached out to me. She'd summoned me to her.

And I'd fallen unconscious.

Strapping on my sandals, I wondered if it had been her that struck me unconscious, or the events that had come before. The dream had been strangely vivid. Could it have been more than a dream? Caught in its throes, I'd ignored all the strange aspects of the world. The city mirrored above... I'd imagined flying through the Pyrthae, I suddenly realized. But of Talan and the long flame with him, the dark figure that tamed the firestorm, the strange, gray woman who had

protected me… It had to be nonsense made up by my imagination.

Unless I'd truly visited the Pyrthae again.

Madness. I pushed away the thought and slowly eased
onto my feet. My aching head made my limbs shaky and
weak, and every movement jarred. My neck felt so stiff it was
difficult to turn it from side to side. I knew my hair was a
mess, but I could only summon enough care to grab a cloth
band to bind it back. My Verifier medallion hung heavy
around my neck.

Just before I left my room, I noticed two things waiting
for me on the floor by the door. Cursing how far away they
were, I bent slowly to retrieve them. One was a knife half a
cubit long, nestled into a plain leather sheath that was
connected to a series of leather bands. The other was a
folded piece of parchment. I picked them both up and
opened the note.

*Remember to report to our clerk Galene as to your expenses the
day before and retrieve today's allowance. If she isn't waiting for
you in the atrium, you can find her in the clerks' chambers off the
Conclave.*

*Wear this knife always. It won't be comfortable, but it won't be
in danger of slipping down.*

*Don't entrust yourself to a cartman. There have been reports of
them delivering patricians and clerks of the law into the hands of
brigands and Guilders. Your feet will carry you safer.*

And who's sleeping late now?

~ Nomusa

Her reminder was timely; I'd completely forgotten about
reporting to our clerk, though I'd noticed the distinct lack of
silver among Nomusa's gifts. I tried reining in my impatience
at the delay. Eltris had called me, and I'd already wasted a

night in answering her. And now, it wasn't only about learning what I could of Famine. I glanced back at the twin sears on my blanket. Best to hide evidence of my channeling, as much as I could — the last thing I needed was Hyrol's suspicion, especially if he did turn out to be someone's agent.

After I'd stuffed the blanket under my bed, the best hiding spot I could manage until after dark, I followed Nomusa's advice and unbound my chiton to strap on the knife. Little good it would do me under my robe, I thought sourly. Once again, I yearned for a tunic and trousers, even if I didn't often walk about in them alone. *But why not?* I wondered. Wasn't the situation dire enough that I should do what was practical, not what was expected of me? Corin regularly wore such pedestrian clothes, after all.

And why stop there, I thought as my hair fell in my face for a third time. *Why not shear my hair short as well?* But in the end, once the knife was securely against my back, the leather rough against my skin, I tied my chiton on again and bound my unruly hair back in a tail. Appearances still mattered to an extent, at least to my mind. For now, I'd preserve them.

The headache still assaulted me as I descended the stairs through the finch tower, the birds' chirps a dozen needles stabbing repeatedly into my skull. But as I entered the atrium, I found my nausea easing and my habitual hunger returning so that I resolved to break my fast.

Then I saw someone waited for me. The woman was clearly a Conclave clerk, not only in dress but in manner. She'd seated herself in the middle of one of the long tables and spread out her work's materials around her. A small strongbox, a ledger neatly arranged, an inkwell and pen sitting at the ready. Her hands were folded before her and her eyes on me, as if she'd been doing nothing but waiting for me to descend.

"First Verifier Airene," the clerk said briskly. "Please be

seated. We have the Aviary finances from the past day to discuss." She gestured to the chair opposite her.

"Galene, I presume?"

The woman gave a curt nod. "Of course. Now if you would, we can settle these accounts straightaway."

"I've only just risen. If you'll permit me a moment for my body's needs."

I couldn't keep the annoyance from my voice. Even if my head didn't feel as if smiths were busily pounding away at it, the woman's disregard for my time pulled at my frayed patience.

Her lips thinned. "Very well. I will be waiting."

I took my time. Once I'd returned from my morning necessities, I snuck back in through the kitchen and made a small meal of what Sizani had prepared. Bread, fruit, and cheese, my mainstay these past few days, continued to be what was served. Torn between haste and a petty desire to make the clerk wait, I let my disturbed stomach set the pace, then returned to the atrium.

Galane's narrowed eyes let me know the delay hadn't escaped her notice. "If you are ready," she said coldly.

I sat. "I am."

She straightened the ledger before her, though it had seemed straight to me before, then dipped her pen in the inkwell. "I believe, First Verifier, you were given an allowance of five silver scions yesterday. If you would tell me how much of it you spent and on what, we can soon be finished here."

"I didn't spend any of it."

She raised an eyebrow. "Then you have no need of an allowance today."

"No, I do. I don't have it anymore."

"I'm afraid I don't understand."

Though I'd been playing coy at first, now I found the

truth hard to admit. "I was robbed. All of it was stolen on my way to the Acadium."

As she noted this in her ledger, Galene's expression plainly spoke her disbelief. "I see," she said as she finished the entry. "I would advise that you be more careful today."

I nodded regretfully. "It is a bad habit of mine, making friends with thieves."

She made no comment, but made another note in her ledger. Then, setting her pen neatly in its stand after dabbing the end with a cloth, she shifted to the strongbox and, turning a key in its lock, opened it. I heard the faint rustling of coins within as she moved it.

"Five silver scions, as is your allowance." She withdrew the coins and set them in a neat stack before me.

I took them. "Do you have a purse as well? I'm afraid mine was taken."

Galene stared at me as if I'd asked her for gold. "I do not carry purses with me, First Verifier. I am not a street peddler."

I found it hard not to roll my eyes. "I'll manage then. If that's all…" I rose to my feet more swiftly than was comfortable. The food had helped my aching head, but the world still tilted violently in my vision.

The clerk watched me. I wondered if she thought me sick from too much wine; I knew I must be displaying some of the signs. Perhaps that was what she thought I'd spent the coin on. "I will see you tomorrow, First Verifier Airene," she said, judgment plain in her voice.

I didn't acknowledge her as I left. With silver in hand, I had what I needed from her.

By the time I'd crossed the bridge and exited the Laurel grounds, my headache had eased, and I increased my pace. Even though a fair number of people wandered the streets, I remembered keenly my robbery from the day before. No need to be on Oedija's streets any longer than I had to.

Keeping to the main roads, I managed to make it to the Acadium gates without any incidents, only stopping briefly at one of the few peddler's stands to buy a small purse. The woman's eyes went wide as I handed her a silver to change, and I wondered if she would have enough small coins to do it. But a minute later, I walked away with nickel, silver, and copper all softly clinking in my purse, tucked safely beneath the neck of my chiton.

Entering through the Acadium gates, I headed directly for Eltris's tower. Reaching it, I found no Acadian apprentice waiting today. I wondered why as I knocked loudly three times at her door.

There was no answer. I waited less than a minute before I tried again. "Eltris!" I called in. "Eltris, are you in there?"

When she still didn't answer, doubts finally surfaced. Maybe it hadn't been Eltris who had called me after all. Maybe someone had tricked me. Or maybe, still caught in the midst of my strange dreams, I'd imagined it.

I rubbed my eyes, temporarily relieving the pressure building in my skull, then stared up the tower. Was she even here? Perhaps she was up on the second floor and couldn't hear my calls. For a moment, I had the mad idea to climb the tower and enter through a window. Instead, I sighed and turned away. If Eltris was there, she wasn't ready to talk. And I had too many other things to do to wait around.

I'd taken only a few steps away when I heard the creak of the door opening behind me. I whirled to see a scowling woman standing in the tower doorway, curly gray hair springing from her head, a frumpy brown robe hanging from her stout, short frame.

"Eltris," I greeted her, trying to hide my surprise. "So you are here."

The Master Augur wasn't as polite. "So you finally decided to come."

"Finally?" My mind spun as I reconciled her words. "Your call — I didn't imagine it?"

"No, you didn't. And I waited all night for you to figure that out."

My shock was quickly giving way to irritation. "You could have sent a finch, like any ordinary person, instead of... whatever you did."

The augur stared at me, her yellow eyes piercing. "No, I couldn't. Not with the danger you were putting us all in."

Before I could ask what she meant, she turned back into her tower. Only the open door gave me any indication to follow.

Apprehensive but too curious to turn away, I entered the dim tower. From the little light, the entry room was as much a disaster as before, like a rat's nest built up over decades. Eltris already limped up the stairs, so I didn't linger, but followed her to the second floor.

Though the boarded windows blocked out the daylight, smokeless braziers filled the room with an intense light. Above, finches sang and flitted among the rafters. A worn rug extended across the stone of the tower floor.

As I looked around, Eltris walked to the opposite side of the room, then turned to face me. "Now," she said without preamble, "channel."

I blinked. "What?"

The Master Augur glared at me, her hands twitching at her sides. "You're a warden now, if you hadn't figured it out. And new wardens are dangerous — as you reminded me last night. So I must teach you to channel. Now—" She gestured impatiently. "—go on!"

"Master Eltris, what do you mean about last night? Was I... was that channeling?"

"Yes. Unguided, unwise, and dangerous channeling, for you and the rest of us. So, though I have much else to do, I will at least show you enough not to get us killed."

"But why was it so dangerous?" I insisted. "Was I in the Pyrthae?"

Eltris stared at me with disgust. "Can you not even recognize that? Then you also must not know who almost claimed you."

A horrible suspicion arose in me at her words. Suddenly, the vast sphere of fire and the shadow within it made all too much sense. "Famine found me. He was going to consume me, burn me away to nothing." I tried to remember the fuzzy details. "But the shadow that commanded him — that was Vusu, wasn't it? He stopped Famine from attacking me."

The augur sniffed. "You're not entirely devoid of intelligence, then."

My questions were insistent enough to ignore the gibe. "But why? Why would he do that? I thought he'd want to kill me after I put a quarrel in his side."

"You're the Finch," Eltris said, lips curling. "You should tell me. Now, if you're done wasting my time with your suspicions, show me how much you can channel."

I knew better than to push my luck, even if the questions still needled me. And, if I were honest, a large part of me yearned to know what Eltris could teach me.

But I could only shake my head. "That's the problem. I don't know how."

She snorted. "Of course you know how. If you're a warden, you can channel."

"But it just happened on its own the first time. I felt my locus opening up and then—"

"Don't use such words," Eltris cut me off. "Not until you know what you are talking about. Tell me of the sensations and where you felt them when you channeled."

I tried to remember. "It felt like an area in the middle of my stomach opened up. Not like a hole exactly; more like a molten stream pressed in and through me into the rest of my body, that I couldn't help but release."

She nodded sharply. "And before that?"

I closed my eyes and put myself back in the moment. "I grew hot, feverish. It made me sweat and itch. I didn't think much of it at the time, though, as I was distracted."

"Distracted?"

I hesitated, then cracked my eyes open and replied honestly. "Someone was trying to kill me."

The augur stared hard at me for a long moment. Then, "Anything else?"

Only Eltris wouldn't question attempted murder. "No," I said with a touch of amusement. "Nothing else that I remember."

"Very well. We must make you hot again then." The augur suddenly raised her hands toward me. A moment later, heat like I'd never felt before pressed in around me. I gasped at the sudden change in temperature and staggered. It was hotter than anything I remembered, hotter than any steam room or sunny summer day. Only the day I'd channeled had been hotter. My headache, which had been fading, filled my head to bursting.

But I knew what Eltris was trying to do. Fighting through the discomfort, I willed myself to open to the fire and force that had poured from me before. As heat washed over me, I pushed away images of my skin blackening and my eyes drying in my skull and tried to channel radiance.

Nothing came.

"It's not working!" I cried out. "How do I make it work?"

As abruptly as the heat had inundated me, it ceased. I gasped as cool air rushed back against my skin and clutched my arms around me, shivering.

"As I suspected," Eltris said calmly. "You're not fully attuned to the Pyrthae."

"Not fully attuned?" I asked through chattering teeth, a pit forming in my gut.

"Oh, you are a warden, there's no doubt to that. But when

first attuned, the locus is not yet developed, and thus won't open on command. Only through repeated accidental channeling does the locus form enough to be controlled."

My worry eased, but only slightly. "So all those accidents — the fire, the dreaming. All of that has to happen again before I can control this? But what if I—?"

"I'm not finished!" Eltris interrupted. "If I'm to train you, you must be silent when I speak. All my pupils have called me 'master' during training, and I don't intend for our relationship to be any different."

I swallowed down the bitter draught, as I knew I had to. "Yes, master."

"Good. Yes, more accidents will happen before you achieve control. But there are some things you can do to limit the damage. Most important will be to practice the exercises I'm about to show you, as they will help give you some measure of control over your channeling when it does come over you." Eltris gestured impatiently. "When you're ready…"

Sweat still coated my skin, chills wracked my body, and my headache pounded inside my skull. But I couldn't waste time with weakness. "I'm ready."

We began with me lying down and breathing through my belly, then tightening my gut. This, Eltris said, was to increase awareness and control over the area where the locus formed. Through controlling the locus, I could begin to channel at will, or stop channeling. She continued to instruct me in building awareness in my arms and hands, then legs and feet, as I would need command over every part of my body to gain complete control.

We kept at it until the Acadium bell tolled, signaling just under a turn had come and gone since I'd arrived. Eltris nodded and bade me to rise.

"Practice this as you lie down to sleep each night. Build awareness throughout your body. Over time, you will learn restraint, and it may prevent the worst of the accidents. So long as they don't come on too strongly."

I wished she'd left the last part unsaid. "Thank you, master."

"But these exercises won't prevent what you did last night. How did the dream come upon you? What were you thinking about?"

I couldn't prevent a flush rising up my neck. "Nothing, really. I was just thinking about... a friend. About how it would be nice to see them."

"Don't think of the Pyrthae. Don't think of channeling. Don't think of daemons or Famine or Vusu. And in particular, don't think about mysterious men."

I stared at the batty old woman, thinking I must have misheard her. But though her mouth was still set in a frown, the corners of it twitched.

Fully blushing now, I said quickly, "I'll try. But I don't know that I can control what I think before I sleep. My mind drifts as I relax."

"Then don't relax," Eltris retorted, all traces of humor gone. "If you must think of anything at all, think of mundane things. But if you are to be safe, you must clear your mind completely. If your mind is a blank slate when you sleep, it will not stray into dangerous waters. Now sit, legs crossed, back straight. You will practice clearing your mind."

Whereas the awareness exercises had been relaxing, clearing my mind proved aggravating. I'd never noticed how many thoughts drifted through until I tried keeping them all out. My frustration mounted as, time and again, I could maintain no more than a few seconds of complete blankness. If I couldn't manage to clear my mind now, I held little hope I'd be able to do so in the darkness of my room, when my fears and worries had an easy time worming their way in.

"It isn't possible." I opened my eyes and looked up at Eltris, who stood over me.

The augur scowled. "Not for the feeble-minded. But you must do it. I've warned you what will happen otherwise."

"But I don't understand how dreaming can lead me into the Pyrthae. Is...?" I hesitated to ask the question, anticipating the augur's chastisement, but there was no help for it. "Is it quintessence I'm channeling?"

Rather than chastising, Eltris scrutinized me for a long moment. "Quintessence, you call it," she muttered. "A suitable name, I suppose."

"What is it exactly? Xaron seemed to think it was the mind, or perhaps the soul."

"No one knows for certain."

I waited for her to explain. I wanted to stand, but was afraid the movement would prevent whatever explanation was forthcoming.

She looked away from me, craning her head back to peer at the finches flitting above. "Quintessence is the rarest and most precious of the Pyrthaen elements. It does not work in the same way as the others. While the abundant energies like radiance, kinesis, and magnesis exist as the fundamental components of the Pyrthae — like water, earth, and air in our plane — quintessence is congregated into entities and seems to be an animating force. In sufficient quantities, it enables control over the other energetic elements."

I opened my mouth to ask the dozen questions racing through my mind, but Eltris continued before I could speak.

"Just as the elements reside within your body, so does quintessence. Perhaps it is what makes us conscious and aware, the substance of our mind. Or perhaps it is, as many of the religions would tell us, our immortal souls." Eltris's lips curled, showing what she thought of the idea. "Whatever it may be, it is the element that enables us to channel — the conduit by which we control the flow of energy, the hammer by which we forge it."

She stopped and stared down at me, seeming to expect an answer.

I nodded hesitantly. "I think I understand. But I don't get how this connects to me dreaming my way into the Pyrthae."

For once, she didn't mock me, but nodded. "Quintessence isn't just used for forming the other elements. As an energetic element itself, it can also be channeled."

Confusion turned my thoughts upside down. "But if quintessence is what our minds are made of, how can we channel it? Wouldn't it mean there is… less of us? That we're giving a part of ourselves away?"

"I say 'channeling,' but it is more like the use of a tool than the flow of energy. Instead of expelling something like fire or force, you use the hammer itself for whatever your ends might be."

"And one of those uses is entering the Pyrthae."

"Yes. Among many others."

"Like passing messages between minds?" I guessed. "Or seeing traces of channeling after the fact?"

She narrowed her eyes, the calm teacher dissipating. "Perhaps. But those don't concern you. For you shouldn't channel quintessence at all."

I raised an eyebrow. "And why's that?"

As she looked up again at the rafters, I could tell her patience was reaching an end. But she almost managed to keep her voice even as she explained, "Channeling quintessence draws dangers that using the other elements does not. When a warden channels magnesis, for example, they draw the energy into our world from the Pyrthae. No part of them leaves Telae, our realm — they are simply allowing Pyrthaen elements in. But when a warden channels quintessence, a part of them enters the Pyrthae. Only by doing so can our minds escape the confines of our bodies." Her gaze returned to me, sharpening. "As you did last night."

I nodded, the thought making my skin clammy and

chilled. "I think I understand. When I entered the Pyrthae, Famine could find me."

Eltris eyed me shrewdly. "As I said, quintessence is the most precious of the elements, and the more you possess, the more power you wield. And it is also what Famine has an insatiable appetite for."

Cold, sharp and sudden as the kiss of the monsoon winds, bit through me. "So that's what he wants. Quintessence."

"Yes. Famine, as all the Quintyr, is oriented toward one aim. His particular obsession is the consumption of quintessence."

"But if it's quintessence he's after, why does he destroy everything in his path?"

Again, that considering look came into Eltris's eyes. I was drawing close to a limit to her secrets, I knew. But I hadn't reached it yet. "In the Pyrthae, quintessence is rare. But here in Telae, everything alive possesses quintessence in some measure. Grass, trees, birds, fish — and in the greatest measure, humans."

I felt so faint I was sure I'd have collapsed if I were standing. "So that's why he wants to return to our world. To Telae."

She wore a bitter smile. "Finally, you understand. And you know why it's so important that you don't stray into the Pyrthae."

The augur turned and walked toward the stairs. Unwilling, I rose, stretched out my stiff limbs, and followed behind. There were so many more questions I had, so many she might be able to answer. But one nagged more insistently than the rest.

I decided to push my luck. "Master, if I could ask one more thing. I understand why it's dangerous for me to channel quintessence. But you said I endanger everyone by doing so."

Eltris didn't turn until she stood by the top of the stairs. I stopped just before them facing her. But I saw from her stiffened jaw and creased brow that I was to be disappointed.

"Practice your exercises and refrain from channeling quintessence," she said shortly. "That's all you need concern yourself with. Now, leave me to my work. I'll follow up with you when I have the time."

I knew I was treading dangerous waters now. But I couldn't leave it there. "Three days. I'll call again in three days, and we can make time then. Master."

Anger flashed in her eyes. For a moment, I thought she'd refuse simply out of spite. "Five," she finally said. "Five days. The second turn after noon."

It was much further away than I'd hoped for. But any promise of her spilling more of her secrets was better than nothing. To say nothing of exploring more of my new magic.

"Fine." I gave her a small bow and turned down the stairs, feeling her gaze follow me into the gloom.

8

ALLEY WHISPERS

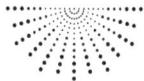

The Seed, even ripped from its source, had gained enough power to assume its own form. Rootless, it roamed the skies, brooding.

'If famine I bring,' it thought, 'then Famine I will be named.'

The daemon Famine thought long and hard as he flew, and finally saw the sacrifice of Tyurn Sky-Sea spelling his own destruction. Though he had not been able to prevent it, he suspected he might be able to use the gift to his advantage.

So Famine sowed seeds of his own among those Tyurn sought to protect, poisoning them and hoping to turn them to his own purposes.

- The Seeds of Famine, a translation from the Lighted-tongue; by Oracle Kalene of deme Hull; 881 SLP

A somber mood claimed me as I set foot again on the cobblestones of the Acadium's main street. Though I'd finally spoken with Eltris and learned more than I thought the batty old woman would ever let on, the knowledge hadn't heartened me. In some ways, knowing Famine's motivations didn't change anything. I'd always known he desired an end to our world. But to know he'd grow more powerful with each soul he consumed brought a creeping chill to my skin, as if a sudden shadow had fallen on me on a sunny day.

And as I thought on it further, I realized I had more questions than ever before. If Eltris was correct about my dream — and I sensed she was — Vusu and the strange woman had stopped Famine from consuming me. And after the trial, the Master Augur had said he'd bound the daemon god to him. The little I knew didn't add up. What was Vusu's hold on Famine? Something allowed him to yoke and harness the power of the god. Perhaps that only went to show that Famine wasn't a god; he was a Quintyr, as Eltris had insisted, though I scarcely knew what that meant.

Most pressing of my questions, however, was why Famine hadn't broken through to Telae, and when and how he would. For I had no doubt he would eventually. He had come many times before, if Eltris had spoken true. And the Master Augur had said after the trial that Vusu wouldn't be able to hold him back for long. I had assumed Famine was returning as soon as I laid eyes on him in the Pyrthae. Now, I felt the trickle of sand counting down each moment until he did.

My headache pounded anew, and my body had grown sore. I wanted to curl up on the ground and sleep. But I kept walking. Even if I could have slept, even if I wouldn't have been afraid of falling into the Pyrthae, I still had work to do, and no time to put it off.

I made for the Acadium exit, forgoing both Tomes and my brother. My head already felt crammed full with what I'd learned from Eltris, and I knew I wouldn't have the focus or attention to decipher the old texts. As for Linos... I could do nothing for him. Until I knew how to rid him of the daemon that claimed him, it would do little good for me to rouse it. Eltris might know how. But I knew my hopes were better entrusted to Talan.

One thing heartened me at least. Though I hadn't channeled or even come close to it, I clutched fiercely to the hope the augur had instilled in me. I would channel, and I would learn to control it. I had no other choice. And from the buoyant elation that filled me, I knew I'd have it no other way.

Exiting the Acadium gates, any lingering excitement quickly dissipated. I was headed for Port and had to cross Iris to get there. What might have been a nostalgic walk back to my decade-long home presently had me looking over my shoulder and checking every passing alley. But dangerous though my path might be, I knew I couldn't put it off any longer. It had been too long since I'd acted the proper Finch.

The day was overcast, and the close press of buildings left many back streets poorly illuminated. Even here in Iris, filthy men watched my progress from shadowed alleys. My hand twitched, ready to seize my hidden dagger, for all the good it might do me. I kept to the main roads and hoped my luck would hold out.

For this journey at least, it did. As I turned a corner, the homey, wooden sign of Zipho's emerged in front of her cafe. A smile found my lips. It had been too long since I'd seen the matronly cafe owner. I doubted even Nomusa had the time to make it out here. Hopefully, the troubles that had seen the rest of the city had left her store untouched.

But as I entered within, I found it was a vain hope. Less than half of her usual clientele was present, and those who were looked up suspiciously as I entered. I averted my gaze and approached the counter.

"Airene!" Zipho came bustling into view from the other side of the tree that grew through the middle of the shop. "Where have you been? And Nomusa — that *fanla* has not been by in half a span! Now is no time to take a break." She gave me a reproachful look before coming around the counter to pull me into a big hug.

I returned it with a startled grin. "Sorry, Zipho," I said as I extricated myself. "We've been busy."

"Sit. I will brew you a cup of coffee thick as mud, just the way you like it, and you will tell me what has happened."

I did as she instructed, knowing there was no way around it. Besides, it felt good to sit, and even better when she brought me a steaming cup of coffee. I took the clay mug in hand and breathed it in. Scents of chocolate and licorice filled my nose. Almost from the first sip my incessant headache began to recede.

Zipho settled down in the chair opposite of me. "Now. What have you to say for your absence?"

I debated how much of the truth to reveal, then told her as much as I thought she'd believe. I spoke of Vusu's betrayal, and Myron's abduction, and Asileia's relative innocence. But of Famine, and my visit to the Pyrthae, I said nothing. Nothing, too, did I mention of the Preservists and the Valemish plotting with Avvad. I had little more evidence than suspicions and couldn't see how sowing discontent among Oedija's population would help us now.

Zipho nodded along for much of it, clearly having heard some of these things as rumors. But at the mention of Vusu, she muttered, "If that man shows up here..." But she let the threat hang unfinished. We both knew how empty it was.

I drank down the last of my coffee and stood, slipping a coin from my purse and sliding it subtly under my mug. I knew she wouldn't take my coin outright, and as no other customer had come in during our chat, I suspected she'd soon need it.

"Thank you, Zipho," I said. "That was just what I needed."

The matronly woman rose as well. "You are welcome anytime. But make sure you send Nomusa my way!" She continued in a lower voice. "Just because she's a queen doesn't mean she can ignore a lowly cafe owner."

I smiled and turned out of the cafe. My smile grew wider

when I heard Zipho's astonished call as she discovered the silver coin I'd left for her. Even the thought that I'd have to report it to that abysmal clerk Galene didn't dim my pleasure.

The gentle drizzle that had begun outside, however, did dampen my mood. I shivered and resolved to sort out clothes from a seamstress, or at the very least a cloak. The monsoons would be here in full all too soon.

I didn't go far from the cafe, but turned into the alley next to it. Before, the alley had been empty of Oedija's vagrants, as the ground here tended to grow muddy during the monsoons. But now, no fewer than five figures huddled down against the light rain, pulling ragged garments around themselves. I stood at the entrance to the alley, squinting at the faces of the vagrants to see if I recognized any of them.

"I wondered when you would come."

I spun around to see a slight woman with her features hidden under a hood leaning against the wall next to me. How she'd managed to come up silently behind me with her limp, I didn't know.

"Hello, Wisp," I greeted her.

Wisp didn't respond, but turned away. It was no more than I'd come to expect from her. My primary informant for over a year now, she had quickly managed to gather a network of informants so extensive and reliable that the rumors she passed along were as good as fact. Yet that knowledge came with a price; a price, I hoped, that wouldn't be inflated by the uncertain times.

"We shall go somewhere more private," Wisp said over her shoulder as she began to walk away.

I followed as she led us to an alley so narrow I doubted I could enter without my shoulders brushing either wall. I eyed it skeptically, but Wisp, narrower of stature than me, easily slid in. Once again, I followed, though grudgingly. Like most of the backways around Oedija, the alley smelled of piss, and it reeked all the worse for the cramped quarters.

Wisp turned back halfway down. "You will watch my back and I yours," she said flatly. "Now. What do you wish to know?"

I kept my eyes behind her. "All that you know. It's been long since we last saw each other."

"Yes. But I suspect there is much you could tell me that I don't know." She cocked her head. "Perhaps we can lower your price for a bit of information of your own."

"Perhaps." I wondered uneasily what knowledge she wished to know. My fingers were suddenly uncomfortably hot and itchy. I distracted myself by slipping out fifteen magnes and holding them out, palm down. "Why don't you start?"

She accepted the coins and secreted them away. "What first?"

"The Manifest."

Wisp flashed a rare smile, as if she'd been expecting the request. "Of them, I hear rumors and shadows. But there are some few facts I can share."

She told me of the Seekers' activities, which were much the same as before, if more detailed than Nomusa provided — of building more permanent housing, and training the common folk for war, and the beginnings of cultivation, despite it being late in the season and with droughts in the fields all around Oedija.

Then she touched on more pertinent things, like how the Seeker wardens displayed themselves openly, with violet tatu inked along their exposed arms and around their eyes, similar to how Vusu himself appeared. They seemed to have taken leadership positions among the Seekers, commanding them in martial and domestic affairs alike. I wondered how such a structure would fare. Wardens were no better leaders than any other person, and some would no doubt prove to be poor at the role. The inefficiency such a hierarchy would produce, as well as perhaps the resentment among the populace, might work to our advantage. Even so, I acknowledged it was a thin hope. There would have to be significant internal strife for it to be of use.

Making the Seeker compound even stranger were the demographics joining it. Even more than commonfolk, honors left their ancestral positions to join the movement. It was hardly surprising considering how many were treated little better than slaves, and some a good deal worse. Yet I wondered why, after a thousand years, honors chose now to cast off their societal chains. Perhaps they sensed the weakening state of the realm. Or perhaps Ariston the Dishonored was the spark to set their desire for freedom ablaze. I tucked the information away for later consideration.

"Of their leader," Wisp continued with a gleam in her shadowed eyes, "all I know is what he is not. He is not among the common followers of the Manifest. He is not seen by anyone but the Seeker wardens, Ariston the Dishonored, and his personal honor, Seda. By their movements, it is rumored he remains entrenched in a room deep in the Wyvern's Claw."

A grim smile forced its way onto my lips. I was not proud of the vindictive satisfaction I felt at the likelihood that Vusu lay suffering, but neither could I deny it. From Wisp's sly look, I thought she knew, or at least suspected, my part in his current condition.

I changed the topic to ask of the Valemish next, but found the rumors were less satisfying. There were movements among the temples and between them, but nothing suspicious beyond that. What might be hidden on the people who traveled between the temples, Wisp couldn't tell me. Only when she hesitated and glanced behind her did my interest pique.

"You've heard rumors," I guessed.

Wisp nodded reluctantly. "I do not like telling anything but fact."

"I won't tell anyone if you don't."

I caught a dubious glance from beneath her hood before she lowered her eyes. "Those who sleep the streets speak of disappearances. Of phantoms in the night who come to claim victims. Of corpses left behind, stripped of their skin and souls."

It sounded ridiculous, but I knew better than to laugh. I'd heard Talan speak of such things before. *Ikoz*, he'd called them in the ash-tongue — Silks, in the sea-tongue. Pyr bound to the will of the Avvadin Imperium, they were so named for the bands of shimmering cloth wrapped around their invisible, ethereal bodies that chained them to service.

As if Oedija needed another danger on her streets.

"Thank you, Wisp," I said, glancing over my shoulder before pulling out my purse. "If you hear anything more, tell me first. I'll make it worth your while." I slipped out two scions and held them out.

With a gleam in her eye, the informant snatched the coins from my hand and turned to walk abruptly down the alley.

But as she limped away, a farfetched idea suddenly occurred to me. "Wisp. One other thing."

She halted with a lurch and half-turned back, head cocked to one side.

I could scarcely believe what I was about to say. But I had to do my part for the Order, if only for Nomusa's sake. "Wisp, I'm now First Verifier to the new Order of Verifiers. I'm sure you already know this."

She gave a curt nod.

"As First Verifier, I'm obligated to recruit others to our cause, those whom I deem competent and dependable. We're seeking how the Manifest came to form, and how former Tribune Vusumuzi was able to finance his movement—"

"No." Wisp turned away and continued her dogged walk down the alley.

A reluctant smile pulled at my lips. It was no more brusque than I'd expected.

"I'll take that as you'll consider it!" I called after her before turning the other way.

As I walked back north, I mulled over Wisp's news. But try as I might, I couldn't put the pieces before me into a pattern. They seemed just a collection of whispers and facts, movements of people and spirits and countries all outside of my control. I could tell the Council what I'd heard, of Silks rumored to be on the streets, but with the Preservist faction's stranglehold on the Demos Council, no good could come of it.

Even less could be done of the movement of honors into Thys. Or, if action was taken, it wouldn't be anything I'd want to be part of. I couldn't condone locking up honors as if they were Avvadin slaves, nor disciplining them with the whip as the imperials to the south were said to.

And of Seeker wardens openly displaying themselves, even that flagrant display of magic could bring no response. Several Shepherds had died during Asileia's trial, while others had joined with Vusu. Only a handful were left in Tribunal control from how Nomusa told it. The Acadians training to fight were not officially condoned and were probably still fledging in their abilities. Even witnessing Isidora's display when fighting the Shepherds, I found it hard to believe many Acadians capable of martial ability. I hoped I'd be proven wrong.

I sighed. Once again, all I learned led me nowhere. And yet I could do nothing but seek to gather more scraps in the hopes they eventually might amount to something.

Despite my promise to Nomusa, I didn't call on patricians, but returned to the Acadium to seek out the library.

There, three ancient texts awaited me. For all the good reading them would do me.

The same guards who had greeted me that morning eyed me skeptically as I re-entered, but I ignored them. They'd grow used to seeing me soon enough.

As before, the pupil Platon eagerly accompanied me down into Tomes. With my wits fully about me this visit, I firmly issued him away to read in peace. Only after he'd repeated the Master Librarian's rules three times did I convince him to retreat to the other end of the shelves, where he paced and talked to himself. After a time, I was able to shut out his murmurs and muddle through the ancient words in the first book I'd selected, *The Seeds of Famine.*

What I learned both fascinated and perplexed me. According to the old book, Famine had first come from "the Lower Realm," some part of what I assumed was the Pyrthae, then tricked the Eidolan god Tyurn Sky-Sea into giving it his power. Only when Clepsammia, Goddess of Fate and Tyurn's daughter, showed her father the truth did Tyurn free himself of Famine's influence, then die giving birth to the First Wardens. Only once he was free did Famine come to know himself. And once he did, he set out to poison Tyurn's Gift.

I leaned back and rubbed at my sore neck. How much of it was truth, and how much fancy? On the one hand, the original composition was soon after the Lighted Passage. But that didn't mean it was soon after the events inscribed. Famine I'd seen with my own eyes and knew him to be real. But the Eidolan gods — were they supposed to be real as well? Of them, only Tyurn was said to have died in the Famine War. So if they existed, where had they hid for over a thousand years?

But some of them had to still exist. After all, wardens were supposedly attuned to the Pyrthae by the gods. And unless my own attunement was a strange accident, a god had done so for me. So perhaps the Eidola were not completely myth, as I'd always supposed.

As I pored over the words, Platon came over begging to return upstairs. I was happy to oblige, particularly as, from the way he danced, I suspected he needed to relieve himself. Besides, my headache had returned, and my eyes felt gritty from staring at the cramped words for so long.

"How long has it been?" I asked as I returned the book to its cubby.

"It must have been three turns at least! You stared at that book for forever! Begging your pardon, mistress."

Consulting the sandglass mounted next to the library entrance, I found the pupil had overestimated; only two turns had passed. Still, I'd read enough. Evening was quickly approaching, and I had to return to the Aviary before night fell. Besides, if I was being honest, part of me was eager to practice Eltris's exercises and make another attempt at channeling. Despite what she'd cautioned, I figured it'd come sooner or later. Better to channel when I intended to than when I didn't — or so I told myself.

I waved goodbye to Platon as he bolted for a chamberpot. On the library steps, I briefly considered visiting Ward before turning toward the Acadium gates. I'd be returning here everyday, most likely. There'd be other opportunities to visit Linos. But I couldn't completely fool myself as to my reasons for avoiding it as I walked quickly toward the exit.

It was shorter to take the back ways to the Laurel Palace so I could cross the bridge back over to Conclave grounds, and for a moment, I was tempted. But remembering my robbery, any desire for a shortcut immediately dissipated. I strode along the main road, looking to either side. The few people still on the streets looked as suspicious of me as I was of them.

It wasn't long before I heard them.

They swept onto the street behind me like a flood,

thrusting torches and clubs into the air and screaming like daemon-masked, drunken revelers at the Carnival of Veils. So suddenly they filled the street with noise that I couldn't believe they were truly there for a moment. As they passed, they overturned the few carts and stands left on the stones, tore down hangings and signs before shops, and banged against the boarded-up windows.

I didn't have to see much to know I'd stumbled in the way of a dusk mob.

Anywhere seemed safer than before that angry mass of humanity, so despite my earlier reservations, I fled into the closest alley. I shared it with nearly a dozen others, all of whom seemed set to squat there for the night.

"Never seen a dusk mob?" one bent woman mocked me from the base of the alley wall. She spat at my feet.

Heart hammering against my ribs, I ignored her and watched the passing crowd. They looked dirty and poor for the most part, and predominantly male. But what unified them most was the rage painted on their faces. I cringed back from it. Their fury seemed almost palpable to me, a noxious air suffocating me as they passed. The only other time I had felt such a depth of hate had been before Famine himself.

Enthralled by the dusk mob, I startled when someone grabbed my arm.

Fear and fury coursing through me, I turned and lashed out, striking my captor with quick blows to the nose then the leg. I didn't even look at his face until after he'd cursed and sprang back, one hand to his face. I didn't recognize his features, shadowed as they were under a hood.

Not caring about propriety, I hauled up my chiton and ripped free the knife Nomusa had given me, then held it before me in what I hoped was a menacing manner. My lips pulled back in a snarl.

"Stay away from me!" I hissed.

The man glowered at me. Blood trickled between the

fingers of the hand held to his nose, while the other had disappeared inside his coat. "They didn't mention you were a feral minx," he snarled, his voice nasally from his dripping nose.

"They?" I demanded.

A blue glow emanated out from the sleeve of his upraised arm. My blood went cold. I didn't need to see the full tatu to know it was an unblinking eye. The mark of the Underguild.

"Tyurn's balls," I said faintly.

The man leered at me. "Now you understand. Be glad the Undermaster wishes to extend you an offer, or I would cut you down where you stand."

The Undermaster — Kalindi, I suspected it referred to, from what Talan had told me. It seemed the Underguild's usurper had taken on a new title.

I glanced at the vagrants who shared the alley with us, but they were backing away, fear plain on their faces. Looking back at the Guilder, I didn't lower the knife.

"Go ahead," I said. "Tell me Kalindi's offer."

The man's eyes narrowed. "The *Undermaster*," he said with emphasis, "knows of your association with the traitor Talan Wraithsbane. He doesn't hold this against you. But he does ask one thing in return for his forgiveness."

It took an effort to hide my sneer. "And what's that?"

"It's simple, really. Tell us where he is."

I almost laughed. Strange as how our friendship had developed, my loyalty to Talan was as strong as to Xaron, Nomusa, and my family. There was no chance that I'd confess his location even if I'd known it. But flat refusal could bring the ire of the Underguild down on me, and at a time when I needed to move about the city freely. I had to proceed cautiously.

"What will you do with him if I tell you?"

The Guilder grinned, revealing a bit of blood that had

seeped between his yellowed teeth. "Show him a traitor's punishment."

Cutting off the offender's hands was the traditional reprimand for the Underguild, but I suspected Kalindi wouldn't stop there. I wondered what Talan had done to warrant the threat.

"I'll consider it," I said finally, reviling the necessary lie.

"Don't take long. The Undermaster is not a patient man. And you wouldn't want to give him a reason to show his displeasure."

With one final leer, the Guilder turned down the alley and disappeared.

The vagrants who had been with us had all melted away, leaving me alone in the alley. On the main street, the dusk mob had passed on to cause destruction elsewhere. I heaved a sigh of relief at the near escape.

But I wasn't safe yet. Cautiously taking to the street again, I kept my knife out as I ran to the Laurel Palace gates.

9
EYES IN THE NIGHT

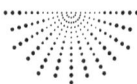

Agmon Brandheart, Foremost of the First Wardens, quickly arose as the leader. A commander and a soldier, he embraced Tyurn's Gift and gathered the other wardens of humanity scattered across Telae to his side. Boldly, they went out to meet their enemy.

Famine had gathered legions of his own to his banner, both human and daemon, for many longed for the power he promised. Many more filled the daemon god's war tents than Agmon Brandheart had managed to marshal.

Even still, they met on the battlefield. Wearing the form of a great scaled beast, Famine flew over the armies, and wherever the daemon-god went, no warden could stand before him.

Agmon Brandheart, most noble of humanity, called a challenge to Famine. But the daemon only laughed and continued his slaughter elsewhere. And no matter how Agmon challenged him, Famine would not face him.

- The Seeds of Famine, a translation from the Lighted-tongue; by Oracle Kalene of deme Hull; 881 SLP

S leep took a long while to come.
    Foremost on my mind was the Guilder's threat. I

worried less about myself than Talan, though I knew the threat meant he was thus far safe. Still, how long would he remain that way with Kalindi bent on revenge and the reach of the Underguild at his disposal?

But even that threat felt almost insignificant when I contemplated the one rising, hidden, for all of us. Famine sought to break into our world, into Telae. And Eltris believed he would do so when Vusu's control inevitably slipped. I wondered if I'd done the right thing now, putting a quarrel in his side. Yet how could I have done any less? Unchecked, Vusu would destroy Oedija just as surely as Famine.

But there remained Eltris's belief that Vusu somehow held Famine in check. How a man, even a powerful warden, could leash a god defied my comprehension.

But I couldn't think about any of that. Not Famine, not Vusu, and especially not Talan. Though I didn't know what danger I posed to the city by straying into the Pyrthae, it was warning enough for me to try to not dream.

But not enough to stop from trying to channel.

I pushed the worries from my mind and set into Eltris's exercises. My body gathered a warm energy as I rolled my awareness through every limb and digit, even to the thin skin of my scalp, imagining my focus like a ball of light wherever it traveled. But the warmth was not the thrumming heat of radiance, and when I tried to open myself to the Pyrthae, my locus remained stubbornly closed.

I sighed and set into the mental exercises, trying to clear my mind of my lingering worries. But no matter how I insisted on emptiness, thoughts clung to me like barnacles to a ship's hull. If Talan was safe from Kalindi's henchmen. If I dared Oedija's streets again when riots and thieves ruled them by day and Guilders, Seekers, and Silks haunted them by night. If the stubborn old Master Augur would ever tell me everything I needed to know to stop Vusu and Famine. If we had a prayer of a chance of stopping the daemon god at all.

Sometime in the midst of my worries, I was carried into an uneasy oblivion.

I blinked my eyes open to daylight, surprised I'd fallen asleep. It felt as though I'd just lain down. No dreams of soaring through the Pyrthae greeted me, nor glimpses of Talan as a flame or otherwise. Perhaps the augur's exercises had worked. Even knowing it was for the best, I couldn't help but feel disappointed.

Rising, I looked in my wardrobe and found, to my pleasant surprise, that Hyrol had found the note I'd left for him and had supplied me a full closet of chitons, trousers, and tunics, as well as an oil-treated cloak. I didn't hesitate in grabbing a pair of tunic and trousers and, after securing my knife, I put them on.

But when reaching for a chiton to pull over them, I paused. Seeker wardens, Guilders, and Silks haunted Oedija's streets, to say nothing of the common cutthroats and cutpurses. If I was to wander the city by myself, I had to give myself the best chance to run.

Tightening my jaw, I took only the cloak and closed the wardrobe.

Walking downstairs, I entered the atrium and found my days were gathering a pattern. Galene the clerk waited to take my account once more.

"First Verifier," she greeted me as she cast a disdainful glance at my clothes.

"Galene," I said pleasantly. "You look as well as could be expected."

After exchanging several more biting sentences, I dispensed of her with flippant haste, then set off for the Laurel bridge. Though fear crawled up my throat and tightened it, I knew I had to go out into Oedija once again. I had to read more of my ancient texts, then do my due diligence to the Order by rooting out corruption. I wasn't sure either would pan out. But trying was better than cowering in my room.

Filled with nervous energy, eager to ease the guilt I felt toward Nomusa, I settled on attending to my Verifier task. But though the command ultimately came from Orhan, I wouldn't do as the Preservist leader desired and find some scapegoat for his corruption charges. I aimed to investigate where the rotten heart of Oedija actually pulsed.

Orhan's estate was located in the center of the Petaled Fence, the richest part of deme Iris. The community was sprawled over a hill that afforded views of both the ocean and the distant mountains, and it was separated from the rest of the inner city by an intricately carved stone wall and guards posted at its gates. Ordinary residents were not permitted access unless they had received invitations.

But as I reached the gates, I thrust my Verifier medallion at the guards, hoping my position would be enough. After exchanging a look, they grudgingly admitted me, and I entered the Petaled Fence for the first time. Walking a little ways down the wide street paved with a black-veined white marble, I tried to repress my awe as I craned my neck to spy Orhan's manor near the peak of the hill, which rose nearly as high as the Laurel Palace to the west. Though it wasn't as grand or opulent as the Wreath's homestead, which stretched over half a mile with its interior gardens, it said much of Orhan's sense of his place in the world that he made the attempt.

I took pains to ascend to it by covert ways, or as covert as I could manage in an unfamiliar place. Available alleyways to sneak through were lacking in a district of manors and the reputable shops that serviced them. So instead, I opted for taking a wide arc through the district, avoiding the main thoroughfare on which Orhan would no doubt have eyes posted, and I approached from the back of the estate. There,

I found a perfect stake-out spot, a conveniently located Eidolan sanctuary with a balcony facing out toward the Low Consul's estate and an open view of his back gate. After stopping by a shop to pick up a peering glass, I made for the balcony, and through frequent and generous donations to the offering plate, the oracle and his acolytes let me be.

Yet for all my troubles, I was little rewarded. Though I watched those coming and going from the estate, I didn't see anyone suspicious enough to follow when they left. Not even Valemish priests came to the Low Consul's manor. Though I wasn't surprised that Orhan was discreet, particularly in broad daylight, I had hoped to see more.

In the frequent pauses between Orhan's visitors, I practiced Eltris's techniques, telling myself that there was little use in wasting time while I waited. A flimsy excuse; I couldn't deny that I burned to channel as easily as Xaron and Talan did. Had not duty and guilt called, my desire would have shut me indoors all day to work at it.

But as the grains in the sandglass slowly counted the afternoon away, I left off both of my pursuits with a heavy heart. A day with nothing accomplished was a sore blow at this stage. Yet I couldn't think of what else I could do. With evening approaching, I stole back to the Aviary for the night.

I began the next day much the same way. Though the oracle and acolytes cast me odd looks, they didn't complain when I put another handful of cullets in the offering plate. Morning came and went. Though I watched Orhan's entrance with rapt attention, not even permitting myself to stray into Eltris's exercises, I found no visitor worthy of pursuit.

As the noon bell rang in the sanctuary tower, I turned from my vantage point and left. Mulling over the problem, I could think of no better way to catch Orhan in his corruption that wouldn't be reckless. No doubt I could convince Xaron to sneak into the estate, but I had only vague ideas of what I'd have him look for. There was little point in risking it until I did.

Little knowing what else I could do, I made for Tomes and pushed guilty thoughts of Linos aside. With Platon as my usual accomplice, I read *The Seeds of Famine*. The book had, however, wandered into the territory of aggravating. For reasons beyond my understanding, it now strayed through the minutiae of the Hunger War, detailing the number of troops on each side, which notables joined which army, where the important battles took place, and the like. Dutifully, I waded through the mundane events, searching for useful scraps and coming up short.

Only one detail stood apart from the rest, the same question that bothered Agmon Brandheart: why Famine avoided confronting him. I dared to hope that, whatever the reason, it would be the key to defeating him once more.

But the hope of that answer couldn't keep me down there forever. Turns later, with an aching back and neck, I left the library. Blinking as I stepped back into the sunlight, it took me several moments before I spotted the man walking down the cobblestones in coarse, brown robes too poor for even an Acadian.

"Hilarion, do a tumble!" I called to him.

Xaron turned and, recognizing me, grinned.

"You're rather pleased with yourself," he observed with a wry smile as I approached. "Yet a jape comes to mind when I see you as well."

I glanced down at myself. I'd almost forgotten that I'd forgone the chiton that day, and my tunic and trousers were visible beneath my cloak. "I'm going through a wardrobe adjustment at the moment," I said dismissively.

"I can see that. I can't say it's flattering, but at least it suits you." He gave me a wink.

I ignored his words and pulled him into a hug to whisper in his ear. "Are you here for what I think you are?"

He hesitated and glanced around as he pulled away, then nodded slightly.

"I want to come with."

"No!" He scanned the area nervously again. Though no one was nearby, he continued in a quieter voice. "Airene, you can't. You're too prominent. You'd draw the wrong attention."

"And *you* don't draw attention?"

"A different kind. I'm a laughingstock. No one really pays attention to where Hilarion goes. But a Verifier means serious business. You only go where there's something to be sniffed out."

"I suppose," I admitted grudgingly. "Fine. I'll leave you to it for now. But it won't be long before I force the issue."

His lips tightened, but he didn't deny it. We both knew the dangers we faced. Once I gained control over my channeling, Xaron couldn't object any longer to my learning to protect myself.

I squeezed his hand briefly. "Come to the Aviary soon. You haven't seen what a dump they've put us up in."

"Nomusa says it's a ruby in the rough, once you carve the crud off it." Xaron grinned. "I can't wait to see it."

"Then come tonight. We can make an evening of it. Since I'm stuck behind walls then anyway."

He shrugged. "Can't argue with that. I'll see you then."

With that, he turned and went to his warden training, leaving me to carry on my own way.

My predicaments rolled round and round in my head as I slipped down the streets back to the Laurel Palace gates. A steady drizzle, barely more than mist, had quickly covered the city and obscured the roads. I pulled up the hood of my cloak and peered around, more on edge than usual, as I could only see people a dozen feet away from me. Yet I was growing adept at avoiding troublesome spots in this new cityscape, circumventing the places where I'd seen or heard of thieves frequenting. Rumors, which had always made my ears perk up, now took on a greater interest. The wrong warning could leave me sprawled in an alley, never to rise again.

Even so, I doubted I could have avoided Guilders if they sought me. Why they might be quiet put me ill at ease. My fears whispered that they'd caught Talan and had no more use for me. But reason asserted itself; more likely, they'd seen no signs of communication between us and had no orders to push the issue further.

Still, I couldn't help but want to search for him, and not only to make sure he was safe. I missed his voice, his warm touch. I missed the safety I felt in his presence. But I wouldn't endanger him by seeking him out, not for those reasons. I sighed and forced the desire to recede to the back of my mind.

Reaching the gates of the Wreath grounds, I mulled over where to go. It felt like a long time since I'd last spoken with Jaxas, but I didn't have anything in particular to report. True that I'd learned more of Famine; but that the daemon god sought to come to our world to consume it was hardly news. Everyone who had heard the tales of the Hunger War knew that was Famine's desire. There was little point in wasting the Archon's time, especially when I wasn't sure how welcome I'd be.

Instead, I turned to the bridge and made my way across. But at the turn to the Aviary, I kept going straight, and headed instead for the broken dome looming out of the mist.

Entering inside the Conclave, I found the place transformed by the showers. Water slicked the stone steps and filmed the benches. The few Servants still present huddled miserably within the few unbroken alcoves, while the honors wore flat expressions as they hurried to and fro, droplets trickling down their shaven heads.

I stood for a moment just inside the doors, staring at the small portal behind the Archon's dais. I couldn't recall if the

Demos Council door was kept closed in times when they weren't in session. But I hadn't been studying it for more than a minute before the door opened, and the Low Consuls began to file out. Feiyan left first, the rest of the Equalists with her, while Orhan and the Preservists followed after.

Not wishing for any trying interactions just then, I pulled my hood down further and stepped into an alcove. I found myself watching Orhan. The middle-aged, portly man took each step slowly, careful on the slick stone, but his resolute smile never left his face. A thought began to itch in the back of my head, then whittled away into an idea. A smile found my lips. Orhan's eyes darted toward me, and I looked away, hoping he hadn't recognized me. I didn't look back until he and the others had filed out of the great double doors.

Nomusa and Jaxas came last, lingering behind the rest and speaking in a low conference. I wondered what they spoke about and if Nomusa would later keep it secret. I hadn't forgotten about the figure in the red cloak in the Laurel gardens.

Stepping from the shadows, I caught both of their gazes and strode toward them. "Evening."

"First Verifier Airene." Jaxas's eyes were flat and unreadable as he gave me a respectful nod. "You just missed the session."

"And a lively one at that," Nomusa added. She looked tired but still elated. I recognized it as how I'd often felt in the midst of a fine hunt. A glimmer of envy wormed its way inside me.

"How's that?" I asked lightly.

"Daelya and Berker were at each others' throats over the organization of the defenses. How much to requisition there, how to organize the supplies, and the like."

"I thought those details were left to the Stratechons."

"For the most part, they are," Jaxas replied. "Which was precisely the Preservist point. But Daelya felt that a more active role might be necessary considering the circumstances."

I kept my doubts to myself. If any defense Oedija could muster would make a difference, I'd be amazed. But saying so wouldn't help anyone.

"Archon, if you wouldn't mind, could I have a private word with Nomusa?"

"Of course." He gave a brief bow, then turned away. Just before he left through the doors, a hooded man I hadn't seen standing there turned out to walk next to him. I studied him with skepticism.

"Who's that with Jaxas?"

Nomusa turned to look. "The new Tribune acting as the handler of the Shepherds — or what remains of them, anyway. He's taken it upon himself to be a guard of sorts. But enough about him. What did you want to discuss? Or should it wait until we're back at the Aviary?"

I glanced around and saw no one near. But after the Tribune had appeared from nowhere, even whispered words didn't feel safe.

"It can wait," I decided.

We hurried across the Conclave grounds, our cloaks pulled tight about us. The rain hadn't relented, but only fell harder. By the time we reached the Aviary's doors, even the oily skin of my cloak couldn't prevent the rain soaking through. Stepping inside, I shivered and peeled the wet fabric off, then slumped into a seat.

"Tea or coffee?" Nomusa offered, already headed toward the kitchen.

"Is mulled wine on offer?"

She rolled her eyes and disappeared inside the kitchen, reappearing a few minutes later with two mugs of steaming tea. I accepted the cup, folding my hands around it and breathing in the pleasantly spicy scent of cinnamon and cloves.

Nomusa sipped her tea. "So, what was it you wanted to talk about?"

I set the mug down. "The Low Consuls. They have solars within the Conclave, don't they? Where they compose letters and keep documents?"

She nodded. "The Servants do as well, though they're often shared rooms." Her gaze grew sharp. "Why do you ask?"

I flashed a rueful smile. "Sounds like you've already guessed why. I staked out Orhan's estate this morning and saw nothing. Unless you'd rather Xaron risk a house-break, his Conclave solar is our only option for evidence of corruption."

She was already shaking her head. "You're not seeing the whole painting, Airene. We can't go after Orhan for corruption, period. He has too much power — in the Council, in the Conclave, and from his own money and influence. Even if we find evidence that he's plotting something, what could we do with it?"

"Act on whatever we learn. Thwart his plans. Anything is better than looking aside from the fact that he might very well be undermining Oedija's defense for his own gain."

"And what if you're caught? Orhan would disband the Order in a heartbeat. Verchlesa and Tychon would side with the Preservists for certain; even the Equalists might affirm the decision. No one wants Finches digging up their secrets."

I'd feared her reacting this way and had hoped for better. "Then what do you think we should do?" I demanded. "Nomusa, unless you have a better path forward, I think we have to do this. We need Orhan and his lackeys out of the way, for Oedija's sake. And this is the only step I've found as to how we might begin unseating him."

Nomusa cast her gaze down at the table, taking a sip of her tea. After a long minute, she sighed and met my gaze. "I'm just afraid, Aire. Afraid of losing all we've gained."

I reached over and took her hand. "So am I. But as Talan would say, it's time to throw in the spokes and pray."

She snorted lightly and squeezed my hand. "You'd do better not to take advice from him."

The front door burst open. Nomusa and I jumped to our feet, my shins bruising on the table as my hand went to the knife under my tunic. But as the man stepped in and threw off his hood, I let my hand fall away. Xaron grinned at both of our expressions.

"Did I startle you?" he asked innocently.

"Next time, knock," I said drily as I collapsed back onto the bench. "Now sit."

"Someone's in good humor tonight." He obliged by sitting next to Nomusa and looked around. "So, this is the place. Ruby in the rough indeed."

"She'll get there," Nomusa said reproachfully.

"You can get a tour later," I said. "We have something else to discuss first."

His eyebrows shot up. "Do we?"

I shared a look with Nomusa. Despite her earlier opinion, she obliged me with a small smile.

I turned back to Xaron. "How would you like to do another house-break?"

～

"It's late enough," Xaron insisted for the third time. "The moons are hidden. It's raining. No one will be out, and the guards will be inattentive, if they're watching inside the grounds at all."

"Just a little longer." I took a sip of my second cup of tea, feigning patience. But he was right; the time had come. From where he, Nomusa, and I waited in the dining hall of the Aviary, we could see the night had grown as dark as Oedija ever saw.

Even the radiant winds were lost amid the drizzling gloom. The patter of rain and the distant tide of the ocean muffled any other sounds. The light from the pyr lamps mounted periodically throughout the grounds seemed subdued. It was as good a night for a house-break as we could have hoped for.

Xaron slumped against the table. "No one tells you the end of a nation involves so much waiting."

"This isn't the end of Oedija," I said without conviction.

"We used to wait this long for house-breaks all the time," Nomusa reminded us.

Xaron gave us a baleful glare. "But then it had been to break in somewhere that would be a challenge. This is a job for a street urchin."

I hoped he was right. Conclave guards only patrolled the fence around the grounds, not around the Conclave chambers. With Xaron by my side, locked doors would pose no issue. Nomusa had talked us through where Orhan's solar was located; all that remained was to break in and rifle the messages. We could be done with the whole task in a turn of the sandglass if all went as expected.

"At least you get to wear normal clothes for a change."

"Normal for you," he muttered. "A fine wardrobe change you've made."

"They're practical," I said stiffly.

"And stylish," Nomusa added with a smirk.

He suddenly stood. "Let's go. Nomusa, you said the clerk locks up at the second turn after sundown. That was two turns ago. The only thing that will come of us waiting longer is less sleep."

I sighed and rose with him. "Fine. But if we get caught because we left too early, I'll expect you to get us out of it."

He grinned and opened the door. A chill monsoon wind swept in. "Why don't you take care of it? After all, you're like me now."

"Not quite," Nomusa said from the table. "She can't channel."

Her words pricked me, but I pretended otherwise as I glanced back. "Wish us luck."

Her expression had grown serious. "'Thae's blessings."

I gave her a tight smile, then followed Xaron out the door.

"You'll channel soon," he murmured as he closed it. "Don't worry."

I nodded and led the way into the rain. It couldn't come soon enough.

As we crossed the grounds, I saw no one within sight, as the border fence and the guards that patrolled it were hidden from view by numerous groves. Yet as Xaron and I made our way toward the cobblestone road before the Conclave doors, we kept a careful watch and both ears open for footsteps in the rain. The grounds appeared empty of any other travelers.

We reached the Conclave doors. "Alright, house-breaker," I whispered to Xaron as I scanned the darkness behind us. "Time to show your worth."

Xaron kneeled next to the keyhole and peered through it. It was many times the size of a regular keyhole; the key to turn it must have been as big as one of my hands. Brow creased in concentration, he wriggled his fingers inside it and felt around for a moment before drawing them out with a smile.

"Simple. All I will need to do is press in the tumblers with some gentle kinesis."

I hoped he was right. "Work your magic then."

Flashing me a wry grin, he put his fingers back inside the keyhole. His brow creased, his smile faded, and his eyes drifted close as his fingers worked inside the lock for a few moments. I looked away and scanned the area again. Though no one should have any reason to be here so late, I couldn't shake the feeling we were being watched.

I heard a series of clicks, then a satisfied grunt from

Xaron. The door rumbled as he pulled one open. "There you are," he said with satisfaction. "Simple, didn't I say?"

"Gloat inside." I pushed him in and heaved the thick door shut behind us.

The thin light that came through the broken shell of the dome did little to remit the deeper darkness around us. Yet relief washed over me at the idea of the doors being between us and any unseen watchers.

I could feel Xaron's eyes on me. "Are you alright?" he asked. "You seem on edge."

I shook my head. "Just feel like something's watching. Can you lock the door behind us?"

"Of course. We'll only be in here a short time though. Is it necessary?"

"Please. For my sanity."

He shrugged and kneeled back before the keyhole. A few moments later, I heard the tumblers shifting, then the click of the lock turning back into place.

"Thank you. Now, a little light would be nice."

"Channel it yourself," Xaron complained, but he obliged with a large flame flaring up from his fingertips. "Would you like me to lead the way?"

I winced at the echo his words produced in the cavernous building. "Quiet now. Our voices carry too much for talking."

We ghosted along the edge of the chamber toward the hallway that held the Servants' solars. From Nomusa's directions, I knew they were situated along a corridor that curved around one side of the Conclave. The Low Consuls' solars were at the far end, positioning them closer to the small chamber at the back of the building where they most often congregated. As the doors were unlabeled and the darkness conspired to confound us, we had to backtrack twice before I was sure we stood before Orhan's door.

"You sure you don't want to check again?" Xaron teased softly as he crouched before the door. Even his slender fingers could fit no more than one at a time in this keyhole, and he seemed to be having an issue with it.

"You can open it, right?"

"Give me a moment."

I glanced up and down the corridor. The feeling of being watched had returned, though I still saw nothing. But seeing as how Xaron had extinguished his flame, that didn't mean much.

"Sorry," he muttered. "I need to concentrate."

I kneeled next to him, staring wide-eyed into the darkness. Blood pounded in my ears. "Hurry," I breathed. "I think someone else is here."

A puff of air caught my cheek as the door clicked. "Aha!" Xaron announced too loudly for comfort. "There we are."

The flame reappeared, showing that Xaron now stood. As light again shown down the hallway, I thought I saw a shadow fleeing into the gloom. A trick of the light, I told myself, as chills crept up my spine.

"Inside, quickly," I urged, following my own advice and slipping inside the solar. "And lock the door behind."

"Again?" he complained. But he shut us in the room and bent to comply. As his flame disappeared, the faint glow of covered pyr lamps cast the room in pallid illumination.

I tried to use Eltris's practice to relax my nerves as he worked on the lock, but it was no use. "Is it me, or are Eltris's exercises worthless?" I griped.

"They're worthless," Xaron readily agreed. "You should try the Shifting Sands meditation."

"The what?"

"Something Isi showed me. You imagine yourself walking through a desert, more or less. It focuses me every time."

I stared at where I knew he crouched in the darkness. "Isi," I muttered to myself.

The lock clicked, then a flame flared back to life to reveal his shame-faced look. "What?" he demanded at my smirk.

"Nothing. We have searching to do, don't we?"

Locating two of the pyr lamps, we began to roam Orhan's solar, which turned out to be a series of three rooms. One hosted nothing more than a washing basin and a clean chamberpot. The other, I guessed, was for the use of the clerks and honors within Orhan's employ from the scattering of quills and small desks. Returning to the main chamber, which I hoped was Orhan's own workspace, I began to peruse the parchments scattered across the much larger desk. I'd assumed Orhan would be a neat and organized person from the way he conducted himself, but found myself sorely mistaken. Papers were in disorderly stacks all across the surface and piled into cubby holes with seemingly no rhyme or reason. I wondered bitterly if he'd done so just to make searching his papers difficult as I scanned one document after another.

I quickly abandoned the larger papers in favor of the smaller finch scrolls. The sort of evidence I sought wouldn't be in formal documentation, but communications between the Preservist leader and any entity in opposition to the Council's stated goals. Yet even his missives contained little of import. One was from a proprietor giving a brief account of the losses to Orhan's estate this past harvest. His lands, like the others around Oedija, seemed to have been sorely affected by the droughts. Another was a letter from his daughter, who was apparently lodging in his manor outside the city. Perhaps it was significant that he didn't wish her to be in Oedija city. But with the Avvadin Imperium marching up from the south, anyone with the means might do the same. My own family was on a Wreath estate in the countryside, after all.

"Airene," Xaron hissed from next to me. He, too, had been rifling through finch messages, and he offered one to me. "Read this one. It's in the ash-tongue."

With skepticism born of the weary slog, I accepted it

from him. I was only just proficient in the Avvadin script and had to struggle to decipher the words:

> *You grow heretical as the end draws near, Sakin. Take care you do not discard your only friends at the turning of the tide. You will have your reward, in this life and the next. So long as you do not displease either of your masters.*
>
> *More arks pass through the gates everyday. Soon will come our time to rise.*
>
> *Be sure you rise with us.*

My chest fluttered, though I couldn't tell whether it was from excitement or fear. The missive was unsigned, but it didn't need to be. From the language used, this had to come from a Valemish priest, a Kul.

I told Xaron what it said. "Good work," I whispered to him. "This is exactly what we need."

He nodded, but his brow was creased with concern. "But what does it mean? 'Soon will come our time to rise' — Will the Valemish attack from within Oedija's walls? And what is within the arks they're smuggling in?"

"Weapons? Money?" I shrugged. "We suspected the Valemish conspired against Oedija. Now we have proof of it, and against Orhan as well."

"Proof, yes. But will it be enough to remove him from power? I doubt it. The rest of his faction would never turn on him. And even if the other five and Jaxas voted to remove him, would he defer to their decision? Or would it just rouse rebellion sooner rather than later?" Xaron shook his head. "This is why I've stayed away from politics. It becomes muddled too quickly."

"It's a bit late to stay out of politics. You've stepped right into them."

"You don't have to tell me that," Xaron muttered. "Its stink is all I can smell. Come on. We can at least tell Nomusa what we found and see what she says."

After we'd put Orhan's solar back together as much as we remembered it, we returned to the door, and Xaron set once more to unlocking it. I neatly rolled up the scroll and tucked it into a subtle pocket in my cloak. Only then did my thoughts turn back to the watcher I'd imagined outside the door. I hoped it was just my imagination getting the better of me. Either way, we had no choice now but to leave as swiftly as we could.

The door clicked open, and I followed after Xaron as we exited back into the hall. As he channeled radiance, the hall flared into light.

A silhouette fled down the hall away from us.

This time, I knew I wasn't mistaken. "There!" I yelled as I pointed. "After him!"

Xaron needed no prodding, but charged forward. I hurried behind, endeavoring to keep up, if only to remain in the light. The figure fled before us, footsteps echoing in the empty hall. Who were they? What had they heard? And worst of all, who might they report back to? Breath hissed in my throat as I sprinted faster.

Reaching the end of the corridor, the figure didn't turn toward the door, but into the main chamber. I stuttered to a halt near the doors, but didn't stare in confusion for long as they leaped impossibly high to grab hold of the jagged edge of a broken wall and haul themselves up.

"They're a warden!" I cried to Xaron. "Be careful!"

With typical rashness, Xaron followed, leaping dozens of feet into the air to land on the same broken wall. The figure leaped outside, and as my friend gave chase, I lost sight of them both. Meaning to follow, I ran to the great double doors when a terrible realization occurred to me. Xaron had locked the doors. As I tried to push them open, I found I was trapped inside.

I stepped back, trying to think of a way out. Fear and frustration clouded my thoughts. I stared into the darkness behind me, trying desperately to detect any movement. The watcher might not have been alone; perhaps, even now, I was being stalked by his companions. I ground my teeth and pressed my back against the solid door. There was nothing I could do but wait and hope it was Xaron who returned for me.

As I waited, I tried desperately to open myself to the Pyrthae. Channeling was my only protection if the other warden returned. Channeling might even get me out of here, if I could use kinesis to trip the lock. But once again, Eltris's exercises failed me. I couldn't stop my constant searching of the darkness to clear my mind nor relax my body. I exhaled in frustration. None of the wardens I'd seen had any trouble channeling on command. But I knew of no other way than Eltris's.

A scuffle of sandals on stone sounded from where Xaron and the warden had exited. My breath caught as I listened in terror to the sounds of someone coming closer. Was it Xaron returning? Or had the errant warden doubled back?

"Airene," Xaron called softly.

I let out my breath and sagged against the door. A moment later, I saw him drop into the chamber and look around.

"Here," I called back to him.

He ran lightly over to meet me. "I lost him," he said, voice tight with frustration. "He slipped over the fence, and I knew I couldn't leave you in here."

"You should have followed him," I said without conviction.

Xaron laughed and pulled me in with an arm over my shoulders. "I knew you'd be scared of the dark."

I didn't dignify his teasing with a response.

"But anyway," he continued, "we at least know something

about them. Seeing as he was a warden, he was most likely a Seeker."

"Most likely. But we don't know."

"No. But everything Finches do is guesswork, isn't it? Now, assuming it *was* a Seeker, what did he want? Was he watching us, or here for something else? I doubt he meant us harm — the Manifest would have sent more men otherwise."

I nodded. "Either way, it seems an awful coincidence, doesn't it? That the Seeker would be here the same night we were?"

Xaron was silent for a moment. "Unless they're always watching," he muttered.

I'd thought the same thing. "How would you feel about running the perimeter at night? Of the Conclave as well as the Laurel Palace. You'll get to channel all you want for a turn or two."

He grinned. "You know just how to manipulate me. Of course I'll do it. I have precious few duties as it is."

I drew him into a tighter embrace. "Thank you. Now, if you could get us out of here—"

A rattle began in the lock of the great doors. Xaron and I froze, staring, before reality set in.

"Guards!" I hissed.

Xaron looked around frantically. "There's nowhere to go. Only a warden could escape without the doors."

A wild idea entered my head. "Carry me! Can you lift me up there?"

The key was turning in the lock, the tumblers sliding into place. Time was running out. Xaron stared at the distance, brow creased.

"I don't know," he whispered. "I could hurt you!"

I pushed him to the wall as the door began to creak open. "No time!"

We reached the base of the broken wall as whoever was outside began to enter. The light from the torches they carried gleamed off their helms, showing them to be Conclave guards, and shone on the tips of their spears.

"Show yourselves!" one of them called, sweeping the torch around. Its light fell over the ruined chamber.

I jumped into Xaron's arms. "Just do it!" I hissed.

The motion caught the guards' attention. "Thieves! Stop right there!"

Xaron didn't hesitate any longer. His wiry frame held surprising strength, for he held me easily in his arms. "Hold on," he muttered, dropping into a crouch.

Then, with a sudden lurch, we were flying. I heard kinesis pounding against the floor as Xaron launched us upward to the narrow ledge. For a moment, it looked like we wouldn't reach the rocky ledge — then his feet almost floated to land on the stone. He swayed back and forth for balance for a moment, then said, "Brace yourself," before leaping down on the other side.

I saw the rubble littering the base of the wall a moment before it was underfoot. Xaron's feet scrabbled against it, then he slipped, sliding down it with a curse. Stone banged against my clothing, ripping and bruising. But as we slid to a halt, me half hanging from Xaron's arms, I knew we were lucky to still be alive.

I scrambled to my feet. "The Aviary!" I hissed, then set off at a run. My knee hurt where I'd knocked it against a rock. Xaron lagged behind me. I hoped I hadn't pushed him to his limits, but I couldn't stop to reconsider things now.

The guards were not quick in following. By the time we slipped inside the Aviary doors, their torches were still near the entrance of the Conclave. Perhaps Xaron revealing that he was a warden had deterred their pursuit. Whatever the reason, I was grateful to slide into a chair and catch my breath.

"That seemed like it ended well."

I startled upright and stared wide-eyed at the figure in

the corner. Only a moment later did I recognize Nomusa's voice. "Don't do that," I snapped, fear sharpening my words.

She uncovered a pyrkin lamp, revealing her amused smile. "Why were those guards after you? Did you make that much noise?"

I explained everything while Xaron was hunched over, still breathing hard. I interrupted the telling halfway through to ask if he needed anything, but he just waved a hand. I kept an eye on him all the same. Hopefully all he needed was rest.

Nomusa held out a hand. "Let me see the note."

I gave it over, unable to hide my surprise. "You can read ash-tongue?"

"I was the heiress to my ishaka," she said with wry amusement. "I was tutored in all of the languages of the Four Realms, though my sand-tongue is poor. I thought you knew that."

As she finished, she looked up with her brow creased. "I agree with you — this must be from the Valemish. But there are still a lot of questions."

"But it's enough to cast suspicion on him. The rest of the Council should see it."

Nomusa bit her lip. "Maybe. But we should sleep on it. I have a feeling all of this will move swifter than we like, and we need to be prepared for it."

I reached over and shook Xaron's shoulder, as he'd slumped onto the table. "Can you make it back up to your tower?"

"Don't make me," he said without lifting his head.

I grinned, realizing he'd be fine. "I'm sure we can make you up a pallet. Come on. I guess it's my turn to carry you."

THE YORANDU HEIR

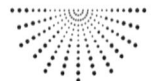

Clepsammia appeared to Agmon Brandheart. Clad in a cloak of night, she was invisible to all eyes but his.

'Why does this daemon flee before me?' Agmon thundered. 'Can he not match my power?'

'More than match it,' the Maiden of the Sands said. 'Famine's power grows with each passing day. It is his destiny to swallow the whole of the world.'

Agmon Brandheart, bravest of all men, paled at this prophecy. 'Then we must fail. He cannot be defeated.'

'No. In the end, all must perish, swallowed by the God of Hunger. But all things end, Brandheart. It is not the end that measures the life, but the purpose fulfilled.'

She thought of her father, gone from this world, but did not impart his passing. For even the wardens, gifted with her father's dying strength, did not know the Ruler of All Realms no longer reigned.

Agmon stood straighter. 'Then I shall fulfill mine, so long as it ends in glory. If I can but force my enemy to face me!'

- The Seeds of Famine, a translation from the Lighted-tongue; by Oracle Kalene of deme Hull; 881 SLP

The summons came early the next morning.

Nomusa shook me awake. "The Council wishes to see us," she said quietly. "Now."

I sat up, immediately alert. "Orhan knows we broke in," I guessed.

"Probably. The guards must have reported the intruders to him." Her brow was creased. "This is moving faster than I thought. And until we know how this will play out, I think we should keep Orhan's missive secret for now."

"Why bother?" I rose and clambered over Xaron, who snored on a makeshift pallet on the floor, and pulled out a tunic and trousers from my wardrobe.

Nomusa gave me a look. I sighed and pulled down a chiton as well. Best not to ruffle the Council's feathers just now.

"Feiyan must be the one to reveal this. We lack the authority to accomplish anything. Well, anything except the Order's dissolution."

I looked sharply at her. "Feiyan? Since when is she our friend?"

Nomusa bit her lip. "Airene, I meant to tell you sooner. But Feiyan… she's allied with us now."

The mystery that had surrounded my friend suddenly came into painful clarity. "The stranger in the red cloak the day I awoke. That was Feiyan?"

"Kako, actually."

"So Feiyan is on our side, is she?" I asked sarcastically. "From what I've seen, she's only ever been on her own side."

"She helped confirm both of us as First Verifiers, if you remember."

"Reluctantly."

"And she gave us the Thulu pyrkin before the Despoina's trial."

"Because she didn't believe in its usefulness." I threw up

my hands. "None of this makes me trust her, Nomusa. I doubt anything will."

"But you must. She has authority and resources that we don't. And she grows closer to Jaxas everyday."

"To Jaxas? I thought she was the Despoina's pet."

"Not anymore. Ever since the trial, her flattery has been directed toward a different Wreath."

I frowned. It wasn't unlike Feiyan to shift loyalties, but I didn't like Jaxas accepting her confidences. Though, of course, Nomusa had as well. Feiyan was a parasite I'd never be rid of, it seemed.

"She'll not betray us," Nomusa pressed. "Not in this, anyway. We both want to keep the city in one piece."

I bit back further words. We had no choice in this matter, I knew, but it didn't make me like it any better. I wiped at the sleep lingering around my eyes.

"I'm sorry. I know you're making the best of a tough situation."

Nomusa nodded stiffly, not looking at me. "Thank you. Now, if you're ready, we'd better go."

"Where are we going?" Xaron asked sleepily from the floor.

"Nowhere with you," I told him. "Sleep."

With a grunt of assent, he turned on his side and curled back up into his blankets.

After a brisk walk, Nomusa and I arrived at the Conclave doors. I felt for Orhan's stolen message, which I'd secured in a small scroll case under my chiton. Though I didn't plan to reveal it, I couldn't trust it to remain anywhere but on my person.

As if there hadn't been a break-in the night before, the guards waved us through as normal. Though, I reflected, they'd hardly accuse one of their own of the deed. The gloomy day peeked in through the broken dome, drizzling rain onto the floor. Few Servants and their staff milled about, their proceedings for the day not yet begun. My own short rest was already catching up with me, my mind groggy and my body stiff. I pushed my discomforts from mind as Nomusa led us down to the Council chamber door. Giving me a final significant look, she spoke to the honor waiting by the door, and moments later, we were escorted inside.

The Council chamber was emptier than usual. Most of the Low Consuls were not yet there, only the five of the Preservist faction. Orhan smiled heartily at us, flanked by his fellows. Berker, sitting at Orhan's right, leaned forward, the smile on his face like a wolf staring at a pair of lambs.

"First Verifiers," Orhan greeted us. "Good morn to you both."

Nomusa and I bowed, mine more perfunctory than hers.

"Good morn, Low Consuls," Nomusa said, her tone nothing but gracious. "To what do we owe the pleasure of your summons?"

Orhan motioned for us to move further inside, and we reluctantly complied.

"An unusual circumstance, to be sure," he said. "It seems that the recent devastation to our chambers here in the Conclave has left us vulnerable to thieves. Last night, guards reported two wardens fleeing the premises."

I kept my face carefully composed. "Sounds like Seeker wardens. Did they disturb anything?"

Orhan's gaze settled on me, a slight smile playing on his lips. "Why, yes they did. I entered my solar this morning only to find my papers in a great disarray. I must confess, I am a rather suspicious man. Thus, I give my things the appearance of disorganization so that rifling hands will be less cautious."

My throat went dry, but Nomusa said smoothly, "A wise approach, and one that has now served us well."

The Preservist leader smiled in acknowledgement, then looked at me. I said nothing, but stared back, hoping my silence wouldn't seem culpability. It couldn't make him more suspicious than he already was.

Nomusa glanced at me, then looked back at Orhan. "Low Consul, if we might ask, did they take anything from your papers?"

"Nothing of import — merely a friendly correspondence. But those unfamiliar with our relationship may read too much into it." His gaze slowly panned from Nomusa to me again. I met it steadily. I'd show no signs of guilt. I couldn't be guilty before a man trying to sell us to a foreign empire.

"I assume you wish us to investigate?" Nomusa inquired.

"No, no, that is quite alright. I don't know what you could discover. The thieves were quite adept. I just wanted to pass on word of it to you, and a reminder to remain cautious."

The way he smiled made my skin crawl.

"We'll keep that in mind," Nomusa promised.

Orhan nodded. "Good. Now, I need not remind you that the Yorandu delegation arrives tonight. I trust we will see you both there?"

Nomusa's smile stiffened. "Of course," was all she could manage.

"Very well. You are dismissed."

We thanked them, bowed, and left the room as swiftly as we dared.

"We have to move quickly," Nomusa said in a low voice when we were outside the Conclave chambers. "It's only a matter of time before Orhan has us searched. He might have even sent someone to the Aviary while we were gone."

I sighed. "Then we'd best speak with Feiyan soon."

Nomusa cast me a sideways glance. "I'll handle it. I know you'd prefer to stay far away from her."

"What tipped you off to that?"

A smile tugged at her lips, but her expression smoothed a moment later. "I suppose we should discuss the Yorandu delegation arriving tonight."

I winced, knowing the depth of the emotions behind her words. I tried to imagine how such an encounter would feel. Something akin to running into Vusu in the midst of a festival, perhaps. But though Vusu had killed or maimed my brothers, he hadn't robbed me of my home, family, and inheritance in the same stroke, and all at a young age. I suspected such wounds didn't heal, but only scarred over, prone to breaking open at the first reminder. Mine certainly promised to never fade.

"I can speak with them," I offered. "Perhaps you don't even have to come."

She shook her head. "As Firsts of the new Order of Verifiers, we are to be presented before the Yorandu Heir. The Council believes we should do our utmost to convince the Yorandu delegation that Oedija is taking active steps to overcome its significant challenges. We are part of that. They may also expect us to report in brief to the Yorandu Heir on the progress we've made on rooting out corruption within the upper echelons of our society. Besides, this will be the first time since the trial that all the most powerful in Oedija have gathered together. If Vusu has been waiting for an opportunity to strike, he may get no better one. I have to attend."

Her jaw stiffened, and I quickly changed the subject. "What time should we meet?"

"The fourth turn of the afternoon. You need a bath and plenty of time to prepare."

I rolled my eyes, but didn't deny it. Nearly a span's worth of grime clung to me, and my hair had been reduced to a frizzy mess.

"Oedija is breaking, and we're spending time bathing." I shook my head. "What a strange world we live in."

"But it's the way things are, so no point in moaning about it. Now come on. I think I have a comb that won't break on those tangles of yours…"

~

The Laurel Palace, resplendent as it was, needed no additional decoration. Yet as Nomusa and I entered inside, we found it had been furnished with further marvels. Braziers, burning with golden flames, lined the walkway through the atrium. As we passed between them, heat pouring over us and sweat beading on my skin, I wondered if it was channeling or alchemy behind them. When I was a true warden, I hoped I'd be able to tell the difference.

Nomusa muttered complaints about the braziers as she wiped at her brow with a hand cloth. Even shining with sweat, she looked as stunning as I'd expected, though in the simple way she'd adopted since becoming a First Verifier. A deep violet peplos of a supple, flowing material flattered her curvaceous figure. She'd curled her hair neatly against her head. Her only jewelry was the Verifier medallion and a bracelet of emerald-colored glass. When I saw a sparkle within them that went beyond reflected sunlight, I'd known she'd been to visit Maesos; no one else used pyrkin to set their works aflame.

I knew I must look plain beside her in my borrowed, pale green peplos. Nomusa claimed the color accentuated my eyes, but I was more concerned with the necessity of leaving both tunic and knife behind. Though trouble from the Seekers was possible, I could see no way to keep either one without it being blatantly apparent. Not that I could do much against other wardens at the moment. But it was reassuring all the same to have a blade close at hand.

We followed the people before us, Servants by their line of conversation, down the carpeted walk to the feast hall. Room after room, the braziers continued.

"The guests must be the feast," I observed drily. "I can't see any other reason to bake us all before arriving."

Nomusa shrugged. "Intimidation. Perhaps Asileia wishes to show her suitor that while Oedija suffers, it isn't weak."

"Only a fool would fall for that." I left the last part of my thought unspoken: that I hoped the Yorandu Heir was a fool, for all of our sakes.

As we arrived at the feast hall, we found it transformed since our last visit. Pyr lamps, glowing the gold and green of the Wreaths, floated around the room, powerful magnets holding them aloft. Banners had been unfurled along the walls, depicting scenes of conquest against fearsome beasts as well as stories of the Eidola and the Lighted Passage. An array of food as vast as I'd ever seen spread before us in a spectacle of color, texture, and shape. My mouth began watering as I saw chocolate, a rare delicacy, adorning a number of desserts that I had no names for. Drinks, too, were more plentiful than I'd ever seen, with honors serving them to guests from platters.

But though the feast invited me to indulge, a sharp guilt needled me. Many starved on the streets of Oedija. Perhaps a show of plenty was one of the necessary frivolities of ceremony, but it did little to ease my conscience.

Forgoing food for the moment, I turned my attention to the dais that had been raised at the far end of the room, a wooden scaffold painted gold that rose half a man's height and creaked with the weight of the people walking across it. Upon the platform, Despoina Asileia Wreath sat in a throne made of wicker wood, the ends fanning out several cubits above her, fashioned like a peacock's feathers. The Despoina had not turned herself gold or bared her breasts as she had for her Ascension, but wore a sober violet chiton, even if the fold across the front did open coquettishly, hinting at what lay beneath. Her face had been painted to exaggerate her features, serving now only to emphasize the bored expression with which she stared over the proceedings.

Next to the Despoina stood one of the few female laurel

guards I'd seen: First Laurel Synne, Nomusa had told me earlier. Her face was all hard planes as she stared at the people milling around her, daring any to approach. A hard woman she must be indeed to fill Lykos's boots.

My gaze caught on the four manacled men surrounding her. Fear and loathing struck through me. The Shepherds' faces were hidden within aqua hoods, but I knew they stared out with dead eyes. Loyalty to Oedija they might claim, but that didn't make them my allies. Especially not with the secret I kept hidden. I didn't know if they could detect attunement just by a looking at a person, and I didn't want to find out. I spotted their Tribune handler lurking around the edges of the dais. He scowled as he stared around him, his head of thinning hair shining with perspiration, his maroon robes billowing loose about his shoulders. A nervous sort, I suspected. Best not to run into him either.

I averted my eyes and sought friendlier faces. Xaron was easiest to spot, and not only because of his Hilarion clothes. As I watched, he spouted a fountain of flames into the air from his mouth, to the amazement of the onlookers. I shook my head. The breadth of his tricks astonished me, particularly now that I was a warden myself. He was clearly reveling in having an audience to perform in front of.

Jaxas was almost as easy to find, if only because of the company he kept. He was absorbed in conversation with a pair of Bali dressed in as strange a fashion as I'd ever seen. The older man wore a robe patterned of a variety of bright colors, and a stole made of a leopard's hide draped around his neck. His peppered hair was braided tightly against his head.

The boy was more extravagantly dressed. Though he was slightly shorter than myself, his feather crown rose high above my head, the yellow and blue quills plucked from a bird I didn't know. Across his chest hung a broad collar of bronze, etched in fine detail with a hundred images, and from the collar hung ribbons of woven silk dyed in as many colors as his older escort's robes. His stomach was bare, revealing a young man's lithe figure, and his arms were revealed as well but for the many bracelets jangling about his forearms and wrists. He wore a skirt of bronze plates, and the sandals on his feet were painted gold.

The Yorandu Heir, Komo. I had known Komo was young, but I hadn't expected him to look no more than fourteen years old. I doubted he even grew hair over his lip. The older man would be an advisor — I doubted a warrior would wear those robes.

I felt Nomusa stiffen by me, no doubt glimpsing the Yorandu visitors as well. "I'm going to mingle," she muttered. "Keep an ear out for anything of interest." She headed in the opposite direction of the delegation.

I sighed and examined them again only to find Jaxas had spotted me. Our eyes met for a moment before he turned away to respond to something Komo had said. I turned away as well. If he wanted something from me, he could find me.

Dozens of patricians, Servants, and other notables of Oedija had grouped together. Most conversed in hushed tones, though from one or two erupted boisterous laughter. Yet in these times, most conversations would be of trade and commerce, of soldiers and strongholds. Between the knots of important and prosperous folk, honors flitted back and forth. I spotted Nikias in one corner scowling over it all. No doubt even this flawless affair wasn't up to the steward's standards.

As I scanned the room, I searched for a quarry oblivious enough to allow a Finch to eavesdrop. The wine in my hand called to me. Though it smelled too sweet, I wanted to lose myself in it and leave behind my worries for a time. Instead, I only drank it in sips. The threat of a Manifest attack weighed heavily on my mind, and I found myself glancing often at the windows and doors.

"A frown at a celebration sticks out like a finch among terns."

I startled and turned to the speaker, who had approached from behind. My mood soured further still at the sight of the richly dressed honor. "Kako."

The man wore a smile that didn't touch his eyes. In flattery of the Wreaths, he wore boldly green robes with a golden stole draped around his neck. Silver chains adorned his neck as well as his wrists, perhaps in mockery of his caste, though he still sported the tin spiral earrings and shaved head of his fellow honors.

"If you can't enjoy yourself at a party of such great expense," he continued, "I don't know what would please you, First Verifier."

"Perhaps I'm displeased *because* of the great expense."

"Ah, you think it wasteful. But is it not more wasteful to attend and not delight in it?"

I was in no mood to mince words with the silver-tongued fool. "What does your mistress want?"

"Why would you assume she wants for anything? No, Airene. The Low Consul has all she desires of you for the moment."

Even knowing he was baiting me, I couldn't help but ask, "What do you mean?"

The honor's eyes glimmered with the light of a nearby pyr lamp. "But that is half the fun, isn't it? My knowing, your wondering."

I shrugged, playing for nonchalant. "You've said nothing to wonder about."

"No, perhaps I haven't." A smile lingered about the corners of his lips. "Perhaps it isn't me you should ask after, but your closest allies. Perhaps you don't keep them as close as you think."

Chills prickled up my spine, but I forced a smile. "If you mean your arrangement with Nomusa, I know all about it."

Despite my hopes otherwise, Kako's smile didn't slip. "Oh, I thought you might. But you have more friends than her."

With that last barb, the honor turned and melded back into the crowd.

Kako had a gift for mischief. I spite of myself, his words stuck in my mind like a sliver under a fingernail. The honor was many things, but he rarely told a lie that did not contain a kernel of truth. But who else could he mean but Nomusa?

Seeking to distract myself, I ghosted near a group who seemed intent enough in their discussion not to notice me. But as soon as I drifted within earshot, one of them cast me a scowl and gestured to the others. I moved on as if I hadn't noticed. But as I approached my second group of targets, I was noticed again and rebuffed, forced to drift further on.

It wasn't long before I realized what I needed. And I knew just the person to help me obtain it.

I found Xaron in one corner of the room entertaining four young women, likely patrician daughters. I stood just behind them and crossed my arms, unable to decide if I was amused or annoyed at how avidly he sought to charm them.

"But what is this?" he declared as he reached toward the ear of one of the girls. She giggled and moved out of the way, then gasped as his hand blossomed in a vision of shifting colored light. It seemed a streaked painting, and I thought I detected images in it — a butterfly settling on a flower, the sun shining golden through waving grass…

One of the girls gasped, and I blinked. The vision had felt like a nudge on my mind, like when Kyros had sent the message to the librarian from his tower. I looked at my friend with fresh eyes. Xaron had just channeled quintessence, I was sure of it. And I was equally sure he had no idea he had.

His gaze slid over to me, and he closed his fist, making the pastoral scene disappear. "Alas, but I require a respite from my service," he said with a deep bow. "If you fine ladies would excuse me..."

"You're not dismissed yet!" one of the girls objected. "You have to entertain us when we ask. Show us more!"

I moved around the patricians and looped my arm though Xaron's. "Hilarion is going to entertain me now," I said firmly, meeting the eye of the spoiled girl. "If you'll excuse us."

As I led Xaron away, I heard the girl whisper loudly, "I know what kind of entertainment *she's* after," and she and her companions burst into giggles. I ignored them as well as Xaron, for he grinned as I led him to as private an alcove as could be found in the bustling feast hall.

"Growing jealous?" he teased me as he stole my cup of wine and drained it.

"Very." I waved over an honor and received two goblets more. "Xaron, I need your help."

"Oh? Not the kind that girl was insinuating, surely?"

I gave him a flat stare, but he just grinned at me. "Teasing, Aire. What did you need?"

"Cover. We need to pretend to have a conversation while I listen in on people around the room. No one will let me get close enough."

"You *are* wearing a rather intimidating scowl," he pointed out. "But I'm sure it doesn't help that you're one of the leaders of an organization who used to put people like them in the stockyards."

"Exactly my point. So can you help me?"

"Help you?" He wore a mischievous look. "I can do you one better. Put down your wine."

Confused, I obliged, setting my glass next to his. I grew even more perplexed as Xaron raised his hands to my temples.

"What are you doing?"

"Helping you hear." He closed his eyes, his face clearing of emotion. "You may want to brace yourself."

I discovered what he meant a moment later. Without preamble, the room shifted around me, then a wave of sound crashed over me. I reeled under the weight of it. The score of conversations had crescendoed until they filled my head, too loud and overwhelming to distinguish from one another. I would have cried out were I not afraid my own yell would provoke further pain.

As abruptly as it had come, the deluge subsided. "Airene?" I heard Xaron's voice so clearly it seemed as if he spoke in my head. "Did I hurt you?"

"What did you just do?" My own voice reverberated in my head, and I winced. While not quite painful, it wasn't a pleasant sensation.

"I amplified the sound around you. Remember when I told you sound is merely vibrations? Just as any Hilarion amplifies the vibrations in speakers' throats, I can amplify the sounds you hear. But are you sure you're not hurt? You're scrunching up your face like you've eaten a lemon — seeds, rind, and all."

"I'm fine," I lied. With the discomfort of speaking, I wanted to avoid explanations as much as possible. But I couldn't help asking, "You're using kinesis then?"

"Yes. A variation of it."

It clicked then. Before, when Xaron had been channeling the light scene for the girls, I'd thought I felt quintessence pressing on my mind. As my present pain subsided, I again felt that same touch, surrounding me like a bubble. Xaron channeled quintessence though he didn't know it. He always had. As Eltris had said, quintessence was the tool that shaped energy. All channeling required quintessence; though some, like this trick, seemed to require more than simpler channels.

I tucked away my questions. Only one person might answer them for me, and I'd have to wait until tomorrow to ask her. "We may as well make use of this. Can you pick out a conversation for me?"

"Yes. Who would you like to hear?"

Only then did I realize I'd squeezed my eyes shut. Opening them, my vision swam as I scanned the room. I picked out the first interesting pairing I found. "Focus on the Despoina and the Bali man she's speaking with."

The sound whirled around me, and I closed my eyes again as the deluge filled my mind. Then, as the voices settled to a manageable level, two came to me clearer than the rest.

"I have heard you are the — what do you call it? The mouthpiece of a god." The man had a rich baritone with a timbre that made me suspect he was fully aware of it.

"A goddess," Asileia responded shortly. Her voice sounded reedy and thin compared to his. "I am the Hand of Clepsammia."

"Ah, my apologies, my lady. And Clepsammia — she is a powerful goddess, no?"

"She claims all the sands of time."

"Powerful indeed." I heard the rustle of the man's clothes as he moved — cloth scraping together, ornaments of some kind clinking. "A perfect matching for a powerful woman."

Suddenly, I realized with horror what this conversation was: the Bali was courting our Despoina. Yet I knew by the masculine voice it couldn't be the Yorandu Heir.

In my surprise, I missed Asileia's response, and the man was saying with irritation, "If the Despoina does not wish me near, I am sure she would tell you."

"Leave him," Asileia snapped. "I would hear his words."

The sound of sandals on wood faded away. Someone had come to intervene, I gathered; perhaps a guard or an advisor, or even Jaxas.

"Is it not wearying, all these people fretting over you, when you have no need to be cared for? Not a woman such as you."

"Yes. It is wearying."

"Why don't you send them away? Or perhaps we could go somewhere they will not bother you. Somewhere more... private."

A long silence fell, telling of Leia's deliberations over his words. "I will meet this prince of yours first," Asileia decided at length. "But you and I will speak again. I would hear more of what you see when you gaze upon me."

"Yes, divine queen of mine eye."

I reached out and touched Xaron, and he obliged by pulling me away from the conversation. "Well?" he whispered.

My head was starting to ache, but I didn't ask him to stop. The evening was only just getting started. "I'll tell you later. Do you see any Low Consuls? Or Kako — I can't get something he said earlier out of my head." The briefest doubt that Feiyan's henchman may have been alluding to Xaron flashed through my mind, but I dismissed it as quickly as it came. Questioning my trust in Xaron wasn't an option.

"No. But there is — Burning hells!"

My senses seared as Xaron's hand lifted from my temples. As the world righted under my feet, I put out a hand to the wall, gasping slightly. Queasiness assaulted me, and for a moment, it was hard to open my eyes.

"Aire." Xaron sounded as if he spoke through clenched teeth.

I opened my eyes. Coming toward us were two Shepherds, the crowd flinching away before them, their dead eyes never straying from us.

"Why approach now?" Xaron muttered. "I've been channeling all evening. I have a right to."

Sharp fingers needled through my gut, but it wasn't for Xaron that I feared. Remembering Eltris's unnaturally keen hearing, and understanding it now for what it was, I didn't dare respond. Shepherds might easily be enhancing their own senses.

The two manacled wardens stood before us, balefully looking out from under their hoods. For the moment, they stared at Xaron. "You have channeled, though you are forbidden," one told him.

"I'm Hilarion!" Xaron responded angrily. "I have every right to channel!"

"Only for the entertainment of others."

Though I quailed inside, I spoke up. "He was entertaining me. Surely that's not outside his bounds."

Icy water seemed to pour over me as both Shepherds turned their gazes on me. "This Hilarion was entertaining you," the Shepherd repeated.

His expression didn't shift. I had no idea if he believed me or not. "Yes," I said firmly. "He was."

"Don't worry about him!" a reedy voice snapped from behind them. Stepping between the Shepherds was the Tribune I'd seen before. "The boy has the right, as he said. Return to your posts!"

The Shepherds moved without hesitation back to where they had previously stood. The Tribune looked between Xaron and me. "Entertaining her, were you?" he asked with a leer.

"Yes," Xaron responded stiffly.

Unperturbed, the Tribune peered at me. "And who are you?" he barked. His eyes wandered down to my medallion. "Ah. One of the new Finches. Friends with Hilarion, are you?"

"I believe I'm the one who gets to ask questions," I said calmly. "You're the new handler of the Shepherds?"

The Tribune sneered. "And I thought you lot were supposed to be sharp. Why else would they obey me?"

"Pray you fare better than the last one. As I recall, I shot him with a crossbow."

The man only grinned wider. "We'll have to see if you get lucky twice." Without another word, he turned and stalked back through the crowd.

I found Xaron staring at me. "What?"

"With Tribune Timon just then, you were a bit... short.."

"You heard the way he talked to us. I can't stand men like him." But the truth became apparent even as I spoke. "I suppose he scares me," I admitted in a whisper. "Because of... you know."

Xaron smiled sympathetically. "Of course I know. But drawing his ire won't do you any favors."

He was right, of course. But I couldn't completely dispel the sudden anger that had filled me, and with my head beginning to ache again, I felt it simmering just below the surface.

"I suppose I'd better try to eavesdrop the usual way again," I said grudgingly. "And you have more tricks to perform."

A grin blossomed on his face. "And more young ladies to amuse."

I rolled my eyes as Xaron sauntered away to be immediately hailed for a performance. At least someone was enjoying their new position.

I hunted around half-heartedly for another group to pester, picking up my wine and sipping at it again. But before I could decide on a target, Nomusa emerged from the crowd. I knew what she'd say from her black look before she opened her mouth.

"It's time," she declared shortly, then turned toward the dais.

Quelling my dread, I followed.

Jaxas and Komo, still conversing at the base of the dais, turned as we approached. The young Bali Heir's face brightened like a boy anticipating a sweet.

"These are the Finches? And one of them Bali!" He spoke with the same accent as the man I'd heard speaking with the

Despoina, and in the same sonorous manner, like he wasn't afraid of his words being heard.

"Yes," Jaxas responded, his eyes briefly meeting mine. I saw caution written there and wondered at its source. "Shaka-Heir Charatta Yorandu Komo, please meet First Verifier Nomusa and First Verifier Airene."

"Two Firsts?" the older Bali man standing next to them said. "That is unusual, is it not?"

"It is," Jaxas acknowledged. "But our First Verifiers work well together, and the times call for unprecedented actions."

"They do," Komo agreed easily. "I am glad to meet both of you. Particularly one of my countryfolk." He extended his hand to Nomusa, clearly seeking to give the usual Bali greeting.

Nomusa didn't look down at his hand, but gave a short, stiff bow, little more than a nod. She said nothing.

As the young Heir's brow knit in confusion, I rushed to say, "We're glad to meet you as well, Shaka-Heir Komo. And which of your warriors do we have the pleasure of meeting?"

The older man laughed, though I noticed the exchange hadn't escaped his attention. "A charming one, aren't you? I am no warrior, First Verifier, but the Heir's advisor. You may simply call me Nkosi. Long have I served his father, and so may I hope to serve him."

But though Komo had lowered his arm, he hadn't looked aside from Nomusa. "Why do you not greet me as tradition would bade?"

Dangerous waters, those. I tried to navigate the conversation away from them. "Nomusa has long since left her homeland, and I'm afraid she no longer practices—"

"Tradition." Nomusa cut through my rushed words, and to my consternation, the other three focused on her. "What do you know of tradition?"

Komo stared at her in astonishment. "I am young, but I

have been well tutored, First Verifier. Yet I do not think this is what you mean."

Nkosi narrowed his eyes. "A Bali in Oedija, resentful of the Heir. I don't have to wonder long to know which ishaka you fled from."

"Nor should you wonder at who is my family," Nomusa shot back. "If you've served his father, their blood is on your hands as well."

"Blood on his hands?" Komo sounded astonished. "Nkosi is an honorable and loyal—"

"Peace, Heir Komo," the advisor interrupted him. His eyes did not leave Nomusa. "What she says is true. Her family's blood does stain my hands, and I am not ashamed to say so."

Hard lines deepened in Nomusa's face as she stared at Komo's advisor. I stood by, helpless to intervene. Jaxas was similarly silent, watching with hollowed eyes.

"Speak plainly," Komo demanded of Nkosi. "Who is she?"

"Nomusa, as she said before. Eshalo Yorandu Nomusa."

The Shaka-Heir's eyes widened. "Eshalo," he whispered, turning toward Nomusa. "But I was told all your family had died."

"No," the Bali advisor said. "Your father and I never conspired to deceive you, Komo. But we always knew the Eshalo scion lurked somewhere within the Four Realms."

Komo bowed his head. "Truly, I am sorry," he said with his gaze lowered. "Just because your family's death was necessary does not mean I do not regret it."

Jaxas looked as astonished at his words as I was. Nomusa's teeth bared in a snarl. "*Necessary*, was it?" she sneered. "You think to dismiss murder with words? To rob me of my homeland and make amends with apologies?" She turned her head aside, fists clenched and arms stiff at her sides.

Komo's head shot up. "No! Of course not! I merely wished to—"

"Heir Komo," Nkosi said, reprimand sharp in his voice. "We will speak of this later." He turned his angry gaze on Jaxas. "You bring us here to negotiate an alliance, yet flaunt this rebel in our face. You play a dangerous game, Archon."

"Nkosi," Jaxas started, but the advisor had already turned away.

"Heir Komo, I suggest we retire for the evening to ponder our future relationship with Oedija."

"As you wish," the boy said, his uncertainty plain. As he turned after his advisor, he cast one last lingering look back at Nomusa. I almost pitied the boy for the pain in his expression.

"Both of you will come with me. Now."

I turned toward Jaxas. Never had I seen anger on such open display from the Archon.

"Of course." I glanced at Nomusa.

She still looked aside, hands clenched in fists. When Jaxas began walking away, she finally spoke, her voice tight. "I will return to my quarters now."

As Jaxas turned back to answer her, she stalked past him and out of the banquet hall. The Archon shook his head sharply and beckoned me to follow him out.

Amid the stares and mounting murmurs around us, the Archon led me off the carpeted path and up the stairs. I breathed a sigh of relief. As terrible as that had been to witness, it had been worse with all those people watching. I'd already gained notoriety from the Despoina's trial. Finches could only operate effectively from the shadows, and the Order was attracting far too much light for my liking.

As we ascended the stairs and entered Jaxas's solar, his ire grew almost palpable. Sealing the door and sharply dismissing Nikias, who had scrambled after us during our hasty exit, he stalked over to stand before the cold hearth, facing away from me.

"Why," he began in a low voice, "in the burning depths of the 'Thae did you not tell me of this before?"

My cheeks burned. "It wasn't relevant before."

"And now?" He turned toward me, eyes catching the yellow light of the pyr lamps mounted along the walls. "Leia already walks a thin line. Her recent trial, her erratic behavior, rumors of Myron's survival, to say nothing of both fronts that Oedija faces — all of these already conspire against this alliance with the Yorandu. And just when I believed we might be making progress, we're thwarted yet again."

I thought of the Bali man courting Asileia and decided now wasn't the best time to mention that additional wrinkle in his plans. "I'm sorry, Jaxas. Things have been moving fast."

"And you've not kept up." The hollowness of his face was made more prominent by the shadows. "You've not been the same since you woke, Airene. You haven't been to see me, and I've heard little of your activities. I need the woman who brought the plans of the Manifest grinding to a halt. I need the Finch who convinced me to put the fate of our city in her hands. Can you be her once again?"

I let his words wash past me as I stared into one of the lamps. I wished I could tell him the truth. But all I had was the same tired excuse.

"You must defend our nation," I said, quiet but firm. "I seek to defend the Four Realms from the threat no one else acknowledges."

His expression didn't shift. "You think I don't know the threat Vusu still poses?"

"Not Vusu. Famine."

We stared at each other for a long moment. The Archon looked away first.

"Famine," he repeated softly. "And what can we to do to stop a god?"

"I don't know. But we must try."

He straightened. "Be that as it may. I know I don't have

authority over you anymore. So I ask you as a friend. Please, Airene. Don't forget about your home city in the throes of your pyr hunt."

Perhaps he didn't mean to dismiss my quest, but I couldn't think he truly understood if he put Oedija above dealing with Famine. All I could manage was a nod before I turned away.

As I touched a hand to the door, Jaxas spoke again. "Tell Nomusa to stay away from Komo. Please."

I only nodded again.

Escaping the palace, I didn't hail a carriage, not knowing which one might bear me, but walked back down to the Aviary. Night had fallen while we'd taken part in the revelry, and though the wind off the sea was cold and wet, and clouds crowded out the lights of the radiant winds and the moons, there was still a peacefulness in the air that I hadn't felt in a long time. Now that I couldn't safely wander Oedija's streets at night, only on Wreath and Conclave grounds could I find solace.

But I couldn't find peace tonight. Though it hadn't been completely my fault, I still felt responsible for what had happened. Somehow, I had to repair it.

But even as I made the resolution, I felt it wilting before my greater purpose. No matter how Jaxas pleaded, no matter how much I felt I was making a ruin of my responsibilities, I had to stay true to my course. Famine was the enemy of all. No other concern could come before him.

As the cold wind bit through my thin dress and whipped my hair into my face, I wondered bitterly how many relationships and people would fall to my quest.

I returned to the Aviary, tore off my borrowed peplos, and unwound my hair, replacing them with a tunic, trousers, and a simple plait. The chill of the oncoming wet season permeated the room, so I pulled on a cloak as well and clung it tight around me as I sat on my bed. I was restless, far too restless to sleep, yet I didn't know where to go. I was as good as a prisoner here at night, and the chains of safety and comfort were tight about me.

I tried to relax with Eltris's exercises once again, but found my mind drifting. Something nudged at the edge of my thoughts. It was the same feeling as if I'd forgotten something important, but couldn't for the life of me remember it. I turned restlessly in my bed, trying to quiet my mind for sleep.

My eyes fluttered open, then went wide. The glow of pyrkin from the cracked pot had reminded me of something. *The whisper finch.* The pyrkin had looked like the glowing patch of feathers on its chest.

They will come for him the night he arrives. The whisper finch's words came back to me now. In the intervening days, I'd neglected to puzzle them out, distracted by everything else that had occurred. Now, the knot began to unravel. *He fears the knowledge he brings to Oedija.* The events and players of the evening fresh in mind, the words suddenly took on new meaning.

What knowledge the Shaka-Heir brought to Oedija, and who feared it, I still didn't know. But Komo was in danger, and I was the only one who knew.

I only prayed I wasn't too late.

11

RIFT

Clepsammia had known Agmon Brandheart would fight until his end. A knowing smile played on her lips, for she knew all that would come, and the destiny he would complete.

'I can help you face Famine,' said she. 'You must find the one who may endanger him most and beseech her aid.'

'How can any being, god or mortal, endanger one such as Famine?'

'Because she completes him. Go find the goddess Harvest. And then you will have the only ally you need.'

- The Seeds of Famine, a translation from the Lighted-tongue; by Oracle Kalene of deme Hull; 881 SLP

I ran back to the bridge through the pelting rain.

What I could do to stop anyone who sought to harm Komo, I had no idea. I still couldn't channel. I might alert Komo's warriors or the laurel guards, but if it were Seeker wardens after him, neither would be enough to stop them.

There was one person who could help, however.

I arrived back at the palace doors, gasping and dripping. The amused guards looked me up and down, but glimpsing

186

my medallion, they allowed me to pass. They didn't even check me for a weapon. What they would have done if they'd found my knife strapped against my back, I didn't know, but it didn't bode well for them to be lax if assassins were after Komo. I caught my breath as I slowed to a walk, ruining the carpet with every sodden step. I'd look mad enough entering the feast hall dressed as I was — no need to be panting like a lathered mule as well.

Reaching the feast hall, I entered within. Finely dressed patricians glanced at me, then looked away with offended expressions. I refrained from smoothing my frazzled hair and looked around. The Despoina no longer sat in her throne, perhaps having found a private moment with the Bali man. But it was Xaron, tucked away in a far corner with giggling girls, whom I sought.

My patience at its end, I wove my way to him, the task made easier by the rich and powerful stepping out of the way, as if afraid of the rainwater dripping from me. Reaching the corner, I pushed past the girls and grabbed my friend's arm.

"Come on. No time to lose."

The bouquet he'd formed of fiery radiance burned away into nothing. "What?" he objected. "What do you mean?"

"You're taking him again?" the same spoiled girl as before complained, then muttered, "Greedy hag."

I ignored her and dragged Xaron through the crowd.

Once we were outside the feast hall's doors, he pulled away. "What's going on?" he demanded, bewildered.

"I'll explain as we walk. Do you know where Komo's quarters are?"

"No. Why would I?"

I sifted through our contacts. "Nikias. Have you seen him?"

"He followed you and Jaxas out after you made that scene with Komo."

J.D.L. ROSELL

"Perhaps he's in Jaxas's solar," I murmured. We didn't have any better chance to find Komo, so I turned toward the stairs. "Let's go."

"He will not be there."

I whirled toward the unfamiliar voice. An honor stood not six paces away. From her position near the open doors, she'd been just out of sight before. Xaron looked between us curiously, as if we might know each other. Perhaps it was the familiarity with which she'd spoken to us. Honors tended to be deferential and to wait until they were spoken to.

"You know where Nikias is?" I asked.

"Yes. But you wish to know where Shaka-Heir Komo resides, do you not? I can take you to him."

Time was pressing; my questions for her would have to wait. I nodded. "As quickly as you can."

The honor quickly led us up the grand stairs, then up a second staircase. Taking the hallway south, we entered the same wing of the Laurel Palace as the guest quarters located on the first floor. I could already tell this wing of rooms was fit for kings and queens. The walls were lined with lavish paintings of notable people and events in Oedija's history, and the floor was thick with golden carpets. The honor pointed at the most extravagant of the doors, which was inlaid with gold. It was also the only one with Bali soldiers outside it, dressed in a similar manner to their prince, though without all the feathers and silk. Curved swords were belted at their waists. Though one was a woman, her only adjustment was an additional black wrapping around her breasts under the broad, bronze collar.

"The Shaka-Heir is within," the honor said in a hushed voice, though Komo's guards had already noticed us.

"Thank you," I said, then began to brush past her.

The honor's voice arrested me. "Remember this, First Verifier. Remember that I aided you in your time of need."

It was my turn to look back, bewildered. But the honor only gave me a nod before turning and striding away.

"What was going on with her?" I asked Xaron.

"No idea."

No time to wonder. I drew in a breath and approached Komo's guards with as close to a smile as I could manage.

"Evening. I need to see the Heir as soon as possible."

The male guard, a veteran with a scar above one eye that partially closed it, looked me up and down. "I do not think you have the authority for that request. Who are you?"

Xaron broke in. "You should speak with more respect, man. This is the First Verifier of Oedija."

The man looked unfazed. "And you are the jester, no? Then perhaps this is why you tell me the First Verifier wishes to see the Shaka-na so soon after she and her companion offended him. To do so would seem a jest to me."

I wondered if this was the First of Komo's guard, as well-informed and confident as he appeared. But until I knew, I wasn't sure I wished to confide what I suspected was coming. "I apologize for that, and will be glad to apologize to the Shaka-Heir myself. But my errand is urgent, and I must see him. Will you tell him we wish to meet?"

The guard looked me over again, then spoke to his companion. "Go to the Shaka-na."

The woman nodded and turned to knock at the door. A call from within admitted her, and she slipped inside.

The veteran guard stared at us as we waited. I couldn't keep from shifting my feet. Xaron looked as if he might burst with questions, for I still hadn't explained what was happening.

"You are as nervous as a *taliga* — an asher, as you call it," Komo's guard noted. "I would wonder but that you do not have the white fingers."

Surprise compelled me to look at him. I could not tell if

the man was joking or not, for his expression was as serious as before.

"What is your name?" I asked him.

"Zolani."

"Zolani. How long have you served Heir Komo?"

"All his life." He pointed at his scar with a sudden grin. "And I will serve him the rest of his life, spirits willing."

I wondered uncomfortably if he had gained that scar killing Nomusa's family. The thought made my favorable first impression of Zolani sour.

The door opened again, and the female guard stepped out. "Shaka-na Komo will see you now."

Xaron and I slipped between the guards to enter within. The decor inside almost made me wonder if we were still in the Laurel Palace and not transported to the Bali plateaus. The room was brightly lit with green pyr lamps. Vines crept along the walls, vibrant and alive, and leafy plants in great decorated pots filled the corners. As we were in the hosting room of the suite, there was a table and cupboard, likely holding liquors and other objects to entertain guests.

Komo stood in the middle of the room and watched as we approached, his young features drawn. He'd discarded the ceremonial garments from before and wore a simple white tunic and loose pants that cinched around his ankles above his bare feet.

"First Verifier Airene," he said gravely. "I am surprised that you visit me so soon after..." He shrugged. "Well, you were there."

Despite the urgency, I couldn't let things lie at that, especially when his advisor stepped into the room with a severe look. Before they'd believe the threat I needed to warn them of, I had to regain some measure of credibility.

"I apologize, Heir Komo. We meant no offense. Archon Jaxas was not aware of Nomusa's heritage, and I didn't think of what trouble it might cause." A quick look at Nkosi included him in the apology.

The advisor did not ease his hard demeanor. "And now you bring us your royal jester to salve the wound. Tell me, Airene the Finch. How many ways do you wish to insult us this day?"

Before I could think of a reply, Komo looked around at the advisor. "Peace, Nkosi. You have taught me to look at people and give time to judge them fairly. I do not think we have given the First Verifier a fair measure yet, nor time to explain herself."

A small smile softened Nkosi's features. "I have not judged her, Shaka-na. I meant to cut to the quick of the matter through sharp words. But perhaps even that was not yet necessary." He looked back to me. "Please, First Verifier. I will assume then you did not come idly."

My estimation of the young ruler-to-be had risen greatly. Even though I knew as Nomusa's friend I ought not to like him and his kin, I couldn't help a begrudging respect forming.

"Thank you Heir Komo, Advisor Nkosi. I do come tonight with urgent news." I paused, gathering the courage to say the words. "I fear your lives might be in danger."

They didn't react with the surprise I expected, but merely shared a look.

"And from whom do you expect this attack?" Nkosi asked calmly. His posture seemed to have shifted minutely, but suddenly, it he seemed as if he might spring forward at a moment's notice.

Time to throw the spokes, as Talan would have said.

"From Seekers, those who ascribe to the movement known as the Manifest. They have wardens among their numbers. And I believe they are coming after you tonight."

"Why so soon?" Komo wondered aloud as he looked again

to his advisor. "Our negotiations may yet fail. Why attack before anything has even been decided?"

The advisor only nodded his head in acknowledgement. "Zolani," he called out.

The veteran guard peered in at once. "Yes, Nkosi-sa?"

But the advisor didn't have time to answer — for the room suddenly split with a shriek like from a great dying beast.

The floor shook under us, making me fall to my knees. Fighting for balance, I wrenched my head up and stared. The ceiling had ripped open — not in fragments of stone, but like the very seams of the world had been rent apart. Every color and light known to humankind assaulted my senses. I knew immediately what it meant as a familiar wave of nausea flooded through me.

Someone had cut open a path from the Pyrthae.

"Xaron!" I shouted.

Just as he looked up, our attackers emerged from the tear, clumsily turning about midair to fall gracelessly to the floor. Three at a time, they poured through, as much as the tear would allow. Violet tatu adorned their faces, and dark robes whipped about them.

Seeker wardens.

The room burst into a frenzy. Zolani whipped his sickle-shaped sword at the closest of the Seekers. The feral screamed and collapsed, but threw up his hands as he fell. A wave of kinesis barreled into the veteran guard, and he flew backward to land against the wall with a faint crash.

I narrowly avoided the erratic wave as I threw myself to the ground. Scrambling to my feet, I saw Xaron slam one into a wall so hard that his skull cracked with red lines, a grotesque parody of his spidery violet tatu. The moment after, Xaron cried out as a line of fire cut against his shoulder.

Nkosi, despite wearing cumbersome robes, fought with

hands and feet, disabling and knocking one of the wardens flat to the ground before striking his throat with a savage jab.

Komo, though a boy, fought with as much prowess as the men, moving with the grace only hard years of practicing Ixolo could have afforded him. He knocked one Seeker to the ground with a sweep of his legs, then leaped and kicked a Seeker just emerging from the rent into the wall. I stared at the force behind the blow, then found my suspicions confirmed as, a moment later, another of the wardens threw kinesis at the boy. Komo turned and met it with open hands, then twisted his body around. The blast dispersed around him. I stared in amazement.

The boy was a warden.

But a Seeker had finally noticed me huddled on the ground and raised her hands toward me, sparks gathered at her fingertips. I desperately willed my locus to open, but I remained as closed to the Pyrthae as before.

The split second of hesitation was enough. Fire leaped toward me.

I turned aside too late. Flames caught my shoulder, searing where they touched. Tumbling to the ground, I gasped with the pain and scrambled away.

A glance back showed the warden readying a second attempt on my life. But before she could channel, someone barreled past me, steel flashing in their hands. As the second of Komo's guard attacked, the Seeker turned the fire on her, but missed. The guard flashed her sickle-blade across her opponent's throat, and the Seeker fell in a red spray.

Gasping with fear and pain, I fled for the door. Every movement of my right shoulder pulled at the scorched skin and sent waves of sickening agony through my body. Yet as I found the safety of the cool stone outside, I gritted my teeth, reached around under my back, and pulled free Nomusa's knife. I held it up in my left hand as the screams and rumbles of channeled energy sounded from within. I'd killed before, but I was no warrior. I was scared near witless just thinking about reentering the chamber. Even though I'd weathered the horrors of the Despoina's trial, I wasn't prepared for this.

But I never would be.

Gripping the dagger tight, I turned into the room again. Five Seekers still fought against Xaron, Komo, and Nkosi. Xaron and Komo often wove into each other's conflicts as they dodged and dispersed the attacks against them. Each had sustained wounds horrible to behold, but didn't seem to slow from them. Nkosi kept to the walls, only striking out when a Seeker came near. Zolani and the female guard lay motionless along the walls. The Pyrthaen tear still hovered above, flooding the room with a strange light. None seemed to notice my return. I ghosted along the edge of the room, the walls now pocketed from errant blasts of fire and force.

As Xaron flung one Seeker toward the wall six feet away from me, I buried my fear and leaped forward, raising my knife with both hands. The pain of my burn only fueled the fury with which I stabbed the knife down into the stunned man. The blade, clumsily aimed, entered between his neck and shoulder, tearing through the flesh with an ease that stunned me. The Seeker jerked his head up at me, horror and wrath and pain twisted together. As he raised a trembling hand toward me, I jerked away, leaving my knife in his shoulder. Before he could try for vengeance, his hand fell away, and his head fell forward.

"Back!" one of the Seekers shouted above the fray. "Back to the 'Thae, fools!" The warden followed her own advice and, with a kinesis-propelled jump, flew back into the rent above.

Her retreat broke the rest. The last three Seekers immediately followed, two crashing into each other in their haste to flee. Xaron gave one a parting burn on the leg before he sank against the wall, gasping.

I stood and watched dully as Nkosi stepped up next to the

Shaka-Heir and placed a hand on his shoulder. They both looked up into the Pyrthaen tear, which had already begun to seal over. Though my ears were dull from the battle, I faintly heard the advisor's murmured words. "You did well, Komo. Very well. Now we must care for our fallen. See to Zolani. I will go to Sunto."

My gaze drifted down to my wet hands. The blood had begun to form a strange lattice as it streamed down my skin, the pattern reminding me of the violet tatu of the Manifest.

"They're both dead," Komo said quietly, but he did as his advisor asked, kneeling by the crumpled body of the veteran warrior. "He has no pulse, nor life in his eyes. He has joined our ancestors."

"Sunto as well." The advisor kneeled next to the female guard, who lay twisted on the ground on the other side, blood pooling under her head. "*Kwagati umya wako umgoda hlahla*. Would they had died under the boughs of the isikhayha."

"They will find their way rootward, I do not doubt. Their spirits were strong and their hearts true."

My gaze lingered on the veteran. He'd meant to serve Komo all his life. A bitter irony it had ceased this night.

But I had my own to attend to. Still feeling as if I walked in a dream, I kneeled next to Xaron, wiped my hands on my trousers, and put a hand to his head. Blood matted his hair.

"Xaron," I said softly. "Are you alright?"

He looked up with a pained grin. "They ruined my outfit."

A small smile crept over my own lips. "I'm sure we can find you another potato sack to wear. Let's get you to a healer."

Ignoring his protests that he could walk, and ignoring my own hurts, I pulled Xaron's arm over my good shoulder and helped him stand.

To my surprise, Komo stood at his other side. Though cuts and burns puckered up the skin of his arms and chest, and his white clothes were splattered with red, he didn't seem much wearied or injured from the battle. He met my eye without hesitation as he extended a hand with a bloody knife in it. I flinched as I recognized the weapon as my own.

"You spoke the truth, First Verifier Airene," he said. "I will remember your warning. Now, let me help you."

I stared at him, not accepting my dagger. "You're nearly as badly injured as he is."

He gave a small laugh. "My wounds will heal." He suddenly looked to Nkosi. "It feels wrong to laugh in the face of death."

His advisor shook his head. "If we cannot laugh now, then what good has laughter ever served? You do no injustice to their names, Shaka-na. The passed do not wish the living to linger, but to move on and be merry when they can."

Komo gave him a small nod, then turned back to Xaron and me. "I don't mean to delay. Let us be off. But do you not need your knife?"

Though my skin crawled, I finally accepted it and clutched the grip hard. If we weren't still in danger now, we would be eventually. I couldn't let the fear of hurting others stop me from protecting myself and my companions.

No matter how much I might wish it could be otherwise.

Several turns later, Xaron was settled into a bed, and I sat next to him. It was the same bed I'd occupied just under a span before. I sat in the same chair Corin had. I wondered if she'd discovered anything of her sister yet. At least she would be safer than us.

Just as she'd led me into the situation that landed me in that bed, so I'd done with Xaron. I glanced at him. He slept finally, though he'd moaned for the previous turn, complaining about being unable to lay on his side from his wounds. The healer had said his injuries were not serious and would heal, and had given him a poppy tincture to help him rest. Yet cracked ribs and seared skin were far more than I wished my friend to suffer because of me.

I stared down at the exposed knife in my lap, clean of blood now. It glinted dully with the green light that crept in through the windows. The storm had broken, and the radiant winds were out once more, pulsing as they streamed over the city. I didn't touch the blade, but studied the sharp edge of it. I had killed a man with it mere turns before. He was the second person I'd killed; third, if Vusu succumbed to my quarrel. It didn't have the shock of the first time, yet I doubted the great emptiness that welled up in its wake would ever depart. I wondered bleakly how many more I could kill before there was nothing left of me to drain away.

Despair covered me as a blanket, suffocating, with no escape. I didn't try to throw it off. I let it bear me down, down to an oblivion where it might ease away.

Only in the midst of that darkness did I see the glimmer of light. It pulsed gently like a star on a clear dusk. Instinctively, I reached toward it, the only light in this place. As I touched it, the light eased a little wider. I grasped eagerly at it, pulling for more. It readily complied. The star cast off a suffusing warmth, one that drove away the shadows. I allowed in more, letting it fill me until it threatened to burn.

I jolted awake, suddenly aware. Half of my fingertips, dug into my trousers, glowed with a dampened light. Trembling, I raised them.

Two fingertips on my left hand and three on my right glowed warmly.

Held in the midst of the comforting warmth, I didn't fear them. Radiance filled me to the brim, but I didn't overflow with it. Easing my tensed muscles, I relaxed and let the energy swirl inside me.

Nkosi had told Komo not to linger on the dead, but to

move on and be merry. The guilt and horror of what I'd faced hadn't faded.

Yet, embraced by the power of the Pyrthae, living the culmination of fanciful childhood dreams, I allowed myself to smile and drift away on a river of light.

INTERLUDE I

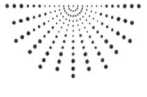

SEDA

S eda balanced the tray in one hand as she slipped the key from her neck. She always carried it under her chiton, hanging cold against her skin, where no one might be tempted to steal it from her. It still made her uneasy, carrying the key to Master's room. She didn't want to fail his trust. But even more than that, it was unsettling that he needed a lock at all. Before his illness, he'd feared nothing, for nothing could harm him.

Now he had not the strength to leave his room.

She banished the traitorous thoughts as she fitted the key in the lock. Such thoughts could sink her into despair, and then she couldn't serve Master. And he needed her as he never had before.

Almost as soon as she entered, he called out to her. "Seda?" His voice was cracked and weak as if parched. Yet the ewers of water she brought to him were always empty when she returned.

"I am here, Master." She pulled the door closed and locked it, then turned too quickly and almost upended the tray. A bit of broth spilled from the bowl onto the crusty bread.

Stupid girl. Clumsy girl. She thought the insults, for Master wouldn't approve of her cursing herself. He had often told Seda that she, like every being, had a spark of divinity within her, and that if she couldn't respect herself as she was, she should at least treat herself well for that. She tried to obey. But when she acted so stupid, so clumsy, she knew she deserved to be punished. As Valem punished his children, as Seda's father had punished her with his fists, so Seda felt she should punish her failings.

She must, for she couldn't fail Master.

She was careful with the tray as she walked to him and set it down. His room was square — fourteen paces each way, she'd discovered during long turns of waiting. Only the light of a single, swinging pyr lamp illuminated the room. Master preferred torches, saying fire was cleansing while pyrkin was crowding, but even he admitted he was too weak to risk it now. And Seda worried even the small amount of smoke from a torch would weaken him further.

"I brought bread and broth, Master," she murmured as she knelt and took the bowl and spoon in hand. Master was facing her, still dressed in the torn robe he'd worn since the night his illness began. Once it had been white; now, it was charred ashy and stained dark with blood. She wished he would let her bathe and clothe him. But it was his eyes that bothered her most. Always open, they stared past her into places that Seda couldn't see, and that she feared no man should ever look.

She stifled her worry and brought the spoon to his lips. "Drink, Master. It will make you feel better."

As soon as the spoon touched his lips, he lapped it up greedily. Seda smiled. A hungry day was a good day. Giving him a few more spoonfuls of broth, she asked, "Would you like softened bread, Master?" She didn't expect an answer, nor did she receive one. Tearing off a bit of the bread and dipping it in the bowl, she brought it to his lips. Master accepted it and chewed, his expression absent and blank.

As she dipped a second piece of bread, his hand snaked out and grabbed her arm, upsetting the bowl of broth. She bit back the curses at herself as she stared into Master's urgent stare.

"Yes, Master?"

"Seda," he said, voice gravelly but stronger than before. "You are still here."

Relief flooded her. This was him, truly him, returned to her at last. "Yes, Master," she said. "Always."

"No." He shook his head slowly. "Not always, loyal one. Soon, you must go to another." He closed his eyes. Seda wondered if he'd fallen asleep.

Then his eyelids fluttered open again. "He tries to claim me," he muttered, more to himself than Seda. "He has his claws in me. I don't know that I can let him go now."

The words stuck like barbs in her. Before she could decide on soothing words, Master spoke again. "Do you remember when you came to me, Seda?"

"Of course, Master."

"A girl nearly killed by her father." Seda was gratified at the fire that burned in his eyes. "You couldn't stay with him, that much was clear. And I saw in you the unbreakable honor it requires to remain a true servant."

"Yes, Master," she replied, and tried to believe it. But she couldn't shake the doubt that nothing in her was unbreakable. Nothing was even whole enough to break.

"And do you know how I knew this?"

"No, Master."

"I knew because no matter what your father did to you, no matter how bruised and bloody he left you, you refused to leave him. No amount of suffering would cause you to abandon those you had dedicated yourself to." His eyes seemed to reach behind her.

"Yes, Master." This at least she could agree with. She

would never leave him. Not after all he had done for her. And she for him.

He sighed heavily. "I hope you do not blame me for taking you away from him and having him killed. He made it simple. A daemon in a man's skin, he was, and few were sad to see him go."

Seda kept very still. If only she could unhear words. But she could not.

"You never told me that before, Master," she said quietly. "That you were behind his sentencing and execution."

Master looked up at her, surprised. "Didn't I? Oh, Seda. I don't wish to give you pain. I… my mind wanders. I'm not as I was…"

Stupid, stupid girl. She had caused him anguish. Why must she always speak the wrong things?

"You should drink more broth, Master," she said, reaching for the spoon with her other hand — her shame-hand, against the teachings of her faith, but he still gripped her right arm too tightly to use. She was glad he had the strength to hold her so firmly.

"Seda, Seda. When will you let him go?"

She froze as the spoon dipped into the broth. She didn't dare look into Master's eyes. She knew by the harshness of the voice that it wasn't his mind she would see behind them.

"Other," she breathed.

"*Other*," the one who had stolen Master's tongue sneered. "Why must you call me that name, *Other*? I am no other but the servant to our true master."

"No one can be master but he who has mastered himself." She repeated it in her mind, the mantra Master had taught her in preparation for this day. When daemons would steal his tongue and tempt her from his service.

"But there is, Seda. If you would but open yourself to me, I could show you I have. But you know it all the same. You know your master serves not himself, but a greater lord, the same as I serve. The same as *you* serve."

"No. Master does not serve the Snake. The Snake serves him. The Snake is bound to him."

"The Snake is wound around his neck!" the Other mocked. "Or is it not his tongue I speak with?"

"Silence!" she hissed through clenched teeth. He held her so tightly she could feel the bruises starting to form. But she would not struggle. She would not leave. Master had barely eaten. He needed sustenance to recover his strength.

As if hearing her thoughts, the Other said, "He'll not rise again, Seda. Look at the wound in his side! See the foul corruption pouring from it, the tainted flesh that pulls back cracked and purple! See the shaft shot deep! That it missed his vitals was a disservice. It has prolonged his suffering, only made it longer before my master can claim him."

"He can heal," she murmured. "His wounds have always healed before."

She saw from the corner of her eye Master's face draw back in a rictus grin. "Ah, Seda. But he won't heal this time. Our true master won't let him."

The truth she'd long suspected hit her with a blow harder than her father had ever managed. She crumpled in on herself, breath coming fast and shallow. *Stupid girl. Stupid, stupid girl.* She should have done something before. She should have stopped the Other and the Snake before it came to this. It didn't matter that she couldn't think of what she could have done differently. All she knew was that she hadn't done enough.

"Seda?"

Relief flooded her. "Master!" She wanted to throw herself on him and burst into tears, but she couldn't burden him with her own sorrow. She had to be strong for him.

"I… lost myself for a moment. I think it would be best if you left me to rest again."

She looked down at the nearly untouched tray. She should have done something to help before he became so weak, it was true. But it wasn't too late to try to do all she could.

Seda drew in a deep breath.

"No, Master. You told me you took me in because I would never stop serving you. Let me show you it is true. I will not leave until you eat all this tray's contents."

Master wore his own smile now. "Seda. What would I do without you?"

You will never have to find out, she resolved as she brought the lukewarm liquid to his lips. She would never leave him.

No matter how much he hurt her.

12

A FINCH FOUND

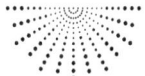

Agmon Brandheart and his most loyal First Wardens left the battlefield in search of Harvest. They combed all the realms for the goddess. Yet nowhere could she be found.

'She has retreated beyond our pleas!' one despaired. 'She will not harken to our call!'

'We will find her,' Agmon boldly claimed, though his own courage faltered. 'If we have to search to the corners of Telae and the heights and depths of the Pyrthae, we will find her!'

- The Seeds of Famine, a translation from the Lighted-tongue; by Oracle Kalene of deme Hull; 881 SLP

I woke to a knock on the door.

Rubbing my eyes, I sat up. My back was stiff and sore, the night spent sleeping in a chair doing little to improve upon what the melee in Komo's quarters had started. As little as I'd contributed, I felt battered and bruised, and my seared skin pulled painfully as I shifted.

The knock came again. "Airene? Xaron?" Nomusa called through.

"Coming," I groaned in response.

Enough daylight peeked between the curtains that I had little trouble finding my way to the door and unlatching it. As the door opened, Nomusa slipped in, her face lined with worry.

"How is he?"

"I'm not sure," I admitted. "I only just woke up."

Locking the door, we walked together to his bedside. Nomusa had found us after the Seeker attack last night, so it wasn't the first time she saw the cuts and burns that ran patchwork over Xaron's skin. I winced as I noticed a spot over his right ear where radiance had burned his hair off. It could have been much worse, yet if I knew Xaron, he would fixate on how that hair that would never grow back. Despite our scrutiny and hushed conversation, he didn't stir. I wondered if we should be worried by that.

"Kallias the Sculptor is coming to see him today after he visits the... Yorandu delegation. Jaxas sent for him last night, but the Acadian healer keeps his own schedule, even for princes." She wore a hint of a vindictive smile as she said it. Nomusa's attitude toward Komo seemed to have improved since he'd fought by Xaron and me, but every transformation had its limits.

I shrugged. "I doubt he'll need it. Komo told me his wounds would heal. Perhaps he has a similar gift as our Sculptor does."

She'd flinched at his name, then shook her head in disgust. "Magic abounds now," she muttered. "Our enemies, our friends... Even people I've known half my life." She gave me a sidelong look.

I held up my left hand silently, putting on display the two fingers that had glowed with radiance the night before. "They've appeared," I said quietly. "My shifts. I channeled last night and controlled it."

Her brow creasing, Nomusa took my hand and examined the fingertips closely. She inhaled sharply. "I see them moving." She met my eyes. "You really are a warden."

"Yes. I am." I drew my hand away.

"Did it happen during the fight?"

"No. After."

Only then did it occur to me how lucky that was. While Xaron was permitted to channel, and Komo possessed some measure of diplomatic immunity, I wouldn't be so fortunate if I were exposed as a warden. Even channeling in defense of Oedija's interests, I'd still be liable to the Tribunal's justice at the hands of Shepherds. And where channeling was done for harm, the only sentence I could expect was death.

"Airene?"

I realized Nomusa had said my name more than once. "I'm fine. Just thinking."

She suddenly pulled me into a firm hug, though mindful of my burn. "Your injuries are less visible, but I know they're there. I'm sorry you had to endure all that. Again."

I sighed and relaxed into her embrace. But almost as soon as I released the worries of the night before, the new day's concerns pressed in. "We have work to do." A moment later, I realized how callous that sounded and amended weakly, "That came out wrong."

"Don't apologize. A few rough words won't offend me." She released me and smiled. But I saw her own concerns weighing on her mind behind her eyes. "I wanted to delay telling you this, but the Council has called you to their session this morning. They demand an account of what occurred in Komo's chambers."

"Why? So they can squawk over it and do nothing?"

"I don't like it either, but you'd do better to find a softer side of your tongue. You'll make no friends among the Low Consuls chastising them, and we badly need friends."

"Fine. But I have some demands of my own. Coffee and food, to start."

Nomusa raised an eyebrow. "Setting your sights a little high, aren't you?"

"That's as high as I'd like to shoot as well," a sleepy voice spoke from next to us.

Nomusa and I whirled on Xaron.

"How are you feeling?" Nomusa asked.

"Feeling?" Xaron groaned as he tried to sit up, then abandoned the attempt. "All too much right now."

"If his humor has gotten this bad, I think he's close to joining the ancestors," I commented.

"How I'm feeling right now makes me wish it. 'Thae above, where did those Seekers learn to channel like that?"

"Vusu," Nomusa and I answered at once.

Xaron grinned weakly. "Right."

Mindful of the approaching Council meeting, Nomusa went to fetch my demands to bring back to the room. We broke our fast together, the meal almost strange with how easy and familiar it felt. How long had it been since we shared a simple meal? How long would it be until our next?

Too soon, Nomusa and I said goodbye to a morose Xaron, then made our way out of the palace and across the bridge. We were quiet much of the way, anticipation of the meeting silencing idle conversation. That there would be a reckoning for the attack, I had no doubt. I only hoped something good would come out of it for once. I snorted lightly. Things were getting desperate if I were hoping for something good from the Demos Council.

Nomusa cocked an eyebrow. "Something amusing?"

"Oh, just the usual irony. How little there is to hope for, and how I can't help but keep hoping."

She shrugged. "A failing of which we're all guilty. But it helps us face things, doesn't it?"

I flashed her a bitter smile. We'd need a good deal more than false hope to face this down.

Too soon, we were admitted into the inner chamber of the Conclave and stood before the Council. Of the Low Consuls, Feiyan was missing, as was Berker. But we had additional guests lining the wall: the five white-haired, red-caped Stratechons, leaders of Oedija's paltry defenses. I eyed them, wondering what their presence might mean for the Order.

Jaxas gave us a look that seemed a warning as we entered. Orhan spoke first. "First Verifiers. I hope you had a pleasant evening."

"I've not changed since then, so you can tell for yourself how pleasant mine was." The words were out of my mouth before I could stop them.

"Yes," Orhan replied lightly. "You do seem to have taken some injuries. But it is no more than one deserves for shirking their duties, is it?"

His disdain twisted my guts with fury, but I struggled to keep my tone even. "Perhaps you could clarify your meaning."

"Oh? But I thought it would be perfectly clear, when our esteemed guest was brutally attacked immediately after you arrived at his quarters."

Cold ran through me with the shock of a sea spray. The gazes on me suddenly seemed like those of a pack of hungry dogs, waiting for their chance to attack. It was all I could do to refrain from licking my dry lips.

"Are you implying I had something to do with the attack?" I asked carefully.

A sneer curled Orhan's lips. But before the Preservist leader could answer, Jaxas cut in. "I am sure Low Consul Orhan wouldn't imply that of our trusted Finches. After all, Airene and Nomusa orchestrated the trap that thwarted

Vusumuzi's ambitions against the realm. Surely, such an action insulates them from any suspicion of collaboration."

Orhan didn't lose his smile, nor did he look aside from me. "Of course. Such an implication would be... ungenerous of me."

"Good. As Archon, it is my duty to facilitate, so I will do so now. The subject before us is now abundantly clear, I trust."

"Quite," Daelya said drily.

"The defense of our guests is paramount, particularly when the visitor is a prince and a potential suitor to our Despoina in a time of great need." Jaxas turned to the Stratechons. "Have you agreed upon your plans yet?"

The white-haired generals looked between themselves wearing a range of emotions — disgust, impatience, even boredom. "No, Archon," the middle one answered, a man with a thick mane impressive for a man of his age. "We are still determining the best course."

"Perhaps I'd better decide for you," Jaxas snapped.

I stared at him. Rarely had I seen him lose his temper, and now I'd witnessed it twice in a day's turn.

As the others in the chamber shared significant looks, and the Stratechons huffed in affronted silence, Jaxas exhaled softly and continued in a quieter, if no less exasperated, tone. "Orhan, I believe you wished to ask our First Verifiers a few questions."

The patrician smiled, not bothering to hide his smugness. "Yes, indeed I would. The lack of information we've received from your Order is, if I may be frank, abysmal. Perhaps you were not involved in the Shaka-Heir's attack." He let the pause linger, leaving no doubt as to what he implied. "Yet it is apparent you received intelligence about it. Why did you not act sooner? And from whence did this information come?"

I didn't wait for Nomusa to answer, though I knew it would likely be wiser. "As soon as I heard the Seekers were coming for Heir Komo, I ran to him. I only had time to find—" Too late I realized my mistake, but I cut off all the same.

But the wily leader of the Preservists smiled like he'd led me right to where he'd wanted. "You only had time to find your friend Hilarion. So he could help kill those Seekers by using Tyurn's Gift, isn't that right?"

Someone gasped; I didn't see who. My eyes were leveled at Orhan. He met my gaze, knowing that I couldn't touch him. But that didn't mean I wouldn't try.

Nomusa cut in before I could reply. "If he channeled in defense of our guest, is that not something to be celebrated? When should magic be used, if not for the good of Oedija?"

Orhan leaned back. "But that is the wrong question, First Verifier. It's not what magic should be used for. It's if it should be used at all. And the answer to that, I think, is clear to all of us."

"No." Again, my tongue leaped before me, and I couldn't reign it in. "No, I don't think it's clear. You're comfortable allowing magic to proliferate north of the wall. You're fine with the Valemish training Tefra and keeping Silks within the depths of their temples. But when Xaron uses his power to save a person you very much need alive, you say it's a crime." I ignored Nomusa's pleading look and spoke over her as she tried to interrupt. "If you wanted to do something about the Manifest and prevent this from happening, Orhan, you would have invaded their compound long ago. You would have put an end to these Seekers before they ever truly started."

Orhan's eyes didn't shift, though the smile had finally faded. "First Verifier Airene, I believe you forget that I do not hold charge of Oedija's forces. The Stratechons do."

I glanced at the old soldiers. It didn't stretch the imagination to guess why they'd done nothing. The Preservists commanded much of the wealth of Oedija, and I suspected that a fair amount of that gold now lined the Stratechons' purses.

I gave a curt bow. "Excuse me, Low Consuls, Stratechons. But you can understand we are very busy at the moment. If you have no further questions, we'll make our departure." Not waiting for a response, I turned and left the chamber.

Nomusa didn't catch me until I'd almost reached to the Aviary. She must have nearly run, for I hadn't slowed my pace even for my injuries. Whirling me around outside the door, she stared at me with a desperation I hadn't yet seen.

"Please, Airene. Don't do this."

My anger hadn't abated, and I found myself speaking sharply. "Do what?"

"Don't throw away what we've worked so long to gain. I know you may not feel so now, but we need this position. Without it, we'd be as insignificant as we were before. You wouldn't be admitted to the Acadium. You couldn't read those ancient tomes or see Eltris again."

I tried to deny her words, but knew I couldn't. So I said nothing.

"I know you must follow the hunt that calls you; your looking into the Despot's murder proved that. And I'll do my best not to let them stop you. Just… don't sabotage us in front of the Council. Please."

I'd never heard Nomusa so conciliatory. I could only nod.

Her furrowed brow smoothed. "Good. We both have things to do. But I want to make sure you're alright."

"I'm fine." I knew it was what she needed to hear.

I hoped it was true.

After I changed into clothes that weren't burned and bloodied, I made my way out into the city and headed for the Acadium library. As each day yielded less, it began to dawn on me how unlikely my quest was to bear fruit. Why would I find something in among the dusty books in a span when others had been reading them for decades?

But I'd visited the Pyrthae. I'd seen Famine with my own eyes. And Eltris, stubborn as she was, might fill in the other gaps in my knowledge. Perhaps there were secrets contained in those books that no other could recognize but I.

So I spent the rest of the morning and early afternoon with Platon down in Tomes, breathing in the slow decay of vellum, parchment, and paper. I'd left off in the middle of the depictions of the Hunger War, and wasn't eager to resume them.

Yet only half a turn into my reading, the text made an abrupt shift. From details of supply lines and regiment numbers, it honed in on Agmon Brandheart and a significant visit by Clepsammia.

> 'I can help you face Famine,' said she. 'You must find the one who may endanger him most and beseech her aid.'
>
> 'How can any being, god or mortal, endanger one such as Famine?'
>
> 'Because she completes him. Go find the goddess Harvest. And then you will have the only ally you need.'

I leaned back in my hard chair, pondering. The twist was unexpected, to say the least. Harvest was a minor Eidolan goddess, one worshipped by farmers and ranchers, who were most affected by her whimsies, real or believed. I'd never heard of her tied to Famine in any of the stories told during the Festival of Radiance. That she would be cited by Clepsammia as the one who could endanger Famine defied belief.

Because she completes him.

The words stuck fast in my mind. Famine's appetite was insatiable, or so the stories always said. Yet now that I thought on it, there was a certain logic to the thought that if anything could temper Famine's hunger, it was the Goddess of Bounty.

But if I were to rest my hopes on Harvest, I had to first know she truly existed.

I leaned forward to my reading again and found my hopes sinking. Agmon and his First Wardens, it seemed, had difficulty finding Harvest. They abandoned their war with Famine and his armies to set to it, but despite months of searching, they couldn't find her. As my reading time wound to an end, they seemed no closer to locating the goddess.

Then, just as I was about to shut the book, Clepsammia appeared to Agmon again. I absorbed the words, squinting as I tried to make sense of them.

'Harvest has sown seeds of herself among you,' she told them. 'To find her, you must find them.'

'But how will we know a Seed of Harvest?' demanded Agmon Brandheart.

Clepsammia, Seer of All, hid her smile. 'She will show herself to you. All you must do is hold to your patience.'

The book was named *The Seeds of Famine*, but it seemed he wasn't the only one to spread his seeds. Harvest, too, had sown of herself among humanity. And in lieu of the goddess herself, such a "Seed of Harvest" could apparently suffice in combatting Famine.

Questions swirled in my mind. What did it mean to be a Seed of Harvest, or a Seed of Famine for that matter? For God of Hunger, it had earlier been implied it was a means of corruption, a way to sway the First Wardens to his side. What would it mean for Harvest?

Then there was the matter of Clepsammia's role in all this. Up until this reading session, I'd taken her role for granted. As the Maiden of the Sands, it made sense that she would help destiny along its course. But her continual interventions prodded me in a new way, invoking memories to turn a new face.

First, my dream, the night Famine almost took me: A woman in gray had intervened when Vusu couldn't stop Famine. Only, I'd sensed even then that she wasn't human. Her features had been strange and altered; human-like, but not quite. And clutched in her hand had been a sandglass.

I knew it couldn't be Clepsammia herself I'd seen. It was one thing to discover Famine was real. It was another to believe the Pyrthae was littered with the gods of legend. Besides, it had been a dream. I wasn't sure I could rely on anything I'd seen in it being real. I had probably imagined her because of my readings.

But then there was the other matter. Despoina Asileia had insisted often enough that she was the Hand of Clepsammia for the claim to become meaningless. But if Clepsammia were real, could it be the Despoina wasn't mad? Could there be a rhyme or reason to her erratic actions?

The answers would have to wait. With a measure of reluctance, I stood and stretched. Eltris's next lesson awaited that evening, and I had another task to handle before then, one I could no longer neglect. With Orhan sniffing after our trail and a government rife with treason, I had to help Nomusa and Jaxas set things right, insomuch as was possible. And since I couldn't leave off my hunt to do it, I'd have to call in an extra set of hands.

I ascended the many stairs to exit the library. But before I left, I convinced Platon to inquire as to when his master, the mysterious Master Librarian, might be available. If anyone could answer questions about legends and lore, it would be her. After the sending the poor pupil back and forth several times, we agreed upon an appointment in two days. I was sure she only relented to it because I was a regular visitor now. From her aloof manner, I guessed the woman's only true love was for books.

The matter settled, I hurriedly left the Acadium and made my way toward Port. When I arrived at Zipho's, the aroma of roasting coffee instantly brightened my spirits. A smile tugged at my lips as I strolled in.

I was surprised and pleased to see Nomusa leaning against the counter running around the tree in the middle of the room. She seemed as startled to see me.

"Don't you have somewhere to be?" I teased her as I came around the counter.

"I could say the same for you. Grow tired of crossing your eyes in that tomb you call a library?"

"Nothing a mug of hot coffee won't fix."

Zipho slyly nodded and turned away to brew my drink. Leaning closer to Nomusa, I asked her, "But really, I didn't think you left the Conclave grounds these days. Zipho was just complaining you never visit her."

"I don't nearly enough. But there were a few things I wanted to... discuss. That only she would truly understand."

I looked away. Simple enough to guess her meaning by her tone. I couldn't fault her for wanting to speak to another about her predicament with Komo, especially as Zipho had also fled during the Yorandu coup. And I was too close to the situation, with too much stake, to offer the support she needed.

But a small ache remained in my chest all the same.

As Zipho and Nomusa bantered next to me, loneliness slowly crept up on me. I didn't want to be forced to sit and drink my coffee while making light conversation, but it was too late to avoid it. Suddenly, I badly wished Talan were here with us. No matter how dark the situation, he seemed able to persist through it. I'd never realized what a steady presence he was in my life until he went so conspicuously silent.

Then a memory of my dream in the Pyrthae surfaced from the depths of my mind. Zipho brought me my coffee, and I sipped it absently as she and Nomusa spoke. If what I'd seen in the dream were true, then Talan had been with someone else. It could have been anyone — a contact, an ally, even an enemy — yet I suddenly wondered if it wasn't another woman. After all, it had been in the dead of night, and the flames had shown them so close as to be intertwined...

A familiar cloak passed by the door. I stood abruptly, mouthing a silent prayer. My coffee was barely touched, and Zipho gave me a severe look, but Nomusa only waved me on. "Go hunt," she said, like an oracle bestowing a blessing.

I nodded gratefully and turned out of the cafe, another silver coin hidden under my mug.

I didn't go far, but turned into the usual alley in which I met Wisp. Once again, paupers littered the filthy ground. I stepped around them, repressing the fear that one of them would rise and hold a knife to my throat. Besides, I could channel now, at least part of the time. I told myself I didn't need to fear a vagrant's blade, and hoped it was true.

Wisp waited at the other end. A second hooded figure stood at her shoulder. Beneath the cloak, I couldn't see much of their face, and I kept a careful eye on them as I approached. I'd meant to push my offer of becoming a Verifier on Wisp again, but the stranger's presence threatened to infringe on that.

"We will meet in the narrow alley from now on," Wisp said, her nose wrinkled. Though she was a denizen of the streets, the reek of urine and nightsoil that permeated the air seemed to needle her.

"Fine." I nodded at the person behind her and asked bluntly, "And who is this?"

Wisp inclined her head slightly. "This is your new Verifier."

As I raised a skeptical eyebrow, the figure lowered their hood. My confusion only increased. For standing there was a female honor, complete with a bald scalp and ears flashing with tin spiral earrings.

"What do you mean, my new Verifier?" I demanded of Wisp. A joke; it had to be a strange joke from my even stranger contact. Surely she couldn't mean for an honor to be a Verifier.

Why not? a small voice whispered in my head. *If you were an honor, would you not still be a Finch?* The incongruity stunned me. Never had I thought about honors in such terms. I didn't like the light it put me in.

Wisp's mouth quirked in as wide of a smile as I'd seen from her. "You asked me to be your Verifier. I refused. You asked me to reconsider. I did not. But I did consider your plight. Now, I have provided you the ideal person to accomplish your tasks."

I looked again at the honor. The markings of her caste did not diminish her gentle, pretty features. Her dark cloak obscured the simple clothes I assumed she wore beneath. Most striking were her eyes, sharp-edged and the shade of light brown of the caramel treats sold in the finest bakeries in Bazaar.

"My apologies," I murmured to her. "I am First Verifier Airene. If Wisp speaks well of you, I don't mean to cast doubt on your skills."

The woman waited a breath after I finished. Though she was an honor, I didn't think it was out of hesitation.

"I am Kelena. Kelena of House Iason." Though her voice was soft, it had a quality that compelled me to listen closely.

I frowned. "House Iason. You don't mean—"

"The Low Consul? Yes."

My mind spun at the implications. Iason was one of the five Preservists on the Council. To have an honor of his house as a Verifier... Yet I shook my head. "Iason would never dismiss you. Not to become a Verifier."

For the first time, a flash of emotion passed over the

honor's face. I wondered at it. Perhaps this was about freedom for her, an opportunity to escape her present conditions.

"Perhaps not," Kelena said evenly. "But perhaps I could persuade you to try all the same."

Considering my relationship with the Council at the moment, I doubted they would permit me so much as a drink of water in their presence if I asked. But she didn't need to know that.

I crossed my arms. "I'm listening."

"First of all, you've already seen a demonstration of the depth and breadth of my knowledge. Perhaps you remember an honor in the Laurel Palace who directed you toward the Yorandu Heir's rooms?"

She spoke with the air of a recited speech, but her words still captivated me. "That was you?" I tried to remember what the woman had looked like.

A smile quirked Kelena's lips, though it didn't reach her eyes. "Do we honors look so similar to you?"

"No, no, I—"

"She was but one of my hands," Kelena continued smoothly over my fumbling, while Wisp grinned outright. "One of the many I can call upon should the need arise. My network spans all of Oedija, even into places I suspect you have a difficult time reaching."

Honors. I had considered the possibility so often before that her web was immediately clear to me. Honors were the perfect network of spies. They were in every major household, every arm of the demotism, throughout the whole of the polis. And many of them were in the Manifest as well, if Wisp had spoken true when we'd last met. I'd never known how to tap into such a network. And now here it was, served on a platter before me.

I pretended to consider it, not wishing the full measure of my eagerness to show through. I knew I should feel more hesitant. Despite Wisp's commendation and Kelena's apparent show of usefulness, I still didn't know her and couldn't be certain of her intentions.

"If I'm to initiate you, I'd like to know some things first. How far does your network reach? What new information can you bring the Order?"

The honor raised an eyebrow slightly. "You wish to know from whom the Manifest receives funding. You wish to know their movements, their defenses, their plans. You wish to know where they have hidden away Myron Wreath, and what the Visage Vusumuzi has been doing since the Despoina's trial. All this and more, I can provide you, if you give me the time and resources."

It was a simple decision. Even if Kelena was serving on someone else's behalf, the promise of all that was worth the risk. And Nomusa had, after all, said we'd have to take risks on whom we trusted.

I would just have to hold my own secrets close.

I clasped my hands together, taking care to keep my fingertips hidden. "Very well, Kelena of House Iason. I must talk this over with my fellow First Verifier, but I'm sure we can come to an agreement. Meet me here tomorrow at the same time and I'll have your answer."

Kelena bowed slightly, though not nearly enough to befit her caste. I was glad for it. Seeing beyond the markings now, I felt a great sense of shame that I'd ever expected such a gesture from her. What made her any less than me, after all?

"I will await your answer tomorrow," she said as neutrally as before. With a nod at Wisp, she turned and walked down the alley.

I looked after her with some concern. "Is she alright traveling Oedija by herself?"

Wisp gave me a sly look. "Safer than you have been."

I turned my face aside, heat flushing my cheeks. The woman was far too omniscient for her own good.

"Thank you for bringing her," I said quickly. "She promises much."

"And will deliver on it." Wisp looked abruptly up and down the alley. "Now do you wish for news or not?"

"Of course." I handed over a full silver. "I want to hear it all."

13

THE WATCHERS

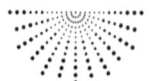

Clepsammia knew of the First Wardens' despair, and appeared to them again.

'Harvest has sown seeds of herself among you,' she told them. 'To find her, you must find them.'

'But how will we know a Seed of Harvest?' demanded Agmon Brandheart.

Clepsammia, Seer of All, hid her smile. 'She will show herself to you. All you must do is hold to your patience.'

'The hardest command of all,' the Hero of Man said bitterly. But at her behest, he waited.

- The Seeds of Famine, a translation from the Lighted-tongue; by Oracle Kalene of deme Hull; 881 SLP

After Wisp informed me of the goings-on of Oedija, I checked in at Zipho's to see if Nomusa was still there, but arrived too late. Catching sight of the sandglass in the cafe, I found I was running behind for my lesson with Eltris. Cursing, I set off at a jog, leaving Zipho calling after me.

Despite Nomusa's warning, I would have flagged down a cartman had I come across one, but they seemed few and far between these days. Perhaps they'd all converted into Seekers, I mused sourly as my breath rattled in my lungs and passersby cast distrustful glances in my direction.

Half a turn after the bells had tolled my appointment's allowed time, I reached Eltris's tower with several stitches in my sides. Gasping to catch my breath, I knocked sharply on the door. "Eltris! I'm sorry I'm late!"

"Not Eltris!" a voice responded sharply from the other side. "What are you to call me?"

My blood up from the exercise, I had to close my eyes and will myself patience for a moment before stiffly replying, "I'm sorry I'm late, master."

The door swung open, revealing the augur's face flushed with anger. "If you wish to be a warden, then you must be here for your instruction. Don't make me wait again."

I pushed down my rearing rebelliousness and followed her as she turned to the stairs. It wasn't an auspicious start to the lesson.

As I mounted the last step, she called back without looking around. "Have you made progress since our last meeting?"

"Yes. I channeled last night."

"I thought you might." Reaching the other side of the room, Eltris turned swiftly. Her eyes glinted in the bright lamplight. "Need seems to bring out the best in you."

She knew of the attack on Komo, then; how, I couldn't say. Considering how little she seemed to socialize, I doubted she'd gotten it by hearsay. More likely, she'd seen the Seekers traveling through the Pyrthae, or divined it by some way of channeling quintessence I knew nothing of. Though if she had, I didn't like to think what it said of her that she hadn't come to our aid.

"I didn't channel during the attack. It happened later that night."

I explained in brief what had occurred, smoothing over

the anguish it had cost me. Somehow, I doubted Eltris would be sympathetic to despair. As I spoke, the augur didn't shift, but nodded sharply as I finished.

"Radiance and quintessence. Very well. We shall focus on these."

"Because I channeled them first?"

"Call me master," Eltris reminded me sternly. "You show an affinity for both, girl. Even more, you show you can control one while you endanger yourself with the other. Perhaps with time you won't be kindling awaiting the spark to burn everyone around you."

I bit back the words searing my tongue.

The augur smiled thinly. "Good. Perhaps you are still capable of being trained. Now show me what you remember of our exercises."

We practiced body awareness first. When performing it while lying down became simple enough, she varied the positions, having me stand, then walk around the room. With each iteration, it grew harder to maintain true awareness throughout my body. I suspected the exercise would only grow more complicated as I mastered each step.

After a long time, she moved to the mental exercises. As tedious as the previous practice had been, this was worse. My thoughts madly struggled against dismissal. It felt as if letting them go completely would scatter everything I'd worked so hard to gather into my mind, never to be reassembled. And no matter how I tried, I couldn't overcome the unreasonable fear.

Eltris seemed to sense it. "If you cannot control your mind, how can you hope to control the Pyrthae?" she snapped, rising from where she'd been sitting crosslegged before me.

"I'll try to do better, master." I gave the words more bite than I intended. As always seemed to happen, the exercises had brought on a headache, and my mood had soured as Eltris pushed me harder.

"You must do more than try!" Exhaling hard like a mule, Eltris turned away and whistled, holding out her arm. To my surprise, one of the finches landed on it, then began to peck at her. Only then did I see the augur had laid seeds along her forearm.

I watched as the colorful bird ate for a moment, then was pushed aside as a larger one alighted next to it. Two more joined the fray, until Eltris shooed them off and spread seed on the ground. Dozens of finches swooped down to feast.

As I watched the birds, I realized my thoughts had come together of their own accord, coalescing into a long-simmering question. "What beings will I draw by channeling quintessence?"

"I have already told you — beings who mean you danger." Her voice did not have as much rebuke as before. She, too, watched the birds peck at the floor.

"Daemons?"

Eltris snorted. "Daemons no more exist than gods do."

I hid a smile. The augur had wandered into my trap. "Who other than daemons would prey on humans from the Pyrthae?"

The augur met my gaze with a hard smile of her own. "Don't think you can lure me into revealing more than I wish to, girl. I'll tell you all you need to know, no more."

I wanted to rail against her stubbornness, but Eltris didn't respond to coercion. I had to tease out her knowledge slowly.

"Very well. No more tricks. But I should know what might harm me by channeling quintessence. Just in case it happens by accident."

"From what I've seen of you, it's more likely to happen by intention. But if it will quiet your incessant questions for a time, I'll feed you a little." She paused, yellow eyes narrowing as she studied the finches hopping about our feet. "Pyr and Quintyr are the primary beings drawn to quintessence."

I vaguely remembered her using that word, "Quintyr," before. "Didn't you say Famine was a Quintyr?"

Eltris startled, looking around at me. "Damned depths of 'Thae," she muttered. "I suppose I did."

Somehow, I had scored a mark, but I was more irked than triumphant. Why must she intentionally keep information from me? But once more, I held back my annoyance. "Why would pyr and Quintyr pose us wardens a threat? What is it about channeling quintessence that makes them dangerous?"

The augur sighed. "It's because they *are* quintessence. As our minds are composed of quintessence, their whole beings are formed from it. It is their animating substance, and it gives them the ability to form the other energies into bodies that suit them. And as our bodies and minds decay from the years, so do they. Unless they halt senescence by gaining more quintessence."

"They remain whole by taking others' quintessence? But wouldn't that kill those they steal from?"

"Don't we also kill to stay alive?" A small smile played on the Master Augur's lips. "Don't condemn them for doing what they must. It's the way of things, not something you can change. But that doesn't mean we must give them what they desire."

I thought uneasily of the presence that had attacked me through Linos's touch. Had it been a pyr seeking to steal my quintessence? And what might it already have done to Linos? I almost asked Eltris, but stayed my tongue at the last moment. It was not only that I desired to keep my secrets as she kept hers. The woman had a coldness about her that made me wonder if she saw me as anything more than a tool. I didn't want to put Linos in her power. Perhaps it was a question I'd ask Kallias the Sculptor, if I could catch him.

I turned to another idea nagging me. "Famine. You said

that quintessence is what he hungers for, too. But he's Quintyr, a god, not a pyr?"

Her smile was gone as quick as it had come. "The Quintyr are not gods," Eltris snapped. "Don't confuse them for each other. Gods are the inventions of small-minded scoria, while the Quintyr are a reality."

There are no gods. But it was a thought for another time. "Then what are Quintyr, exactly?"

"They're older than humanity, far older — for they were already ancient when our world was young. They are the original occupants of the Pyrthae, and thereby rule it. Their minds do not work as ours do. While ours flit about to this intent and that, theirs are fixed upon a single purpose, and bend all of their significant wills toward that purpose."

Chills made chicken-flesh of my skin. "And Famine's purpose is consuming our world."

"Consuming all quintessence. But yes, our world included."

Not wanting to consider that again, my mind flitted back to my reading. "But Famine isn't the only one? There are more Quintyr than him?"

"No, Famine is not the only one."

I waited for her to say more, but when it was clear she'd keep her lips sealed, I opted for a more straightforward tactic. "Does Harvest exist?"

Her surprise was gratifying, her mouth opening and closing before she found a response. "Why would you ask that?" she snapped. "Where did you hear that name?"

I shrugged. "She's the Eidolan Goddess of Bounty. It might be handy for her to exist when droughts are afflicting the Four Realms."

"Would it?" Eltris mocked me. "How unfortunate, then, that Harvest is dead."

All my smug satisfaction vanished instantly. "Dead?" I repeated.

For once, Eltris seemed solemn and sincere. "Yes. From all I've observed, from a lifetime of searching, Harvest long ago succumbed to her enemy. The one most bent on her destruction."

"Famine," I murmured.

"Yes. She was supposed to be able to complete him. And for a time, it seemed she had. The Hunger War ended with Harvest binding Famine. But a thousand years later, Famine has reemerged, while Harvest has not."

In one stroke, she had all but robbed the meaning from everything I'd read in *The Seeds of Famine*. Even if I didn't yet know the end of the story, I knew its results.

I shook my head. "There has to be more to it than that. Perhaps she's just hiding somewhere. Like Famine was all this time."

"I doubt it, girl. I've been to what may as well be her grave marker. I don't think we can rely on Harvest to bind Famine for us again."

"Then what of the other Quintyr?" I insisted. "Which others exist? Surely one of them will intervene. If Quintyr can kill each other, they must want to save themselves from Famine."

Eltris was shaking her head before I'd finished. "They won't intervene. Those who still exist have long ago retreated deep into the Pyrthae, beyond human grasp, or settled so firmly into our world that they have begun losing sight of what they once were. The few who don't sleep and haven't forgotten have no concern for Famine or are too weak to challenge him." The augur suddenly seemed old, her shoulders slumping forward as she stared at the birds still hopping about the stone, searching for any remaining seeds. "We're on our own, girl. We have to find our own way this time."

My head throbbed, and my mind spun. But I couldn't let things lie there. I couldn't give up hope.

"Vusu. He's held Famine captive for years — decades, if he's really Yama from the stories. He's the most powerful warden I've heard of. But if he can do it, perhaps others can."

"He's as strongly attuned as he is *because* of Famine, girl. And he only holds Famine because Famine wills it."

I looked up from the birds to stare at her. "Why? Why would he let himself be held?"

As I watched her, I sensed her teetering on the balance of whether or not to tell me. I waited in silence, knowing a nudge would likely send her in the wrong direction.

Finally, she sighed, long and slow. "Because Famine knows that, should his opportunity arise, he can use Vusu as a conduit into our world."

I listened to the tweeting of the birds, so at odds with the cold dread twisting my stomach into knots.

"So when Vusu dies…" I said faintly.

"Perhaps Famine breaks into our world. Or perhaps not." Eltris shrugged. "But I would hope for Vusu to hold on, so we don't have to find out."

Another thought cut even deeper. "It's my fault. I forced the confrontation with Vusu. I shot him through with a crossbow."

"Yes. You did."

After a moment of somber quiet, she turned away. "I think that's all for today. Come back in three days. And mind my warning, girl. Do not stray into the Pyrthae."

I nodded, numb with all I had learned, and turned toward the stairs. But a sudden thought gave me pause, and I found myself turning back.

"You said before I could endanger all of Oedija by entering the Pyrthae. But I don't understand why. Can Famine use me as a conduit as well? Can he use any warden?"

Eltris didn't look at me for a long moment. When she did, her eyes were impassive, her mouth set in a firm line. "Any warden who channels quintessence or enters the Pyrthae is endangered by Famine and hungry pyr. But you are right; most wardens are not a danger to more than themselves. Famine cannot use any warden to break into Telae."

"Then why is it different for me?"

The Master Augur stared at me, and this time she didn't answer. As the silence dragged on, a realization welled up in my gut, cold and hard. I'd neglected the mystery that had plagued me when I first awoke. Now, I could no longer ignore it.

"How did I become attuned?" I asked quietly.

Eltris shook her head. "And you imagine yourself a Finch. There's only one way you could have become a warden, girl."

With that, she turned and walked down the stairs.

I watched her descend into the gloom below, unmoving, consciously forcing myself to take deep breaths. Only once she'd gone out of sight did I descend the stairs myself. In the dim yellow light below, Eltris was a shadow moving among the books and other scholarly implements. She didn't look as I rattled open the door and exited.

Outside, the cool air of the season drove the cold deeper into me. I left the alley and wandered aimlessly about the Acadium campus. As I passed by Acadians and pupils going about their business, traveling between the modest halls and well-tended towers, Eltris's parting words circled in my mind.

There's only one way you could have become a warden.

Talan believed the Buyujinn, or greater spirits in Avvad, were responsible for attuning wardens. Here in Oedija, the Eidolans believed their gods were behind it. But if Eltris was right, there were no gods, only Quintyr and pyr. Yet at least one of the Eidolan gods of old was Quintyr. Perhaps others existed as well — or had, before they disappeared. And if gods were Quintyr, then it stood to reason that the Quintyr must be attuning wardens.

And I knew of only one Quintyr in Oedija.

No. I increased my pace and turned onto less populated paths. I couldn't accept it. Yet I couldn't deny it must be what Eltris believed. Why else would she look at me with pity, with revulsion? Why else would I endanger the city by entering the Pyrthae?

But though logic herded me toward that one conclusion, I grasped for other explanations. Only two seemed vaguely promising. The boy who had spoken through the whisper finch — he had visited me twice before my attunement. Perhaps he was behind it. Or perhaps the gray woman from the Pyrthae, the Clepsammia pyr — perhaps she was the goddess in truth.

The Seeds of Famine. I'd read the book for days, read that Famine had corrupted Tyurn's Gift and meant to use it for his own gain. But I'd never stopped to think what it meant.

Now it seemed all too obvious.

As I entered a courtyard, my gaze happened on a familiar figure walking quickly ahead. Relief flooded through me. *Xaron.* If anyone could distract me from these thoughts, it was him.

I hurried over to fall in step with him.

He glanced over, not seeming surprised. As before, he wore Hilarion's garb, though a cloak covered much, the drawn hood even hiding some of the wheat-crown on his brow. He didn't seem much the worse for wear after what had occurred the night before.

"I'm surprised to see you up," I remarked.

"Kallias saw to me." He shrugged. "Apparently my wounds were simple to fix."

Looking him up and down, his gait seemed slightly unsteady. "Maybe so, but he can't make you well in a morning, Xaron," I reprimanded. "Even if he healed your wounds, you still need rest."

"I'll be fine." He glanced at me. "You're probably worse off. You haven't had your burn seen to."

I shrugged. My clothes had irritated the raw shoulder all day, but it was it the least thing bothering me at that moment. "I'll be fine. Where are we headed?"

His eyes flickered to either side, watchful and wary. I knew of only one place that might draw out such hesitation.

"Don't say I can't come. I'll follow if you try to forbid me."

"It's too dangerous," he said in a low voice. "What if you get us all caught?"

Doubt almost made me give it up. But as my recent revelation burned inside me, I felt a reckless desire to do something, *anything.* Desperation overcame the doubt.

"Any of you might be followed and caught," I pointed out. "I won't change that. I need to learn, Xaron. *Actually* learn."

"You *are* learning! Or isn't Eltris putting you through those body and mind exercises?"

"Yes. But it's more than that. I…"

The confession was on the tip of my tongue. But, with the knowledge still fresh and raw, I couldn't bring myself to say it. I didn't want to see the horror I felt reflected back in his eyes.

"She holds back most of her secrets," I said instead. "She knows what's out there, what's breaking free — but still, she keeps them."

"Have patience with Eltris. She's not easy, and it may not feel like you're learning anything. But she has a method to her mad ways. You'll learn everything you need to. Eventually." He gave me a sympathetic smile.

"I have a feeling our definitions of what I need to know are different."

We walked in silence for some time. When I glimpsed the same fountain twice, I glanced at Xaron. "So are you going to take me there, or are we just going to walk in circles?"

He at least had the decency to look sheepish. "Sorry. It's just… I don't think you should channel in front of anyone we can't trust, Airene. You could lose everything if the wrong person sees you."

"You don't think you can trust everyone training with Isidora?"

"I do trust them," he amended hurriedly. "But I'm not risking as much as you are. I'm already known as a warden, even as a warden who has channeled in a fight. It might not even impact me to be discovered here. But you put your life on the line. Is it worth it?"

As much as I hated to admit it, he had a point. And part of me wondered if I should be channeling at all. "You're right. It would be stupid to expose myself." As his expression began to grow hopeful, I hurried to say, "So I'll just watch everyone else. I won't give any indication that I'm a warden. Isidora already knows I'm aware of your group and that I know the danger Vusu poses. I'll just say I'm there to see what we have to fight against the Manifest."

His obstinacy melted away, and he shook his head with a rueful grin. "You always could talk me into things against my better judgment."

I shrugged. "What are friends for if not to get you into trouble?"

Xaron set our path straight now, taking us off the main road and into a rundown section on the south side of the campus. The sky had clouded over, and the alleys we traveled through were dark and shadowed. I took care to peer around each corner. We ought to have been safe behind the Acadium fence; even a determined and clever vagabond would be hard-pressed to circumvent the barbed tops of the metal wall. But it wasn't common thieves that worried me. Seeker wardens knew no boundaries, and I doubted the Imperium's Silks did either. Even Guilders could make their way in if they wanted to. With all the adversaries populating the city, it paid to always remain cautious.

Finally, Xaron stopped midway through a moldy alley in

front of a plain wooden door with a greeting hole. The building was made of limestone that looked a century unwashed. Its mortar suffered from neglect, and several sections of its walls seemed liable to fall at any moment. Yet it was large enough for its intended purpose, and far enough from the usual paths of Acadians to avoid casual notice.

Xaron knocked three times. A moment later, the door opened.

"About time," Isidora said, a hand resting on her hip. Unlike the last time I'd seen her, she now wore a homespun tunic and trousers. They did as little to accentuate her figure as the Acadian robes before, yet she wore them without any evident self-consciousness. I envied her that. Despite wearing a similar set of clothes, there was still part of me that wished to pull my cloak tight about me so others couldn't see.

As the Acadian's gaze slid over to me, her smile faltered. "Ah. And you came as well."

"I hope that's alright," Xaron said in a low voice. "Seeing as how she already knows about, you know..."

"Of course. Come in — we can discuss this more freely inside."

Isidora stepped aside, and I followed Xaron in. The atrium was gloomy and poorly lit by a few scattered torches. I could barely see the high ceiling in the flickering light. Something soft pressed beneath my sandals: carpet, an odd luxury for the poor conditions of the place. The air was thick with mildew, and dust streamed through the light.

We were not alone. Fourteen silhouetted figures stood among the stone columns, watching as Xaron and I entered.

"Hello, Watchers!" Xaron called cheerily as he approached them.

A few answered back, their voices friendly. "Ho, Hilarion!" a young man's voice called above the rest.

Xaron just grinned in response. He seemed comfortable

here, which helped put me further at ease.

"Good. We're all here then." Isidora strode past us into the center of the columns. "Watchers, we have a guest tonight. Meet First Verifier Airene."

The shadowed Acadians muttered among themselves. I shifted, suddenly nervous. I would have preferred to have kept my identity hidden in this dark room, but it was evidently too late for that now.

"If you don't recognize her name, you may know her title," Isidora continued. "That might alarm some of you. But rest assured, she's on our side. Even if Xaron didn't already attest to her good faith, even if she didn't already know what we do and make no moves to oust us, then shooting a crossbow through the Visage of the Wyvern should be proof enough that she's one of us."

The murmurs seemed to take on a different note. I glimpsed a few nods and smiles from the shadowed faces. I nodded back, glad for the darkness as my face flushed with pride. For, no matter the ramifications of my shooting Vusu, part of me was still glad I had.

"She wanted to see what we Watchers have to fight the Seekers, so let's show her. We're starting with the usual — the Shifting Sands meditation."

One or two Acadians groaned, and Isidora shot them a look. "You need the practice most of all, Heron. An eight-year-old boy could put your focus to shame."

"Bring one and we'll see," Heron retorted. But he folded down onto the floor with the rest, crossing his legs and sitting with his back straight. Xaron joined them. It left me alone standing, unsure of what to do.

Isidora seemed to sense my discomfort. "You may join us for this first exercise, Airene, if you wish."

I nodded and quickly sat, though more meditation was the last thing I wanted after my lesson with Eltris. But it was better than standing and watching.

"Close your eyes and clear your mind," the Acadian began, her tone softening. "Listen to my words and feel as I feel."

The experience was entirely different from Eltris's mediation. Instead of attempting to empty our thoughts, Isidora filled them with a vividly described scene. At her prompting, a wide desert expanded across my mind's eye. Waves of sands poured over the crests of dunes. The hot sun beat down on our heads. Dry air filled my lungs with every breath. There was no end to the horizon before me. I followed an unseen path toward a destination I'd never reach.

"All may shift around you," she prompted us several times. "You alone are still."

And I was, for a time. When Isidora told us to dismiss the scene and we stood and stretched, I marveled at how much more effective it had been for me than Eltris's stubborn repetition for me to stop thinking. Perhaps I'd have to paint my own scene during my next lesson, no matter what the Master Augur instructed, though I doubted I'd manage it was well on my own without Isidora's guidance.

The Watchers, as they referred to themselves, then moved into the next phase of their training, one that I could also participate in. Mirroring Eltris's exercises, this was intended to prepare our bodies. We moved in ways I hadn't since I was a child, pushing ourselves off the floor, running in place, and circling our arms until our muscles were warm and limber. Despite sweat beading on my forehead, I found my tension easing and my headache dissipating. Again, I found it superior to Eltris's method. I was beginning to wonder if the augur knew what she was about at all.

Then began exercises I couldn't participate in. Leaning against a column, I watched as Isidora led the gathered Acadians through the intentional channeling of each of the elements. This, at least, wasn't unlike what Eltris had made Xaron do during the lesson I'd witnessed. Isidora instructed them in the steps for making their radiance a single stream so it had no seams that an opponent could use to pull it apart, then how to sharpen your kinesis to ward against dispersion.

When they arrived at magnesis, I was surprised to see Xaron step up next to her and instruct them in polar charges and magnetic fields. True, he'd successfully channeled lightning against Vusu. But to see my friend as an authority on the subject meant seeing him in a new light. Talented and strong as he might be in his attunement, he had barely a season of training. It went to show how novice all these Acadians were in their magic.

I tried not to think about my own inability as they channeled, but found it impossible. My hands flexed and relaxed as the Acadians practiced each energetic element. A longing to join them ached in my chest. I watched their every gesture and hung onto every word of Isidora and Xaron's instructions. Never had I listened closer to my friend. Though I'd heard much of it during Xaron's lesson with Eltris, it took on a different aspect now. I wanted to test my own mettle. I wanted to know if I could channel at will yet, and where my five shifts would rank among the others. If I had this gift, I wanted to know how I measured.

No matter who had given it to me.

My anxiousness only increased as Isidora moved them into what seemed the most anticipated part of the practice: sparring. Xaron paired off with Heron and beat the joking young man a dozen times in a row. Other pairs were more evenly matched. Two on the opposite end of the room were barely able to muster flickers of magic against each other. Isidora moved from pair to pair, supervising as best she could. I paid particular attention to the intense matches. My fingertips itched with anticipation as blows were turned aside or met. Even in their Acadian robes, many of the men and women moved nimbly as they wove in and out of their channeling.

But even in practice, channeling was far from safe. A cry filled the room as an errant beam of radiance clipped a woman's shoulder and sent her spiraling to the ground. Isidora was by her side immediately, and the sparring died down for a moment. But as she crouched next to the young woman, Isidora snapped at the others, "Why are you standing around and staring? You're supposed to be sparring! You think Seekers will stop fighting if one of us gets hurt?"

The cold reality of what they trained for sprang the room back into action. The Acadians took to the practice with new abandon. It inflamed me as well. My toes had begun to itch along with my fingertips. I rubbed my hands against my trousers as I watched Xaron send Heron tumbling through the columns, wincing as the young man hit the floor again and again, clouds of dust rising around him. Xaron looked about, but his gaze didn't settle on me. Isidora watched him and nodded approvingly, at which my friend grinned. I looked between them and wondered at the uncomfortable feeling in my gut.

Only then did I realize what had been building up inside me without my realizing it. As if a dam broke, radiance suddenly flooded my body, filling me with a warm elation unparalleled by anything else I'd experienced. The energy coursing through me tried to burn away my sudden anxiety, but I clung desperately to it. If I let go of that worry, I knew I would channel outright. Already I could feel the heat pressing against my fingers and toes. With horror, I looked down and saw light seeping through the skin. I curled my toes into my sandals and balled my hands, squeezing shut my eyes as I did. I couldn't channel here. I wouldn't allow it.

But the more I tensed, the more the energy intensified. I couldn't close off my locus to the Pyrthae, not this time. More radiance crowded into me with every moment. It felt as if my very organs must burn from it. I couldn't hold anymore, but I couldn't release it. Fear clawed through me. I'd die if I didn't release it now. I had to.

NO!

The denial surged out of me in a rush. Dimly, I was aware I'd collapsed to my knees, and my body trembled with sustained tension. But though something had escaped me, I found some of the radiance pressing back through the opening inside me. Strained but emboldened, I mustered my will and pressed against it further. The warmth and peaceful-ness of radiance leeched away as I pushed it back into the higher plane. Exhaustion rushed into its place, but I didn't relent. I pushed the last of the energy back through the locus, then blocked it off. I didn't know how to seal the gap in me, but I meant to dam it for as long as I could.

"Airene? Airene!"

Slowly, I opened my eyes. Xaron and Isidora kneeled next to me. Even the flickering torchlight pained my sensitive eyes. But I didn't relax. If I let up my concentration even for a moment, I knew radiance would flood through me again. And this time, I wouldn't be able to stop it from escaping.

"I'm fine," I said through clenched teeth.

"Whatever that was seems to have affected her most," Isidora commented. She looked in pain as well, eyes squinted and her brow creased. "I suppose it makes sense. She wouldn't have any defenses against it."

Xaron didn't say anything, but his eyes betrayed his suspi-cions. "I'll escort her home," he offered as he slid an arm around my waist. "Airene, can you stand?"

"Yes." I wouldn't have been able to without his support. My legs were wobbly from my struggle with radiance as if my very bones had melted. Step by step, Xaron led me from the room, the rest of the Acadians watching me.

But I couldn't worry about that. Breath hissing through my teeth, I walked out, hunched over like an old woman, fighting every moment to keep from burning them all alive.

14
TWIN FLAMES

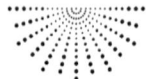

As with all of Clepsammia's prophecies, this one came to pass, and swifter than expected. Eleven days after the Goddess of Fate came to them, as Agmon Brandheart sat at his war council, a girl boldly entered.

'What is this?' Agmon demanded. 'Who are you?'

'I am Aika of the Green,' the girl said. Her voice spoke of the country folk living in the hills, a poor and uncivilized people.

Agmon grew enraged. 'We return to war in the morn. Why have you disturbed us at such a dire time?'

'Because I am the one you have been seeking. I dreamed of a snake devouring fruit from a great tree and woke to fire in my veins.'

'So did it happen to many of us,' Agmon replied. 'But though we possess godly power, none of us have the seed of a god within us. How are we to know the Seed of Harvest has planted within you?'

'No words can tell; only my actions will. Take me before Famine and I will show you.'

Her courage swayed even the iron will of Agmon Brandheart. 'Very well,' the Hero of Man said. 'When we ride on the morrow, you will ride at the fore — and may Harvest keep you safe.'

- The Seeds of Famine, a translation from the Lighted-tongue; by Oracle Kalene of deme Hull; 881 SLP

T he walk home was long and hard, my locus not closing until we'd already stepped through the Laurel Palace gates. Xaron had to support me the entire way. From the smirks and coarse words of the laurel guards, I knew they thought me drunk.

"Even you can do better than a drowned Finch, Hilarion," one of them japed.

"Very funny," Xaron replied wearily. The journey home had been no easier on him, and we had to go a ways to the Aviary yet.

But as my connection to the Pyrthae severed, I found I was able to walk. My legs still wobbled, and my head hurt worse than it had since I'd woken from my three-day sleep, but at least I could remain upright.

As we mounted the bridge and the wind hid our words from any eavesdroppers, he finally asked, "Were you damming your locus?"

I nodded, too weary for words.

He smiled sympathetically. "I told you about when I had to do that as a kid. It was a brief phase for me; you shouldn't have to do it for long. And who knows, maybe as an adult, you'll master it faster. That you didn't channel tonight was a marvel itself. I had three accidents before I managed to put a lid on it."

I nodded to his compliment and kept my eyes on my feet. Though the bridge had sides high enough to stop me from tipping over, I didn't fancy falling to the stone all the same. My knees hurt enough from collapsing in the Acadium earlier, and that had been on carpet.

"Don't worry about Isi and the others guessing," he continued. "They seemed to think that whatever you did came from somewhere else, and that scoria would be more vulnerable to it."

"Good," I murmured. At least that much had been achieved from my efforts.

He looked sidelong at me. "What *did* you do, anyway? Was that quintessence?"

"Don't know."

He shrugged. "I guess it doesn't matter."

We lapsed into silence for a few tottering steps.

"I shouldn't have brought you," he mused aloud. "I should have known it was too early, that it would be too taxing."

"You think you should have known that seeing other people channel would make me channel too?" I asked sarcastically.

"But you didn't just watch, Airene. Isi put you through the beginning exercises. Your body and mind were made as ready to channel as any of ours. Besides, there's something about being around other wardens that makes it come easier. Feeling the energy coursing through the air... It brings it out of you."

I didn't regret attending, no matter what had happened. I'd learned more in those turns than I had in my two lessons with Eltris. But my mind clung to another thought.

"Are you close with Isidora?"

He glanced at me. "We work well together," he said carefully.

"Apparently you're her authority on magnesis."

"I guess. Airene, is everything alright?"

"Everything's fine." My head hurt, my body was sore and weak, and what was supposed to be a gift was barely under my control. But none of that had to do with Xaron. It wasn't fair to take out my frustration on him.

Xaron knew me well enough to let things lie. We walked the rest of the way to the Aviary in silence. He bid me a brief farewell when we arrived at its weather-worn door, and I managed to paste on a weary smile before turning inside. It had only just grown dark, but after I ate a brief supper of the cold food Sizani had left out for me, I trudged upstairs to my room, intending to tuck in. I'd just have to make an early start of the next day.

But when I reached my room, I found Nomusa's door cracked open and yellow light streaming out from within. Since she was awake, I knew I should talk to her about our potential new Verifier. And, if I were up to it, my new revelation. Sighing inwardly, I knocked lightly on her door and pressed in.

Nomusa looked up from a series of finch scrolls scattered on the floor around her. She seemed as much at ease curled up on the floor as standing straight among a group of Servants. "You're cutting it close to dark," she observed, then narrowed her eyes. "You look awful. Did you get mugged again?"

"Worse — I ran into Xaron."

I slumped onto her bed and reported the evening to her, though I had a feeling I wouldn't like her response. Sure enough, it followed the lines I'd feared.

"You shouldn't have gone," she said reproachfully. "Not only was it risky for all of them, but look what happened to you."

It annoyed me how closely her response mirrored Xaron's. "I had to go. Not only is it good to know which wardens are on our side, but I need to learn to channel. Didn't you say we have to take risks?"

"That's not what I meant, and you know it."

I knew I wouldn't keep my temper much longer and quickly changed the subject. "But that's not what I wanted to talk to you about. I think we should take on a new Verifier."

"Oh?" Nomusa arched an eyebrow. "And who has gained your trust?"

"She hasn't gained my trust yet. But what she offers is enticing."

"You have my attention."

I drew in a breath. "Her name is Kelena. And she's an honor to Iason."

"An honor? To Iason?" She looked dumbfounded. "Why would she be a good Verifier? And where did you even find her?"

"Wisp brought her to me. I know it's strange, but I think we should give her a chance. She's already aided us once. You remember last night, when that honor led Xaron and me up to Komo's rooms?" I flinched as I said the Shaka-Heir's name. Nomusa's face had gone carefully blank, and I pressed quickly on. "She said to remember that she helped us. Then Kelena brought up the incident and said she was responsible for the honor's aid."

Nomusa's brow creased. "Are you saying this Kelena was able to contact an honor within the Laurel Palace to help you at the drop of a copper?"

Now that she mentioned it, it didn't seem likely. "I guess I don't know. Maybe this is another time we're being set up to be betrayed, like with Vusu. Maybe we shouldn't make her a Verifier after all."

"Perhaps. But if she's telling the truth, if she's able to make use of other honors so quickly... that could be invaluable. And you said she presently serves Iason? Think of the information and access she could provide. We might even be able to make headway on the Council's mandate to find corruption. Though not the way they'd like us to." Wicked humor lit her eyes.

"All true. And Vusu did help us as well as manipulate us. Even if she isn't on our side, we still might get some use out of her." I put my head in my hands and kneaded my temples. Hard enough to make a decision like this, much less when I felt as I did just then.

Nomusa spared me the burden. "Let's bring her on. I don't see how she could put us more at risk than we already are. And I doubt the Council will confirm her anyway. But if we try, it will prove we're serious about working with her."

"Fine." I rose, my body screaming in protest. "Now I'm going to collapse in bed."

She rose smoothly and gave me a hug, sniffing as she did. "Make time to wash tomorrow. You haven't gone since the fight last night, have you?"

"I didn't have the time," I said, slightly affronted. But I quailed at the suggestion. Time wasn't the only reason I hadn't ventured to the baths. With the city in turmoil, bathing was a risk I didn't like to take.

Nomusa sensed my reservation. "We have baths here at the Conclave, you know. I can show them to you tomorrow if you like. Who knows, it might be good for your wounds as well."

"If you insist."

"I do." She looked at me with her head cocked like bird. "Your hygiene is growing almost as poor as our old Guilder friend's."

I smiled at the thought of Talan, even as a sudden ache woke inside me at his absence. "Please let me never get that bad."

"You won't while I'm around. Now go; get some sleep. Tomorrow will come soon enough."

I woke with Talan's flame in mind.

Nomusa's reminder of him seemed to have wormed its way into my thoughts, and likely my dreams. I smiled to myself for a moment as I remembered his roguish smile and knowing eyes, the soft touch from his rough hands. Wherever he was, I hoped he was keeping himself safe, though I knew it was a vain hope.

Then I remembered the last I'd heard of him.

I sat bolt upright. How many days had it been since the Guilder had passed on Kalindi's threat? In the whirl of activity, I hadn't given more than a thought to warning Talan. But would it be better to warn him, or would seeking him only further endanger him?

Only when I rose and thought of what the rest of the day held for me did I realize how impractical the idea to find him was. Once I bathed, I knew I should squeeze in what I could of my research in Tomes, then give Kelena the news with enough time for the Council meeting that evening, and finally attend the meeting. I wished I could skip the latter, but if I wanted to be taken seriously as a First Verifier, I had to appear before the Low Consuls.

But if I truly valued my friend, something had to give. I decided to take off the morning and hunt him out. As he'd said his hiding holes were compromised, I knew visiting his old places would get me nowhere. If I assumed he wasn't still in Hull, where I'd seen him in the Pyrthae-dream, that left just one place to check. Failing that, I'd could only hope he'd show up soon.

I readied myself as quickly as I could, rushing the clerk Galene through her accounting and dragging Nomusa from her bed to the Conclave baths. My being in a hurry wasn't a new development, and she didn't question where I rushed off to. I barely noticed the fluted columns and finely carved pediments around us as I sloughed off the olive oil from my hair and skin.

As soon as I'd cleaned and dressed, I bound up my damp hair and hurried off toward Port. With crowds still gathered about the Conclave gates, as they had been except for the few turns when the Conclave guards had driven them away, I had to take the long way around from the lesser-known gate

Corin had shown me. This time, the guards didn't taunt me, but eyed me apprehensively as I, a lone woman, went out into the city. I was growing more comfortable with navigating this new Oedija, but a lump of fear always sat in my gut.

I hurried through Iris's streets toward my home deme, keeping an eye over my shoulder the whole way. Instead of turning inward toward Zipho's, Maesos's, and Canopy, I turned toward the Lighted Sea. My destination was at the far end of the harbor and took several turns to reach. I hoped I wasn't wasting my time.

Remembering from my last trip the safest route down the cliffside, I took one last look around before descending the slippery rocks. That I'd traveled it successfully before made it little easier. Every foot- and handhold I sought carefully, and my limbs trembled with more than exertion. But it was no more than a quarter-turn before I lowered myself to the edge of the cave's mouth and carefully folded my way inside.

As my eyes adjusted to the dimness, I found an unkempt man facing me, a knife bared in his hand. Dark stubble layered his chin, and his hair, bound back in a tail, was shiny with grease. His eyes were narrowed in suspicion, their golden color almost hidden in shadow.

Upon seeing me, though, the man sheathed the knife with a flourish and a half-cocked grin. "I wondered when you'd find me."

"Hope the delay didn't disappoint." A smile found its way onto my own lips as I stepped toward him. Filthy or no, Talan was a sight for sore eyes. "I have so much to tell you."

"As do I." His eyes flickered back deeper into the cave, where the faint glow of firelight came from.

"What? Are you burning breakfast?" I teased, stepping within reach of him. Nomusa was right; the man's hygiene was appalling. But still, I reached out to embrace him. The things I had to tell him were bursting to get out. But for a little while at least, all I wanted was to hold him.

Just as I was about to touch him, he stepped away. I flinched, then lowered my arms. There was apology in his eyes, but it didn't lessen the hurt suddenly rising inside me.

"Airene," Talan said quickly, "there's something I should tell you—"

"Is this the Airene I've been hearing so much about?"

My hand went to my knife as a figure emerged from the darkness of the cave — a woman, nearly as tall as Talan and darker of skin than Nomusa. The part of myself that wasn't dumb with surprise wondered if she were Bali or from the southern provinces of Avvad. Her sharp features were scored by many scars, but her beauty and air of confidence were unmarred by them. She wore a rough-spun tunic, fraying trousers, and well-worn boots, and carried them with all the confidence of Feiyan in her fine robes. Her dark, round eyes studied me with a hint of amusement.

I remembered the other flame I'd seen with Talan in my dream and cursed myself for a fool.

"Hello." The word came out half-choked.

"I've startled you," the woman said. "My apologies."

"Airene, this is Sule. Sule and I have known each for a long time." Talan had lost his usual self-possession. His eyes looked anywhere but at mine.

"A very long time," the woman agreed.

"I see." I looked back toward the mouth of the cave and out over the sea. I wondered if I should leave before I gave vent to the anger suddenly roiling inside me.

"Sule, could you give us a moment?" His gaze found me, but I didn't meet it.

"Of course," the woman said easily, retreating back into the cave. Her eyes gleamed as the rest of her was lost in shadow. Even retreated, with the echo and the size of the cave, she would likely hear everything we said.

I lowered my voice anyway. "I didn't mean to surprise you."

"Let me explain," Talan said, barely softening his voice. "It's not what it looks like."

I finally met his eyes. "I'm listening."

He ran a hand over his greasy hair, as if attempting to tame it. "It's as I said. I've known Sule for a long time. She and I were... childhood friends."

"You're not making this sound any better."

"I know, I know. But the tale is far stranger than I know how to tell you." He drew a breath. "Here's the short of it. You remember how I lived for some years in Erimis?"

I nodded.

"My home is actually some ways south of there, in one of the provinces long ago conquered by the Imperium. Sule and I knew each other from our hometown. We were in a cabal and—"

"A cabal?" I interrupted.

Talan waved his hand. "Just a group of children, really, who thought we were hard and worldly. Anyway, for a while, we were close. But... a situation came up. She made one decision, I made another. When we parted, I never expected to see her again. I moved to Erimis then, for a fresh start, and made a name for myself."

"I'll say. Wraithsbane, isn't that the one?"

He groaned. "Not exactly what I meant. But after a number of bad turns and foolish decisions, I found myself in a poor way, and taking on a job I knew I shouldn't. Just then, Sule showed up again."

"And you made up and were friends again."

He gave me a wry grin. "Not as I remember it. Though I wouldn't say we parted enemies..." He shrugged. "Again, I never thought I'd see her again."

"Yet here she is."

"She showed up here in Oedija soon after the Despoina's

249

trial and came to me. At the time, the situation with Kalindi was particularly precarious, and I judged it best to take her in to keep an eye on her."

"Why?" I demanded, not caring that I spoke louder. "Why couldn't you just wave and pass by?"

Talan closed his eyes. "Because she can find me no matter where I am."

It took a moment for that to sink in. "Why?" I asked in a hushed voice. "Is she a warden?"

He nodded. "Not only that, but she — She isn't the Sule I knew before." Talan glanced back at the woman, who crouched next to the fire in the back of the cave. "She's different."

"Different how?"

"Perhaps it would be easier for me to explain."

Sule stood and turned back toward us. Annoyance spiked through me, but I held my tongue.

"I am both Sule and another," she continued. "It has been a long time since we thought of ourselves as separate, but I suppose you would see us as jinni and human in one body."

Cold realization dawned on me. My hand strayed back to my knife. "This is the Damask Esir who tried to kill you back in Erimis?" I demanded of Talan, though I kept my eyes on the woman. "The one possessed by a Qarin?"

"Yes. She won't harm you, Airene. I told you, we have an understanding."

"I don't see how you could come to an understanding after that."

Sule, or the one who called herself that, took a step forward. "Then perhaps you've never had to band with an enemy in the face of a greater threat."

Despite myself, I thought of Feiyan. I shook my head free of her face. It wasn't at all the same as lying down next to her at night, next to this... *thing*. This abomination that was what the daemon sought to make of Linos.

"You're evil and twisted." I nearly spat out the words. "You stole that woman's body for your own."

"Not quite. She who was once Sule was broken. I cared for her body as I mended her, and she sustained me and brought me back my memories. Yes, I benefit as well, I don't deny it. But now neither of us can exist without the other."

I wanted to look away from the woman. The very sight of her repulsed me. I felt I could almost see the daemon that prowled behind the human eyes. But I could do nothing against her. Not only was she not human, but she was trained as a Damask Esir, one of the elite soldiers of Avvad enslaved to loyalty by the pyr known as Qarin. And she was a warden. My knife would be of little use against her, and though I tried to open myself to the Pyrthae, my locus now remained stubbornly closed. I could only hope I could pull the wool from Talan's eyes.

"She's manipulating you," I told him. "She's still Esir, can't you see that? The Qarin controls her. How can you trust anything she says?"

"I can't." Though he looked tense, he didn't seem wary of Sule. "But I have no choice. She can find me, Airene, no matter where I am. Unless I keep her close, I endanger myself."

"Then kill her."

Talan's head shot up, his eyes wide. Behind him, a rueful smile twisted onto the woman's face.

"That would be difficult," he admitted weakly. "But even if I could, I don't want to, Airene. Sule is a valuable ally."

I could scarcely believe what he was saying. "She's not an ally, Talan! She's our enemy!"

"No," the Esir interjected. "Our enemy is Avvad. The Kahin-Shah bound Sule and I together. I was enslaved as much as she was at the hands of the Tefra. Now we wish to take our revenge."

"Then take it elsewhere," I shot back. "Anywhere but here."

"Airene." Talan's tone was almost pleading. "Avvad's armies advance on Oedija. Vusu and his Seekers grow stronger with every passing day. Kalindi and his minions spread like a disease throughout the city — thieving, coercing, murdering. We need allies, any we can get. Sule has agreed to aid me in preparing to meet Avvad. I'll not cut her loose."

I felt something tear inside me.

"Then keep her," I snapped. "You're welcome to each other. Just don't expect me to save you when she stabs you in your sleep."

I backed toward the entrance, feeling for the wall behind me. Talan didn't follow. His bright, honey-hued eyes watched me, brow furrowed. Sule, standing behind him, shook her head with a small smile.

But as angry as I was with him, I knew I had to warn him. "Oh, by the way, a Guilder found me. They're searching for you, Talan. Don't let them find you."

His eyes widened, and he took a step forward. "Airene, wait. It's not safe—"

"Nowhere is safe," I cut him off bitterly.

I'd reached the cave entrance and reluctantly released my knife. My hand trembled as I seized the stone wall, but my grip held. I looked back once more at Talan, wishing there were words to show him the depth of his mistake. But anger sealed my lips shut.

Without another word, I turned and started the slow climb up from the cave.

15
HONORARY VERIFIER

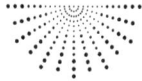

Just before the two armies clashed in what promised to be the final battle, Clepsammia again appeared before Agmon Brandheart as he sought to read the stars.

'Your Seed of Harvest has appeared,' he told the goddess. 'Now we will see if you have spoken the truth.'

'I have,' Clepsammia replied, 'but I have not spoken all of it.' Her smile grew wide with anticipation.

'Tell me,' Agmon demanded.

'The gift given to you by my father, the power for a mortal to wield a god's power, was his last act. Tyurn Sky-Sea, Ruler of All Realms, is dead.'

Agmon Brandheart felt hope grow cold in his breast. 'What can tame Famine's appetite if not the Lord of All? We are doomed!'

'You have not yet heard everything, noblest of mortals. There is an uglier truth still to behold.'

'Then speak it and leave me to despair!'

'Despair... do you believe that to be your destiny, Agmon Brandheart?'

Clepsammia drew nearer still.

'The truth, bravest of men, is that even as Tyurn Sky-Sea bestowed his last gift upon you, Famine was in him. Your skill in

wielding the elements of my world is as much of the God of Hunger as my father.'

Agmon's heart wrenched in his chest so that he thought he would collapse. 'Our enemy is in me? In all of us?'

'All of the First Wardens are Seeds of Famine. Other gods have touched your kind and opened you to the Higher and Lower Realms. But you, Agmon Brandheart, are born of my father's guilt and your enemy's gluttony.'

The Hero of Man sank to his knees. 'He will turn us to his cause. That is why he has not destroyed us.'

Clepsammia did not hide her smile. 'Perhaps. But this flaw cuts both ways. Famine does not stay away only to make you an ally. He cannot deny one born of his seed. Within your heart, Agmon Brandheart, lies the power to restrain a god.

'But to restrain Famine, you must offer him something in kind. A sacrifice of spirit, or an offering of blood...'

- The Seeds of Famine, a translation from the Lighted-tongue; by Oracle Kalene of deme Hull; 881 SLP

R eaching Zipho's cafe a half-turn before Kelena was due, I sat and brooded over a cup of coffee. The cafe owner, sensing I was in no mood for gossip, left me alone after she'd served me.

As I stared into the dark, steaming liquid, regret slowly seeped through me like a stain into wood. Yet as soon as I thought of that strange, beautiful woman huddled next to Talan at night, my blood began to boil anew. Each sip tasted more bitter than the last. We needed allies, true. But we didn't need abominations like her.

Abomination. Did that make Linos an abomination as well?

I remembered the harsh words that had come from his tongue, the presence that had tried to take me. Was he even now yoked, as Sule was by the Qarin? Had I saved Linos only to doom him to a life as a daemon's slave?

Draining the rest of my coffee, I bade my farewells to Zipho, left the cafe, and made for the narrow alley.

Coming to the end of the alley, I peered in and saw a hooded figure standing midway through. So full of misery and self-loathing, I almost didn't care if was a Guilder or thief waiting to waylay me rather than my contact. Turning sideways, I sidled through the narrow space toward the figure.

When I was a few paces away, Kelena pulled back her hood. "First Verifier Airene," the honor greeted me. Despite her impassive tone, she twitched with nervous energy.

"Hello, Kelena." I paused, awkward suddenly. I'd been aloof and suspicious when we'd first met, but now we were intending to throw in our lots together. I'd have to start acting much warmer toward her. "Is your day going well?" I asked her tentatively.

She seemed surprised by the question. "Fine," she said shortly. "And yours?"

"Not well."

We lapsed into silence again. So much for friendly sentiment. I ignored the flush rising along my neck and said quickly, "Nomusa and I have decided to take you on. So long as you're still interested."

As I regained my composure, Kelena regained hers. "I am," she said, drawing herself up straight.

"Good. Before it can be official, we need the Demos Council to confirm you. Nomusa is setting an appointment with them for the sixth turn this evening. Can you be there?"

She seemed startled by the mention of the Council. I wondered how much hell Iason would raise.

"Yes," she answered stiffly.

"I'll see you at the Conclave gates then." I began to slide back the way I'd come before I remembered something else.

"There's a side-gate on the north end of the Conclave grounds. I'd suggest making your way there rather than the main gates."

Kelena nodded and turned away. I glimpsed a small smile playing on her lips before she pulled her hood back on.

When I exited the alley, I let out a long sigh. I hoped Nomusa and I could make good on our promise. Despite myself, I found I was beginning to trust the woman.

Yet if we were to work together, we had a hard battle ahead of us yet.

~

Though there was too little time before the Council meeting for my usual activities, I still made for the Acadium campus. If I hurried, I had just enough time to make it there and back. The daemon-possessed woman still haunted me so that despite days of ignoring Linos while visiting Tomes, I suddenly felt the urge to visit him.

Already wearied from the day's walking and my climb to the children's cave, my legs and lungs were burning by the time I reached the Ward. The same clerk as before sat in attendance, and she eyed me as I approached.

"Are you seeking healing?" she asked with false sweetness.

I brushed back a stray hair that had come out of its braid. "No, thanks. I'm here to see Linos. Ward three, bed sixty-four."

After the clerk confirmed it, she let me find my own way in, though I felt her eyes follow me. She wasn't the only one to cast looks my way. A disheveled woman in tunic and trousers wasn't the usual visitor here. I tightened my jaw and stared straight forward, refusing to acknowledge their stares.

Reaching Linos's room, I found a healer's assistant attending to my brother. She bowed out as soon as I explained who I was, though not without a wary look of her own. I ignored her and looked down at Linos. He seemed in much the same condition as last time and lay flat on his back, eyes set in their webs of violet lines and staring at the ceiling. I didn't come close. I hated that I feared even to touch him.

"Linos," I murmured. "What has been done to us?"

He didn't answer, as I'd known he wouldn't. As I'd hoped he wouldn't. If he had, I knew it wouldn't be him speaking.

"I think I understand more about how you've become the way you are," I continued. "You've been hollowed out by him, haven't you? By Famine. But I don't know why. I wish you could tell me."

My little brother had always pretended to know more than he did, but I was sure he knew things that might help me now. If he could only rouse and tell me.

"Linos," I whispered. "Little Lion, can you hear me?"

His head snapped toward me so quickly that I jumped.

"He can't," the daemon that seized his tongue crowed. "But I can, sweet nectar to my soul."

My chest tightened so it became hard to breathe. "You don't have a soul," I hissed.

"I'm nothing *but* soul," the daemon corrected me. "But soon, *very* soon, I'll be more. I'll have a body of my own."

I wanted to shake the daemon from my brother. "Leave him alone!"

"Oh, no, Airene. I don't mean to leave him. As you well know." The daemon stretched Linos's mouth into a wide smile.

I wanted to scream and strike at him. I wondered desperately if channeling quintessence could harm the pyr, or at least dislodge him. But even if it might, I couldn't channel at will. I was helpless.

"You won't have him," I warned as I backed toward the door. "I won't let you."

"I'll be waiting!" the harsh voice called as I fled from the room.

Putting the door between my brother and me, I stood panting behind it for a moment. Healers and assistants passed by, casting odd looks my way. When one actually stopped to inquire if I was well, I decided I had to move on. Time was already short as it was.

But I couldn't leave my brother like this without doing anything.

I stormed up to the clerk at the front. Someone had arrived there before me, so I waited impatiently for them to finish before walking up to her. Rather than smug and superior, the woman looked frightened at my expression. I tried to soften my scowl, but it was etched into my face.

"When was the last time Kallias visited my brother?" I demanded.

The clerk blinked. "Kallias the Sculptor?"

"Who else?"

Lines formed on her brow, but she flipped open her heavy book and began to search through, her finger scanning the lines. "Sixty-three, sixty-four..." Her finger stopped, and after a moment, she glanced up nervously. "It seems the Sculptor hasn't visited your brother since he was first admitted."

The cold fury of an ocean's swell swept through me. I had another appointment to make. "Thank you," I said, then began to turn away. But something under the entry caught my eye. The clerk had begun to close the book, so I thrust a hand out to stop it. "Wait. Who visited him there?"

The clerk stared at me with a scandalized expression, but she obliged by folding the book back open. "Master Augur Eltris. Is that whom you're referring to?"

I stared at the name in the book. Eltris had been to visit my brother and hadn't told me. How much did she know? What did she plan for him?

"Thank you," I said woodenly, then turned away.

Outside, I stepped to the side of the entrance. My vision

tilted drunkenly. Even within the Acadium, my brother was in danger. I shook my head and set off at a fast walk, knowing I had no more time to stand around and consider it. All I knew was that somehow, someway, I had to protect my brother.

Especially from my supposed allies.

My mind was in as bad a way as my appearance when I arrived at the Conclave north gate. Kelena already awaited me. Her expression was carefully blank, but I was sure she saw every errant hair and mud splatter up my trousers. I put it from mind. If the Council put me out for a rough appearance, they were even pettier than I'd thought.

"You ready?" I asked as I drew out my Finch medallion for the guards, who were less reticent about expressing their skepticism of my dress.

She nodded and followed.

Nomusa met us at the Conclave doors. "Hello, Kelena," she said, nodding as the honor bowed her greeting to her. Then she turned to me. "You're racing the sandglass to the last speck. I was about to hunt you out myself if you didn't show up soon. What happened?"

"A long day. Weren't you saying we're running short on time? Let's go recommend a Verifier." I gave Kelena an encouraging smile, but she didn't return it as she stared around the Conclave. Even as an honor to Iason, she'd likely never seen the grand seat of the demotism before. And she had a big trial before her. She couldn't be blamed for missing a few things. My smile slipped away.

We hurried down the Conclave steps to the Council's small door. As we neared, the same male honor as before stepped forward. "The Council awaits you, First Verifiers," he said, rebuke plain in his voice.

"We know," I said, my forced good humor evaporating.

Nomusa halted me with a touch to the arm. "Remember what we discussed before," she warned softly. "Let me do the talking."

She was right. I was in no condition to speak to the Council. I pushed down the mutinous feelings that rose in me and nodded.

Her smile formed a thin line. "A good start. Kelena, if you'll follow me."

We entered the Council chamber. All ten of the Low Consuls were gathered along with Jaxas. No one smiled or spoke as we filed inside. I met Jaxas's gaze and was surprised to see cold consideration there. I lowered my gaze to the floor. The room had a chill feel to it that had nothing to do with the monsoon winds spiraling through the open windows.

"Demos Council," Nomusa began with a bow. "Thank you for your time. I'll be brief. We bring before you one we hope to be the first to join the new Order of Verifiers. This is Kelena of Iris. By all accounts, she is—"

"Kelena of Iason, you mean!" Iason, usually stuttering and uncertain, was neither now. His fury made him tremble as he stared at Kelena. "I assume I will return to a sooty kitchen this night, won't I, honor?"

Kelena flushed, but didn't flinch away from his stare. "Perhaps," she said in a quiet voice nearly swallowed by a sudden gust. "But that will no longer be my concern if you confirm me."

"If!" Iason sputtered, looking around with wide eyes. "There's no question of i-it!"

"I would not say that, old man." Feiyan leaned back in her chair, amusement dancing in her eyes. "Some of us are more open to equal opportunities for all."

Berker leaned on the table, his face growing purple with

rage. "She's an honor!" he snarled. "She can no more be a Finch than a dog can be a Servant!"

"Peace, please," Orhan interjected. A mocking smile played on his lips, and I wondered what he had in store for us. "We have not heard out the First Verifiers."

"Thank you, Orhan," Nomusa said graciously, though her eyes betrayed her unease. "It's plain that Kelena is an honor. But this is her advantage. She's established a network of honors that span the whole of Oedija, giving us eyes and ears into places we hadn't previously." She paused, letting the suspense build.

As with most things, Berker was deaf to it. "Like what?"

"Like the Manifest compound," Nomusa said smoothly. "And the Laurel Palace. Thanks to Kelena's foresight, an honor was waiting to bring Airene up to the Yorandu delegation's quarters the night the Seeker wardens attacked. With her aid, we may know well before the next attack and be able to prepare for it."

The Low Consuls exchanged looks, and Orhan's smile grew. Too late, I realized why. These ten people, the most influential in all of Oedija, had more secrets between them than the rest of the city combined. To be told the honors of their households might double as spies only weakened our case. Even those among the Council who wished the Order success wouldn't sacrifice their own privacy. Nomusa seemed to sense the same thing, while Kelena's expression remained impassive.

"For the good of Oedija," Nomusa continued hurriedly, "we should elect Kelena of Iris as a Verifier of the Conclave." She fell silent, neck darkening with a blush as she stared stonily at the opposite wall.

Jaxas moved minutely. "We are called to a vote," he said in a soft voice. "Those in favor of electing Kelena to the position of Verifier?"

Feiyan immediately raised her hand. I gave her a

grudging nod, and she smiled sweetly in return. But it seemed our accordance was in vain. Daelya raised her hand hesitantly, and Zehaar only followed suit after her two fellow Equalists stared at her. Yet no other hands ascended. My hopes sank.

"All opposed?"

Iason's hand was up first, with the rest of the Preservists following. I waited for the last two hands to raise, and inevitably, they did. Verchlesa of Thys and Tychon of Hull didn't seem as vindicated like Orhan and his faction, only resolutely determined. Too much risk, too much change. I glanced at Kelena, but she was a statue in her stillness.

"The honor Kelena's appointment is denied," Jaxas said. "Thank you, First Verifiers. You are dismissed."

I felt his eyes on me, but I didn't meet them. I could guess what the Archon meant by his gaze.

"J-just a moment!" Iason cried. The old man stood shakily to his feet and pointed an accusing finger at Nomusa. "You t-try to steal my honor, make her one of your F-Finches, and expect there to be no c-c-consequences? Kelena was my most reliable girl! Yet in light of this betrayal, I am f-forced to dismiss her. Now that I am sh-short-handed, you will have to supply someone in her p-p-place." He smiled wickedly at this idea of vindication.

Nomusa bowed stiffly. "Very well. We will find an honor to replace Kelena in your household. Anything else, Low Consul Iason?"

He had already sunk back down, the smug smile still on his wizened face. "N-no. That is all."

Nomusa bowed again, and I followed after. The bow Kelena gave was stiff but to the exact angle required. It seemed that the more fate beat her back into the role decreed for her, the less human she became.

We didn't speak until we were outside the Conclave

doors. "Come with us," Nomusa said, then turned toward the Aviary.

Though Kelena gave no indication she'd heard, she followed her after a moment. I trailed behind.

A short while later, we were inside the Aviary's atrium, and Nomusa invited us to sit as she slid onto one of the tables. She picked up a slice of mango from the platter next to her and thoughtfully bit into it.

"Kelena," she said after a moment, "I'm sorry."

"You presented it poorly. You made it seem threatening to them." Kelena didn't look at either of us as the bitter words spilled forth. "You didn't think through the barriers being an honor to one of the Low Consuls would pose. You didn't think how resistant they would be to change. You should have let me speak. If they'd heard me speak, they would have known I'm not a silent maid with a shaved head and tin earrings. They would have heard what I am. They would know how I could help them." Tears glistened in her eyes, but she resolutely stared straight ahead.

Nomusa looked surprised. "You could have spoken if you wished. Neither of us prevented you."

Kelena finally looked over at her. "It would have been unseemly!" she hissed.

I gave a sardonic laugh. "The Order is nothing if not unseemly."

The honor turned her hateful eyes on me. "You haven't been told all your life to remain silent until spoken to. You haven't been taught to give the utmost respect to authority, or risk a slap across the face. You move through the world with assumptions that it will give as you require, and it complies. You think it must be this way for all." She jerked her head away. "It is not."

I listened in astonishment. She was right. I'd expected the same treatment for her as for myself. It was no more than she deserved. But that didn't mean it was what others would give her.

Yet as I exchanged a worried glance with Nomusa, it wasn't for this gap in our vision. We both knew that if we didn't act quickly, we'd lose her.

Looking back to Kelena, I said the only thing I could. "You're right. And I'm sorry we weren't able to initiate you into the Order."

Kelena's eyes narrowed, and her mouth parted, but no words came out. An apology was likely the last thing she'd expected.

"But that doesn't mean you can't be a Finch," Nomusa quickly followed up. "For most of our lives, Airene and I have acted as Verifiers without official recognition. I wish we could have given it to you, but we don't have to let it stand in the way of working together as if you were one of our own."

The honor's eyes slid over to Nomusa now. "You would still take me on as a Finch?" she asked slowly. "You would risk the Order's dissolution to bring on an honor?"

"It's not charity," I admitted. "We need you. You have access, contacts, and knowledge that we sorely require."

After looking between us for a moment, Kelena nodded. "I have no other place now. If you'll have me still, I'll join you. But I'll need food and shelter."

"And coin," I stated firmly. "Nomusa, can we tap the remaining five silvers to our daily allowance?"

"Galene will question it. It would be safer to give her coins out of our own allowances. Perhaps one and a half each?"

I nodded. "Is that sufficient, Kelena? Three scions per day?"

Her eyes were wide. "What would I use them for?" she asked in a small voice.

I realized with a start that she may never have possessed money of her own before. Some honors worked at the banks sorting money, but no honor was permitted possessions of their own. Any money she'd spent before had been Iason's.

"Whatever the work requires," I said. "Surely even honors take bribes."

She shook her head. "Not coin. Favors we exchange, and small items we cannot obtain except through barter. What use could an honor have for coin?"

"To stash it," I suggested. "To save up enough to escape to another life, or to at least have the choice."

Yet again Kelena shook her head. "Where would they go? Oedija is home. Our families and friends are here. Our lives are here. We don't know the world beyond the polis's walls, except for those of us who have lived on the estates. We'd be more slaves than here, for our masters would be the hateful Fates."

I closed my eyes. I didn't know the Fates she referenced, but the rest made all too much sense. Every man, woman, and child wanted the freedom to do with their life as they would. But not at any cost.

"Very well," I ceded. "But you will get the coin nevertheless. If you must say you're spending it on another's behalf, so be it. But it's yours to use how you see fit."

"Just don't buy clothes like Airene's," Nomusa suggested. "Get something a bit more fashionable."

As I shot her a dirty look, a smile slowly crept onto Kelena's face. It brought out a smile of my own. Perhaps we'd gained a new Finch after all.

Nomusa grew serious again. "We'll need a cover story. But I can think of only one that's suitable."

"I'll do it," Kelena said abruptly. At Nomusa's surprise, she clarified, "You wish me to be the Order's honor, do you not?"

Nomusa nodded slowly. "Only for appearances. In all other ways, you'll be a Finch, with full rights and responsibilities. But you'll have to keep that from everyone, including Hyrol, the Aviary's current honor."

To my surprise, Kelena smiled. "No need to worry about that. Hyrol is part of my network."

Chills prickled my skin. Though some part of me was gratified to be vindicated in my suspicion of Hyrol, most of me wondered at what we'd gotten ourselves into.

Nomusa masked her own reaction. "That's settled then. Now we have to assign duties. Airene, I assume our responsibilities remain the same?"

I nodded and said nothing. Until I knew how our recent inductee would take the news of Famine, I didn't want to risk ruining my credibility with her.

Nomusa looked to Kelena. "Then that leaves your duties. We have a glaring gap of knowledge where it concerns the Manifest. Our top priority is to anticipate when the Seekers will make their next attack, and where. Any additional news you can gain of the Despot's whereabouts and Vusu's doings would also be invaluable."

Kelena nodded, though her eyes darted between us, clearly wondering what we'd kept for ourselves. I resolutely looked away, not meeting her gaze. There would be time enough to tell her later.

"Good. Then I have one last piece of news." Nomusa cast me a look. "The Archon approached me earlier today. He informed me that the Council has deemed it necessary to elect the last Low Consul. As the typical manner of doing so — by consensus — has left it open, it will require a simple majority among the remaining unrepresented eleven Servants to win."

I listened, stunned. Was this why Jaxas had stared so intently at me? I grasped immediately what it meant for him. So long as the eleventh seat of the Council was empty, Jaxas had the power to break ties. Once it was filled, he returned to little more than a glorified moderator. It was the way our demotism was supposed to function, true. The Servants were of the citizens of Oedija, elected to power rather than inheriting it as the Wreaths did. Yet despite all those lofty ideals, I knew Jaxas was who we needed in that position right now.

"Is there no way to delay it?"

Nomusa shook her head. "The date is set. Three days from now, the last Low Consul will be elected. With times as desperate as they are, nothing is likely to change that. I'm working with the Equalists to find a suitable candidate, as well as with Tychon and Verchlesa, if they're willing. We won't allow Orhan and his Preservists to determine the course of Oedija."

I hoped she was right. For if they elected one of Preservist leanings, I feared Oedija would already be lost.

1 6

A SUMMONS AT DUSK

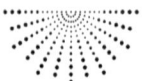

Clepsammia released Agmon Brandheart from his vision. 'It is for you to decide, Hero of Man. You must make your choice soon.'

Agmon opened his eyes and found they'd arrived at the battle-front. The enemy soared before them in the form of a great serpent. All trembled as Famine's eye, black as a stormy night, fell upon them.

But one stepped before the others: a girl, of no great height or import. Only as he saw her did Agmon Brandheart remember Aika of the Green riding in his vanguard.

Fearless, the girl challenged the God of Hunger soaring above. 'Daemon! I offer you a chance to sate your ravenous desire! I will tame the hunger that commands you, if you but dare to come near!'

Famine immediately dove at the girl like a hawk at a mouse, his jaws opening wide. Agmon, staring inside his gaping maw, saw the end of all times within. He quailed and waited for the girl to be consumed.

But Aika of the Green stood her ground. 'Famine!' she called again. 'I offer myself as Sacrifice! My blood and my spirit are yours!' And upon these words, she raised a knife as white as bone, then plunged it through her own chest.

*- The Seeds of Famine, a translation from the Lighted-tongue; by
Oracle Kalene of deme Hull; 881 SLP*

I lay in bed, sleepless, Isidora's mind-painting exercises faltering in my mind. Despite night having settled over Oedija, Nomusa and Kelena had gone out to sway the upcoming election, insomuch as they could. The honor, knowing many secrets of the Servants, promised to be useful if it came to coercion. It left me alone to think over the day — or avoid thinking about it, as I'd opted to do.

Yet after my thoughts became so distracted that I couldn't remember if I was supposed to be imagining a desert or a sandy beach, I sighed and sat up. Images of what was happening to Linos kept asserting themselves every time I tried to focus. The barbs of Eltris keeping information from me and Kallias the Sculptor being too important to treat my brother followed quickly behind.

But imaginings of Talan with Sule were what stirred me to anger. How the man could be foolish enough to trust a daemon, I couldn't understand. If he wouldn't listen to reason, I didn't know what could sway him.

Helplessness and frustration conspired to keep me from sleep as well. Finally, I relented to their tide. Rising, I bound my sandals and threw on my cloak, then left.

I only made it to the tower before something drew my eye. In the low light of the pyr lamps, among the many finches settling down for night, I glimpsed a tightly bound scroll attached to the leg of a green-plumed bird. Ascending nearer the top of the tower, I took some seed from a nearby trough and cooed softly, trying to coax the bird toward me. Eventually, I succeeded. The finch ate contentedly as I untied the scroll, then withdrew my knife to cut the unfamiliar seal, a tree with its branches formed into a sphere — the shape of the Bali isikhayha trees, if I wasn't mistaken. The script was strange to me as well, written in large, flowing letters barely recognizable as Oedija's sea-tongue.

> *First Verifier Airene,*
>
> *The Shaka-Heir bids you visit his quarters this night, if you are able. If this missive arrives too late, he wishes you to come at your earliest convenience.*
>
> *~ Faluwa Yorandu Nkosi, Advisor to Charratta Yorandu Komo, Shaka-Heir of the Yorandu*

I lowered the small scroll, considering. When this message had arrived was critical to know. Though Nomusa made liberal use of our finches, I'd found little reason to, and I hadn't been watching for scrolls. Either way, I could ill afford to delay. The turn wasn't too late as to attempt a visit, and I clearly wasn't going to fall asleep.

Finally having a purpose, I hurried toward the Laurel Palace. The green radiant winds streamed across the cloud-dappled night sky, lighting my way as I crossed the bridge and ascended the hill to the golden Wreath estate. Though I didn't recognize the guards, they admitted me at a flash of my medallion. Recalling my steps from two nights before, I found my way back up to Komo's quarters.

But as I traveled down the hallways of the opulent wing, I found the Bali guards stood in front of a different door. I froze as I realized why. Memories of the fleeting battle crashed through my mind. Screams filled the air. Blood splattered the floor. Bodies slammed into stone walls with sickening squelches. The perfumes of burned flesh and fresh death filled my nose.

I nearly doubled over. It must have only been a moment before the panic passed and I was able to draw in a ragged breath, yet the moment dragged on and on. But eventually, my eyes again saw the hallways before me. The unfamiliar guards watched me. They could have been carved from wood for all their expressions shifted.

Feeling as if I walked in a dream, I put one foot in front of the other until I stood before them, grasping for words. "Heir Komo summoned me."

One of the guards raised an eyebrow. "And you are?"

Recognition of his voice startled me from my daze. Incredulous, I stared at the man, words completely escaping me now. Without having to search, the traitor guard who competed for the Despoina's affections stood before me.

It was easy to see why he thought he stood a chance, even with royalty. In addition to his honey baritone voice, he had strong features and bright, lively eyes. The hardened muscles of his arms and stomach were on fine display in his warrior's garb. He looked dangerous and alluring all at once. A smile played at the corners of his lips even as his eyes narrowed at me. Yet scorn didn't diminish his beauty, but somehow enhanced it.

"What do you think?" the would-be seducer asked his fellow guard. "Which of the sea-city herbs did this one take?"

He clearly intended offense by speaking in my own tongue. Yet still, I found myself tongue-tied.

The other guard didn't answer either. A taller, thinner man already balding despite his youth, his brow knitted together as he studied me. "Are you well?" he asked, his words heavily accented.

I finally rallied. "Yes. I just... I was remembering what happened here before."

The guards exchanged a look. The younger man said something in a low, excited voice in the Yorandu tree-tongue, but the traitor guard just shook his head, amusement plain in his expression.

"My friend believes that you remember this as the Shaka-Heir remembers," he informed me, speaking with exaggerated slowness. "That you feel the violence of places."

I knew he mocked me, yet in my stunned state, anger couldn't reach me. "Remembering as *I* do is enough," I told him. "I was there with Heir Komo when the Seekers came."

The traitor guard's smile slipped, and his eyes flickered to the medallion at my chest. "First Verifier Airene?"

My name and title returned some semblance of my dignity. "Yes. Now will you admit me?"

The traitor guard spoke rapidly to his companion, and the younger man shot me an inscrutable look before knocking on the door, then entering within. The traitor and I were left in silence. With each passing moment, I felt more myself. If the memories hadn't faded, they'd lost some of their cutting edge.

"What's your name?" I asked him flatly.

The traitor guard seemed to have recovered his mocking confidence. "Why? Do you wish to report me for my suspicions?"

"What's your name?" I repeated.

"Bhaka." He said it as if it were of no importance.

I didn't respond, but waited until the door opened again. The younger guard stepped out and motioned to me. "Shaka-Heir will see you."

As he held the door open, I stepped inside. I felt Bhaka's gaze on me as I passed him, but I didn't look over as his fellow closed the door behind me.

"First Verifier Airene."

Komo wore a loose white tunic and short trousers, similar to what he'd worn the night of the attack. The Shaka-Heir's boyish voice had none of the buoyancy from when I'd first met him at the feast. I wondered if his "feeling the violence of places" was taking its toll.

"Heir Komo." I bowed and approached. The room was not as richly adorned as his initial quarters had been, lacking the vines covering the walls. Komo's advisor Nkosi stood in one corner of the room next to a bookshelf. He didn't look up at my entrance, seeming engrossed in a small book cradled in his hands.

Komo noticed my study of the room and shrugged. "Do not fear — we are comfortable here. I am more worried about you. How do you fare? I saw the man they call Hilarion up and walking."

"I'm fine. My wounds were not so dire. And yes, Xaron was healed without complications, thankfully. I see you're well yourself."

Komo nodded absently. "Yes. As I said, it does not take my body long to heal. I had feared I would call you from your bed with the note, but I could not wait."

"You needn't have worried. What did you wish to speak of?"

The boy glanced back at his advisor, but Nkosi continued to ignore us. "Asileia Wreath," he said with some reluctance.

I tried to hide my surprise. How strange that the topic should come up now, with the Shaka-Heir's traitor standing outside his door. But as I considered telling him, I realized I couldn't. We needed the Yorandu as allies, and the surest way to tie the bonds was through marriage. To confess our Despoina might have a dalliance with his guard could only serve to undermine our burgeoning relationship.

I tried to ignore the guilt that assailed me as I stowed the admittance away. "What would you like to know about the Despoina?" I asked lightly.

Komo's brow creased. "You seem reluctant to discuss her, as do most Oedijans I have encountered. Is it considered rude in your customs to speak of your leaders?"

I thought quickly. "It isn't offensive exactly. But people might be reticent because they don't know her personally. She's a figurehead, and most recognize her as little more than that."

"And you?" the boy pressed. "You have spoken with her, have you not? What has been your impression?"

I strained to think of which of her qualities might be put in a positive light. "I have only spoken directly with her once, and she hasn't worn the Evergreen Wreath long. But she seems a driven woman, and one intent on making Oedija strong."

"So I have heard. Yet what others tell me and what I see do not match." He shifted, his gaze wandering from me. "She seems... distracted. And she often speaks of being the Hand of Clepsammia. Is this a title of some importance to your people?"

His mentioning her self-proclaimed title stirred an idea that sent cold fingers crawling down my spine, and for a moment, I lost the line of my thoughts. But now wasn't the time to consider it.

I scrambled for a way to spin this hiccup. "She means that, as the Despoina, she is the ambassador of the Eidolan gods. A recently adopted title, but one steeped in tradition."

Nkosi's book snapped closed. "Enough," he said, his tone halfway between annoyance and amusement. "Enough dancing around the truth. The Shaka-Heir wishes to know whether or not he courts a madwoman."

My tact was nearly banished before the bold question, but I clung resolutely to it. "Some might be offended by that question."

"But I do not think you take offense easily. Tell us, First Verifier Airene. Is the Despoina god-touched?"

"Nkosi," Komo said nervously. His eyes darted between us.

"It is under control, Shaka-na. The question, Finch."

Nkosi knew. If I was to salvage our relationship, I had no other choice but to confess the truth. "I don't know. But once, I believed her mad enough to attempt to murder her father."

The two exchanged glances.

"I wondered when you would speak of your missing

Despot." Satisfaction warmed Nkosi's tone. "Myron Wreath is alive, is he not?"

My mind spun. Who would have told him that? This game raced ahead of me. Until I found a way to get ahead of it, the truth was the safest route. "We believe so."

"Yet you have not recovered him."

I saw my chance then and seized it. "We haven't the strength. The Manifest hold Myron Wreath captive. There's been no demand for ransom, so freeing him by force has become the only option. We need you, Heir Komo, to rid the traitors of our city."

"But if Myron Wreath is freed, does he not resume his position as the Despot?" Nkosi pressed. "Would not Asileia be forced to cede the crown back to her father?"

Curses ran through my mind. I hadn't considered that angle before. "I don't know. You'd have to pose the question to the Archon."

"Jaxas Wreath. The man in line after Asileia, is he not? I wonder if there are not other reasons Myron has yet to be recovered."

For a moment, I could do nothing but stare. The implication was an insult to the man who had sacrificed so much for Oedija.

"I would not fear that," I said coolly.

"Please, Nkosi," Komo urged. "Do not repel everyone in Oedija. We may yet make this alliance."

"When we have been met with little but lies and deceit? I do not see what we would have to gain, Shaka-na."

The boy turned to his advisor. "We have not been honest either. Tell her. Tell her what only one of the Bali would know."

Nkosi seemed taken aback, his night-dark skin flushing darker. My curiosity grew as I looked between them.

"You are right," the man admitted. Then he approached me and held out the small book he'd been reading.

I hesitated a moment before accepting it. Though it seemed well-cared for, the cover was time-worn, the words and images faded beyond recognition. "What's this?" I asked.

"*Tales of the Desolate,* you would call it in the sea-tongue."

Everything fell into place. I knew what they thought they withheld. "The story of how the eleventh ishaka became the Unnamed. The story of Yama and Lophe and their Serpent God."

They stared at me, eyes wide. "Then you know?" Komo pressed.

I nodded slowly. Yet the weight of the admittance held back the words. If they didn't suspect what I suspected they did — what I hoped they did — I might still drive them away. But as it was, they hesitated over the marriage and alliance. They might leave us. I suddenly resolved that if they did, it would be knowing the full extent of the threat that Oedija and the entirety of the Four Realms faced.

"Heir Komo, the Serpent God that assailed the Bali ishakas didn't leave this world. And Yama didn't die in obscurity. He came to another place and continued to serve his god. He came here, to Oedija." I drew in a breath for the final confession. "The former Tribune Vusumuzi is Yama in another guise, and the Dragon he and the Manifest revere is the Serpent God returned."

Komo stared at me, features lifted almost in awe. "You knew. All this time, you've known. And yet you do not fear to face him."

Nkosi seemed to have aged. "It is as I feared then. The world again buckles beneath the tightening coils."

I held the book out to him, but the advisor pressed it back into my hands. "No. You are familiar with the stories, but you have not read all. This is an older version than the one you will have seen. After Yama and Lophe fell, the Shakas agreed that the Twins' words were too dangerous for any to hear. So a copy in our tree-tongue was disseminated that stripped their speeches away, leaving only the history and the warnings against the Serpent God. The book you hold now is the original, written from firsthand accounts in your sea-tongue, in case it fell into the wrong hands of our countrymen. It contains the very words spoken by Yama and Lophe."

The tome suddenly felt heavy in my hands. I considered what this might mean. "How do you know it's accurate? How do you know this additional material wasn't an author's invention?"

"This book has been handed down through the line of the Shaka's family, unblemished by history's workings, that was written by the advisor to the Yorandu Shaka at that time," Nkosi said. "It is uncorrupted."

I looked the advisor in the eye. The time for half-truths was over. "But you broke that bloodline. You murdered Nomusa's family."

Nkosi didn't flinch as I expected him to. "Madness does not prey only on Oedija's rulers," he said softly. "My Shaka did what had to be done."

I looked aside. The man spoke with far too much belief to be comfortable. Could he speak the truth in this as well? Had Nomusa's father been as mad as Asileia was becoming?

"I need to think this through," I found myself saying. I bowed stiffly, not meeting their eyes. "Thank you for the book."

"Keep it safe, First Verifier Airene," Nkosi responded. "Read it. And when you have, we will speak of this further."

I nodded, then turned from the room.

17

THE SAME COIN

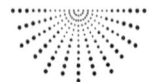

As Aika of the Green fell to the earth, unmoving, Agmon Brand-heart found his courage. Calling the charge, the First Wardens surged forward to meet the enemy.

But as Famine swooped down to accept the girl's body, the ground suddenly trembled. A tree, as shining and brilliant as the sun, grew where none had stood before. As all stared in awe, they saw the God of Hunger plunge onto its branches.

Famine screamed, and raged, and lashed his great serpentine body back and forth, but he could not break free of the white limbs thrust through him. Slowly, his movements grew sluggish; then he ceased to move at all.

Agmon Brandheart stared into his enemy's black eyes, but could not tell if he lived or had died, for he had never seen life behind them before. 'Is it over?' he whispered. 'Is it done?'

The Hero of Man sank to his knees and wept. For all they had lost. For the girl who had saved them. And for the coward he had showed himself to be.

- The Seeds of Famine, a translation from the Lighted-tongue; by Oracle Kalene of deme Hull; 881 SLP

ECHOES OF CHAOS

I read through the night.

The previous copy of *Tales of the Desolate* that Nomusa had lent me had been intriguing and vivid enough to haunt my dreams. This original was utterly engrossing. Now that I knew Yama and his Serpent God for what they were, everything took on new meaning. The will that drove the Twins to conquest their fellow people, the hunger for power and vengeance, were all too familiar.

Yet there was more still in this first edition. Yama and Lophe's own words were littered across every page, and when Yama spoke, it was as if I heard the words from Vusu's own lips. *All that is great comes with sacrifice*, he whispered into the still air of room, and I had to look around to ensure he wasn't there.

Though most of what I read made my skin crawl, one revelation comforted me. Again and again, Vusu spoke of being haunted by Famine — by his hunger, by his promises of power, by his thirst for violence and blood. I'd felt none of these things since my own attunement. Surely, it could mean only one thing.

I wasn't a Seed of Famine.

The earlier suspicion I'd held loosened and relaxed inside me. Despite the heaviness of the rest of the text and the sleepless night, I felt almost light as I closed the fraying cover and sat up. Another Quintyr must have opened me to the Pyrthae. No matter who was responsible, it couldn't be worse than the God of Hunger.

As for the rest... I had to think over what I'd read and pick apart the sentences. Almost, I could understand Vusu's motivations, his purpose. What was written here, in a century-old book, both corroborated and undermined what I knew of Vusu.

I pitied him.

I shook my head of the strange feeling. There wasn't a man in Telae less worthy of pity, that I knew well. I rose from bed, a nervous vigor coursing through me. Sleep was impossible now, and I had a full day ahead of me. Despite all I'd learned, there were too many gaps in my understanding. The meeting with the Master Librarian might fill those in.

Yet I could face anything now that I knew I was uncorrupted.

Tucking the book protectively under my arm, I donned my cloak and, still in my clothes from the night before, quickly left the Aviary. I drifted along, nearly dizzy with the lack of sleep and food, but I didn't take the time to stop. Answers were the true sustenance I needed.

When I reached the Yorandu wing, I approached Komo's door, where a different pair of guards now kept watch. At my request, one inquired within, then soon ushered me inside.

Komo rose from a chair to stand with his hands clasped behind his back, a boy trying to appear a man. Heavy-lidded eyes and slumped shoulders told me he'd claimed as little sleep as myself. His advisor was nowhere to be seen.

I bowed briefly and produced the book from beneath my cloak. "I read it last night."

"Then you have done more than I." The boy tried on a smile that failed to reach his eyes. "I know the stories of the Unnamed, of course. But I've not received close instruction."

"Perhaps you'd like to." I held out the book.

The Heir hesitated before stepping forward to receive it. "Nkosi might want you to keep it," he said dubiously.

It struck me then how much of a child he still was. The sympathy that filled me cut with its sharp edges. Too closely it mirrored the guilt I felt for not being able to protect Linos.

"You take it for now," I said gently. "It's safer here with you. If I want to read it again or Nkosi wants me to have it, I can always return."

Komo nodded wearily and turned to set it on the shelf in the corner. "Nkosi has already gone to the Conclave this morning, or so I have been told. I have only just risen. If you wish to speak to him, perhaps you should seek him there."

I contemplated it briefly. "I'll visit later. I don't wish to be caught in the web of politics at the moment."

"A bit late for that."

"Far too late."

We shared a fleeting smile.

"I'd better be on my way." I bowed again. "But I'll return this evening if you're available."

"They have a walk planned for me in your Laurel Groves with the Despoina." Komo tried to keep his voice composed, but dread seeped between his words. "But perhaps after."

"Just as long as it isn't as late as last night's meeting. I must sleep sometime."

His brow knit together. "Of course. Forgive me — you must sleep then."

I smiled. "Only teasing, Heir Komo. I doubt any of us will rest much anymore."

The sun had crept into the sky by the time I left the Wreath grounds, its low angle casting the alleys in shadow. Despite my thoughts conspiring to distract my weary mind, I tried to keep watch. In daylight, I was safer out on the main streets, but nowhere was truly secure in Oedija these days.

Luck was with me, and I made it to the Acadium without incident. First, I went to the Ward. Linos was much the same as when I'd visited the day before, still staring up at the ceiling. I didn't venture close but sat in the corner of the room, watching him. Now more than ever I wished him to rise and flash his mischievous grin, to give some sign I hadn't completely failed him. I'd glimpsed the depth of Vusu's madness and had some inkling of what he was capable of.

Fear for my brother grew further still as I wondered what he'd gone through.

And why. Despite all I'd read, I still had no answers as to why both of my brothers had been targeted by Vusu. I wondered if I ever would.

Leaving without disturbing him, I found my way to Tomes. My appointment with the Master Librarian wasn't until that afternoon, but I knew I was getting close to finishing *The Seeds of Famine*, and was eager to be done with it, even if deciphering the ancient words sounded interminably tedious. Platon had learned to leave me to my studies as he wandered the great library, humming to himself and playing small games that he dashed aside at the slightest sound, fearing his master was coming down to chastise him.

But if I'd feared the words would be dull, I was wrong. I hadn't squinted long in the yellow light of the pyr lamps before my heart began to thump hard in my chest. A girl, Aika of the Green, had appeared before Agmon Brandheart and proclaimed herself to be the Seed of Harvest he'd been looking for. Despite his doubts, Agmon sent her to the front lines to prove her worth against Famine.

Then Clepsammia once again appeared before the First of Firsts, and made yet another revelation: that the First Wardens were all Seeds of Famine as well as of Tyurn Sky-Sea, Tyurn's Gift corrupted even as it was given. But it was her next words that made my breath catch:

The Hero of Man sank to his knees. 'He will turn us to his cause. That is why he has not destroyed us.'

Clepsammia did not hide her smile. 'Perhaps. But this flaw cuts both ways. Famine does not stay away only to make you an ally. He cannot deny one born of his seed. Within your heart, Agmon Brandheart, lies the power to restrain a god.

'But to restrain Famine, you must offer him something in kind. A sacrifice of spirit, or an offering of blood...'

Blood pounded in my ears as I read the lines again. *He cannot deny one born of his blood. Within your heart lies the power to restrain a god.* They were true; I'd seen they were true. I'd wondered how Vusu was able to hold Famine to his will; now, I had the barest shadow of an answer. Being a Seed of Famine, it gave him the power to restrain the God of Hunger. Why and how that could be, I didn't yet know. Eltris clearly thought she understood, believing Famine stayed of his own will, seeking to break into Telae. But now, I wondered if there wasn't more to it.

And Clepsammia's last words — *"But to restrain Famine, you must offer him something in kind. A sacrifice of spirit, or an offering of blood."* I had seen that, too, proved true. At the Despoina's trial, Vusu had cut Linos's arm, spilled his blood, and declared it a sacrifice for Famine. Then Famine had come, opening a path into the Pyrthae, and I'd followed.

I leaned back and rubbed my eyes. If these things written in the ancient text were true, what else that it declared might be? Had Tyurn Sky-Sea existed, and died to attune the First Wardens? And Clepsammia — was she real as well? Had it truly been her I'd seen in the Pyrthae, who had protected me from Famine? Was it she who hounded the Despoina into madness? *The Smile of Fate*, Clepsammia's expression was called. And so it had felt when I'd looked upon it, even when I'd not believed her to be more than a dream.

And Harvest, and the Seeds of Harvest — this book said they could complete Famine. Could they be what we needed? But if that were true, if Aika of the Green were a Seed of Harvest, then why had Famine returned when he'd been restrained?

My appointment drawing to a close, I bent back to the book and kept reading, hoping the answers would be in the text.

The battle came, and Aika rode at the front of the army.

283

She encountered Famine, and her called words to him burned into my mind:

> *'Daemon! I offer you a chance to sate your ravenous desire! I will tame the hunger that commands you, if you but dare to come near!'*
>
> *Famine dove at the girl like a hawk at a mouse, his jaws opening wide. Agmon, staring inside his gaping maw, saw the end of all times within. He quailed and waited for the girl to be consumed.*
>
> *But Aika of the Green stood her ground. 'Famine!' she called again. 'I offer myself as Sacrifice! My blood and my spirit are yours!' And upon these words, she raised a knife as white as bone, then plunged it through her own chest.*

Breathless, I continued on, seeking what her sacrifice would bring:

> *But as Famine swooped down to accept the girl's body, the ground suddenly trembled. A tree, as shining and brilliant as the sun, grew where none had stood before. As all stared in awe, they saw the God of Hunger plunge onto its branches.*
>
> *Famine screamed, and raged, and lashed his great serpentine body back and forth, but he could not break free of the white limbs thrust through him. Slowly, his movements grew sluggish; then he ceased to move at all.*

I scanned the words after, but little else was written. The Hunger War ended there. The land fell into ruin from the battles, and the people were forced into exile. They began a journey across the sea, led by their remaining gods, Clepsammia among them. And so my ancestors embarked on the Lighted Passage and came to found Oedija.

I returned to Famine's defeat, mulling over the words. Now that I'd reached the conclusion, instead of the elation of discovery, I found myself filled with a vague disappointment.

Perhaps these passages held clues to defeating Famine once more, but the answers it offered were riddled with holes. What was this "knife as white as bone" with which Aika sacrificed herself? Why did a white tree grow in her place, and why did Famine die on its branches? And if Famine *did* die, if the Seed of Harvest completed him, how had he returned?

Scooting back my chair with a screech, I stood and began to pace. One question after another filtered through my mind, and one by one, they unfolded into a widening fear. I didn't push them away, but let each blossom inside me. My chest felt full of them; my gut ached. My palms sweated with the effort of holding them in.

Realization suddenly dawned on me. *My locus* — it opened inside me and the Pyrthae's energy filled me. Once again, I'd managed to channel when I least meant to.

In a fit of abandon, I let it suffuse me, unable to release the soothing warmth. Radiance, I recognized it, as my head began to grow light, and the pains of reading faded to buzzing numbness.

But as the energy urged me to draw more, the comfort drained away. I couldn't channel; not radiance, not here. A thousand years or more of literature was housed in this library. All it would take was a stray ray of radiance for it to all go up in flames.

Remembering my training, I unclenched my fists and sat back in my chair, forcing myself to relax. My limbs went slack and heavy, and the muscles of my abdomen released.

For a moment, nothing changed. Then slowly, ever so slowly, the warmth of radiance drained away, until at last my locus sealed itself shut again.

A weary smile crept onto my face. I'd stopped myself from channeling.

"First Finch Airene?"

I startled, then relaxed as I saw the library's boy coming

cautiously down the hall. "You don't have to use a title, Platon. Especially not one you made up."

The boy grinned. He knew me well enough to realize I wouldn't press my authority on him. I was glad for the familiarity, though it made me remember how ornery Linos had been at his age. My chest gathered a different ache.

"Sorry." The unrepentant boy bowed mockingly and grinned even wider. "I thought maybe you'd want to go up. I think it's time for the appointment."

I rubbed at my sore neck. "Has it been that long?"

"Has to be! You were napping for a while."

"I wasn't napping."

"Uh huh." The boy rolled his eyes. "Anyway, it's my job to get you there on time, or Master Hagne will have a fit."

We ascended back to the main floor of the library. In the wake of the near accident, my questions upon finishing *The Seeds of Famine* had fled me. But as Platon prattled on and my weary legs mounted stair after endless stair, they found me again. At least I might soon have someone to discuss them with.

Platon led me to the Master Librarian's solar, a tiny room that seemed built from the wall as an afterthought. Entering within, I found the space crammed full of books. There was barely room for me to stand. A single pyr lamp hung above us, leaving the corners of the small solar in shadow. Master Hagne herself sat among the stacks, a hood pulled over her face. When it slipped back, I saw what Xaron had mercilessly poked fun at. Her skin was pocked with what looked like scales, and her eyes glittered yellow from the shadows like a rabid animal. Though pity rose in me for her mistreatment, I kept my distance, hoping whatever ailment had struck her as a child was long gone.

As we began to haltingly converse, I quickly realized my hopes for the meeting were unfounded. Master Hagne dismissed my interest in legends and, speaking rapidly, tried to divert my interest to areas that held her concern more, particularly Qao Fu poetry of the eighth century — which, if she was to be believed, was the premiere art of any civilization that had existed. I nodded and agreed until I could work her back around to my own area of interest, each time in vain. If the woman knew anything of Famine, Harvest, and the rest of the story, she wasn't likely to turn to the topic soon.

But the meeting wasn't entirely in vain. After the fifth time I turned back to the topic, the Master Librarian irritably suggested I go speak with the Master Historian, or as she put it, "that hack who pretends to know history." I sensed a rivalry between the two and hoped it was one-sided. If the Master Historian was as petty as this Acadian, an entire afternoon would be wasted.

Thanking her, I beat a hasty retreat, only to be intercepted by Platon. "Well?" he asked eagerly. "Did she get you the answers you needed?"

"Closer," I hedged, not wanting to hurt the boy's feelings. I gathered that ascertaining a meeting with Master Hagne was no mean feat. "Thanks for all your help."

The pupil beamed. "I'll see you tomorrow!"

After I extracted directions from the boy, I made straight for the Master Historian. Acadian Helene — she allegedly didn't like to use the title "master" — lived near the front of the Acadium in a square limestone house. Glancing up at the second-story windows, I glimpsed a head bent to work, and dared to hope she'd pause to admit a visitor.

I wasn't disappointed. After one of her apprentices inquired upstairs, Acadian Helene came down to greet me. She was just past middle-aged and had black hair streaked with gray, a round face with plain features, and a smile that warmed me immediately.

"First Verifier Airene, I understand?" she said with a respectful bow. "It's a pleasure to welcome you."

"Thank you." I bowed in return. "I was told you prefer to be called Acadian Helene?"

"Just Helene is fine. Come. From what I've heard, you have some questions that may take a long while to answer."

Mystified, I followed her upstairs. Her solar was nearly as small as Master Hagne's, but lacked the same cramped feeling. Where the librarian's room had been dank and dark, Helene's was light and airy, with open windows admitting a cool breeze. Books were neatly aligned on shelves except for two open on her desk. A pen and ink sat ready to be used, and a leaf of parchment was filled halfway down with neat lines of letters.

Helene requested tea from her apprentice, then sat us down in a corner opposite of her desk. "Now. I'll let you ask what it is you need."

"Thank you for your time, Helene."

"Not at all! My hand was just beginning to cramp, and I always smear the ink when I don't let it rest."

I nodded, smiling in spite of my heavy thoughts. "You may have heard already, but I'm looking into legends surrounding Famine from before the Lighted Passage."

"Yes, I did hear." The Acadian studied me, a shrewd look coming into her eyes. "But as to why you're pursuing it, I'm not yet certain."

Something stayed the admittance on my tongue. The historian seemed an open-minded woman, but I wasn't sure if she'd take me seriously if I told her the truth. "A persistent curiosity, let's say."

"An odd time for an odd curiosity." Helene lightened her words with a smile. "Particularly for a First Verifier."

"Perhaps. Is it the wrong time to ask?"

"Not at all. I wouldn't discourage interest in history at any time. Please, ask your questions, and I'll do my best to answer them."

I considered where to start. Which query would be the

least likely to arouse derision? And what did I most need to know?

"How was Famine defeated before the Lighted Passage?"

She tilted her head to the side, like a finch considering seed spread before it. "'Defeated' is not the word I would use — 'repressed' is more like it. According to the writings we have — *The Seeds of Famine* being the foremost source — the phenomenon our forebears labeled as 'Famine' was suppressed through the ritual of Sacrifice."

"Sacrifice?" I imagined Aika of the Green plunging the dagger into her chest. "What does it mean, to offer oneself as Sacrifice?"

Helene smiled. "You speak as one familiar with the text. You've read *The Seeds of Famine?*"

"I just finished it, actually."

"A persistent curiosity to carry you through all that cramped script! But to answer your question, no one truly knows what it means to be a Sacrifice. But as those who acted as Sacrifices were written thereafter as if dead, I believe it must involve suicide."

"It seemed that way with Aika of the Green."

"Ah, yes, the girl from the hills. It is a common motif in Oedijan stories, the ordinary child coming from nowhere and nothing to save the kingdom. I doubt *The Seeds of Famine* was the first to use it."

"Could you tell me of its particular rendition?"

She nodded with an easy smile. "We know little of Aika of the Green but that she was born in the hills of the western lands to a poor farmer's family who was forced to move to the city when their lands became fallow. There, she lost her parents to disease and violence, leaving her alone in a dangerous city. Aika was hungry, thirsty, with no home but a muddy alley, when she sank down to sleep for what she thought would be the last time. Then she dreamed of a snake.

"In this dream, the snake was wound around a tree

branch, gnawing at the orange fruit hanging heavy there. As Aika approached it, it didn't seem to notice, but finished the first piece of fruit before starting in on the next. Its long tail swung down far enough that it hung just before the girl.

"Approaching it, Aika stretched out a hand to touch the snake's tail. As her finger made contact, the snake immediately left off the fruit and swung its head around to face her. The girl fell back, staring wide-eyed at the serpent. It was large enough that it could swallow her whole. Just before it struck, Aika startled awake, only to find her hands were glowing with fire. Somehow, during the course of the dream, she had become attuned to the Pyrthae.

"Aika claimed that the snake was Famine himself, and that she became attuned by drawing close to his presence. Though none of the First Wardens seemed to believe this, her startling beginning is the only characteristic that sets her apart. Her channeling was not very strong, nor did she seem gifted as a warrior, healer, or crafter. Yet when she offered herself as Sacrifice to him, it was enough to tame Famine and drive him from this world."

I found my brow had furrowed and tried to smooth it. "I don't understand. I thought Aika was a Seed of Harvest. But what you say makes it sound like Famine attuned her."

Acadian Helene cocked her head. "So it does. But it's a matter of some debate as to whether or not Famine and Harvest are separate beings, or two sides of the same coin. The theory makes a certain sense — many cultures' deities occupy dichotomous roles within their pantheons. The merciful judge. The trickster champion of the people. The bloodthirsty savior."

Despite myself, I found disappointment churning in my gut. "You think this is nothing but stories. Tales told to children."

The Master Historian laughed. "Well, I wouldn't tell this one to my children, if I had any! But yes, of course I do."

She seemed to sense my disquiet, for she continued kindly, "I understand the hope, First Verifier. With drought and war coming, it's only natural to seek comfort in stories. But I would caution you against taking these legends as anything more than tales told to explain the troubles that the world brings."

I looked out the window. Acadian Helene was a warden herself; she wouldn't be in the Acadium otherwise. If she could reach into the Pyrthae, she'd know how very real the enemy we faced was. But how long had it been since she channeled? She was an Acadian through and through, skeptical of all she could not see. I wouldn't convince her of the truth when I had but scraps of it.

Glancing back toward her, I put on a strained smile. "Of course. As I said, it's no more than a passing fancy."

Helene smiled in return. "Of course. Now, I apologize, but I have a treatise that I should return to. The events around us will one day be noted in history, and I mean to be the hand that writes them."

I rose and bowed. "I'm sure you will be," I said, though I wasn't sure of it at all. "Thank you for your time, Acadian Helene."

The Master Historian finally stood. "It was a diverting discussion, First Verifier. Do visit again."

The day grew golden as I left the Acadium. I still had a couple of turns until night took hold, but I'd have to hurry unless I wished to encounter the dusk mobs once more. My attention wandered as I walked. All I'd learned over the past day and night swirled in my tired mind. Almost, I felt I had the answer to the problems before me, if I could only have a clear moment to think. But nothing was clear; I walked as if in a fog, the sleepless night finally catching up to me.

I was halfway back to the Laurel Palace, the sun sunk behind the roofs, when I noticed the street around me had emptied. Alertness cut through the mind-fog. I tried to be furtive as I glanced behind me.

Two men walked on either side of the street, keeping a dozen paces away. Hoods were pulled over their faces, but I felt their watching eyes on me.

My limbs went weak, but I quickened my step. My breath came swift and shallow. I couldn't help looking behind me, though it would betray my awareness of them. They didn't close the distance between us, but kept pace with me. I didn't dare run.

After glancing back yet again, I found before me two more figures had materialized. Breath stuck in my throat. Terror robbed the strength from my limbs. I stumbled to a halt. Four men surrounded me, with no help in sight. I hoped it was only coin they wanted.

But when they closed in around me and I glimpsed the glowing, blue eye inked into their wrists, I couldn't fool myself any longer.

One of the Guilders grinned as he neared. "Hello, Finch. Remember me?"

I didn't have the wits to respond. I knew I should reach for my knife. I knew I should try to channel. But both seemed impossibly out of reach. I'd never channeled upon command. I couldn't manage it now. The anticipation of what they'd do to me filled my head, fear pushing out all else.

"Ah, she has gone silent. And I was hoping she'd struggle." The Guilder, the one whose nose I'd bloodied, grinned at his companions. They let out low chuckles.

"What do you want?" The words came out as a plea.

"What do I want? A dangerous question." I could see the hairs on his chin, he was so close. "I want to pay you back for breaking my nose. I want to make you scream. And I want to make sure you know that crossing the Undermaster when he makes you a deal has one end." The grin stretched wider. "But I'm not going to make it quick."

At that, the men surged forward.

Only as they moved did I spring back to myself. Desperate animal rage suffused me as I reached for my knife. But as I tugged at it, it stuck in its scabbard, and before I could wrench it loose, hands seized me and crushed me to the ground.

The Guilder got his wish as I screamed. The smell of unwashed men's bodies filled my nose, and dust filled my mouth as they pressed me against the cobblestones. Shrieks, barely recognizable as my own, erupted from me until a hand pressed my head down hard. Sudden pain; my forehead wet; dizziness washing over me. I ceased to struggle, my limbs grown too heavy to move.

"You know," the Guilder said over me, "your lover thought that you'd put up a better fight. He *screamed* that you wouldn't let us take you alive when we put him under the knife. Yet here you are. A ripe fruit for the plucking."

Helpless rage seized me again, and I bucked and struggled anew. Someone wrenched my hair, then stars flooded my vision as something hit it. Sickening pain washed down me. Head blazing, I gasped, fresh blood dripping down my face.

"That's better," the Guilder crooned. "Nice and quiet while we put you in your place. If there is an afterlife, I hope your Talan is watching from it."

I felt a tug on my trousers, but my belt kept them in place. Groggily, I batted at their hands, but my fingers had grown too clumsy to pry them off.

"Not here!" the first Guilder snapped. "What if those damned mobs come? Pull her into the alley."

"I wasn't having a go!" a gruffer voice protested. "Keep your damned britches on."

"Quick!" a whiny voice cried. "Someone's coming!"

The street lifted away, and I didn't fight as the Guilders

dragged me along. I glimpsed a streak of red splattered on the stones before shadows closed around me. As the shock began to wear off, pain assaulted my head and ribs in a steady, pounding throb.

Disorientation didn't stay anger flooding back in once more. I thrashed suddenly, dislodging one man with an errant kick. But there were too many. As soon as we were in the alley, they pressed me against the ground again. The choking stink of nightsoil and urine filled my nostrils, and though I tried to cry out, they seized my hair again and pressed my face into the grime.

"Flip her over!" the first Guilder commanded. "I'll have the first turn."

"Why?" the gruff voice responded. "Because you were stupid enough to let her hit you in the nose?"

"Because Kalindi would have you flayed and hung up if I let him know all the dirt I have on you. Now get her pants off — I don't want to smell this shit any longer than I have to."

"Do it yourself. I'm not going to undress your whores for you."

I clawed back my wits and tried to focus on my gut. With pain radiating from my side, it was the last thing I wanted to think about, but I strained to open myself to the Pyrthae. It was no use. I couldn't call upon the exercises of Eltris or Isidora. Magic remained as aloof as it always had.

The Guilders must have sorted out their problems, for I was flipped over and my belt pulled open. I thought I would pass out from fear, almost hoped I would. My trousers were just beginning to follow when the Guilders exclaimed again.

"Burning riot's passing!" the whiny voice called.

"Don't bloody call them over!" the gruff voice hissed. "They'll leave us be if we don't call attention to ourselves."

I knew then what I had to do. Hoping a broken rib wouldn't puncture my lungs, I drew in as deep of a breath as

I could. But before more than a screech could come out, a gloved hand clapped over my mouth.

"I don't think so," the first Guilder whispered in my ear, words dripping with venomous satisfaction. "No one's coming to save you."

I clamped my jaws down on his hand, but the leather of the glove was too thick to bite through. In vain, I wished desperately for someone to come. *Talan* — would he know? Was he watching out for me as he'd done before? *Eltris* — would she sense something was wrong and appear from nowhere?

But no matter who I thought of, I knew there was no chance of them finding me. I was out in the city on my own. The Guilder was right.

No one was coming to save me.

INTERLUDE II

CORIN

Corin sat in the dimly lit storefront, staring into the vase's shifting light. The smooth curve of the glass was dappled blue, the pyrkin inside shifting their hues and vibrance with each passing moment. Her sister might have seen something in the patterns, Kari having the gift for reading the signs. Corin had never envied her sister the ability, as it had always been as much a curse as a gift. But now she wished she could see as Kari did. She wished something, someone, could show her the right path forward.

It had been a full span since she'd betrayed Airene to keep Kari alive. A full span during which anything might have happened to her sister for her failure to complete her betrayal.

And what had Corin done to save her?

The old anger, ever simmering below her stony facade, bubbled up once more. Only now, it had nowhere to go. She couldn't push a cart until she was dragging with exhaustion. She couldn't spar with the other outriders of her company and thrash her rage away. She'd spent full spans in the freezing rain when training with her comrades, accepting abuse from the gods and the Forerider of their band without complaint. She'd endured starvation, thirst, and every hurt known to woman. But there'd always been a path to follow, an enemy to fight, an objective to accomplish.

It was the waiting that drove her mad. The waiting, and not knowing what she waited for.

Corin stood, fists clenched at her sides. She longed to reach out and dash the vase against the wall. But she was better than that. However much time passed didn't change what she was. She was an outrider, one of the *yaendul*. She didn't cede control to anger — not in the heat of battle, not in the middle of a glass shop. Picturing an icy cave, she found the frost's calm. For a time, she stood and imagined water dripping from the icicles that hung like teeth from the caves of Jolduun.

Calm slipped away as she realized which cave she'd imagined. The cave she'd hidden her sister and mother in before leaving.

The anger rushed back in with acid words. *Fool woman.* Why had she trusted the chief's word? Why had she believed his fear and honor would be enough to leave Kari and Mother alone? Why was she so stupid as to ruin everything she'd ever touched? She'd failed her fellow outriders when she refused to kill her sister for the sorceress she was. She'd failed her sister when, after two years, she couldn't raise the funds to bring her and their mother over. She'd failed Airene, who had given her a home when she'd had no other in this foreign city.

Corin blinked, eyes burning. She wouldn't shame herself even in private. She wouldn't let tears fall. *If saltwater is to fall, let it fall as sweat,* her Forerider had often said. Right he'd been then, and right it was now. She didn't deserve to weep. She didn't deserve pity, especially not from herself.

She had warning of Maesos's approach by the creak of his forge door opening.

"Corin? Are you still sitting out there? Come in, you'll catch a chill!"

The old glassblower emerged into the room. He'd been laboring in his forge down the hall as he often did, and his ragged work shirt was stained with sweat.

Even after three years in the city, she struggled to find the right words in the sea-tongue. "No, thank you. I'm going out."

"Out? The streets aren't safe now, my girl, not with evening fast fading. Even for you — or perhaps especially. Outlanders aren't especially well-loved, you know."

"I'll be fine."

Maesos squinted at her. "Very well. I can't stop you. But where are you off to so late?"

Corin looked aside and held her tongue.

After several long moments, the glassblower sighed. "I suppose it's none of my business. But take care of yourself, Corin. Anything can happen these days. I gave Airene my promise to watch over you, and I mean to keep it as much as I can."

She nodded, not meeting his gaze. She hoped he'd go away. She had one thing left to handle before she left.

But instead of turning away, he reached into his soot-smeared apron and began scooting around the displays of his glassware toward her. Corin fought down the anxiety that reared at his approach and made herself stand still.

Maesos pulled his hand out, holding up a stoppered vial. "Here. Take this."

Corin didn't reach out to take it, but only eyed the green, swirling mixture suspiciously. "Pyrkin?"

"Not just any pyrkin. Do you remember the special bolts you carted for me the day of the Despoina's trial? This is the last of that strain. I've sent for more, of course, but that may not arrive for full spans yet. Perhaps not before the Imperium does."

She stared at it, uncomprehending. "Why give it to me?"

The glassblower took her hand. Corin flinched, but didn't pull away.

If Maesos noticed her reaction, he didn't comment on it as he placed the vial in her hand. "For protection, Corin," he said gently. "Should you run into anything out there like we encountered in Vusumuzi."

Despite herself, Corin held up the vial. The green pyrkin pulsed with light, the patterns mesmerizing. Almost, she felt she could read what they tried to tell her. *Fool woman.* She covered the light with her hand and slipped it into the pocket inside her trousers.

"Thank you," she said quietly.

"Of course. Now come back safely. I'll need your help shouldering a delivery to Bazaar in the morn." His smile widened, but his eyes watched her carefully.

Corin looked away. The emotion behind his eyes was far too much like pity. "I will."

After a moment, he retreated back to his workshop. Corin waited until she heard the creak of his door closing before kneeling and reaching behind the counter. Her hand closed upon a bundled item. Drawing it out, she loosened the ties on the long knife, but didn't withdraw it from the bag. Should she be stopped by the city guard, concealing the weapon might save her from detainment. Not that she intended to let anyone detain her.

Clutching it, Corin swept her gaze around the shop, knowing she only delayed the inevitable. If this was the last time she was in this place, the last time she saw the glassblower, so be it. He'd shown her kindness, but her first loyalty was not to him.

She opened the door and strode out onto the evening streets.

〜

Corin padded softly through the growing shadows. She wasn't a small woman, and years had passed since she'd thrown aside her wolf-skin cloak. But still, she remembered the long instruction in stealth and misdirection. Then it had been for shadowed forests and frost-gnawed hills in the twilit winter. Here in the city of Oedija, surrounded by worn stone and rotting wood, one lesson remained.

If you must expose yourself to an enemy, never let them know you see them.

She didn't shift her gait when she detected her pursuers. They gave themselves away with small sounds: pebbles scuffed and sent tumbling from roofs; the swish of their clothes; hushed pants of exertion. Among the nearly empty streets, fleeing before the coming dusk mobs, even small sounds stood out. Perhaps they meant her harm. Perhaps they wondered what an outlander woman was up to walking the streets so late in the day.

It didn't matter. She couldn't afford to be tracked now. Corin feigned interest in something on the other side of the street and crossed, moving away from her pursuers. As soon as she came to a street crossing where they couldn't follow on rooftop, she took an alley off the wider road. Unless they were more skilled than she knew, she'd lost them for a time.

As a cartwoman, she knew only the main thoroughfares of Oedija that were wide enough to allow a cart through. But with the Pillars rising high from every deme, she didn't fear getting lost. It was who might find her that concerned her. She gripped her hidden knife tightly and strained her senses.

In the alleys, noises came from the destitute who had made their homes there. The mutters between huddled figures. Small scuffles for prized alcoves. Grunts of people taking comfort where they could. All of it set her nerves further on edge, for they disguised the noise any tails might be making. And, she admitted to herself, she feared these people themselves. She remembered all too keenly her helpless rage as the five boys had robbed her and Airene of all the coins they'd had. Had she then possessed a weapon, she might have killed them all, or attempted to. Even for an outrider against untrained lads, those odds were long.

A woman's muffled scream suddenly sounded from the alley she passed. Corin's hair stood on end. Despite herself, she glanced over. Four figures pressed down someone struggling in the dirt.

Her back tightened, her hands bunching into fists. But four on one — long odds, too long, when those men looked armed and dangerous. And she wasn't here for a stranger in an alley. It wasn't worth the risk.

Corin tightened her jaw and looked aside, pushing down the guilt and self-loathing. A bitter drink she was used to swallowing.

It wasn't long before the temple square came into view. Corin remained out of sight in the alley and scanned the area. Dusk had fully arrived. Two city guards stood at their post at the temple stairs. Corin crouched down to wait.

She didn't have to wait long. An acolyte exited the temple and, with an anxious look either way, scurried down the steps. As he neared the guards, they turned with stony expressions toward him. One extended a hand. The acolyte fished inside his robes for a moment before producing a bag. The guard took it with a grin and pocketed it. With a cursory look around, they sauntered away.

It was the same routine they'd followed the other two nights she'd staked out the temple. If the rest of the routine held, she had less than a quarter-turn before four acolytes arrived with a covered ark. Corin found the frost's calm. She was hard and cold as the age-old ice high upon Jolduun's mountainsides. When her worries had stilled and her focus had sharpened to a fine edge, she stood and strode toward the temple entrance.

No one stepped out to stop her. Sweeping her gaze

behind, she found no watchers. Yet in an exposed square of this size, there were many places from which she could be watched. Corin lengthened her stride and took the stairs to the entrance two at a time. Reaching the doors, she looked around once more, then slipped inside.

The corridors within were oppressive, especially for a woman of her height. Corin stifled her usual panic inside closed spaces and continued forward. Of the three passages, she took the left one, then followed it around a bend and down to the level below.

After a narrow stairway, a square, unlit room opened up. Corin backtracked for a torch, then returned and looked about. The room had been used for moneylending when she'd last visited; now, it lay abandoned. Misgivings rose in her, but Corin pressed on, moving aside the curtains that hung at the back of the room and slipping into the narrow passage beyond.

This corridor was lined with doors, and Corin moved slowly as she passed them. While she'd been to the prior room three times, she'd never been back here before. Always an acolyte had sat before the curtains, attending the ledgers for the debtors coming in. Corin had never been desperate enough to see what was beyond. Her pulse quickened. Would there be gold enough here to buy her sister's freedom?

A door behind her opened.

Corin whirled, ripping the knife free of its concealing bag and holding the torch up behind her. Her face was cast in shadow, while the stocky man in robes she faced was blinded. He cried out and flung up a warding hand.

"Who's there?" he demanded.

Corin considered him for a moment. Though he was not in his red robes, she recognized the priest who had given her the order to betray Airene. The same as who threatened her sister's safety. The frost's calm thawing before her anger, she drew herself up to her full height.

"Corin. A debtor."

"A debtor? Come back in the morning then." The priest's eyes darted to the steel glinting in her hand.

She released the blade and let it fall. As the priest watched it clatter to the floor, Corin stepped forward, seized him by the robes, and shoved him roughly against the wall.

The priest barely resisted, the futility of it plain in her strong grip. "What?" he sneered, his eyes wide. "Do you think to intimidate me?"

"Tell me where you keep my sister, and I will not kill you."

The priest's eyes widened and his mouth twisted. She could smell the fear in his sweat. "Kill me? If you do, you'll never recover your witch sister!"

She slammed him against the wall so hard his head bounced against the stone. His eyes rolled once, and a groan escaped him. Corin held him pinned there with one arm, the torch held close to his face, the heat uncomfortable and the light half-blinding.

"Tell me where you keep my sister," she repeated slowly.

"I don't know!" The priest's voice had grown shrill. "I never knew! I was just to deliver you the messages. I never knew their plans for her—"

"I need more information," Corin informed him. "Or I do not need you alive."

The priest blinked rapidly, his eyes wandering. She wondered if she'd shoved him too hard.

"I — The high priest! He will know. We must ask the high priest!"

"Where is the high priest?"

"In the sanctum."

Corin considered it. It was likely to be a trap. The acolytes with the ark could even now be entering the temple. Others might be guarding the sanctum. Yet she'd come this far. She couldn't leave without knowing how to get to her sister.

She stared hard at the priest. His eyes shifted away from hers. He wasn't telling her all, she was sure of that. She wondered if she should kill him even if he told the truth. But as much as she wished to make him pay for the wrongs he'd dealt her sister, for the wrongs he'd made Corin perform, he was more useful as a hostage. For now.

Using the weight of her body, she heaved him to the ground. The graceless man barely caught himself as he tumbled. While he scrambled to his feet, she retrieved her knife and swiftly stood over him again.

"Lead the way," she commanded him. "And remain silent."

The priest went before her, ascending up the narrow stairway and back to where the passages met. There they took the center passage, the hallway only a little wider than the last. The priest seemed to regain more of his injured pride with every passing moment. Corin considered reminding him why he'd lost it in the first place, but decided it wasn't worth the noise. They continued forward in silence, the priest only stopping to give spare directions. Her nerves were on end as she gazed into each shadowy corridor they passed. Nothing was ever there, yet she felt watched, as if invisible eyes peered out from the walls.

The passage slowly widened, then opened into a tall chamber. Cool, almost fresh air rushed around her as she entered. Corin shot rapid glances around the room. There were too many places a crossbowman could hide.

The priest suddenly burst into a run, dashing away from her. "Intruder!" he yelled. "Murderer!"

Corin cursed in her own tongue as she heeled in pursuit. "Stop!" she shouted. "Or I'll kill you!"

He ran slowly across the circle chamber, and she sprinted after him, thinking to catch him before he entered the next doorway. Before she could reach him, however, something moved out of the corner of her eye. Crouching and whirling around, Corin let the priest go as she took full stock of her new opponent.

Her blood ran cold as her eyes fell upon it.

It wasn't human. She wasn't even sure it was a spirit. It seemed little more than two long bands of shimmering cloth, crossed and intersecting as if around an invisible body, drifting slowly through the air as if gliding through water.

A Silk of Avvad, she realized. A daemon made manifest. One of the bound pyr that made the Imperium feared across the world.

An unfamiliar lust reared inside her. She suddenly wanted to throw herself upon the Silk. She wanted to be consumed in its folds. Before she realized it, she'd taken several steps toward it, the torch and knife fallen from her hands as she reached out. She wondered how soft it would be when she touched it.

The outrider in her reared, and she jerked back.

The Silk quivered, seeming to sense her resistance, then drifted forward quicker. The desire redoubled inside her, almost overwhelming her tenuous control.

Gasping for breath, she thrust a hand into her trouser's pocket. Her fingers closed around the vial secreted there. But even as she pulled it loose, she didn't know what to do with it. The pyrkin could dampen a warden's channeling. But what could it do against a daemon?

She was barely aware of pulling at the vial's stopper, her hands numb and weak. The Silk was mere paces away, the ends of its strands reaching toward her. Her skin shivered with anticipation.

Then it touched her, and her skin began to peel away.

18

NO ONE

We have told ourselves this before: We do what must be done. But by our hand, how will the worlds be forged anew? But by our wills, how will the gods be appeased?

All that is great comes with sacrifice. Better that the nation of our forebears falls than for these to be the final kingdoms the world knows.

- Tales of the Desolate, uncensored; 1092 SLP

As they finally pulled off my trousers, the cold, wet mud on my bare skin awoke a new depth of terror, vast and numbing.

Even as I squeezed my legs closed, I knew the futility of it, and was confirmed as their rough hands forced them apart again. My cries went unheard, their leader still having his hand clamped tight over my mouth. The dusk mob passed by the alley entrance. Enraptured with rage, none of them noticed the four figures hunched over in the alley. Or perhaps none of them cared.

I felt the fight dying inside me as a man kneeled between

my held-open legs. My mind fled my broken body, seeking any escape it could from its ending. And it would be the end, I had no doubt. I'd crossed Kalindi. I'd visited Talan and hadn't told the Undermaster of his location.

Now I'd pay the price.

I watched as if from a distance as the man untied his pants, his three companions standing around him. Time slowed, drawing out the pain of the moment so thinly I fooled myself into thinking I no longer felt it. It was all I could do to stare at the scene. I was a warden. Yet I couldn't stop the rape and death that were swiftly closing in on me.

I pulled further away. The man moved as slowly as if through honey. *Why prolong it?* I despaired at my thinning sanity. *Why make this moment linger?* I wanted it over with. I wanted all the pain to stop. I deserved at least that dignity, didn't I? I deserved to become nothing, no one.

I deserved not to exist.

I wrenched my gaze away, no longer able to watch. As I looked up, surprise dampened the despair. Around me, Oedija had become mirrored, a thin layer of emptiness filling the gaps between them. I glanced down again at the scene below. The Guilder kneeling before me had still not fully taken off his trousers. On the street next to us, the dusk mob flowed like a river of molasses.

I'd fled into the Pyrthae, and time had slowed. I'd channeled quintessence.

But I couldn't wrestle with what that meant now. My body was still below. I had to do *something*.

But if I was going to do anything, I'd have to work quickly. I stared at the men surrounding my body. What quintessence could do to them, I didn't know. I'd just have to try.

I threw my Pyrthaen self down at my assaulters, heedless of what the speed might do to me. I aimed first for the man kneeling before me, his pants halfway down his thighs, his desire open for all to see. Screaming soundlessly, I reached my ghostly hands forward as I crashed against him with all the force I could muster.

I lost myself.

Flashes of scenes filled me as I dove inside his mind. A boy skipping down a muddy street. A man beating a woman into the dirt floor of a house while a boy cried in the corner. A boy winning his first fistfight and feeling the glow of victory as the other boys clapped him on the back. The first whimpering girl he took in a dark, dirty alleyway.

Rage brought me back to myself. I wrenched myself apart and felt the Guilder's pain briefly, then awareness ceased as I broke the connection. Soaring back into the sky, I glanced down to see the man collapsed over my legs, senseless, even as my body lay prone, eyes staring into nothing.

I had to struggle hard to keep myself together. The foray into the man's mind had left me weak and strained. I didn't know if I could survive another attack. But seeing as I had no other weapons to fight with, I braced myself for a second dive.

Cold as I'd never experienced before pierced my arm.

Shocked, I tried wrenching myself away from whatever had seized me as I looked around. An amorphous cloud of flickering light hovered next to me. Only the hand thrust from it was distinguishable as human. But as its presence flooded me, I knew it was far from mortal.

I've been waiting, the daemon gloated. *Waiting for when your foolishness brought you here again. Now you are in* my *plane, human. You can't escape!*

I cried out wordlessly and tried to resist. To my horror, I was losing my shape. My feet and hands began to grow indistinct, melting into glowing mist. Memories leaked from me in wisps of light. I began to forget as they trailed away from me. *Who am I?* I thought desperately. *Who am I supposed to be?*

You are mine. That is all you ever need be again.
NO!

Denial surged within me, shutting out the comfort of the lie. I pressed against the pyr's foreign presence. Bit by bit, I forced it out of my awareness until I reached the boundaries of my body.

Then I wrenched my arm away and floated to the side.

The daemon didn't follow, perhaps stunned by what I'd done. I didn't wait to see if it would attack again but looked down, desperate for a way out. My body still lay prone beneath the Guilder I'd knocked unconscious, but no one else surrounded us. Not sparing a moment to wonder, I dove toward my body. I felt the pyr stirring behind me, but didn't turn as the world below rushed closer. Even as I neared, I didn't dare slow.

I crashed into my body.

As my mind melded with it, returning to its natural form, a flood of sensations washed through me. Everywhere hurt. I gasped and fought to keep above the pain. A ringing filled my ears, and my vision blurred.

But as strong as the agony was, my revulsion for the man draped over me was stronger. Summoning the last of my willpower, I heaved the limp man off of me and snatched up my trousers as I scampered back. My body shook as I pulled them back on, emotions twisting with searing heat inside me. I shoved the feelings down and dressed as quickly as I could, the mud smeared over my legs making the trousers stick and catch.

I kept a fearful watch as I dressed, expecting at any moment to see three hooded figures running down the alley toward me. Why the Guilders had left, I couldn't tell. Perhaps they thought both their companion and myself dead and didn't care enough to check. Or perhaps they feared something — magic, or a daemon — had gotten to us and feared for their own lives. It didn't matter. Either way, I had to flee before they gathered their courage and returned.

I turned toward the street. The dusk mob had passed, leaving the road clear for me to travel upon. But something made me hesitate still. I glanced back down at the unconscious Guilder. He still lived. I sensed I'd have felt it if I'd killed him by entering his mind, or whatever I'd done.

Before I could consider it further, my vision suddenly doubled. I reeled as the world tilted beneath me. As my eyes fluttered open, I saw the mirrored Oedija again hung down above me.

The daemon — he must have done something, pulled me out of my body! But as I looked around, I didn't see him, and I felt myself anchored firmly to the ground.

But *someone* watched me. Spinning around, I saw a shape floating in the strange light of the spirit realm. Eleven strands of gray cloth trailed from her robes, and her tilted eyes watched me with avid interest.

"Clepsammia," I muttered aloud, the name reverberating in my mind.

The gray spirit smiled at me. Something in her expression made me uneasy, as if she knew something I had yet to discover.

I stared up at her, waiting, expecting something to happen. My skin prickled with the danger. I knew Clepsammia, or whatever pyr took her form, might mean me harm. But I couldn't summon the will to flee. With my head craned back, I felt so tired all I could was stare up at the Goddess of Fate and wait.

Clepsammia drifted closer. Still wearing her eerie smile, she gestured, twisting around her hand with a finger extended like a spoon stirring a mug. I could only watch dumbly. Whatever she meant to say was beyond me.

When she rushed forward, I was barely conscious enough

to startle. Yet I couldn't escape. Clepsammia neared too rapidly.

She crashed into me.

I stumbled backward, but felt myself lifting up. Exhaustion fled before the invigorating fire that filled me. The fire in my ribs eased, and my head ceased to ache.

A moment later, the heat faded, but some of its effects lingered. Though pain crept back in, I had the strength to remain standing, and my ribs didn't threaten to double me over at every moment. The double-vision lingered though, and I looked up again at the gray woman floating through the Pyrthae.

Clepsammia put a finger to her smiling lips. Then the Pyrthae shredded once more out of existence.

I blinked as my vision returned to normal, and my mind returned to the present. The Guilder still lay at my feet. Dusk had taken hold, the afterglow of the sun fast fading. I'd escaped one trouble, but I had many others to evade. And though Clepsammia, or whoever that pyr was, had bolstered my strength, I felt it once more fast fading.

Yet despite the urgency, I looked down at the Guilder. Part of me wished to finish what I'd started. Fear, pain, and anger were a caustic solution burning as it wound its way through me. The knife Nomusa had given me still pressed against my back.

It would only take a moment, part of me whispered. *Just a quick slit across the throat. You've killed before. Why not end this despicable man's life? He would have raped and murdered you. Why leave him alive? He'll only do it to someone else.*

I wrenched myself away, sick at the hate roiling inside me. I couldn't do it. I'd never wanted to kill before, but then I hadn't had the choice. Now I did.

Besides, it was a small mercy. With the state that Oedija was in, another might easily kill him if they passed by. Or perhaps he'd never wake from the slumber I'd thrust upon him.

Before I could convince myself otherwise, I limped away and left the man to his fate.

~

I didn't collapse until I reached the bridge.

Amid the other hurts holding me in a half-conscious daze, the pain of my knees hitting the stone was barely noticeable. I'd only made it halfway across. Perhaps I was within a quarter-turn walk of the Aviary, but it felt like miles away. Terror and Clepsammia's gift of strength had driven me past the Laurel Palace's gate, but since I'd entered the Wreath grounds, I'd been losing the battle to exhaustion. My fight with the Guilders and the daemon had left me nauseous and weak. The ringing in my ears had faded to a whine, and my vision blurred around the edges. My ribs hurt with each breath. If the Guilders hadn't broken them, I guessed they were sorely bruised. My hair was matted with dried blood, and my head ached. That was the last time someone would yank me by my hair, I promised myself, though there was little fire in it. A deeper exhaustion assaulted me. Channeling quintessence had a cost, Eltris had said. Now I was paying it.

I clutched the stone railing to remain upright and stared through the balusters over the gently lit sea. The cloud moon glowed with violet light just below the clouds, while the two white orbs were lost somewhere above. Flashes of green showed where the radiant winds struggled to break free of the overcast sky. It would have been beautiful were I not drowning in pain.

The turning of my stomach suddenly became too much. I pulled myself above the railing and heaved out the little left in my stomach. My ribs were aflame with each retch. When it passed, I was nearly too tired to wipe at my mouth. I wanted to lie down where I was and fall into a deep sleep.

Only by berating myself did I stay upright. *Stupid woman. Stupid, stupid woman.* Why had I remained out so late? I'd known the dangers and ignored them. I'd grown careless, and it had nearly cost me my life. Sobs suddenly rose and choked me. The truth of how close a call it had been finally settled in. Never had I felt so alone. Before, others had intervened before I came to any real harm. Xaron, Nomusa, Corin, Talan — my friends had always been there to save me when I needed it most.

But this time, I'd been on my own. And now it was up to me to get myself home.

I forced myself back to my feet. *Just one more step,* I bargained with my weary body. *One more, then you can rest.* Slowly, painfully, the distance between me and the Aviary closed. When the moldy, lopsided building loomed from the darkness, tears of relief trickled down my face. Warmth and comfort were close. I was almost safe.

Reaching the door, I limped inside and looked around. A lone pyr lamp illuminated the room. Taking it in hand, I staggered down the hallway, dragged myself up the finch tower steps, and approached my room at the end. I wanted nothing more than to lie on my bed and lose myself in a long, deep sleep.

But as I cracked open my door, I saw a figure hunched on my bed and froze. It was too late. The person within, noticing the squeal of the door, stood swiftly and walked over to it. I made a pathetic attempt at yanking out my knife before the man's face came into the light.

"Talan," I murmured. My knees gave way to my sudden relief.

"Airene? Airene, are you alright?"

Talan hurried forward, wrapping an arm around my

waist. I cried out as he squeezed my injured side and weakly pulled at his arm. "Ribs," I gasped.

He cringed, then shifted his grip under my arms. Taking the lamp from me, he helped me inside. Once I'd settled onto the bed and lay down, he thrust the light next to my head, examining my wounds. I winced as he trailed the light down me, taking in every detail. Part of me was mortified for him to see me in this condition. The greater part would rather it be no one else.

When he finished, he set the lamp down and shut the door, then strode over and glanced out the window. At length, he returned and crouched beside my bed.

"Who did this?" he asked, voice stripped of emotion.

I hesitated. I recognized that tone. Men had died the last time Talan had spoken like that.

But I couldn't lie to him. The word came out in a whisper. "Guilders."

He suddenly looked away, his fists clenching so tightly his knuckles popped. Before I knew what I was doing, I shrank away from him. It was all I could do to sit there, dazed, as he faced whatever boiled inside him.

It took him a long time to turn back to me. A haunted look lingered in his eyes. "How can you ever forgive me?" he asked in a low, choked voice.

"Forgive you?" A laugh forced its way out from my raw throat. "It's not your fault."

He bowed his head. "It is, Airene. It is."

We sat in silence for a long time before he spoke again. "I've been waiting since it started to get dark. Ever since you visited the cave, something nagged at me. I didn't think of it at the time, considering everything else happening. But finally, I realized the danger you might be in. I came as soon as it was safe and waited. And when you didn't return, I began to worry."

"My fault," I mumbled. "It was my fault. I shouldn't have gone. I exposed you."

He just shook his head. "If you hadn't come to me, I would have gone to you. I couldn't have stayed away much longer."

The world suddenly lurched. Talan cursed under his breath as he steadied me, then gripped my hand. "How can I make you comfortable?"

My throat was dry, and my stomach settled enough to feel ravenous. But the thought of sending him away terrified me. I imagined Guilders climbing in through the window to finish what their fellows had started. I imagined invisible fingers clawing at my mind.

I clung to his hand. "Stay."

He took my hands and kissed them, heedless of the grime that covered them.

"As long as you like," he murmured.

When I awoke the next morning, Talan was gone.

Cool, gray daylight pressed in around me. I stared up at the ceiling, absently tracing the shapes of the lichen. Countless times I'd awoken throughout the night and only fallen back into an uneasy slumber once I'd seen Talan standing or sitting at the window, staring out into the darkness. Once, he hadn't been there, and I'd sat up despite my ribs, panic making it impossible to breathe. But he'd returned moments later, reassuring me he'd just been to the outhouse, that he was only gone for a moment. Still, sleep had been longer in coming.

But now that it was light, the mysterious man had once again disappeared, like a pyr that only haunted the night. As I stared up at the ceiling, I wondered if I'd imagined the entire sequence. I'd heard of people hitting their head and seeing things. If I hadn't imagined him, it was an odd coincidence that he'd been waiting for me, even with his explanations.

But when I glanced at the door, I saw a small scroll tied to the handle. My ribs spread fire through my body, and a moan escaped me as I sat up, but I resolutely rose to my feet and tottered to the door. Clumsy fingers, abused during the fight, fumbled to untie the string, then unrolled it and stared. The letters swam, and I had to squint to read the text.

I didn't want to leave you. But you won't be safe so long as Kalindi lives. I'll do what I must to protect you.

We shared far too little time. I should have moved sooner. But always, I have treasured what moments we had.

Care for yourself, my Finch.

The parchment trembled in my hand as I stared at it, torn between tearing it to shreds and carefully tucking it away for safekeeping. It was unsigned, but I knew which idiotic man had written it. *I'll do what I must to protect you.* The damned fool thought he could kill Kalindi. Never mind that the new Undermaster of Oedija had all of the Underguild's resources at his disposal. Hundreds were in his employ, many of them hardened killers. Even a warden like Talan couldn't overcome those odds.

I returned to the bed and gingerly lowered myself back onto it. Talan had to be stopped before he got himself killed. But who could find him in time? The only person I knew with that significant of reach was Wisp. But how might I reach her quickly?

The answer came a moment later. *Kelena* — she might have a way. I had to find our honorary Finch. Then, I promised myself, when Talan was safe, I could rest.

With a groan, I pushed myself from the bed once more and fetched my sandals. I still wore the dirty clothes from the day before, but I felt soiled by more than that. Stripping them away, I cleaned off what I could in my washing basin and put on a fresh tunic and trousers. Every movement sent pain cascading through my limbs. My ribs weren't the only thing to hurt — the burn on my shoulder had been rubbed bloody from the scuffle, and several of my toes were red and swollen from kicking the Guilders. My jaw ached and my head throbbed, particularly where they'd hit my skull against the ground. I was lucky to be alive, much less walking. Yet I couldn't help the frustration that it would all slow me down.

As I limped out of my room, though, pride slowly welled up in my chest. I'd survived. I'd survived four Guilders, and a daemon as well. A small smile crept onto my face. Perhaps I wasn't such a terrible warden after all. I didn't even care how god-struck that pleasure might make me seem.

But the smile faded as I remembered the helplessness, the pain. The man wrenching down my trousers and placing himself before me. I staggered and caught against the wall, overcome for a moment. I'd never felt so unclean. Even if I had time to visit the baths, even the secluded Conclave baths, I doubted I could undress. I wondered if I would ever feel comfortable naked again.

But Talan needed to be saved from his damned foolishness, and I was the only one who knew it. I heaved a sigh, girded myself against my ailments, and descended the stairs of the tower.

It didn't take me long to reason out that Kelena would be in the Conclave. With the eleventh Low Consul to be elected tomorrow, I knew she'd be there, politicking beside Nomusa. Ignoring the stares of the guards, I limped into the vast Conclave chamber and scanned the people scattered across it. It was far busier than I'd seen it since the trial, with nearly half of the Servants in attendance. The hushed conversations hummed with tension, like a hive of hornets stirring. I ignored it. At the moment, the election wasn't my concern.

I spotted Nomusa at the edge of a knot of Low Consuls. *The three Equalists*, I realized as I studied them. Feiyan's honor Kako stood at his mistress's shoulder in bright yellow robes. Even at this distance, he seemed to be smirking. Feiyan herself looked to be in intense conversation with my fellow First Verifier. I saw many other honors in the Conclave, but of Kelena, there was no sign. I rubbed at my eyes as my vision started to swim again.

"First Verifier."

I startled before I could catch myself, then turned to the voice at my shoulder. Kelena stood in a plain white robe, her face impassive.

"Kelena," I greeted her with relief. "I was just looking for you. I expected you to be with Nomusa."

"I cannot be. I've been deemed offensive to my former master's eyes, and a risk to our task." She didn't bother hiding her bitterness.

I needed to turn that around. I wracked my aching head for a way, but nothing would come to me.

Then Kelena seemed to notice my appearance. "Have you been attacked?" she asked, brow creasing as she looked me up and down.

I grimaced. "Is it that obvious?"

"There is blood in your hair. Are you well, First Verifier? I can send for a healer."

I tried not to think of what it said about my state of mind that I'd missed blood crusted in my hair. "Never mind that. I need you to find someone. He'll get himself killed if I don't stop him."

Kelena stared at me without answering. I had the uncomfortable feeling she was trying to decide if I was delirious or not. She glanced aside and made a small motion with her hand. I followed her gaze and saw an honor approaching.

Before I could say anything, Kelena asked, "Who?"

"Talan Wraithsbane." I winced at saying his epithet, but it was my best hope for identifying him. "Formerly a Guilder."

She nodded, her expression blank. "And if I find him, what message am I to convey?"

"Just tell me where he is. I'll deliver any message in person."

The honor stood by Kelena, and she leaned over to whisper in his ear. When she leaned away, he nodded and departed, making for the main doors. I watched his progress. "Is it that simple?" I asked in amazement. "You have but to whisper to an honor here, and word will spread?"

"No. He has gone for a healer. First Verifier, I will look into your missing Guilder myself, but you must rest with someone watching over you. Who can I call to look after you?"

It took me a moment to understand. "Rest? I don't need rest. We need to go after Talan."

"You're hurt, First Verifier. You need to wash those wounds before they corrupt, and you need rest. I won't hunt down Talan Wraithsbane until you return to your bed."

It was mutinous behavior, and I opened my mouth to lambast her for it, but stopped myself just in time. I swayed on my feet. Mud and who knew what else still crusted up my legs. My stomach turned uncomfortably, and my head pounded so that it was hard to think. I would have ground my teeth if my jaw didn't hurt too.

"Fine," I relented. "Maybe I do need to rest."

She nodded, a crease wrinkling in her brow. "Good. I will send someone to escort you to the baths first—"

"*No*. No baths."

Kelena looked exasperated. "You must clean yourself, First Verifier."

I looked down, unable to find the words to explain. "Please. No baths."

Her voice was gentle when she spoke. "Let me walk with you. But whom should I send for to stay with you while you rest? I will need to go after your former Guilder."

I turned my mind back into gear. Nomusa was too busy right now. Talan was obviously not an option. "Xaron. The Wreaths' Hilarion, if you didn't know."

She nodded. "Very well. He'll be sent for. Now come; walk with me."

After she pulled aside another honor with whispered instructions, we followed her out of the door. I suspected Kelena still meant to bring me to the baths, and I wasn't sure what I would do when we arrived. I knew I should clean myself. But to expose myself again... It seemed beyond what I could endure.

We were quiet until we'd left the guards behind and walked along the promenade. Only the wind and the calls of seabirds surrounded us.

Kelena didn't look at me as she spoke. "Honors are considered property by some of their masters, and we are often used as property. Our labor doesn't belong to us, nor the fruits of it. And some masters even take away the rights of our own bodies."

My stomach turned. I risked a glance at her, and saw her expression had grown stony.

"Did Iason...?" I hesitated, unable to ask the question.

"Rape me? No. His sons did."

Dizziness passed over me again. She said it matter-of-factly, as if it were an ordinary occurrence. For her, I supposed it was. I suddenly felt like I'd been false. I hadn't actually been violated. Even now, could I imagine what that was truly like?

"I'm sorry," I said lamely.

"I don't mention it for pity, First Verifier. I tell you to say that I have felt what you feel, many times before. And in the end, you must take the bath."

"They didn't rape me. They didn't get that far."

From her expression, I wasn't sure she believed me. "All the more reason to bathe and be rid of their filth. Will you wash it away, First Verifier?"

I almost felt silly. The feeling didn't lessen the discomfort, but it made it somewhat more bearable. "Yes. I'll wash it away."

Kelena smiled a smile that went no deeper than her skin, then led me into the baths.

19

ELECTION

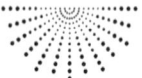

I am not an evil man, nor a vengeful one. I am a man trying to forge the world anew. I am the man who does what is necessary for all to survive.

- Tales of the Desolate, uncensored; 1092 SLP

Kelena saw me through my bath, then escorted me back to the Aviary. Guilt wracked me for keeping her from hunting down Talan, but I couldn't form the words to send her away. It was bad enough to sit on a bench and let her fellow honors rub olive oil into my skin and wash my wounds. I couldn't send away the one person who brought me some comfort in that moment.

Xaron waited at the Aviary's door. Upon seeing us, he ran over and immediately began to fret over me. "The healer's inside. Airene, what happened? Who did this? And when?"

I answered his flurry of questions as best I could, though my tongue and mind were growing sluggish. The pain, kept at bay by urgency and awkwardness, swept back in. I took shallow breaths and told him everything — all except how near I'd come to being violated. He was enraged enough as it was, and I had no wish to recount it.

Kelena left us at the door, and after I'd thanked her as sincerely as I could, she set off toward the Conclave gates. Xaron helped me to my bed, where the healer met us and began her examination of my wounds. I was grateful it was a woman inspecting me. A stranger touching my bare skin was bad enough; I doubted I could stand it if the healer had been male. The healer made me breathe in deeply with my tunic raised while she watched. Running her hands over my wounds, she determined my ribs weren't broken, but only bruised.

"There will be pain, but you must not breathe shallowly," she told me. "That will only foul your humors further."

My head seemed as fine as it could be, considering the circumstances, though the healer warned me I might feel strange for four spans still. For the pain, she provided a poppy tincture and instructed me to drink it that very moment. At first, I refused. Part of me wished to keep my wits about me. Another part feared Guilders coming to seek revenge. But at her and Xaron's insistence, and as my pain continued to wear on me, I relented. The healer left Xaron and me then, promising to check back later that day.

I settled down and blinked blearily. Sleep already had a grip on me. But I couldn't rest yet.

"Xaron."

He kneeled next to my bed. "Yes?"

"Talan is in danger. He…" I closed my eyes, fighting off a wave of drowsiness. "He's going after Kalindi. Fool man. He's going to try to kill him."

"Bold," Xaron breathed. "But after what they did to you, I almost want to follow him."

"You can't." I took his hand in mine, my sense of touch already half-numbed. "You have to stay and watch over me."

He clasped my hand with both of his. "Gladly."

Oblivion edged in, but once again I fought it off. "Xaron?"

"Yes?"

"Are you in love with Isidora?"

His grip tightened on my hand, then loosened as he let out a laugh. "Maybe," he admitted, almost sounding surprised at his own admittance.

I gave a soft snort. "Only you wouldn't know."

"Oh? Then you know if you love Talan Wraithsbane, do you?"

A smile found its way onto my face. "Perhaps."

"You're impossible. Go to sleep."

Releasing my resistance, I did.

I didn't fully awaken until the next morning, though I rose several times throughout the evening and night to take care of necessities. Xaron stayed by me the entire time. Once when I awoke, he was humming to himself and channeling a line of flames into a circle. Another, he was pacing the room.

"You can go," I'd told him groggily.

He'd stared disdainfully at me. "Go to sleep."

Once more, I obeyed him.

When I awoke the final time, birds called outside. The sky was overcast, but bright enough to dazzle my eyes. Xaron sat slumped in a chair he'd dragged in from downstairs, his chin to his chest. I winced at the crick in his neck he'd no doubt wake up with.

For a moment, I was content to lay back. Pain needled my sides and head, though it was still dulled by the poppy tincture. I feared it would return when I rose. But suddenly, I remembered what today portended, and couldn't stop from sitting up with a groan.

Xaron awoke at the sound, sitting bolt upright and staring around in alarm. "What's going on?"

"The election. When is it?"

He blinked at me. "Election?"

"For the Low Consul, cotton-head."

He rubbed a hand over his eyes. "Ah. Right. I think it's at the fourth turn of the morning."

"Fourth?" I stared out the window. "It has to be nearing the third, don't you think?"

He shrugged. "Either way, I guarantee Nomusa has tied herself in a knot by now. You didn't wake during her visit yesterday. She's worse off than you in some ways."

"She stopped by?" Sympathy and guilt rose in me at the thought of my friend. I'd seen little of Nomusa of late, and done nothing to ease the burdens she carried for our Order.

"Briefly. She rested for a few turns, then rose to work again, writing finch messages to send come morning. I've never seen her work so hard, Aire. She's almost a different person."

"No, not different. Just the person she was always meant to be." I glanced at him. "Before your corrupting influence, that is."

He cocked a smile. "If anything, *she* corrupted *me*."

I swung my legs off the bed. I'd slept in my clothes, so only the sandals remained to don. But I stared at them balefully across the room. Bending over to lash them to my feet didn't promise to be a pleasant task with my ribs.

Xaron saw my look and rose. "I can get them."

"I can put on my own sandals," I protested.

"But not helping would be like neglecting to flip over an upturned turtle. Allow me."

When we'd finished readying ourselves, we walked across the grounds to the Conclave. The hubbub could be heard from outside the great cracked doors. I clung to Xaron's arm as we entered and stared around us.

Once again, around half of the Servants were in atten-dance, along with their staffs of clerks. With honors moving between them and providing refreshments, it almost seemed the Conclave of old, but for the ruined dome above. I tried to find heart in it. But I knew a functioning demotism wouldn't be enough to save us from Famine, nor Avvad. I doubted it could even save us from ourselves.

We spotted Nomusa, but as she appeared in the midst of an animated argument, we didn't venture closer. The thin man near her, however, looked up and saw us, then began to ascend the curved stairs around the outside of the Conclave chamber toward us.

"I'm glad to see you up, First Verifier," Jaxas said as he neared. "I'd feared the worst when I heard what happened." He was dressed in plain robes today, and his eyes seemed on the verge of disappearing within the dark circles around them.

I let go of Xaron's arm to stand on my own, even though it taxed my paltry strength. "I couldn't stay in bed for this. How are we doing?"

"I'm not allowed to take sides," the Archon reminded me with a wry smile. "But if I were, I'd be happier to be an Equalist. The contest is close, but your fellow First Verifier seems to have swayed the critical vote. If only the election could occur now."

I studied him and his bowed weariness. "And you. Are you content to return to being a moderator rather than a voice on the Council?"

All traces of humor disappeared from his expression. "Do I have a choice?"

I shrugged. "You always have a choice."

He studied me for a long moment. "Have you had any word of the Despoina?"

I blinked, taken aback by the abrupt change in conversation. "I've been resting in the Aviary. I'm not liable to hear many whispers when I'm unconscious."

He bowed his head and stepped closer. "It's a vain hope.

Still, I must ask. Airene, if you know anything of her, please, tell me. I've not had word of her since last night."

"Last night?" I dredged up a vague memory. "Wasn't she with Komo last night?"

He nodded gravely. "They met in the Laurel Groves. I attended as well."

"Very romantic," I observed wryly.

"Leia did not appear pleased either. She stared away from the Heir much of the time, often ignoring his words to make some idle comment of her own." He shook his head. "I don't know my cousin anymore, Airene. I fear we're losing her to whatever inner daemons plague her."

He spoke with the familiarity we'd gained before the trial. That familiarity, and the things I knew that he didn't, emboldened me to speak.

"I don't think we'll gain her back, Jaxas. I think we have to move forward anyway, and act in spite of it."

"Act in spite of it," he murmured. "What do you mean?"

I considered my next words. "Komo's advisor gave me a book two nights ago. I stayed up all that night to read it."

The Archon studied me silently, waiting.

"It was called *Tales of the Desolate*. I'd read another version of it, but that one had been censored. It didn't have the words of Yama himself in it."

Xaron shifted next to me, but it was Jaxas who muttered softly, "Vusu's words. From when he first began serving Famine."

"Exactly. And what it says… I don't know how he's lasted this long. Famine eats at his mind, Jaxas. Between that and the wound I dealt him, he won't have the strength to hold on much longer."

"I'm afraid I don't understand. Why would we want him to?"

"Because even though he's using Famine for his own gains, Vusu is also holding him back from the world. If he stops, then we will have the daemon god himself to contend with, unbridled."

The Archon rubbed at his temples. When he pulled his hands away, he looked older and more tired than I'd yet seen him. "First we wish to defeat him, now we wish to keep him alive. What's the right course, Airene? What can we do against this threat?"

I little knew myself. But I answered the only way I could. "What we have been doing. Preparing. Learning what we can. Struggling on."

He shook his head. "It's not enough. How could it ever have been enough?"

"It has to be." Another thought occurred to me. "Jaxas, if the ruling Wreath somehow becomes unfit for service to the demotism, what happens? Does another take over?"

He didn't seem surprised by the question. "They serve until death, Airene. Taking the Evergreen Wreath before then is insurrection."

The gargantuan bell tolled from the dais. Even broken, the deep sound resonated throughout the chamber. Jaxas looked toward it.

"The fourth turn of the morning," he murmured. "It's time." He glanced back at me, then walked away without another word.

"Cheery conversation," Xaron observed.

"You'd think you'd be more worried about the end of Oedija."

"What's the use?" The smile slipped from his face as we watched Jaxas and the Low Consuls enter the small, cave-like room behind the dais. "Those gray-heads decide our fates, don't they?"

The eleven Servants voting for the new Low Consul had lined up at the door. The first of them filed through.

"Only if we let them," I said. "Come with me. I need to talk to someone else."

Komo and Nkosi stood in the far corner of the chamber, silently observing the proceedings. Except for Nomusa, they were the only Bali there, and their dark olive skin and ornamentations made them stand out like toucans among pigeons.

Xaron and I approached and bowed. "Heir Komo. Advisor Nkosi," I greeted them.

"First Verifier Airene." Komo smiled genuinely, though it remained small. The worried creases between his brow didn't smooth. "Or may I abandon your title?"

I returned the smile. "Call me what you like."

"'Little finch' is what she prefers," Xaron said confidentially.

Komo laughed softly as I arched an eyebrow at my friend.

"I think I'll stick with Airene," the Heir said. "What can I do for you?"

"I wanted to speak with you about your meeting with the Despoina last night."

His expression fell. "Ah. What do you wish to know?"

From his reaction, it seemed Jaxas had been accurate in his account. "Did it go well?" I asked lightly.

"No," Nkosi broke in. "It did not. As you well know, First Verifier."

"Nkosi," Komo rebuked him. "But he does have a point. It is no more than we expected after our earlier discussions."

I felt Xaron looking at me questioningly, but I ignored him, only half-feigning a wince from a stab of pain in my side. "Did she seem distracted by anything in particular?" I pressed.

"Not by any one thing, but by everything. The only time she carried a real conversation was with one of my guards."

My stomach sank. "Do you mind if I ask which one?"

Nkosi looked at me sharply, but Komo just cocked his head. "His name is Bhaka. I believe he stood guard when you visited the other night. Why do you ask?"

"First Verifier," Nkosi said, his tone edged with reprimand, "if you know something, it would be better to tell us now."

I'd been too direct. But I knew I couldn't reveal what I suspected yet, even if it damaged the trust we'd built. "I don't know anything. But if I find something out, I'll be sure to tell you."

The advisor eyed me suspiciously, but Komo, good-hearted lad that he was, just nodded. "I trust you will," he said.

The dais bell tolled again. As the gathered crowd quieted, I glanced down at the platform and saw Jaxas leading the Low Consuls up its crumbling steps. My stomach lurched. I found Nomusa standing behind the platform, her expression stony. I felt her nervousness as if it were my own. Behind the Low Consuls followed two unfamiliar Servants. When they moved to stand slightly before the Council, I assumed they were the candidates for the office.

As Jaxas stepped forth, the bow in his shoulders even more pronounced than before, my stomach sank. I already knew what was coming.

"In a vote of six to five, the eleventh seat of the Demos Council has finally been filled," he spoke, only audible from the echo of the chamber. "Rusen of Bazaar, if you will speak the oaths and accept the responsibility, we welcome you as a Low Consul of Oedija."

Most of the gathered people clapped loudly, while the rest remained silent. The man who stepped forward nodded solemnly. He was tall, thin, and obviously Avvadin from the cloth wound around his head.

I stared, scarcely able to believe it. We'd lost. The Preservists controlled the Demos Council.

My gaze wandered to Nomusa and found her leaning against the wall, looking dazed. The sight of her pained me more than the results. I knew how she'd struggled to win this, and still, she'd failed.

As Jaxas finished taking Rusen's oaths of fealty to Oedija, Orhan stepped forward from the others. "As the Council is finally complete, we have many things to decide in these tumultuous times," he declared. "You may expect our pronouncements soon."

Dread filled me at the words. What new obstacles would Orhan put before us? Suddenly, I felt the same weight Jaxas had shown to feel earlier pressing down on me. At every turn, a new challenge presented itself. When would they stop? When could Oedija face its enemies with its full strength and not rip itself apart?

Xaron gripped my arm. "Airene. The honor, Kelena. She looks frenzied."

All concern for the election swept from my mind as I followed Xaron's gaze. Kelena hurried toward us, much of the composure she typically bore cast away. Fear made me almost dizzy. I knew what news she must bring, given the task I'd set before her. I almost turned away, not wishing to hear the words, but her address arrested me.

"First Verifier," she said, panting slightly as she stopped before us. "There's been an attack. Seekers at the Acadium, in the Archmaster's tower."

"The Manifest attacked Kyros?" I asked blankly. Despite the direness of the news, I thought only of one thing: this wasn't about Talan; he wasn't dead, not yet. Relief washed through me.

Kelena's eyes were wide and panicked. "I didn't know this was coming. I didn't notice any increase in activity. Perhaps they know not to trust the honors."

I thought over it quickly. "If Ariston leads the Manifest, he likely would know. We'll look into it. But did you hear anything of Talan?"

"No, not yet." Kelena's expression made it evident which

she thought was the more important of the tasks. I had to bite my tongue as my temper flared up. Even knowing that she was probably right, it didn't change the fact that I wished I could hunt him down myself.

"We'd better go," Xaron said. "I'll fetch Nomusa."

I worried still for Talan, but I had no choice but to nod. There was nothing more I could do for him. Considering all of our other concerns, I had to accept that. Xaron slipped through the crowd toward Nomusa.

"Kelena, come with me," I said. "I have to tell someone else the news before we go to the Acadium."

We found our way through the crowd up to the dais. The Low Consuls had begun to file back into the chamber, and we had to hurry the last steps to catch Jaxas before he entered after them. I hissed at the pain in my ribs as we jostled people out of the way, but didn't slow as we neared.

"Archon Jaxas!" I called out breathlessly, hoping my words weren't lost in the hubbub of the Servants. The noise had increased following Orhan's announcement. "Wait a moment!"

Jaxas slowly turned back. His eyes were flat and cold. "Yes, First Verifier?"

I leaned forward, hoping others wouldn't overhear. But there was no time to find a more private place.

"There's been an attack at the Acadium. If Kelena is correct, Kyros's tower has been assaulted by Seeker wardens. I'm going over there to see into it now."

He didn't show any surprise or horror, but considered me with the same flat stare. "They've attacked again," he repeated. "And we didn't anticipate it."

I winced. "Yes. But we are still—"

"I'm not chastising you. I'm seeing a piece to a puzzle I've long stared at, but never known how to place. It is coming together now, whether I will it or not." He stared at me with sudden sharpness. "We must do what we must. Is that not what you said to me, Airene?"

"Yes, it is," I answered uneasily.

He nodded as if to himself. "Go. Learn what you can. Anticipate what must be done next. I'll meet you at my solar when the Council is finished here." He turned to Kelena. "Kelena, can you send an honor to Tribune Timon? Tell him to bring his charges here to see me."

As Kelena nodded, I looked between them with confusion. Jaxas seemed familiar with Kelena's network. Had it just been what we'd told him when we'd tried to make her a Verifier? Or had Nomusa informed him of Kelena's informal status as part of the Order? Even though he was our ally, I would have thought she would run such a decision by me first.

Jaxas looked back to me. "I'll see you soon," he said, then abruptly turned away.

"Jaxas, wait."

The Archon paused, then turned back expectantly. "Quickly, now."

The words spilled forth. "I think I know where the Despoina is. Or rather, whom she's with." I nervously scanned the crowd until I found Komo and Nkosi standing out of earshot. "I fear one of Komo's guards has seduced her. There have been signs of it. I thought you should know in case this danger spreads wider than we know and she needs protection."

Jaxas stared at me for a long moment in the midst of the hubbub. In that motionless gaze, I saw anger flaring to life. The smile that pulled at his lips was more fearsome than a snarl.

"Protection?" Acid dripped from the word. "But she's already accompanied by a guard."

Without another word, he turned into the Council room.

I stared after him. But as Xaron and Nomusa approached,

I turned from the closing door and put it from mind. Time enough to think on it later.

Seeing the defeat in Nomusa's posture, I winced. "You alright?"

She stared woodenly at me. "If there's been an attack at the Acadium, we'd best look into it. After all, we're not much use here, are we?"

Not knowing what else to do, I nodded, then led the way out of the Conclave, one limping step at a time.

20

THE BROKEN TOWER

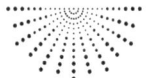

Yet if I thirst for their blood, if I hunger for their spirit, does that stain the righteousness of our task?

- Tales of the Desolate, uncensored; 1092 SLP

T hey came in broad daylight?" Xaron asked with eyebrows raised.

"Bold, I know."

My answer was weary. We'd only just left the Conclave gates, but already, I felt my body tiring. As the morning went on, each breath came more painful than the last. But I was determined not to return to bed, nor to let fear stop me from leaving the Conclave grounds. I'd wasted too much time already.

I glanced at Kelena and Nomusa, but both were silent. "What do you think?" I asked Nomusa.

She shrugged, offering nothing else. I let it be. All she needed was some time to nurse her pride; she'd be back to normal soon, I was sure.

The walk to the Acadium was tense and quiet. It couldn't be anything else with Seeker wardens at large again. If they dared to attack Kyros in broad daylight, who knew where they might appear next. The shadow of the Underguild lay over me as well, and I peered into every passing alley, expecting to see blue tatu glowing in the darkness. If the Guilders didn't already know I was alive, it wouldn't be long before word spread. And Kalindi wasn't one to leave loose threads, to hear Talan tell it.

Talan. I took as deep of a breath as I could manage as a different sort of pain spread through me. That damned fool had better take care of himself.

A touch on my arm. I glanced over to see Xaron's brow creased with concern. "Are you alright?"

"Fine. Just a moment of weakness."

His gaze lingered, but he looked away without another word.

By the time we reached the Acadium gates, my misery had augmented. Agony crawled up both legs and pounded in my head, to say nothing of how each labored breath burned in my chest. I feared even the journey back to Laurel Palace might prove too much for me. If only Clepsammia, or whoever wore her guise, could bolster my strength now.

As the Acadium gates came into sight, the changes there jolted me back to alertness. The guards at the gate had tripled, and some of them wore no armor, but only leather and heavy cloth. *Those trained to fight wardens,* I assumed. By wielding no metal, they insulated themselves against the devastating effects of magnesis upon ordinary soldiers. I'd rarely seen the Acadium's premier guards. Usually, they only emerged if there was an incident with a warden on the campus, and that was a rare enough occasion to warrant few sightings. They eyed us mistrustfully as we approached, particularly Xaron, upon observing his Hilarion clothes. Yet when Nomusa and I showed our Finch medallions, they waved us through.

The campus was more disorderly. Acadians milled about

the paths, walking in knots and muttering among themselves. They, too, looked upon our group with suspicion and passed quickly by. These were the same people who would have held a pleasant conversation with a stranger only a few days before. I shook my head and continued on.

We saw signs of damage from the Archmaster's tower long before arriving. The tall spire, black against the gray sky, spouted dark smoke. Kyros's rooms had burned; perhaps they still did. I wondered how our quarrelsome warden had fared. Little as I liked him, we could ill afford his death.

Seeing the tower again awoke a new dread in me. Twenty-two floors it rose, if memory served. I didn't know if I could manage them in my condition. But I knew I had to try.

A small crowd had formed at the base of the tower. I only recognized one among them.

"Isi!" Xaron called. He pushed through the crowd to embrace the Acadian. She returned it with a weary smile. Some small, protective part of me found it strange to see another woman being so familiar with him, but I pushed it down as Nomusa, Kelena, and I followed after him.

"You came," Isidora said as we reached her.

"Of course." He looked her up and down, and I saw what he must have: dust and soot coated her clothes. "Did you fight them?" Xaron asked apprehensively.

She shook her head. "I arrived afterward and helped put out the fire."

"Was anyone killed? Anything in particular damaged or taken?" I broke in.

"It's hard to say. It's still a mess up there. You're welcome to see for yourselves." She eyed me with a skeptical look.

Was my weakness so obvious? But I didn't need her doubts on top of my own. I nodded at Isidora and walked inside unassisted. Behind, Xaron made his farewells as Kelena and Nomusa followed me.

As I set my foot onto the first stair, Nomusa stopped me with a touch. "You don't have to go up."

"I do," I responded. "I visited his quarters before. I might notice something amiss."

"Not likely from one visit. And look at you. You're barely standing, and this tower is twenty-two circles tall."

I was uncomfortably aware of Kelena watching us and pulled Nomusa closer. "What else am I going to do? Ariston and Vusu aren't going to be content with biding their time much longer. If they're confident enough to attack Kyros, who knows where they'll strike next. I have to know why they came here. It might help us anticipate what they'll do next."

"Even still, you have limits, Airene. Don't push past them."

I closed my eyes, trying not to sway as I did. I was exhausted to the bone. I wasn't at all sure I could make it. If only I'd mastered channeling, I might be more assured. Then I'd be able to bolster my strength with kinesis, as Xaron sometimes did. Or perhaps I could will my body to heal, as Komo was able to do, and as I'd done during my first, long sleep.

But there was no use in wishing for rain. I had to make the decision and stick with it.

I drew in a deep breath and winced. "I'm going. I'll take it slow. I'll rest at every circle. But I'm going up."

Nomusa looked at me with a mixture of bemusement and fondness. "You always keep going," she said quietly. "How do you do it?"

I shrugged, a flush creeping up my neck. "I can't rest when something needs doing, that's all."

She wrapped an arm around me, gingerly avoiding my ribs as best she could. "At least let me help."

It took a full turn to reach the top of Kyros's tower. Xaron and Kelena went ahead to confirm we could enter inside, though I wasn't about to wait for permission after the torment I endured ascending. True to my word, I rested at each circle, and not of my own volition. Pain unlike anything I'd experienced before cascaded through me, and I was drenched in sweat. I hoped I wasn't doing permanent damage to my body. But I couldn't turn back. I had to see the Archmaster's chambers.

Finally, with Nomusa supporting me every step of the way, we arrived. I tried to hide my wheezing breaths as we entered within the scorched doorway.

The scene soon made me forget my suffering. Isidora had been right; it was difficult to tell if anything had been targeted, as the whole room was a wreck. The expensive carpets were burned and smeared with soot. The seared tapestries curled in on themselves like sun-withered grass, still trailing smoke. The pyr lamps, once levitating, were overturned on the floor, white pyrkin gleaming where it was strewn over carpet and stone. Bookshelves were broken, smashed in as if by a gigantic hammer. Books were scattered and torn all across the room. Four Acadians moved about the chamber and picked these up, carefully flipping through the pages as they evaluated them for damage.

Despite the open rent in the ceiling that admitted the cool air outside, the room was as hot as Maesos's forge. Red coals still smoked near the opening. I tried not to cough, fearing the pain it would bring.

Xaron and Kelena stepped from the corner where they'd been waiting. "Pretty bad, huh?" he murmured.

I nodded distractedly. My gaze moved to the cabinets of strange trophies Kyros held and saw the glass smashed in and the items missing. I tried to remember what had been there before. *An empty glass orb. A red mask with the aspect of a daemon. A white, wooden dagger—*

I drew in a sharp breath, then hissed it out painfully.

Nomusa took my hand. "What is it? Is it the smoke?"

I shook my head, wondering if I should say what I

339

suspected in front of Kelena. I decided to risk it. "I think I know what they were after. What they took."

My companions' eyes widened.

"What is it then?" Xaron exclaimed.

"A wooden knife as white as bone. It would look like a child's toy."

Nomusa raised an eyebrow. "A wooden knife?"

"Just help me search for it, in case I'm wrong, or they missed it. I'll explain later."

"Perhaps we should ask him first." Kelena nodded to the figure standing in the center of the room.

Kyros Brighteyed, clad in soot-smeared bed robes, glared about his chambers, his eyes once again filled with Pyrthaen light. "Leave that one!" he snapped at an Acadian as she picked up a book.

The young woman startled and dropped it, then scurried to the next one.

Kyros seemed to notice us as our gaze fell on him. His eyes lingered on me. "What are you doing here?" he growled. "Just can't keep your beak out of anything, eh?"

Nomusa spoke first. "It's our duty to investigate, Archmaster Kyros."

The man snorted. "Then figure this out. Seven of those 'Thae-damned Seekers showed up, tried to kill me, then left. Why'd they do that?"

I swept my gaze over the room. "They did a fair deal more than that." I pointed at the smashed display wall. "What did they take?"

The Archmaster' scowl deepened. "Everything they didn't break. As they should — that was a valuable collection of artifacts." He waved a hand. "Now get out. We're trying to clean up around here."

"I think I need a short rest from the climb," I said lightly. With a parting smile that felt more like a grimace, Nomusa helped me over to sit on a trunk, Xaron and Kelena following.

Kyros's eyes stayed on us for a moment before he turned to bark at another Acadian. I didn't doubt he could eavesdrop if he wanted to, but I wouldn't be saying anything he didn't already know.

"He's not telling the full truth," Kelena said quietly. "I think he knows what they wanted."

Xaron nodded. "According to what Kyros told Isi, the Seekers seemed surprised the Archmaster was in. Kyros thought it had to do with him being up and about again — they probably didn't expect him to still be in his room late in the morning. She also said that he didn't understand why they'd taken what they had."

"Did she say what that was?"

He shrugged. "She didn't know. Maybe it was that knife."

"But why the knife?" Nomusa asked. "What use is it?"

I glanced at Kyros, but I was thinking about Kelena. Perhaps it was past time she knew the truth.

"I think it has something to do with Famine," I said quietly.

All three of them stared at me. I thought I saw Kyros startle as well.

"I read about it in an ancient tome, *The Seeds of Famine*, written just after the Lighted Passage. To defeat Famine, a knife like that was used to… sacrifice someone."

"Sacrifice someone?" Nomusa's brow furrowed. "Like kill them?"

I nodded.

She shook her head. "What good would killing them do?"

"Perhaps it was an artifact with some latent power. Talan spoke of a chalice once that could pour any substance from it. And there are stories of other magical artifacts."

"But that's just it — they're stories."

"And so was Famine, until he wasn't."

"Airene might be right," Xaron broke in. "I know the Qao Fu wear veils that are made partly by channeling to keep out the sand."

"The *ikoz* are bound by a certain cloth," Kelena spoke softly. "And there are legends among our people of items that brought men and women in contact with the Fates."

"The Fates?" Xaron queried.

"The spirits of death among my people, the Kalthuae." She smiled thinly. "We honors have become well-acquainted with the Fates ever since our enslavement."

An uncomfortable silence fell between us, broken only by the shuffling of the Acadians around the room and Kyros's reprimands.

"We should head back down," Nomusa said, her expression neutral. She glanced at me. "Are you well enough to try?"

I nodded, though I felt far from well. The thought of all those stairs sent chills of dread through my body.

But before I could rise, another figure emerged from the stairwell and threw back her hood. I stared in astonishment as Eltris irritably brushed back the wispy gray hairs that sprang into her face and strode toward Kyros.

The Archmaster looked surprised as well as displeased. "My rooms have become a spectacle, have they? Birds and bird-watchers settling the place! What are you doing here, Eltris?"

"What did they take?" The Master Augur spoke as if Kyros were her subordinate, rather than the reverse.

His face purpled with rage. "What gives you the right to—?"

"It's far past time for that, Kyros. Time is of the essence. Did they take it?"

The Archmaster's glowing eyes flickered toward us. Eltris looked around for the first time and visibly startled. Her expression darkened as she saw me sitting behind the other three.

"What are you doing here?" she demanded.

Xaron stammered a greeting, but I spoke over him. "What do you suspect they took?"

"Never mind," Eltris snapped. She looked back to Kyros. "I expect an answer momentarily. Don't block me out as before or I'll break down your barriers. And that won't be pleasant for either of us."

Turning on her heels, the augur made swiftly for the door.

My head spun. *The bone-white dagger* — that had to be what Eltris meant. But did that mean she knew what it was used for? And if she knew, who else might have knowledge of it?

"Eltris, wait!" I rose and lurched after her, my legs nearly buckling beneath me. Xaron and Nomusa caught me and held me upright.

The Master Augur whirled back. "Stop this now, girl! Are you still so blind? Don't you see what will result from your foolish pride?"

"Pride?" I could scarcely believe her words. "You think I act out of *pride?*"

"Of course it's pride! And pride will be your undoing." She turned abruptly to leave.

"I'm not done with you!" I said angrily. My ribs ached, but I pushed through the pain. "Why did you visit Linos and not tell me?"

Eltris paused and glanced back. "It's none of your concern."

"Damned if it's not! He's my brother!"

"Not anymore. He's empty, girl. He's what Vusu called him — a vessel. A shell waiting to be filled." The flickering light of the dying coals caught in her eyes. "You know who Vusu intends to fill him with."

My breath caught. All the knowledge I'd gathered suddenly spun together.

He cannot deny one born of his seed...

Within your heart lies the power to restrain a god...

A sacrifice of spirit, or an offering of blood...

She raised a knife white as bone, then plunged it through her own chest...

My knees went weak. I would have fallen but for Xaron and Nomusa's support. Yet though I struggled to deny Eltris's words and my conclusions, I could only whisper it. "Liar."

The Master Augur shook her head and turned back down the stairs. The slapping of her sandals faded as she descended the stairs.

I drew in a shaky breath and recovered my balance, then extricated myself from my friends. "We'd better go."

Xaron hovered at my shoulder. "Airene, about Linos... I'm sure she didn't mean that."

I closed my eyes and felt myself sway, exhaustion threatening to claim me. "She meant it, Xaron. I don't think Eltris is the wise woman you hoped she was. I think she's a recluse so used to keeping her secrets that she won't reveal them until it's too late."

I opened my eyes and found my vision swimming. "We have to meet Jaxas. I don't want to keep him waiting." I glanced at Kelena. "Will you come too?"

The honor nodded. "My network watches the Manifest. And for your Guilder," she added with a look at me. "I can do no more than wait until I receive word back."

Xaron and Nomusa exchanged looks across me, but I ignored them and turned for the door. "Fine. Then we'll wait."

"We may hear back by the time we get down this tower," Xaron noted lightly.

Even his levity could do little to lighten my mood. Yet I took his arm all the same as we began the long descent.

∾

Xaron and Nomusa took turns supporting me as we walked back through Oedija's streets to the Laurel Palace. Dark, overcast skies added to the uneasy feeling in the air. Brawls and robberies broke out in alleys as we passed. Along most streets, shop windows were broken in, and carts and stalls lay abandoned.

All around us, the city was tearing itself apart.

My heart hammered from more than exertion. At any moment, I expected Guilders to emerge from the shadows and surround us. A knot of four men drifted by, leering and calling jeers after us. But when Xaron flared fire to life in his hands, they scampered back the way they'd come, cursing "damned daemons" until their angry shouts faded away.

It seemed a miracle that we reached the Laurel Palace unscathed. The guard at the gates had doubled, and they shouted and pushed back at the crowd as they admitted us. More than one of the gathered people received a hard crack from their spears. I winced and hurried past to ascend the hill to the palace.

The last of my strength was fast fading. My anger with Eltris had only sustained me through the descent of Kyros's tower; ever since, it had been a losing battle. Each step became less steady than the last. A haze had settled over my thoughts. I barely heard Xaron and Nomusa as they spoke. Only the worry and fear cut through the cloud and kept me moving forward.

We pushed on until we reached Jaxas's solar. Wits dulled, I barely recognized Nikias standing before us as Nomusa and Xaron led me into the room and to a chair by the hearth. I didn't notice Jaxas until he moved into the firelight and sat next to me.

"Rest," he said as he leaned forward in his chair. "All you must do is rest."

I had no choice but to obey. My head lolled back on the chair, and my eyes closed.

When I opened them again, pain greeted me. My ribs seemed truly broken this time, fire radiating from them through the whole of my midriff. My neck had joined the rest of my body in stiff discomfort. Someone had draped a heavy blanket over me and propped up my feet with a stool. I groaned as I sat up and gingerly stretched my sore limbs.

"You're awake."

I tweaked my ribs as I startled and looked around. Jaxas stood before the glass balcony doors, hands clasped behind his back. He glanced at me, then looked back out over the metropolis. His posture was erect, his chin held high.

I tried to sit up straighter with little success. "Where are the others?"

"They'll return soon."

There seemed more unsaid in his words. I waited.

He glanced over after several long moments. "Do you believe in fate, Airene?"

I blinked, my sleep-fogged mind trying to follow. "I believe we forge our own fates. I believe what happens to us is the result of cause and effect. It's not written in stone, nor threaded by divine hands."

Even as I spoke, I thought of Clepsammia and wondered if I still believed that.

"Perhaps it is both," Jaxas said. "For every action and every event seems to have been drawing me in one direction. I've seen this juncture arriving for a time, yet always I thought, 'There is time, there is still time.' But the sieve has narrowed. There is no other choice now but the one before me. One choice that will change the course of my life, and of everyone in Oedija."

"I'm sure you'll make the right decision." I hoped I sounded more confident than I felt. His vague words seeded disquiet in me.

He turned and smiled, skin tight against his skull. "I hope I already have. But enough philosophizing. The fully formed

Demos Council has met, as you know. The Low Consuls have issued a number of decrees. The first was the dissolution of the Order of Verifiers, on account of insubordination and ineffectiveness of its Finches."

I stared at him, my mind turning in slow circles.

"I'm no longer First Verifier," I said slowly. "Or even a common Verifier."

"No longer."

It didn't matter. With enemies closing in on all sides, the title didn't matter. But though I told myself that again and again, it still hurt. I'd striven my whole life to become a true Verifier. I couldn't cut away that childhood dream with logic. I could only imagine how Nomusa must be feeling.

"There's more," Jaxas continued. "The Low Consuls also decided that, with enemies besetting us from both within and without, they require every resource and shred of authority. Thus, the power of the Laurel Palace has been curbed, its resources staunched. We Wreaths will lose all staff but the minimum required to support our family and lands, and the guard will be stripped as well. All of our funds in the banks will be confiscated. Only the small coffers kept within the Laurel Palace remain to us. And as the Archon, I no longer possess any right to voice my opinion, but am relegated purely to a role of moderation."

I stared at him. I had at least known the disbandment of the Order was possible. But this went far beyond that. "Orhan is boxing us in. He's taking away any tool we have for resistance." I slumped in the cushioned chair. "You have no soldiers or resources. I have no access or authority. What are we going to do, Jaxas? How can we fight anyone like this? The Avvadin Imperium? Vusu? Famine?"

The Archon was wreathed in the soft evening light that glowed from his balcony doors. "We make the one choice remaining to us," he said quietly. "We act as you so recently advised. We do everything in our power, no matter what others might think of us. No matter the consequences we might suffer."

Cold fingers crawled up my spine. "What do you mean?"

He didn't answer, but shifted his gaze back over the city. "Hilarion Xaron has gone to fetch the Watchers. First Verifier Nomusa inquires into the glassblower Maesos, to see if he possesses more pyrkin bolts such as we used at Leia's trial. Verifier Kelena goes to Heir Komo to see if he will lend his strength to ours." He glanced at me. "Shall we join their gathering at the Laurel Groves?"

My unease grew greater still. "Why are they gathering?"

"We cannot allow Vusu to command the battle anymore. We cannot wait for the Council to take action. Avvad marches north within the span; we must be ready when they arrive. The Manifest must no longer plague us when they begin the siege." He stared into my eyes, seeming to search for something behind them. "We shall strike now, before the Seekers can take the next step in their plans. We will cut the head from the snake and hope it kills the body."

His intentions hit me, sudden as a bird crashing into a window. "You mean to kill Vusu."

Jaxas nodded slowly. "Kelena's honors report of his continued weakness since the trial. If he is killed, the Manifest will lose its Visage. Perhaps it will lose its will to resist as well. But more than that, we cannot afford them to keep Myron Wreath hostage any longer. It has tied our hands for too long. With his safety secured, action against the Seekers may proceed unhindered."

I was stunned. Boldness was not what I'd come to expect of Jaxas Wreath. Hearing his plans, I wondered if I knew the man at all.

"But how can we do this? We don't have the strength."

"Watcher Isidora informs me that her wardens are ready for this. I have no choice but to believe her. With help from the laurel guard and Heir Komo, I hope it will be enough."

Watcher Isidora. I hadn't realized Jaxas was in communication with the Acadian, much less close enough to command her. And he'd clearly been communicating with Kelena at length. I had the creeping suspicion that I was missing something right before my eyes.

"Vusu is in the heart of the Wyvern's Claw, and you don't know where the Despot is," I pointed out.

"Kelena's contacts inform us of this as well — that Myron Wreath is held in a warehouse in Brinecoast."

I couldn't believe I hadn't heard it from Kelena herself. Still, I struggled to mask my annoyance. "If you want to do both, you'll have to split your forces."

"We will. And in the middle of the enemy compound, no less. Yet we must do these two things at the same time, or we will lose both opportunities." He considered me for a moment. "I don't think it's as impossible as you seem to believe. The Seekers are not an army. They post sentries, but are untrained and ill organized. And our forces will have a significant distraction to use as cover."

When had the foundations for these plans been laid? As I studied the unshifting determination on the Archon's face, I couldn't say. Perhaps, locked away in the depths of Tomes for many long turns, I'd missed far more than I knew.

"You seem to have thought this through." The words sounded vapid even to my own ears, and I continued quickly, "I suppose we'd better go to the Laurel Groves then."

Though I made to rise, Jaxas arrested me when he spoke again. "Airene. I didn't mean to exclude you from my plans. But you have been…" He searched for the word.

"Distracted," I supplied. I wondered why he felt the need to apologize to me. He owed me nothing.

Knowing we could delay no longer, I pressed out of the chair, a groan escaping me. My chest, the pain of which had been a slow burn with each breath in the chair, spiked, but I fought it down.

"Not distracted," he said at length. "You strive against a greater problem. I didn't wish to pull you away from it with my own concerns."

I turned to look at him with watering eyes. What was he thinking behind that calm demeanor? What other plans did he keep hidden even now?

"We'd better go while I'm still standing," I advised.

Jaxas nodded, his gaze not leaving me. "The carriage is waiting out front. It's not far."

I suppressed a grim smile. Not far, perhaps, if every breath weren't agony. But I let him believe the comforting lie, and tried to believe it myself, as we began our slow descent.

21

BURN

There is power in hunger. It is a truth our people have denied for
too long, brother. They believe our hunger makes us weak. That,
starving, we have no hope for sustenance.

But we know they are wrong, brother. In our God, we have
glimpsed power only we can grasp. And I know you hunger for it
as much as I...

- Tales of the Desolate, uncensored; 1092 SLP

The others appeared from the gray twilight as Jaxas and
I rolled into the Laurel Groves.

At every lurch of the carriage, I had to hold back a gasp,
my ribs seeming to puncture new holes inside me. But I
forgot my pain when rows of dark figures emerged from the
dusky light. For a moment, I couldn't help but doubt those
silhouettes were on our side, but rather Seekers or Guilders
waiting in ambush, though none of them moved toward us.

"Our army," Jaxas said softly next to me.

I glanced at him. With a single pyr lamp lighting the
carriage, shadows obscured his features. *Our army* — an odd

thing to call them, an army. And if this were an army, it was his, not ours.

I exited as soon as the carriage rolled to a stop, leaning heavily on the hand of the driver to set foot on the ground. Every breath burned in my chest, but I tried to not let it show. These were our defenders against the Seekers. I wanted to be strong for them, or as strong as I could manage. I walked between the rows of figures, then stopped to look at those who had gathered.

To one side, the fourteen Watchers stood silently under the boughs of olive trees. Isidora stood before them, and Xaron next to her. They seemed to be holding hands, but when I looked again, their arms hung by their sides. Xaron had changed from his Hilarion clothes to as simple a tunic and trousers as I'd seen him wear, and a hood and cloak were pulled over his shoulders. The Acadians had disguised themselves similarly. With the dark cloaks on, I was uneasily reminded of the Seekers wardens we'd fought in Komo's quarters.

This is different, I reminded myself. We were fighting for the right side. Even if we also used our forbidden magic for violence.

The laurel guards had gathered as well. I vaguely recognized the woman who stood before them: Synne of Gate, the First Laurel. She possessed a calm confidence and met my gaze with cool consideration. A score of armored warriors stood behind her, their armor gleaming dully from the pyr lamps mounted periodically along the garden road. They bore spears and bucklers, and short stabbing swords at their hips, like a taxos ready for war.

The group of warriors Komo stood before starkly contrasted with the laurel guards. His Yorandu soldiers wore peculiar armor of feathers, tassels, bones, and brass. All of them, Komo included, had one side of their faces painted green, which seemed almost to glow in the low light, so they appeared as otherworldly spirits more than soldiers. I nodded at the Shaka-Heir, and the boy nodded solemnly in return. My heart wrenched for him. He was so young, yet he didn't flinch from this, even though it would likely require him to kill again. I hoped he could endure it.

All of them would go, and I would stay. It pained me to admit it, but I knew better than to imagine I might go with them. I'd be more of a burden than help. I couldn't reliably channel, or even walk far at the moment.

Yet the relief that flooded through me brought with it the heat of shame to my face. I was glad for the darkness to hide it.

Nomusa stood next to Kelena, still clothed in the fine, simple robes she'd worn to the Conclave. I'd hoped to see Corin with her, bearing a cart of Maesos's goods, but my hopes were in vain. My friend glanced my way with hooded eyes, then looked away. I feared to think what that look meant. Kelena wore a dark cloak, the hood hiding her shaven head and tin spiral earrings. Her eyes were pools of darkness as she stared at me.

"Good. We are gathered." Jaxas stopped next to me and surveyed the small army, then glanced at me. Without saying a word, he strode over to speak with Komo.

Not knowing what to make of the Archon's behavior, I put him from mind and approached Nomusa and Kelena.

Nomusa watched me, her brow creased with concern. "I don't think you should be up and walking. I worried when we left you asleep in Jaxas's solar, but now I wish you'd stayed."

"Glad to hear I'm welcome." I grimaced as a fresh wave of pain washed over me and hoped she took it for a smile. "Are Maesos's goods still coming?"

She shook her head. "No. He had no more of the pyrkin strain. And unless he can find someone to smuggle more from the Thulu, we won't have those bolts again."

The disappointment was sharp, but I tried to push it from mind. "And Corin? I expected her to be here."

Nomusa shrugged. "Maesos hadn't seen her for two days. I suppose she's found some other place to stay."

"Perhaps," I managed, and tried not to think about it further. There was nothing I could do for her now. Just as there was nothing I could do for Talan. Cold fear clawed through my gut. How many friends would I lose before this war was over?

I stepped forward and wrapped my arms around Nomusa, drawing her in as close as my ribs allowed. "You'll be safe at least," I whispered.

She returned the embrace as carefully. "Perhaps. But I'll be in the lion's den. Someone has to watch the Council and make sure they don't interfere."

"You're the bravest of us all then." Releasing her, I turned to Kelena and took a breath to compose myself. "You seem to be in close contact with Jaxas."

The honor's expression remained blank. "I believe you attached yourself to Archon Jaxas as well when you wished to be involved in events of importance. I had resources that could be of value to him, and so I offered them."

That took me aback. She thought I'd tried to reprimand her. And perhaps I had, I realized too late.

"I don't fault you for it," I amended. "In fact, I'm grateful. We need anything to strike a blow against the Manifest."

She smiled thinly. "This will be more than a blow, Airene."

I was surprised at how thin my name sounded without my recently acquired title. It didn't matter, I reminded myself. Before Kelena could see the effect of her words, I turned and made my slow way toward Xaron and Isidora.

My friend flashed me a cocky smile as I approached, but it was too wide to be believable. Isidora looked a little more certain, though her fingers danced against her legs. But I'd seen her kill without hesitation during the trial. I trusted she'd keep her wits about her in a fight.

"You're awake," Xaron observed. "I thought that climb might have done you in."

"Not yet." I looked him up and down. "You look good out of Hilarion clothes. More yourself."

"I *feel* more myself. You have no idea how scratchy sackcloth is. Especially when it's rubbing against your—"

"Glad to see you'll be watching over him," I interrupted quickly, addressing Isidora. "Make sure he comes out alive, will you?"

She flashed me a thin smile. "I will. I want him to stick around, for some reason beyond me."

Xaron shrugged. "It's no mystery. You're in love with me."

The Watcher leader flushed, while Xaron grinned at her.

I smiled too, then seized his hand. "Don't do anything stupid."

He pulled me into an embrace. "Unlike your own clandestine love," he murmured into my hair.

I nodded wearily, letting him take some of my weight. But as he was the one going into danger, I knew I couldn't lean on his strength. Reluctantly, I pulled away and glanced over at Komo and his warriors. "I should thank him for being here."

"Then go. We'll come back, never fear."

I tried not to think about it as I turned toward the Bali regiment. The boy watched my slow approach, his expression brittle. Even his sense of control, incredible in his youth, couldn't hide the fear behind his painted face.

I stopped a respectful distance before him. "You didn't have to come."

"I did," the boy replied heavily. "You showed me that. Even Nkosi said honor compelled me to go."

"Nkosi did? It's hard to believe that old root came around."

A smile flitted across Komo's lips. "I am glad he knew better than to try and come with. He can be too stubborn for his own good."

"I know the kind. Take care, Heir Komo."

"And you, Finch Airene."

I turned away, not having the heart to correct him, and found Jaxas standing not far behind me. But the man next to him, and the four hooded strangers behind them, made me stop in my tracks. Even in the dim light, the aqua color of the cowls made their identity clear.

"What are they doing here?" The words came out as a demand.

"Tribune Timon has come at my request," Jaxas said, his tone neutral.

The Tribune leered at him, his pinched features only worsened by the heavy shadows clinging to his hollowed eyes. "Hello again, Finch. Or should I even call you that now?"

I barely hid my distaste. "Why?" I asked Jaxas bluntly.

The Archon studied me for a moment. "You'll understand soon."

He turned from me to the rest of those gathered, and I stared at his back. I didn't like how mysteries were piling up around the man, the one Wreath I thought I could trust. I hoped I still could, no matter the secrets he kept from me.

"Thank you all for harking to my call tonight," Jaxas began, his voice loud and strong, almost reminiscent of Myron. "I know it is on short notice and the message was vague. But we must act quickly if we are to take advantage and get ahead of our foes."

"You mean the Manifest." Isidora posed it as a question.

Jaxas nodded. "And others. The Avvadin Imperium marches on our city. We cannot hope to prevail if Oedija stands divided against its armies. We must strike at the heart of the Manifest now and hope it is enough to begin its unraveling."

"What is our quarry?" First Laurel Synne asked, her words precise and clipped.

Jaxas swept his gaze slowly over his audience. "The head of the dragon," he said, quiet but carrying in the silence. "We strike for Vusumuzi himself."

As murmurs bubbled up around us, I feared the news would break this tenuous fellowship. But even though they shifted their feet and glanced nervously at their compatriots, no one backed away. A warm glow of pride began in my chest. I stood among Oedija's bravest, I knew that now. I tried to ignore the squirm of guilt that I wouldn't have to put my own courage to the test tonight.

Jaxas gestured to Kelena, who still stood next to Nomusa. "Kelena has eyes and ears among the Seekers, and has learned of the traitor's location. She has also heard continual reports that he remains in a room at the heart of the Wyvern's Claw, the wooden amphitheater off the shores of Lake Thys. By all accounts, he remains ill from the bolt Airene shot through him."

My face flushed as all eyes turned toward me. I struggled to remain properly dignified, though Xaron's grin didn't help.

"Isidora, Xaron, and the other Watchers will enter by stealth into the Claw," Jaxas continued. "Following Kelena's instructions, you will navigate your way to where Vusu lays ill, then execute him in the name of Oedija's justice. When you are finished, you are to go to the lake's shore, where Kelena has planned an escape."

Some of the Watchers visibly shivered. Even having shot Vusu once, my skin broke out into chicken flesh. *Execute him.* The order sounded cold, military. The command of a king.

Xaron spoke up. "What is this escape? Always best to know your escape when you house-break."

The Archon nodded at Kelena, and she cleared her throat. "There are boats on Lake Thys that none will expect to aid us," she said, a slight shake in her voice. "The honors on these boats will direct them to the shore at the appointed signal: the waving of a torch at the landing point."

"What kind of boats?" Xaron pressed. "Fishing vessels?"

Kelena hesitated. "Lotus Ships."

Xaron's eyes widened, then he let out a laugh. "This isn't the way I expected to spend my first night on a Lotus Ship!"

Isidora cast him a bemused look, then asked, "Why would these honors risk their lives for us?"

"Because they are whores." Kelena seemed to have gained back her bite. "And no one is more despised and mistreated than an honor-whore."

I cringed, imagining how true that must be.

"In exchange," Jaxas said, unperturbed by Kelena's vehemence, "I have promised them freedom from their class and profession, with both financial support and the opportunity to learn another trade."

I turned my gaze to the Archon, eyes narrowed. Considering how significantly the Council had clipped his power, he had no way of making good on such promises. Perhaps it was necessary, but the lie didn't sit easily.

Yet Jaxas gave no sign of guilt as he turned to the last of the gathered. "First Laurel Synne, Heir Komo and his guards have agreed to accompany you on a separate mission. There's a warehouse in Brinecoast where Vusumuzi keeps an important hostage, someone you might believe to be dead — Despot Myron Wreath."

The First Laurel's stiff expression broke as her brow creased. Yet she only gave a nod in acknowledgement before turning to Komo. "I have developed a strategy for entering the warehouse, Heir Komo. We may discuss this before we embark."

The Bali prince nodded, his face drawn. "That would be

good." His words were only undermined slightly by a boyish crack in his voice.

Jaxas bowed deeply to each gathered group. By their astonished expressions, I knew all comprehended what it meant. It was a singular honor for any Wreath to bow to anyone, much less foreign soldiers, outlaw wardens, and common plebeians.

"Thank you all for your unbelievable faith and courage," he said as he straightened. "These are dangerous tasks I ask of you. Many of you are not trained for battle. Yet to a one, you have borne the burdens I've laid at your feet. Whatever the results tonight, each one of you will be remembered as heroes, your deeds forever memorialized."

"You save Oedija," I suddenly interjected. As all eyes turned to me, I fought down a flush and continued softer, "You save her when she most needs it."

Nomusa arched an amused eyebrow, while Xaron smiled openly. I let out a breath and smiled back. Whatever embarrassment I might have cost myself, it was worth it see a little levity from my friends.

Jaxas glanced up at the dark sky. "The sands are running low. Go while we still have time."

At his words, they dispersed. I hugged Xaron one last time before he and the other Watchers swept after the Yorandu soldiers and laurel guards. Nomusa came to stand by me as we watched them disappear into the gloom. Soon, only Jaxas, Tribune Timon, and the four Shepherds were left, their manacles clinking softly as they shifted. I glanced at them mistrustfully, but looked away as Jaxas bent toward the Tribune to speak.

"He didn't name their task," I muttered to Nomusa.

"I wondered at that as well."

We waited in silence until their conversation finished. Timon, noticing our gazes, grinned wickedly at us before turning down the cobblestone path, the four Shepherds following silently behind. I suddenly wondered how he managed to control them. It made sense that Vusu had been able to. But Timon? He seemed little more than a small, spiteful man.

"They have perhaps the most important task tonight," Jaxas said as he walked up next to us.

Before I could ask what he meant, he continued. "Come. Airene, we will drop you off at the Laurel Palace on our way to the Conclave."

My jaw nearly dropped. "What? I should come with you."

"No," he said firmly. "You're still unwell. The safest place for you is in my solar tonight. Rest there and trust that we'll do our parts."

I felt the truth of his words. My limbs shook with the simple act of standing, and my pain worsened with every passing moment. Yet I couldn't let it go at that.

"There must be something I can do. I wouldn't rest tonight even if I were stepping over death's threshold."

The hard lines in the Archon's face softened. "I'm sorry, Airene. It is what's best for you."

Nomusa's expression spasmed, clearly torn, yet she remained silent. I couldn't find a good excuse to delay them any longer. At a motion from Jaxas, Nomusa and I piled into the carriage and soon rumbled down the garden path.

Someone had lit the hearth in Jaxas's solar, and the room had filled with a suffusing warmth. Yet I couldn't find comfort in it as I let the door swing shut behind me with a heavy thud. My heart hammered painfully in my chest, and each labored breath sent waves of pain throughout my body. The guilt was worse still. I staggered over to a chair by the fire and slumped into it, closing my eyes and resting my head back.

Everyone had a role in this night, the night we would tear

down the Manifest. Everyone — except for me. It showed just how little consequence I was. What had I done this past span but muddle through old books and speak with batty spinsters? I'd thrown away the Order and a lifelong dream. I'd failed to discover how to defeat Famine and learned little enough besides. I could barely channel to save my life, as I'd found out.

Now it was clear why I had no role. There was none I could perform without bungling it.

Wallowing in self-misery and pain, I considered calling for a poppy tincture. *If I can do nothing but rest, let me rest like the dead*, I thought. But something held me back. I'd told Jaxas I couldn't rest while the others risked their lives. I'd stand by that, no matter how futile the gesture.

Yet as time dragged on and the warmth from the fire seeped into my bones, I found my eyelids drifting closed. Visions of the horrible things befalling my friends couldn't stay the exhaustion. Even as I despised myself, even as I sat upright to try to stay awake, gasping at the pain from my ribs, I could barely keep my eyes open.

Then something boomed like thunder outside.

My eyes flew wide open. A moment later, the windows and doors rattled, and vibrations pulsed through the stone under my feet. Fear and vigor flooded me, compelling me to stand and hurry to the balcony doors.

It took but a moment to find the source of the eruption. Over the wall, across the dark lake in the deme beyond, a conflagration greater than any I'd seen blazed and spread. I stared as the flames and smoke billowed up. *We have no volcanoes in Oedija* — it was all that I could think in the daze.

The truth hit me a moment afterward.

My knees buckled as I saw it was true. The wooden amphitheater, the one I'd once feared would catch flame, finally had.

The Wyvern's Claw burned.

INTERLUDE III

TALAN

Aknife in the back. A hand clasped over the gasping mouth. Warm life spilling over his skin.

Talan held his breath as the man jerked his last in his arms. So long as he didn't breathe, he could keep calm. So long as he didn't smell the bitter, coppery stench, his stomach wouldn't purge itself clean.

His lips twisted into a bitter smile as the man grew still and heavy in his arms. If only he could believe his own lies.

He released the limp man to the ground. As he sucked in a breath, the stink of blood filled his nostrils. *The perfume of a killer,* he thought, and coughed as bile hit the back of his throat.

He didn't startle as someone came up next to him in the darkness, moving on silent feet, but acknowledged his companion with a nod.

"You've changed," noted Sule, or the one who wore her skin. She glanced at the body lying still on the ground. "You're more like how Sule remembers you."

He tried to ignore her words and looked down the tunnel. He didn't see any silhouettes against the dim pyr lamp at the far end, but that didn't mean much. The Underguild's network of tunnels, caves, and forgotten caverns was riddled with holes in which an enterprising street urchin or malevolent dwarf could listen.

"The quieter we are, the less chance of discovery," he reminded his companion softly, then motioned for her to follow. He pretended not to notice the small smile the Qarin-possessed woman wore as he turned from her and set off down the tunnel.

His footsteps were nearly silent, a steady flow of kinesis cushioning his footfalls. Behind him, Sule did the same; he could only hear her following by the soft rustle of her clothes. All else was silent but for a slow drip of water somewhere ahead.

He heard them before he saw them — a sudden patter of feet approaching from either end.

Talan whirled and channeled, sending seven sharp darts of kinesis hurtling down the hall. From the cries, a few found their marks. On his other side, metal sang softly as Sule drew her sword from its cloth-wrapped scabbard and charged at the men approaching from behind. The cries echoing down the tunnel told of her blade finding its mark.

Talan barreled toward the three figures limned with lamplight ahead of him and threw forward radiance. Yellow flames surged from his fingertips and leaped up to embrace his attackers. Their screams crescendoed to join those of the men Sule cut down, then abruptly stopped as Talan sent out another round of kinetic darts. The three figures collapsed, silent but for the crackle of their burning flesh.

Sule sauntered up behind him, no longer bothering to cushion her steps. "They know we're here."

Talan flexed his hands, fingers numb from the quick channeling. "We'd best hurry then."

But he hesitated. He could taste the foul aroma of blood

and burned meat. The smoke made his head light and dizzy. He tried not to think of how it must feel to burn, or for pure force to rip through your gut.

Find your center, he reminded himself. The words of his long-ago mentor came to mind after: *If all the world is whirling, what can you do but turn with it?*

He took in a shallow breath, then leaped over the flaming corpses with a kinetic push. He didn't look back as he set into a jog.

The necessity for silence gone, they moved more quickly. They were close now. He knew these catacombs as well as any part of the city. He'd held an audience with the Guild-masters on dozens of occasions and could have followed the winding paths with his eyes closed — had he ever trusted his fellow Guilders enough to attempt it. It would all be settled soon. He couldn't keep a self-loathing smile from his lips.

No one waited before the great doors to the final chamber. The entryway stood wide open. Talan halted and raised a hand, and Sule heeded his warning. A line of torches implied a path toward the open doors. He scanned the rest of the greeting chamber, squinting into the shadows that gathered around the edges, but saw no one. Unless Guilders hung like bats from the black ceiling above, this room was empty.

He turned halfway back to his companion and studied her from the corner of his eye. The Qarin had given him its word that it would cooperate and help him undermine the Underguild. But Talan could only rely upon it hating Avvad. Beyond that, he wasn't sure what the jinni possessing his childhood flame desired, much less if it aligned with his own goals and well-being.

"Perhaps they wait in ambush beyond," he whispered to Sule. "Will you continue?"

He could almost see the spirit gazing out from the woman's eyes. "I gave you my word, and it is binding. Let's meet this ambush together, Talan Wraithsbane."

Talan closed his eyes. Despite all he'd seen and done, the fear had never gone away. He didn't want to die. Least of all to scum like Kalindi; least of all now. But he'd made a promise to Airene, and he meant to stick to it.

He'd keep her safe.

Yet he couldn't help but wonder at himself. When had he become so resolved to protect her? In some ways, he barely knew her. They'd spoken little of their childhoods, of their fears and hopes and dreams. Most often, it had been business that brought them together.

But there was a spark in her that he'd seen in no one else. It was a gamble to throw away his life to save hers, a gamble that the spark was real. A gamble that they would have the chance to fan it into flame.

He'd always been too much of a gambler for his own good.

"Let's," he said softly. Then, standing, he walked into plain view and crossed the chamber to the door. Sule's footsteps echoed softly behind him.

As he entered the grand chamber at the heart of the Underguild, he saw the five thrones of the Guildmasters were filled. The putrid smell of decay told him who occupied them. His smile curled into a snarl as he witnessed what had become of his former leaders.

In the center slouched Hax, the man who had brought about an unprecedented period of order and civility to crime in Oedija. He'd survived dozens of attempts on his life. He hadn't survived Kalindi.

On the left sat what remained of the woman responsible for Talan's induction into the Underguild. Peralda had been one of the most fascinating women he'd met, able to manipulate the worst of humanity into doing her bidding — including Talan, as it turned out. He suspected she had wanted him to take her place as Guildmaster after her. He'd never know now, nor if he would have accepted the dubious honor.

The figure in the rightmost seat shifted in the shadows. Sheltered from the lamplight, he couldn't make out the man's features. But Talan remembered who had always sat in that seat.

"Kalindi."

"*Undermaster* Kalindi," the hidden man corrected him softly. As he leaned forward, his face came slowly into the light. A sweep of black hair fell over features that might have been handsome, had Talan not known what lay beneath them.

"I wondered when you'd try for me, Wraithsbane. Everyone said you were unpredictable. But I knew you'd come slithering to me." His lips curled into a sneer. "All I had to do was threaten your little Finch to ensure it."

His heart hammered in his throat. "Predictable or unpredictable," he said with forced calm. "Either way, this ends the same."

"Does it? And how is that, Wraithsbane?"

Talan ignored him. The conversation was a ruse, meant to do nothing more than buy time as he observed the corners of the room for assailants lying in wait. Unless they hung from the ceiling high above, he saw none. Kalindi's arrogance had no limits. The fool still didn't know what Talan was capable of. But he couldn't rely on the man's stupidity for his own safety.

Opening his locus wider, he spread his awareness around him. It strained his mind to do so for long, but for a moment, he glimpsed every living thing around him, including the two dozen men creeping toward them from the former chamber. Guilders had been lying in wait after all.

But they weren't what made his blood run cold. Something else lurked beyond them.

A familiar desire suddenly suffused him. *Come,* four voices whispered in his mind. *Come. Become one with us.*

He sealed his locus, cutting off the connection with a gasp. The edges of his mind felt torn and frayed, but the fear cut worse. *Ikoz,* Silks — here, among the Guilders. He'd long suspected the Valemish harbored them within the city limits. But he hadn't thought to find them in league with the Underguild. Avvad's reach was greater than any of them had realized.

Kalindi's grin grew wide, and he leaned forward as if to loom over them. "Is something wrong, Wraithsbane?"

"Silks," Sule breathed next to him, the Qarin having sensed them as well.

Talan nodded and risked a glance behind. Without his awareness spread, he had no idea how close the men creeping up on them were. Tentatively, he opened himself to Valem's power again, allowing in trickles of radiance and kinesis. Without spreading his awareness, the spirits would be hard-pressed to assault his mind. Even if they could find a way, he had to channel regardless; otherwise, he'd be nothing to the score of men closing in.

"Now, now, Talan," Kalindi suddenly addressed them. "It does not have to end like this." His tone had changed, from sneering to conciliatory.

Talan trusted this side of Kalindi even less. Yet he found himself looking up at the self-proclaimed Undermaster and asking flatly, "What?"

"I don't throw away good tools. I could make use of you. If you agree to my terms, I'll spare your life."

Anger suddenly flared back to life within him. "And what terms are those?"

"You have connections in many places. The Laurel Palace. The Conclave, through the new Order of Verifiers. Eyes and ears in these places would serve me well. So here's my proposal, Wraithsbane. You spy for me, and I swear to let you and your companion here go free, and to never touch your Finch again. I think that's more than fair, don't you?"

Talan closed his eyes and bowed his head. The tendons in his jaw felt like they'd snap. Veins pulsed in his forehead. For a moment, he couldn't breathe for the hatred that poured through him. The image of the Guilders kicking and throwing Airene to the ground, of ripping her clothes off, filled his mind with a force so that he could think of nothing else. Only his revulsion that he considered Kalindi's offer for a moment cut through it, that his fear of death and killing would give him pause.

But he knew better. If he'd learned one thing in Avvad, it was that the best way to kill a snake was to chop off its head.

Opening his eyes, he raised a hand. He opened his locus wider and pulled on the stream of energy that poured in. Kinesis formed at his fingertips, honed until it reached a fine, narrow point.

Kalindi's eyes grew wide, and he scrambled out of his chair. But he couldn't avoid the bolt of force that sped from Talan's fingertips and caught him in the temple. A red spray fanned out from where it entered. The Undermaster spun from the dais, landing headfirst on the stone floor below with a sickening crunch, and his limp body fell after.

Talan watched impassively as Kalindi twitched, then stopped moving. This corpse didn't fill him with revulsion as the others had, but an ugly pleasure. *What have you made of me?* he thought to the dead Undermaster. *What did this place make of us all?*

"They're coming." Sule faced the doors behind them, her curved sword held aloft, and slowly backed away.

Talan turned as well, feeling strangely disconnected from his body. He heard them now in the chamber beyond, their stealthy approach abandoned. His hand moved into his pocket and drew out a long shard of obsidian, then channeled radiance into it. It began to glow.

"We may die here." His voice sounded far away. A strange, sardonic smile tugged at his lips. He didn't bother to hide it.

Sule stared at him. As he met her eyes, he saw the Qarin there again. "Hold yourself together," she commanded. "I'm not ready to leave this world again."

He nodded even as the odd mood clung to him and grasped for the urgency that had driven him before. *The spark. Remember the spark. Remember what this gamble was taken for.*

As the first of the Guilders slipped through the doors, Talan raised the glowing shard and channeled. Radiance, gathered in a blinding beam, blazed forward, burning and cutting through shadowed figures. Screams from the doorway told of others dying in the chamber beyond.

But some had slipped through and spread out around them, knives and crossbows coming up. Talan cut off the stream, nearly staggering with the exertion. Exhaustion pulled at him. The long route in and the effort of continuous channeling had drained him. But he pulled for more still, gathering kinesis and throwing it up before him. Waves of pure force caught and turned aside the bolts and knives that hurtled their way, then knocked the Guilders roughly against the wall. Not enough force to hurt them, but hopefully enough to daze.

Tucking away his obsidian shard, he drew out a long, curved knife and sprinted forward. Behind him, Sule screamed as she ran to engage Guilders on their flank. He threw small waves of kinesis before him until he reached the first of them. The man, off-balance from his relentless magic, had time for his eyes to widen just before Talan whipped his knife across his throat.

The other Guilders were scrambling to flee from him, heading for the door where their fellows had gathered but didn't dare enter. No doubt Kalindi's corpse and two wardens gave them pause. Weariness dulled his mind, but

Talan moved his leaden legs after them and forced a wide grin onto his face.

"Come on, friends!" he called to them. "I have a red smile for each of you!"

They broke. Like a herd of panicked cattle, they rammed against each other in their eagerness to escape. Sule was the herd-dog driving them on, her sword cutting down those too slow or stupid to run. She stopped just shy of the entrance, breathing heavily, but still firm and upright.

"They're still coming," he reminded her.

Sule met his eyes and nodded, then quickly backed away from the clearing entrance.

He felt them before they drifted through the doorway. Desire seeped into him, so subtly that, even though he was aware of what would happen, he almost took a step toward them. They looked like little more than strands of shimmering cloth floating through the air. But Talan had felt their touch before. As they came nearer, he struggled to keep his mind straight. The desire to go to them, to lose himself in their oblivion, nearly overwhelmed his weary will. *Rest*, their voices whispered in his head. *Rest, and worry no more. Struggle no more. Feel no more.*

He wrenched his mind from their grasp and was dimly aware of falling to his knees. Reaching desperately back into his memory, he tried to recall how he'd warded himself against them before. But his head felt full of cotton. The fire of Valem that had burned inside him had dampened so that it was little more than coals.

Sule had backed away to the Guildmasters' thrones. "Talan!" she cried, her voice shrill with fear. "You must fight them! They'll destroy me!"

He forced himself to rise. The knife dropped from his numb fingers, and he fumbled in his pocket for the obsidian shard. *It begins with the spin*, he thought he remembered. Or was it the hook? It didn't matter that he'd practiced the banishing technique countless times since leaving Erimis. With the weight of four Silks bearing down on him, he couldn't wake the cleansing fire to free them from their bonds.

Talan sank to his knees and closed his eyes as the Silks drifted closer.

22
SEEDS OF FAMINE

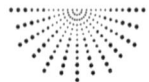

Can any man survive this endless hunger?

- Tales of the Desolate, uncensored; 1092 SLP

I stared at the burning amphitheater, thoughts floating through my numb mind.

Xaron, Isidora, and the Watchers had been tasked with entering the Wyvern's Claw. They'd sought Vusu's room at the heart of it. They'd meant to kill Vusu.

But I couldn't put the thoughts in any order that made sense of the sight before me. I wanted to believe they meant nothing.

Yet the haze cleared, and the truth asserted itself. I couldn't fool myself any longer. I sank to my knees. It didn't matter what had started the fire. Perhaps it had been stray radiance from one of the Watchers, inexperienced as they were. Perhaps it was a trap set by Vusu's minions. Or perhaps Vusu had been undiminished in his power and paid his would-be assassins in kind. But it didn't matter.

No matter what had happened, it didn't change the fact that Xaron was likely now burning within.

Sobs wracked my tormented body, but I fought them off as I crawled to the chair by the fire. I had to see for myself. I had to know if Xaron was still alive.

Dragging myself into the chair, I closed my eyes and tried to slow my hysterical breathing. Focus, Eltris had reminded me during our lessons, was only possible when your mind was not controlled by other things.

But I couldn't wrest back control. Fear and shame and guilt twined inside me and pulled my thoughts into terrible imaginings. I saw each of my loved ones — Xaron, Talan, Nomusa, my family — tortured and killed at the hands of hooded shadows.

Only my anger was stronger. I ceded to it, let it fill me. I cut away the nightmares and squeezed my eyes shut tighter. I could do nothing if I couldn't focus.

I had to enter the Pyrthae. Even if I couldn't save them, I had to see.

I abandoned Eltris's techniques and tried Isidora's. I painted a desert in my mind, brushing in dunes and a clear blue sky in broad strokes. Almost as soon as I'd visualized the rough sketch, the scene carried me aloft like a leaf on a strong gust, as if it had been waiting for me all along.

I found myself ascending a dune. The pains of my body disappeared, and a thin strength returned to my limbs. Hot wind whipped dust into my face. My throat was parched with thirst, eyes gritty and dry. The sands slipped beneath my bare feet, each step losing ground.

But I carried on. Dusty air wheezed in my lungs, but with each passing moment, breathing grew easier. I tilted my head back and saw nothing but the sharp edge of the dune above me. I scrambled up the last few steps to the crest.

As soon as my foot touched the top, I felt myself lift away, the ground losing its grip on me. Panic rising, I bent down to the sand, desperate to grab hold. It was too late. The sky took me with greater force with each passing moment, its weight having reversed. I fell upward into nothing. Barely able to breathe, I closed my eyes and let it take me.

All may shift around you. You alone are still. Isidora's words as she led us through the scene came back to me. I held them tight in my mind. All shifted around me. But I was still. My fear could not touch me.

Opening my eyes, I looked above me, only to see there wasn't sky, but a desert, seen as if I looked down from a tall tower. *All may shift around me, but I am still*, I told the panic that tried to wrest back control. My ascent — or descent, it seemed now — slowed as I repeated the mantra in my head. As I came to a halt, hovering midair, I gazed down at the landscape below me, blinking in sudden recognition.

Oedija had become a wasteland.

I barely recognized it in the dull light that suffused the barren city. But I knew the shape of its shoreline and the circle of the city wall too well to deceive myself. Tall dunes of ashy gray sand had built up around the inner city as high as the wall itself. The Half-Wall on the south side was nothing more than a long, tall mound of sand. The Lighted Sea was drained, the cliffs at the edge of Oedija marking where it had once been. Only an endless brown basin remained of it now. The Pillars were strange here, melding with their mirror images into seamless bars of dark gray stone. The Laurel Palace below me was still recognizable upon its hill away from the consuming sand, though its towers were broken and its walls eroded. The Conclave's dome had almost completely caved in.

Movement drew my gaze eastward, to where a huge storm of sand turned above the city. Stretching the size of an entire deme, sand billowed slowly from it, yet I felt sure the force of its winds could tear the skin from my body. The twister reached into the mirror Oedija above as well, forming a shape like a spinning top that swayed back and forth from its connecting points. The center of the tornado seemed to project the light that filled this place, for the further away from it the land was, the more it fell into shadow.

Fear ran through me as I recognized what it meant. When I'd dreamed my way into the Pyrthae before, Famine had appeared as an inferno. I guessed that I now gazed upon the daemon god's new form.

I glanced down at myself and startled at the form I'd taken. I didn't have a body, but was a vague figure of spinning sand and wind. Seeing my form, I felt, too, the boundaries I put around it to keep it to that shape.

I tore my gaze away and studied the landscape again. Now that I knew what form wardens might take, I saw the other swirling patches dotting Oedija. Three hovered around Famine. Dozens of others fluttered to the northeast. Fear and exhilaration gripped me as I recognized who those must be, and what they must mean.

I willed myself toward Xaron and the Watchers, trapped deep in the Claw, but somehow still alive.

As I neared, I sensed the danger they were in. Xaron, whom I intuitively knew as I'd known Talan's flame before, seemed barely able to keep turning. I descended fast toward him, though I didn't know what I could do. Xaron I might recognize, but I couldn't distinguish between the Watchers and the Seeker wardens among the other shapes that spun against each other. If I threw myself at any of them, attacking them the only way I knew how, I might as easily harm an ally as an enemy, and leave my allies and friends worse off than before.

I halted a couple of dozen feet above and watched Xaron's life fading, urgency hammering through my form and threatening to break it apart. Ideas spun through my head, but I dismissed each of them in turn. Just as I'd suspected and feared, I could do nothing more than watch.

Then I felt something pressing against the boundaries of

myself, and I startled and looked behind. The gray, twisted face of Clepsammia smiled her mocking smile at me as she gripped my sandy shoulder. Somehow, it became more solid under her touch. I felt I could almost hear her thoughts this way, for all the good it did — her thoughts were in no tongue that I understood.

I didn't try to pull away. Now that she was here, I remembered the last time the Maiden of the Sands had appeared before me. When I'd struggled even to stand after the Guilders' attack, she had done something, something that gave me the strength to make it all the way back to the Aviary.

As if sensing my thoughts, Clepsammia's smile tugged unnaturally wider. She twisted her hand through my shoulder, and the sand where she'd touched spun faster. A warm glow of energy suffused me from the spot.

For a moment, I didn't understand; then realization hit me like a crashing wave. I stared, dumbstruck, at the thought of a goddess aiding me. But remembering Xaron's plight below me, I didn't waste a moment longer, but turned and dove for him.

Strength flowing through me, I rushed at Xaron. I barely knew what I did, but as I reached him, I summoned forth my energy and *pushed* it into him, spinning his wind into a fury as I flew by. Passing, I looked back, and for a moment, I feared I'd dispersed his slowly swirling sand.

Then his spiral reared up and surged, his twister growing stronger and more distinct.

Exhilaration surged through me. I'd given Xaron back his strength! I sent a silent thanks to Clepsammia, then turned my gaze to the other fluttering gales below me. Some of those would be Watchers, some of them Seekers. For Xaron's sake, I didn't dare give any others wind. I glanced back at where Clepsammia had floated, wondering if she might guide me again, but the goddess had disappeared. Hoping I'd done enough, I reluctantly ascended back into the sky.

Famine again drew my gaze. I couldn't tell if it was my imagination, but his twister seemed to be growing larger, its winds stronger, with every passing moment. Only then did I wonder why Famine, bound as he was by Vusu, wasn't in the Wyvern's Claw as well. Wincing, I considered Famine's sandstorm closer. Near its base rose a Pillar; but if it was Bazaar's, Iris's, or the Acadium's Pillar, I couldn't tell. It was too hard to distinguish among the force of his winds.

Another thought jolted me back to myself. Xaron wasn't the only one in danger. I scanned Oedija, searching for more signs of wardens. To the northwest, one twister still spun strongly: Komo at Brinecoast, attempting to save Myron, I guessed. As he didn't seem in danger of fading, I continued my search, moving in a wide berth around Famine back toward the Laurel Palace, then onward until I hovered near the Conclave's Pillar.

Finally, I spotted him. To the southeast, small, fluttering sands, little more than a gust, were about to sputter out.

Talan.

As I threw myself toward him, I recognized Sule and her Qarin, a thin spiral reaching up to the mirrored Oedija. Its connection seemed so thin a small breeze might sever it. I ignored it. The daemon would have to take care of itself. I wouldn't assist it, no matter whose side it claimed to be on.

Talan's winds stirred, then faltered, stilling and falling to the ground. Fear flooding through me, I didn't slow my fast descent as I neared. Where before I'd breathed energy into Xaron, I now thrust it into Talan, throwing the whole of my being into him and filling him like wind in sails.

A storm of emotions flooded through me. Senses flashed through my mind. The putrid stench of rotting corpses. Exhaustion heavy in my limbs. But something else pulled at me strongest, an intense desire to lose myself and finally find peace...

NO!

They — whatever they were — flowed like gentle zephyrs into Talan's sputtering wind, sapping his strength and will. I moved to block them, their whispers only tantalizing to me, the separation provided by the Pyrthae enough to resist them. And though I'd given of myself to both Xaron and Talan, my will seemed to have only grown stronger.

As I sheltered Talan from whatever assaulted him, I stirred him back to life. His being still flowing through mine, I knew he'd pushed himself too hard. Maybe beyond what I could repair. I suffocated my fears and pressed more of myself into him.

He suddenly grasped toward me, touching my mind roughly like a blind man gripping my face. *Do I know you?* He flung the question around him clumsily, not knowing how to direct it at me.

Rise, I told him. *Kill Kalindi. Then return to me.*

I felt his amazement and recognition. *Airene?*

My heart soared, but I knew I couldn't keep him longer. The Silks — as I'd identified his foes from his mind — battered against my wall, but I knew it was only he who could contend with them.

Go! With the command, I lifted away, giving him one last burst of wind before I disentangled our spirits. One last glance showed Talan rising once more, his sands billowing with strength.

I reluctantly turned my attention away from him and back north. Famine had grown ever greater. The middle of the tornado extended out, bloated with lazily rolling dust. But I could see how the winds whipped fast near the ends of it. Whatever was happening, Famine was gaining power — and quickly.

I had to go to him. I had to see what was causing Famine's

rapid rise in strength. Did Vusu grow with him? Or had Famine already broken free? And what did the source of the storm mean, that it was not within the Claw?

Maintaining a careful distance, I brought myself closer to the daemon god. I could feel the pull of his winds from far outside the storm's bounds. I studied the area from which it came. The Laurel Palace was to the west of it, the Conclave southwest. Now that I was closer, I could barely pick out Bazaar's Pillar beyond, showing me the storm rose from—

The Acadium.

Heedless of the danger, I threw myself toward the storm. I didn't know what Vusu and Famine were after, or what was augmenting their power. But they'd claimed Linos once before.

I wouldn't let them have what was left of him.

I flew through the desolate city. Famine's pull on my mind became stronger as I neared, threatening to split it asunder. I had to fight every moment to keep myself together. The ethereal light within the twister pulsed brighter, like the beating heart of the sun. I dove low, dipping below the burgeoning middle of the tornado, and soared within the channels of sand covering the city.

Reaching the base of the twister, I halted, trying to make sense of the scene before me. Famine was weaker here at the base, for he rose from another spiraling wind — Vusu, I guessed. Two other winds contended with Vusu, diving into him again and again, each time weakening him a little more. One other held back a small distance. Vaguely I recognized these, but I couldn't place who they were.

Then I saw the small, fluttering breeze flowing around Vusu, and I froze, caught between fear and hope. I knew who that tiny squall was.

Linos!

I cried out to him, unable to stop myself from drifting forward. I hadn't known that any part of my brother was still alive. To see him, to know him, brought me more strength and hope than I'd had in a long time.

LINOS!

I felt him stir in response, and my hopes soared. There were no words to his reaching, no conscious thought. But recognition was enough. My brother was still alive, and some part of him still knew me.

But he was in danger. His slow squall seemed to depend on Vusu's winds to continue swirling, and again and again, the two other gales attacked Vusu. Anger surged through me. There were too many unknowns, too much to consider.

But I had no time. Linos was in danger.

Gathering the errant winds of myself and tightening them so that a tempest roared within me, I threw myself toward the melee. I flew faster than I'd dared let myself before, gathering speed and force. The others noticed me as I approached, but couldn't leave off their fighting.

Suddenly, the gale that had held back lashed toward me and twisted into me.

Airene! Eltris's voice boomed into me, nearly enough to tear me apart. *Stop, STOP! Before you ruin us all!*

Her tendrils pulled at me, tilting me from my course. I struggled to shake her loose, but couldn't manage it.

Let me go! I snarled, flinging my rage at her.

She flinched, but didn't release me. *You don't understand what you do!*

How could I? You never told me!

Inexorably, I pulled her toward Linos and the others. Before, when I'd first strayed into the Pyrthae, Eltris had been able to collapse me into unconsciousness. But either she'd weakened or I'd grown stronger; now, she couldn't resist my efforts.

Release me! I commanded her. *Let me go to him! I'll save my brother!*

Your brother is dead! His spirit is fragmented. He's gone,

Airene! Now you must let him fulfill his purpose. You cannot interfere!

I pried her consciousness from me one strand at a time. *So you've plotted with Vusu this whole time!* I threw at her. *You always meant to kill my brother!*

Her anger stirred and strengthened her, and she clung so tightly that I couldn't pry her loose. *Vusumuzi means to seal away Famine, fool girl! He's sought to end Famine for decades. As a young man, he foolishly accepted the Quintyr into his being in exchange for power. But since then, he has seen his folly and the ruin Famine would bring if loosed upon the world. He seeks to be rid of him forever!*

As much as I wanted to, I couldn't deny the truth of her words. With our minds entwined, the force of her conviction filled me. It didn't help that I'd begun to suspect as much since I'd read Nkosi's book.

Even as Vusu and my brother were attacked again and again by the two opposing spirits, I knew I had to ask. *Why destroy Oedija then? Why kill hundreds of innocents? Why mutilate and maim two of my brothers?*

It would take too long for you to understand. You must trust me, Airene. Do not interfere!

Rage suddenly flared up in me again. *Trust you? You've done nothing to earn my trust!*

Summoning all the force of my disdain, I threw Eltris off with a mighty gust. I felt the augur's surprise just before our connection severed and she was tossed away like a cast-off rag.

Not wasting a moment, I soared forward. But as I neared the struggling gales, I slowed, then stopped. Vusu seemed to be protecting Linos from the other two. But he'd been too long my enemy to trust his intentions now. Knowing Eltris was just behind, I knew I had to make a choice.

Diving, I threw myself into the fray.

I tangled with the winds, fighting and pushing back as

they tried to toss me and shred me. But I had only struggled a moment before something like a strong gale swept over me, and the turbulent scene shifted.

Suddenly, the sands began to drain away below me, revealing figures caught in a struggle.

Vusu emerged from the sands first, his arms raised, something slender and white clasped in his hands. He was even thinner than before, so skeletal that it seemed the barest blow must shatter him. He wore the same peplos as the day of the Despoina's trial, only now the white fabric was soiled and stained with crusted blood. The source of his weakness was plain, the broken bolt still emerging from between his ribs.

The arms of another man parted from the sands after, holding Vusu's wrists. Kyros Brighteyed, I recognized him, as his balding head, loose jowls, and glowing eyes came into view. The Archmaster was clad in rich robes and purpling in the face from exertion. Strange as it seemed, the thick man was barely able to match Vusu's strength, though the traitor looked halfway a corpse.

Then the last of the sands parted, revealing a prone figure lying on the bed beneath the uplifted arms of the men. Vusu and Kyros struggled over my brother's bed as he stared, unseeing, up at them.

I hovered, entranced with horror, as I watched their struggle. I felt their wills clash, over and over, each weakening, neither breaking. The other presence I'd sensed was nowhere to be seen, though I felt it still, searching for an opening in their defenses. Staring down at Linos's scarred face, I guessed who it must be. The daemon who had seized Linos's tongue now sought to fully claim my brother.

What I had to do crystallized in my mind. I pooled all the hate, the fear, the fury surging inside me and drew on its fire. I'd do whatever I had to, not knowing the cost.

I would save Linos.

Drawing myself away, sand flooded the scene again, all three swallowed within them. Back in the Pyrthae, I searched the ruins of Oedija. Eltris still hovered above, watching, waiting. But it wasn't her I was looking for. Just above me, staying at the perimeters of the whipping winds of Famine's sandstorm, lingered the swirling sand of Linos's daemon.

Anger pulsing through me, I threw myself after it.

Sensing its danger, the pyr fled into the blighted buildings. I pursued, speeding far faster than I could have run, faster than a diving hawk. But as the buildings opened into a desolate forum, the daemon was nowhere to be seen.

I swore loudly as I looked for it, even knowing it was futile. Here, it was in its element. I'd have to settle that score another time. Turning, I threw myself back toward my brother and the contending wardens.

Though I felt Eltris's focus on me, she didn't try to stop me, perhaps knowing she could no longer match me. I gathered speed and force as I dove toward Vusu and Kyros struggling over my brother. Famine's fell light pulsed above, as if in delight of the struggle. I didn't slow, didn't let myself think of what might happen when I collided. I formed myself into force and fury and threw myself into the fray.

My aim was true. As I collided, I managed to avoid Linos and Kyros and cut through Vusu's winds alone, carving through to the center of them. I felt the pain ripping through his awareness as if it were my own, deep and wide enough that I almost lost myself in it. But momentum drove me deeper still, until finally, something gave way.

I felt him break.

Some part of me became aware of Kyros throwing Vusu back against the wall in the real world, and Vusu's head hitting against the stone, his arm flopping out at an unnatural angle. The Visage of the Wyvern didn't rise, but stirred sluggishly to look down at the item in his hand. *The white-wood knife*, I suddenly recognized. The one the Seekers had stolen from Kyros, that Eltris had called the sacrificial knife. The same as Aika of the Green had thrust into her own breast. Kyros strode around Linos toward the traitor. I watched, unable to look away, eager to see him make an end of my enemy.

But I'd lingered too long — for suddenly, I felt Vusu seize me. Even broken and dying, his grip was too strong for me to flee. Panicking, I struggled, but still he bore me up.

Up into the the storm above.

As Famine loomed around me, I stilled, like a hare spotted in the open streets. A dark storm of sand and wind walled us in. Above, a heavenly sphere, the source of the strange light, glowed like the sun and pulsed like a beating heart.

Hunger and hate suddenly burst through me. I felt myself draining away into the abyss of the daemon god. There seemed no end to his horrible desire. But Vusu still held me.

You. The word was resonant with bitter irony. *Again, it is you who stops me.*

I had too little of myself for speech, my will draining into the ravenous hunger around me.

Keep hold of yourself, Airene of Port. Listen well. There will be only two Seeds of Famine when I am gone. Only your brother, and you. One of you must become the Sacrifice, then descend stoneward. Only this can contain the Serpent, and only for a time. Do you understand?

Horror brought me back to myself for a brief moment. *No!* I cried out, as much in answer as denial.

I felt his bitter laugh echo through me. *You doom us and do not even know how. Seek my honor, Seda. She possesses all that I could tell you. You must do this, Airene, if you wish to stop Famine. I cannot hold him for much longer.*

The sphere of light above pulsed violently, as if it were a grotesque, enormous egg, and what was contained inside struggled to break free. Dread washed over me anew.

Go! Vusu commanded me, both weakness and strength in the word. *Go, and do what I could not.*

He ripped me free and sent me tumbling away from the tempest. Dazed, I struggled to find myself, my winds scattered about me. Only one thought, stubbornly clung to, forced myself back together.

Linos. I had to make sure he was safe.

Though my awareness strained at the seams of my form, like a skin too full of water, I cobbled my consciousness back together and looked around. Famine's storm raged stronger still, the wind and sand whipping at me and eroding my strength. Pulling back further, I saw at the base of the storm Vusu's winds faltering, but still spinning. Linos had begun to spiral wider, free finally of his master. Kyros swirled strong.

As I dove at them again, the sands parted just in time to see Kyros closing the last of the distance to Vusu, lightning sparking on his fingertips. Vusu glanced up at where I watched, as if he could see me, then raised the wooden knife in his unbroken arm. His body trembled as he positioned the knife above his chest.

His whisper cut through me. *"Famine, I give myself to you as Sacrifice."*

Then Vusu plunged the dagger into his chest.

The Pyrthae vibrated for a moment, the tremor rattling me. Then the tempest that had raged above us disappeared without a trace. The orb of unholy light dissipated as well, and the Pyrthae fell into sudden darkness. I was lost in the black, yet I couldn't move, shock and disbelief rooting me in place.

Famine was gone, truly gone. I couldn't feel him at all.

I roused myself to take stock of the situation. Vusu, too, had vanished. Giving himself as Sacrifice had killed him, or taken him somewhere I couldn't follow. The daemon that had plagued Linos had long since fled. Kyros was melding away as he returned to our world. I felt myself fading as well.

Suddenly, all that I'd done caught up with me. I couldn't even muster the energy to fear for myself.

But I wasn't allowed to slip into oblivion. Someone seized me, anger burning me awake.

Idiot girl! Eltris raged against me. *You damned fool! What have you done? You've ruined us!*

They're gone, I thought wearily. *Famine and Vusu both.*

You don't understand! You never will!

She let me slip through her fingers, and I didn't resist as I melded with the darkness.

23
THE DESPOT OF OEDIJA

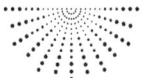

Every man has the chance to remake himself, but few do. To be reforged is to be melted down to the essence of what you are, the impurities burned away, so you may be made stronger.

You and I may be reforged again, brother, should we have the daring to seize this moment, and the courage to face the pain of being born again...

- Tales of the Desolate, uncensored; 1092 SLP

I woke with a head stuffed full of wool. Blinking through the stars in my vision, I stared around me. A moment later, I recognized where I was. *Jaxas's solar.*

Yet I had the distinct feeling I'd been somewhere else entirely a moment before.

Footsteps scuffled behind me. I started, sitting up in the chair I'd been slumped in and groaning with my body's protests. A pair of familiar beady eyes stared down at me, a look of rebuke plastered on his pinched features. Yet with my head in a fog, I found myself uncertain.

"Nikias?" I asked tentatively.

The steward sniffed. "Good, you're awake. Come. The Despot has summoned you."

His words were nonsense to me. *The Despot?* I searched my memory, hoping to make sense of things.

The Claw had burst into flame. Xaron had been in danger.

And I'd gone to him.

I'd entered the Pyrthae. I'd saved him and Talan by channeling quintessence as Clepsammia showed me. I'd felt powerful there, more so with each passing moment.

But then I remembered the rest. The cavernous hunger permeating me as Vusu held me in the midst of Famine's storm. I remembered the traitor's words. *There will be only two Seeds of Famine when I am gone. Only your brother, and you.*

Seeds of Famine.

Eltris's despising words after our last lesson came back to me. *And you imagine yourself a Finch. There's only one way you could have become a warden, girl.*

The suspicion I'd held and dismissed was true.

As I sat, numb with the realization, more pieces fell into place. In *The Seeds of Famine*, Aika of the Green had awoken as a warden after a dream of Famine. *A Seed of Harvest*, she had claimed to be. But I suspected now whose Seed she had truly been.

I slumped down in my seat, all strength leaving my body.

"First Verifier Airene. Are you listening?"

I barely heard Nikias through the tempest of my thoughts. What did it mean? What did it mean that Famine had opened me to the Pyrthae? Was I tainted? Were his fate and mine now bound together? Did he even now worm his way into my mind and spirit, hollowing me, turning me to his cause? Linos, too, had been attuned by Famine — I believed Vusu that far. Perhaps I was doomed to become what he had, little more than a scrap of spirit left to me, little more than an empty vessel, waiting to be filled.

"Airene!"

I dragged myself up from my heavy thoughts. "Yes, Nikias. I hear you."

Nikias didn't bother hiding his disapproval. "His Radiance wishes for your presence immediately. If you are not well enough to stand, I shall order you an invalid's litter."

The strangeness of Nikias's words drew me further from my stupor. *His Radiance?* Even for the Wreaths, the address went too far, particularly when the Laurel Palace had lost even more power by Council decree.

But oddity aside, it was welcome news. It must mean that Komo and First Laurel Synne had succeeded in recovering Despot Myron Wreath. I could only hope Xaron and the Watchers had returned as well. But what had Myron done to earn so much respect upon his return?

I turned through the possibilities. There was another explanation: that this all a charade put on by Orhan and the Preservists to disguise their crimes. But I didn't see why Nikias would comply, unless Jaxas had ordered him to.

The steward turned from me, a disgusted look on his face. "I will send an honor for a litter then."

"Wait — I can stand."

Not sure if I actually could, I lifted myself from the chair and turned to face him. Pain didn't drown me as I'd expected. My ribs still throbbed dully, but it barely hurt to breathe anymore. The back of my head, tender from where the Guilders had struck it against the ground, only smarted. I smiled grimly. My body had healed itself once again, at least partially.

But any pleasure I took in it was tainted by the knowledge that it was only by Famine's gift — or curse — that it was possible.

My legs still unsteady, I leaned on the chair. "Where are we going?"

Nikias watched me as if he expected me to collapse at any

moment. "As I said, we go to meet the Despot. He waits before the palace to make a pronouncement to his people."

That seemed like Myron at least. He'd always basked in the attention of the people at ceremonies. Though why he would care about me attending him, I hadn't the slightest clue.

But I was more interested in other things at the moment. "Nikias, I'm sorry, but I have other places to be. My brother — I must see to him."

Displeasure gleamed in his eyes. "You serve at the Despot's pleasure now, First Verifier Airene. It won't do to stir his displeasure."

His words gave me pause yet again. *First Verifier? I serve at the Despot's pleasure?* Had the Laurel Palace taken up the Order of Verifiers after the Conclave cast us off? There were too many questions, too many things I didn't know. Much as I wished to check on my brother and friends, I needed to attend to these mysteries. Linos wouldn't be in danger for the moment now that Vusu had given himself as Sacrifice. And if Xaron, Nomusa, and Talan weren't safe, there was nothing more I could do.

Besides, I didn't think Nikias meant to give me a choice.

My throat dry, I managed to keep my tone light. "By all means, Steward, lead the way."

Though sunlight barely pierced the gray of the overcast morning, the crowds had already gathered for Myron's announcement. As Nikias and I emerged from the Laurel Palace doors, we were assaulted by the tumultuous sound they made, cascading up the hill from below. Even outside the gates a quarter-mile down, the noise was astounding. And the swell of the crowd — there seemed no end to the gathered people. I felt dizzy standing above them all, as if I were the focus of their attention. Fear, too, was part of it. Since I'd seen what the Manifest and dusk mobs were capable of, I didn't trust crowds. I wondered if this one had gathered merely to greet their returning Despot, or for a more nefarious purpose.

"I'm glad to see you up and walking," said a soft voice by my side.

I glanced over, recognizing Jaxas's voice, but I had to look twice to be sure it was he. The Archon stood as tall and proud as I'd ever seen him. No longer did he seem sickly or bowed by life or duty. The thinness of his features held strength, like a slender tree standing strong after a storm. His robes were rich but simple, decorated in the green and gold that signified the royal family. He wore a golden chain studded with emeralds, and rings glittered upon his fingers. I'd never seen him so ornamented, nor ever expected to.

"Jaxas," I started, but a scowl from Nikias silenced me. My confusion only increased as the steward bowed nearly level with the ground.

"Your Radiance, I have brought the First Verifier," the man said, his tone subdued and formal. "If you will excuse me, I must be about other arrangements for the announcement."

"Of course. Do what you must, and with my thanks, Nikias." Jaxas inclined his head to the steward.

Nikias seemed to take it as a great honor, for he walked away with his chin upright.

I turned back to the Archon. "When did you earn that respect? *Your Radiance*, I mean."

Jaxas smiled, but his eyes remained untouched. For the first time, I wondered if I'd spoken too familiarly.

"I wanted you to be here," he finally said. "You most of all, Airene of Oedija."

I wondered at that curious epithet, but it was the least of the abounding riddles. "What for? What's going on, Jaxas?"

He turned his gaze toward the roaring crowd below. "A change in the tides, I hope. A new dawn for our realm, and not our last."

I stared, at a loss for words.

He looked again at me. "All will be made clear soon. Did you rest well? Nikias said you slept for a long time. I don't fault you for it," he continued quickly at my expression. "You're severely injured, Airene. You need rest."

"I wasn't resting."

The truth suddenly played on the tip of my tongue. I knew what it meant if I told him what I was. I'd have to live with the consequences, for good or for ill. I thought I knew Jaxas. But he'd surprised me many times in the past span, and he kept many more secrets than I'd suspected. Did I know him well enough to entrust him with my life?

As I opened my mouth to speak, I realized I did.

"I channeled. I walked the Pyrthae in a dream, Jaxas. I saw some of what happened at the Claw and Brinecoast. And I was there at the Acadium with Vusu, Kyros, and Eltris, when..." I struggled to put what I'd seen, what I'd done, into words. "When Vusu died," I finished lamely.

Even trusting him, I couldn't meet his eyes, dreading what I'd see. Revulsion? Fear? But when I finally met Jaxas's gaze, I saw a fierce joy there, deep in his dark, recessed eyes. I nearly flinched back from the bluntness of it.

"Thank you," he said quietly. "Thank you for you trusting me as few others would. You cannot know what it means to me."

My mouth opened, then closed. "You knew?" was all I could manage to say.

He nodded. "There were many signs. The circumstances of how you suddenly fell ill. The conferences with Eltris and Isidora's Watchers. But it was the burns in your blankets seen by your honor, Hyrol, that confirmed it."

Anger stirred me from my shock. "You were spying on

me? I suspected Hyrol might be watching for someone else. I didn't think it'd be you."

The Archon held me in his gaze until the anger flickered uncertainly in me.

"I watched for your protection," he said, so quietly his words were almost lost in the tumult of the crowd. "You thwarted Vusu's plans, Airene. The Manifest might still decide to kill you at any moment. I couldn't let you go to the Conclave, knowing they couldn't protect you."

I stared at him, trying to see the truth in his eyes, desperately hoping it was as he spoke it. That Jaxas had sought to protect me, not keep track of my movements. But even after my confession, I'd never felt less certain of him.

An honor walked from behind a column, startling me. Without hesitation, she approached and whispered in Jaxas's ear. Though his eyes didn't leave me, Jaxas nodded once, and the honor hurried away.

"The time has come," he said to me. "I'd appreciate if you stood nearby, Airene. As close as is courteous." He paused. "Can you project voices yet?"

I flinched and glanced over my shoulder to be sure the honor was out of earshot. "I don't think so," I muttered. "And I don't want everyone to know what I am besides."

He nodded slowly. "I'll respect your wishes. Just know that the time for secrets may soon be over."

I doubted he would ever be past keeping his. But I nodded all the same.

"It's nearly time for the speech," he said, turning. "We should be heading down."

"Just one question," I said hurriedly. "Xaron, Nomusa, Komo — where are they? They must have returned with Myron Wreath if he's to make an announcement." I looked around. "Where is he, anyway? Is he set to make a grand entrance as usual?"

The amusement in Jaxas's eyes irked me beyond measure,

but his words set me at ease. "They are safe, never fear. Nomusa is doing me a favor at the moment, and Xaron has need of rest. The Watchers didn't fair well in the Wyvern's Claw, as you have probably surmised from your... dream-walk. Just over half of them survived, Isidora among them."

I nearly folded over with the wave of relief that washed over me. They were alive and safe. Tears burned at my eyes. "High heights of the 'Thae, but I'm relieved to hear you say that."

"Heir Komo and First Laurel Synne also survived and completed their task."

"I figured they, at least, had succeeded." I gestured at the crowd below us.

Jaxas gave a thin smile that didn't reach his eyes. Again, I wondered what I was missing.

He turned. "We must go. The people are waiting."

I had no choice but to follow.

As Jaxas emerged from the columns and started down the main stairwell from the Laurel Palace, the crowd suddenly roared even louder. Jaxas nodded and smiled. Despite being a Wreath, he showed none of the showmanship of Myron, nor the gaudy ostentatiousness of the Despot's daughter. He was a soft-spoken man, and presented himself as nothing else. Yet there was no denying his regality as he walked slowly ahead of me.

I followed at a distance. Laurel guards lined the way, and two Shepherds had taken up post at the next landing. Tribune Timon waited there too, his slithering gaze finding me as I approached. I looked aside, remembering Jaxas's private words with the Tribune. Why was he here with his Shepherds? What task had Jaxas set them to before? I hadn't noticed them during my dream-walk, but I hadn't been searching for them.

My gaze wandered to the person standing next to him. First Laurel Synne's stare was cool as she nodded to me after bowing low to Jaxas. She looked somewhat the worse for wear from her journey into Brinecoast, a dark cut still trickling red down her forehead, her armor crusted with dried blood. Yet her posture only slightly sagged from the night's expedition.

Jaxas stepped down next to the Tribune and leaned toward him. I stared hard, wishing my head wasn't pounding so I could make sense of the situation.

"Airene."

Recognizing the voice, I turned with a relieved smile. "Heir Komo. I—"

The smile froze on my lips at the sight of him. The boy had fared far worse than the First Laurel. Bruises and cuts littered his skin, visible from his ceremonial warrior's garb. In places, his flesh had turned ashy. The eye set in the midst of the flaking green paint was purpled and swelled almost shut. His bottom lip was puffy on one side, making his smile look more like a grimace. His nose was bent and trickled blood.

"It will heal," he said hurriedly at my horrified expression. "Nothing is permanently broken."

"That's good. But still…"

It wasn't just his wounds. Only a boy of fourteen, and he suffered as a man. No — he *was* a man, with all the responsibilities and maturity of one. Despite myself, I felt a glow of pride for the Bali prince. I hoped Linos would act as well as Komo when he came out of his stupor. Perhaps without Vusu, Famine, and the daemon plaguing him, he would even soon rise.

Nkosi, two steps behind the boy, nodded to me. "Our *Shaka-na* is strong, as his father and mother raised him to be. He has done our ishaka proud with his actions tonight."

I nodded in agreement. "But where is the Despot? I was told he'd be making an announcement soon."

Komo and Nkosi exchanged glances. "He is," the boy said, seeming confused.

Before I could ask anything further, silence dropped behind me. Turning, I saw Jaxas stood at the edge of the dais, one of the Shepherd's hands touching his throat, and flinched as his voice crashed over the gathering.

"People of Oedija! You will have heard many rumors why we gather here today. You have heard my uncle, Myron Wreath, is not dead. You have heard my cousin, Asileia Wreath, has fled the city. You have heard the Wyvern's Claw of Thys burns to the ground, and that a battle has taken place north of the wall. Perhaps you have even heard that Shepherds have visited the Conclave." He paused, letting the words sink in. "I come now to tell you all of this is true. The Claw burned at the hands of wardens I sent to kill the traitor Vusumuzi."

For a moment, I stopped breathing. The crowd stirred, but the noise was conflicted and confused. Some shouted angrily, but most seemed uneasy. *How else had the Wreaths used wardens?* they must be thinking. *How else have they played with fire?* I couldn't believe Jaxas would throw this brand onto the tinder of the crowd's temper.

Jaxas continued as if he hadn't noticed the commotion. "Vusumuzi, who called himself the Visage of the Wyvern and led the rebel faction the Manifest, was the most powerful warden of our time. Yet he fled before our Watchers, wardens of the Acadium who were trained to defend us against him. Vusumuzi burned his base of operations as he left, but the Watchers escaped. Vusumuzi, in the end, did not. Though he fled to the Acadium, he died there with a knife in his chest."

Scattered cheers pierced the uneasiness, but not nearly as many as I'd hoped for. A century and a half of distrust of magic couldn't be undone with a single action. Even if they had seen Vusu as a great threat, taking him on with any wardens other than the Shepherds was too much to swallow. I wondered if Jaxas knew what a grave error he was committing. But there was no stopping it now as he continued.

"With Vusumuzi's death, we hope to dismantle the Manifest. To any of you who know those who followed him, tell them: their leader is dead. They should disperse and return to their lives, so that we may prepare for the other threats against Oedija.

"But the traitor's justice is not all we gained last night. Myron Wreath, my uncle, has been recovered from the clutches of the Manifest. However, to our great sadness, he has suffered horrible mistreatment at their hands. For now, he deems himself too ill to serve as your Despot, and has asked another to Ascend in his place. Yet further tragedy finds us. Asileia Wreath, your erstwhile Despoina, has fled the city. So it falls to the last member of our family to take up the Evergreen Wreath."

Suddenly, Nikias bustled past me. I stared down at his hands to see a vibrantly green crown of leaves and twigs. He passed the Evergreen Wreath to Tribune Timon. The Tribune, with an inappropriate grin plastered over his face, raised the crown aloft. Jaxas turned and bowed his head so that the shorter man could set it atop his brow. He turned back to the almost completely silent crowd, a quiet echoed in myself.

"I stand before you as your new Despot, people of Oedija, to act on your behalf, and to protect you from the many enemies who threaten us."

He paused. If he expected applause, he was disappointed. Too much had happened too quickly for them to know how to react. I myself could only stare.

"And already I do so," Jaxas continued relentlessly. "As my reign begins, I have put necessary decrees in place. Beginning with the Demos Council. In ordinary times, their laggardly way of conducting the nation's business might suffice. In war, it does not. Henceforth, I have disbanded the Council and suspended the power of the Conclave. All such power will return to the Laurel Palace as was done in the days of our ancestors."

Finally, the crowd roared. I watched the gates below rattle as people pressed against them, shouting and screaming. A few even started climbing them before laurel guards jabbed them back with the blunt end of their spears. This was a cauldron ready to boil over, and Jaxas only fed the fire.

"Avvad marches on our city!" Jaxas called above the noise, his voice thundering down the hill. "We must prepare for war! I will lead us through this trial. With your help, people of Oedija, we will turn aside the Imperium!"

I doubted the renewed cries were from enthusiasm. I could do nothing but stare at our newly Ascended Despot. He'd done it. He'd done what some part of me had hoped he would do. And from what he'd said earlier, he'd done it in part because of my words and influence.

But now that he'd finally acted, I couldn't help but wish he had not. Rather than unite Oedija, it promised to break it in a way that could never be mended.

Famine might be suppressed, but the tremors of his arrival still wracked the city apart.

His pronouncements finished, Jaxas turned away, and his gaze found and held me. I returned it, though I was sure he could read the fear behind my eyes.

His expression didn't shift as he approached me. "Wait for me in my solar," he instructed, then started up the stairs. I cast one last look back at the roiling crowd, then obeyed my new Despot's command.

I stared out through the balcony doors of Jaxas's solar. Watching. Waiting.

Nikias had filled me in on some of the vaguer details of Jaxas's speech. Myron had indeed been recovered and was in critical condition. Presently, he was under bed-watch by order of the Wreath healers. As for if he was sick enough to serve as Despot, the steward professed belief that Jaxas spoke truly. I kept my doubts to myself.

As for his daughter, Asileia had officially fled the city with Bhaka, Komo's traitorous guard. In some sense, this was true. Both had left the city — but not together. The former Despoina was now being kept at the same Wreath manor in the northern prefectures as my family. As for Bhaka, Komo had sent him back home with three of his guards to accept Yorandu justice.

Now Jaxas met with his new circle of advisors. Among them were, to my dismay, Feiyan and Timon. The former Tribune was now acting as the High Tribune, and Feiyan moved to occupy the premier counselor position of old, First Consul, which made her authority second only to Jaxas's. My blood boiled every time I imagined her smug smile at achieving such a high level of power. I hoped our new Despot knew what he was doing. Feiyan might be a useful tool, but only so long as her interests aligned with our own.

I tried to deny the last of my feelings toward it, but I was too weary to lie, even to myself. That he had chosen Feiyan for such a position over me smarted, even as I knew it was preposterous to feel that way. I was no counselor, no second-in-command. I was injured and a liability as a warden, among a host of other reasons.

Yet I couldn't drown the jealousy and resentment.

More aggravating still was that I couldn't reach Linos, nor had I heard more from Xaron and Nomusa, or anything from Talan. Corin, too, was still missing from before the night's action had begun. My weakness was only one part of the reason for not leaving to find information for myself. Despite watching for several turns as I absently ate from the array of food laid out in Jaxas's solar, the crowds around the Laurel Palace hadn't dispersed. In fact, they only seemed to swell greater, as if the spreading word brought more curious eyes to glimpse the Despot who had taken back his family's ancestral power. I could only hope all my friends were safe, and that Linos was out of the hands of those who wished him harm. I even dared to hope he'd awakened at last.

A creak sounded from the far side of the room, and I turned to see the door opening. But it wasn't Jaxas who walked through. Worries momentarily forgotten, I crossed the short distance and wrapped Xaron and Nomusa in a tight embrace.

"You're late," I chastised them, not letting go.

"Come off it," Xaron complained. "You weren't worried about us. You knew we'd make it out."

Nomusa pried me off with a small smile. "I'm sorry to keep you waiting. Jaxas gave us a task to immediately attend to."

My spirits sank further. Yet two more people had been given priority over me. That they were my friends only made it worse. "And that duty was?"

They exchanged a glance. "Establishing the Watchers as an official order of Oedija," Nomusa admitted with reluctance.

I blinked. So much was changing, and all at once. Suddenly, I wanted to hear nothing more of it. "Never mind that. Tell me what happened last night."

They exchanged another look, no doubt surprised at my lack of curiosity, but obliged. Xaron began with what I suspected was an exaggerated account of his foray into the Wyvern's Claw. According to him, they'd had to overcome Seeker wardens at every turn until they finally arrived at the center room in the tallest part of the amphitheater, where Vusu was supposed to be lying ill in bed. Instead, they'd encountered a room empty but for an intricate trap that shattered dozens of pots filled with oil on the wooden floor, then set them to flames. They'd been forced to flee to avoid being swallowed by the chasing inferno. To make matters worse, Seeker wardens closed in behind them, and they'd had to fight their way out. Six of the Watchers hadn't returned. Recounting this finally seemed to dampen Xaron's mood. He morosely confessed that they hadn't even killed Vusu for their troubles.

Nomusa's story was no less eventful. Having gone to the Conclave at Jaxas's behest, she'd stood in the great chamber and borne witness to the overthrow of the Demos Council. Tribune Timon had marched his four Shepherds down the stairs to the small door behind the dais and entered without invitation. Nomusa hadn't seen everything that occurred, but it wasn't long after that the Low Consuls were marched out. Only Feiyan had been missing — for, as usual, she was ahead of the game. They'd come out quietly for the most part, but only after Berker had been made an example of. One of the Shepherds burned his arm badly when he resisted, and none of the others risked it. I felt some small measure of vindication at Berker's punishment, but it was tainted with the realization that Shepherds were free to use their magic against even the elected officials of our demotism. Even if the Low Consul was an ass, it was a dangerous precedent. The Conclave guards, having witnessed the devastation wardens were capable of during the Despoina's trial, didn't resist either, but let the Demos Council be led away.

At their urging, I reluctantly revealed that, despite being chair-bound, I'd had my own notable night. They stared at me in incredulity as I described entering the Pyrthae and the Oedijan wasteland. Xaron's eyes widened as I confessed I'd uplifted his flagging spirit. He pulled me into a tight embrace.

"You saved me, Airene. I was tamping down flames so that others behind me could escape and thought I would fall on the spot. Then suddenly, I felt energy sweep through me. And to think that was you!" He shook his head. "You've grown into your gift so quickly. It's amazing."

I flushed. "I can't really claim the credit. Clepsammia showed me how."

"Clepsammia?" Nomusa cut in. "The Eidolan goddess?"

I nodded and explained my encounters with her, my suspicions of her role in Asileia's madness, and that, perhaps, other Eidolan gods were not all myths.

Nomusa shook her head slowly. "Gods and daemons among us. You can't have anything more incredible to say."

"Just wait."

It was then I told them of how I'd hopefully saved Talan, then turned to face Famine and saw the conflict beneath him, and what I'd done about it. I told them Vusu's words and actions, and how he'd taken his own life with the white-wood knife, and how immediately Famine had disappeared. Only his words concerning me and Linos as Seeds of Famine did I hold back.

"Just like that, he contained a god," Xaron breathed. "I can't believe his power."

"But why?" Nomusa demanded. "Why would he break apart our city, then sacrifice himself to save it?"

"I know some answers." I had yet to tell them all I'd learned from my readings, but it would have to wait. "And we might discover the rest if we find his honor Seda."

Xaron frowned. "If she's still alive. She might have burned with the Claw."

"I doubt Vusu would have been that shortsighted. No, I bet she's somewhere safe in the Manifest compound, waiting for her master's return."

Before we could continue, the door creaked open. Seeing who it was, all three of us quickly stood. Jaxas — *Despot* Jaxas — stood in the doorway. As we began to bow, he motioned irritably.

"Please, sit down. I've enough of that bowing and scraping from everyone else."

We slowly sat again. I watched him warily. He'd caught me off-guard many times in the course of a day's turning and might hold further surprises still.

Jaxas paced over to stand in front of the fire. For a minute, he did nothing but stare into it. We didn't resume our conversation, too conscious of the potency of our subject. We couldn't discuss Famine before I reported to Jaxas, and I didn't know when that might occur. But then, it was my duty to tell him when I had something to report.

I steeled myself. "Despot Jax— Your Radiance, I mean—"

"Didn't I say enough of that?" His voice was soft, and he didn't turn around, but it somehow made the words more threatening. I swallowed and waited. I had a warden's gift burgeoning inside me, yet this unattuned man could still put the fear of the gods in me.

He suddenly turned. "Xaron. Nomusa. Thank you for your work earlier. Is all well in establishing the Order of Watchers? Have you discussed with Nikias the establishment of living quarters for them in the palace garrison?"

"We have… sir." Her words fell flat as she searched for the proper address.

The Despot's hooded eyes fell on her. "Call me Jaxas if you must call me anything. But that is good. The Watchers will be of utter importance in keeping my rule. I shall call on them soon to discuss their duties." His gaze turned on Xaron. "And you shall pass on my orders to them."

Xaron looked startled. "Me?"

"Who else, but the First Warden to the Despot?" He smiled slightly as Xaron's eyes widened. "You may keep Hilarion's tower, Xaron — but I would discard the robes. They can't have been comfortable."

"You have no idea," my friend muttered. "I mean, thank

you, Jaxas. I hope I will — That is, I'll do my best to serve you."

Jaxas nodded absently, his gaze turning to Nomusa. "And you, Nomusa. I may have suspended the powers of the Conclave, but I will still need their bureaucratic expertise in governing the city and state. As my Archon, it will be your obligation to persuade them to perform their duties. Will you help me?"

She accepted her new position with more grace than Xaron had managed. "Thank you, Jaxas. I will do all I can."

Anticipation filled me as Jaxas's gaze turned finally to me. "I will speak further with both of you in a short while. But now, if you would grant me a private moment with Airene."

My friends glanced at me, questions in their eyes, but they swiftly complied.

As the door closed behind them, I wasn't sure what to feel. What could he have to say that he would wish to keep secret from Xaron and Nomusa? Or perhaps, I mused, the privacy was for my sake — to save me from embarrassment.

Jaxas stared at me for a long moment, silhouetted by the firelight. "I mean to make Kelena my new First Verifier."

I blinked rapidly. My throat had gone completely dry. It had been the one position left that I could imagine him giving me. "Very well," was all I could think to say.

"I need you to know, Airene, it's not because I think you incapable. But the last span has shown me Kelena's value. I need her and the connections she possesses. She's hungry to prove herself. Deny her this chance, and I fear I'll lose all she has access to."

"I understand." I did. I couldn't have admitted it before, but this turn of events forced me to stare the truth in the eye: Kelena was a far better Finch than I'd ever been. I felt adrift. What did that mean for the past decade? What had I been striving for?

"But I have another task for you, Airene," he continued.

"One I would trust only to you. You must find the way to stop Famine, if one exists."

A laugh escaped me, and Jaxas stared at me in surprise.

"You're well-informed, but not well enough," I told him. "Famine is gone, Jaxas. Vusu made a Sacrifice of himself to lock him away, as was done of old."

The Despot stared at me until I shifted uncomfortably, then turned his gaze out over the city.

"You're sure?" he asked quietly.

"I saw it happen. Though… Vusu said he wouldn't be able to hold him long. I don't know how long that means. The last Sacrifice trapped Famine for a thousand years as far as I know. Perhaps only a little while may give us a year, or a decade."

"Perhaps. I will set you to the watch all the same. But if it is in vain, then I will give you another impossible task beside it." He turned a sudden wry smile on me. "After all, you work miracles, do you not?"

I shrugged uncomfortably. "What is your wish now?"

The smile disappeared as swiftly as it had come. "I wish you to stop an empire, Airene. I wish you to find the way to defeat soldiers who cannot be seen or killed. I wish you to dispense of the Silks before they pour over our walls and end our defense before it's begun. And I wish you to counter the Tefra who command them."

I stared at him. Another impossible task, indeed. "As easily ask for the moons," I muttered.

"Only this. Will you try?"

"Of course." I knew no other answer to give.

He nodded grimly. "Of titles, I know of none to give such a position."

I thought for a moment, then startled at a realization. "Give me none. I don't need any, so long as I have access to where I need to go and the requisite resources. In fact, it's probably better I have no title. Perhaps I can escape the attention of prying eyes."

Jaxas considered me for a moment. "Chaos becomes you," he murmured.

He spared me the need to respond by stepping quickly toward the door. "If your report of the night can wait, I have much other business to attend to. As do you."

"Yes," I said, still somewhat flustered by his enigmatic words. "But I must see my brother first."

"Of course. Ask Synne — she will grant you an escort to the Acadium. And if you feel your brother's accommodations are not adequate, you have my permission to bring him here."

The Despot didn't give me time to thank him before he turned from his solar and departed.

24

REBORN

He came to me with promises of power. He whispered dreams of vengeance while I lay sleepless in my thin wraps. I could scarcely eat and drink for how he tormented me with hunger and thirst for him.

What else could I do but turn and serve my God?

- Tales of the Desolate, uncensored; 1092 SLP

I contemplated my rapid changes in fortunes as I rode alone in a carriage to the Acadium. Before, in Jaxas's solar, I had despaired of ever reaching Linos. Little had I known that, in a few turns, I would have access to a carriage and armored guard at a moment's notice.

It was the least of the things stirring about me. With Xaron and Nomusa about their new duties, I had no one to distract me. I looked outside in an effort to escape my worries, but Jaxas Ascending had not stopped Oedija's degradation; if anything, it had accelerated it. The number of houses I saw with busted shutters and doors hanging off of their hinges made chills run up my skin. The dusk mobs would be out tonight, I was sure, and in greater numbers than before. People crouched along the street, staring up with unbridled resentment at my passing carriage. I let the window drape fall closed again and sat back, wondering what I would do if they charged. They wouldn't dare do so with three guards riding with me. Or so I hoped.

Arrival at the Acadium came as a relief. After a brief pause, the Acadium guards waved us through, and the carriage rolled up the hill onto the campus. I couldn't hear how the guards explained who I was. Refusing a title had seemed a noble thing before. Now I wondered if it was simply impractical. But unless I wished to go crawling back to Jaxas, I'd have to live with my choice.

A short time later, we pulled up in front of the Ward, and I stepped out of the carriage. My ribs were still sore and my skin bruised, but I felt surprisingly hale otherwise. Yet I couldn't help a rueful smile imagining what a sight I looked, with my dark clothes and hair falling just above my shoulders.

Then I thought of whom I went to, and all humor faded.

My step quickened as I entered and found Linos's room, ignoring the clerk who called after me. I found his door hung slightly ajar. Only then did I wonder if danger might not linger here. My fingertips suddenly itched, and I rubbed them on my trousers as I stepped toward the door and eased it open.

Two people waited within, standing over the bed in the center where Linos lay, staring unseeing up.

"Finally she comes," Kyros Brighteyed growled as he turned. "I'd have thought you cared more for your brother, Finch." The Archmaster's remaining hair was tousled and his robes rumpled. From the looks of him, he'd been here all night.

"I do," I replied calmly. I turned my gaze to Eltris, who

also stood silently by Linos's bed. "What are you two still doing here?"

Eltris's eyes flashed with an emotion too quick to read. *Anger? Disgust?* I wondered why I even cared anymore.

"Watching," the augur replied at length. "Waiting."

"Something at which you're well-practiced." The sneering words were out of my mouth before I could second-guess them.

Kyros laughed hollowly. "She's finally found her bite, has she? Calm yourself, Finch. Vusumuzi died trying to get to this boy, so we have stood guard in case his pet Seekers come to finish the job. Better to thank us than strike out. It's clear we're all on the same side."

"I wouldn't say that." My gaze stayed on Eltris. "You would have let him sacrifice my brother. You would have let him die."

The Master Augur said nothing, but only returned my stare coolly.

"That's in the past now," Kyros said impatiently. "First Verifier Airene, we have questions for you. First, when did you become attuned to the Pyrthae? And how? I only detected hints of it a span ago when you visited, but that has certainly changed. Did you keep it hidden before?"

Cringing at how brazenly Kyros announced my secret, I quickly closed the door and glanced at Eltris. It wouldn't have surprised me if she'd exposed me simply from spite. "I didn't hide it. I wasn't sure I was a warden when I saw you."

"You weren't sure? Do you mean to say you've only just become attuned?" He snorted. "Impossible! You wrestled this old augur and won!"

"I did," I agreed, hoping I hid the vindictive pleasure warming my chest. "But nevertheless, I'm still fresh to this. Channeling on command still comes with difficulty."

"A rare talent then." There was a new note in the man's

tone. Not admiration or respect, exactly, but the hunger of a collector staring at a prized find.

"Or a singular Quintyr sparked her," Eltris said quietly.

Fire built inside me as I stared at the augur. Kyros looked between us, a scowl deepening his face.

"What does that mean?" he demanded. "How would you know which it was?"

Anger seized my tongue. "Are you so sore that I bested you that you would resort to this?" I railed against Eltris. "Are you that upset the pupil so quickly eclipsed the master?"

Her eyes widened. "Fool girl! Did you not wonder why your power had augmented? *It was because you were near him!* He was close to breaking free, and stronger than ever before! Look at your shifts now — see if they have not spread!"

"Who?" Kyros demanded again. "You can't mean—?" His eyes widened. "But that daemon can't attune wardens! Can he?"

My temples throbbed so that I couldn't think straight, couldn't hold the biting words back. "At least I'm not a bitter old woman sacrificing young boys so she doesn't have to risk her own pathetic life!"

I looked away, unable to stand the sight of the crone. Silence fell between us. My chest heaved as I struggled to master myself. I regretted the words as soon as they'd left my mouth, but I couldn't deny them. Every word had been true, as far as I believed.

But no matter how I might wish to, I couldn't afford to drive her away. At length, I looked up to find the augur still staring at me.

"I can't trust you," I said, my voice pitched soft but firm. "Not after what you meant to do. But I need you. Vusu said he couldn't hold Famine for long. When he returns, we need to be ready."

Eltris studied me without blinking, her yellow eyes like a

raptor's. Kyros's, meanwhile, blazed with Pyrthaen light as he looked between us. I wished he hadn't heard everything. Yet perhaps it was for the best. We'd need everyone we could muster if we were to survive Famine's return.

"Fine," the augur said shortly. Without another word, she strode past me and out of the door.

I stood completely still until I was sure she was gone. Even then, it was hard to let my fury slip away. I shook my head. What a pair we made, my tutor and me.

The Archmaster stepped toward the door, but hesitated at the entrance. "It is true, then? You were attuned by Famine?"

There seemed little point in denying it now. "Yes. As far as I know."

Kyros laughed like a man before the gallows. "I didn't believe the old augur when she told me he was here in Oedija. Famine, returned to the world. It was the stuff of children's stories! But last night, I felt Vusu approaching the Acadium. And when I moved to stop him, I sensed a vast presence behind him, thwarting my every attempt to defeat the old Bali. I knew it then. I knew the Quintyr had returned to meddle in men's affairs."

"So it appears."

He moved once more for the door, but stopped and said gruffly, "Your brother is still in there. I felt him when I fought Vusu." He lingered a moment longer before nodding and briskly departing.

I watched him go, mute with surprise. Perhaps there was a heart in the irascible warden after all.

Heartened by the Archmaster's words, I moved next to Linos, but stood just out of reach. Too well I remembered what had happened the last time I'd touched him. Though I'd driven away the daemon that had plagued him, still I hesitated. I drew in a breath. I couldn't live in fear of my brother forever.

Slowly, I stepped forward and reached toward him. My finger brushed the skin of his arm.

Nothing.

I smiled in relief. My brother was free of that horror at least. For now. But the joy was fleeting. I raised my hand to smooth the hair from his brow. I wished I could close his staring eyes. I wished I could wash away the violet scars around them. But wishing would gain me nothing. I had to learn more to be able to help him. Even from a woman who would have let Vusu kill both of my brothers.

Did you not wonder why your power had augmented?

Eltris's words in mind, I turned my hands over and peered at my fingertips. Breath caught in my throat. All ten of my fingerprints shifted now, the skin moving like ripples on a pond's surface. I was *shur*, a ten-shift warden, with as much potential for channeling as Xaron.

I dropped my hands and took Linos's hand in my own, clutching it as if it were a line thrown out to a drowning sailor. A thought struck me. I turned his hand over to expose his fingertips.

All five prints on the hand I held shifted.

I flipped his hand back over. "Let's get you out of here," I murmured, hating the tremble in my voice. "I'll keep you safe, Little Lion. Trust your big sister."

Almost, I fooled myself into thinking his eyelid twitched at my words. But, despite what Kyros had said, I knew it was nothing more than my imagination. Linos clung to his body, but just barely. He likely wouldn't wake until I figured out a way to help him.

I sighed and, turning from him, summoned the healers.

Once Linos was secured inside the carriage, we made our way back to the Laurel Palace. I tried to ignore the world outside for a few moments of peace. I held Linos's hand for the trip and tried not to listen to the shouting and sounds of struggle interspersed by the creaking of the carriage. My mind lost itself in a sea of vague fears and worries.

I woke from my uneasy rest to the squeaking of the palace gates. Sitting up straight, I waited for the carriage to ascend the long way up the hillside.

But before we had gone far, the carriage rolled to a halt.

If we hadn't been inside Wreath grounds, I might have been worried rather than curious. Just as I was about to poke my head out and see what was the matter, a knock came at the door. I opened it to a laurel guard standing stiffly at attention.

"Lady, there's a man here who says he must deliver a message. He told me to tell you that he bears, ah, 'a chalice of unrequited intoxication'—"

I pushed past the guard before he'd finished and saw him standing just beyond. His hair was ragged and singed, his clothes torn and stiff with dried blood.

It didn't matter. He was here.

He was alive.

Talan flashed me his half-grin as he pulled me gently into his arms.

"Not too gentle," I told him as I squeezed him harder. "My ribs are healed."

"They healed?" He chuckled into my hair. "Ah, Airene. You never cease to amaze me."

I was barely conscious of the guards and driver watching as I held onto him. He reeked of smoke and blood and grime, but I didn't care.

"How did you survive?" I whispered into his chest. "You were so weak. I thought you'd never rise again."

I felt him nod. "Four Silks bore down on me. I was already drained from fighting my way into the Underguild.

Dismissing one *ikoz* is difficult. I've never dismissed more. I thought I was dead; I'll admit, I'd given up. I'd done what I'd set out to do. I thought to myself that, as long as I saved her life, that might balance out the scales of my life."

I pulled back and tilted my head back to look into his amber eyes, shimmering with emotion. My eyes burned as well. I opened my mouth to speak, but I couldn't find the right words.

"But then someone came," he continued quietly. "Someone rushed into my being and demanded I rise. You didn't speak with words, but bared the secrets of your life to me. Of a childhood fraught with death and disappointment. Of an unsettled youth searching for something more than an ordinary life could offer. Of the loneliness you never dared show to anyone lest they think you weak."

My knees felt as if they couldn't support me any longer. "I showed you all that?" I asked faintly.

"And more. You left nothing of yourself hidden. Every part of your being, Airene, wished me to rise again." The smile crept onto his lips again. "So I must reveal my little secret in recompense. I never could refuse you."

Fire filled my body, a very different kind than I'd experienced recently. For the moment, I didn't care that the world teetered on the balance. All I wanted was for this moment to go on.

I leaned up and kissed him.

Our lips lingered on each other's. Underneath the sweat and stench of battle, something earthy and wholesome and entirely of him filled my lungs. I didn't want to stop breathing him in.

He pulled away first, clearing his throat lightly as he glanced behind me. A flush crept up my neck as I followed his glance. The driver was busy pretending not to notice, but all three of the guards were openly grinning and watching.

"I'll find you later," he offered. "For a walk," he added pointedly as the guards began to snicker.

"I'd love that." My smile was beginning to make my cheeks ache.

How I found the strength to turn from him and enter back inside the carriage, I didn't know. As the driver cracked the reins and the mules began to pull us away, I watched out the window until Talan disappeared around the hill's bend.

The rest of the day passed in a blur of activity. Arriving with Linos, I tracked down Nikias, settled my brother into a room, and secured proper care for him. The steward irritably reminded me that there were guards injured from the foray into the Manifest, but I didn't stop pestering him until he promised he would send a healer by as soon as one was available.

By the time I returned to the room I'd taken as my own, I found a message waiting for me.

Meet me at the Silvencrest. Eighth turn. I'll be waiting.

I marveled at Talan's quick sleuthing in discovering my quarters even as I wondered at the location of our rendezvous. The Silvencrest on the Conclave grounds was where the largest wave on the Oedijan coast crashed into a breakwater on evenings when the three moons were aligned in the sky. By some fortune, it seemed such an event was happening tonight. But that was the least thing that excited me. I smiled to myself, but knew there wasn't time to indulge in fantasies at the moment.

Quickly heading to the dining hall, I found Nomusa and Xaron there. As I ate a hasty meal, I divulged all I could of the afternoon's events.

"That rogue," Xaron groaned. "I always thought that

whole thing between you two would just blow over. You just kissed him on the cheek, surely?"

"That's not how I remember it." I winked at him.

Xaron received his own share of teasing when Isidora came up behind him and wrapped him a hug. Nomusa and I grinned at each other.

But having finished the meal, I was eager to be away. Just before I could escape, Nomusa stood and wrapped me in an embrace. "I'm glad you both can find some happiness amid all this," she said, the smile fading from her expression. "Don't be your usual self and feel guilty about it."

"I hadn't until you said something. But now..."

She snorted and turned me toward the door. "Just go."

I took her advice and pushed worry from my mind as I headed for the exit. Avvad marched on Oedija. People starved in the streets. Famine lurked somewhere out of sight, restrained for the moment by Vusu's fading strength. But, I told myself, I couldn't always delay my happiness for the world's problems. Jaxas had charged me with two impossible tasks. One night away wouldn't harm my prospects of accomplishing them.

As my walk went on, passing down the hill of the Laurel Palace to the bridge across to the Conclave, my rationalizations grew thinner. Yet I clung resolutely to them. *One night of rest,* I begged myself. *One night with Talan.* Yet I couldn't dislodge the feeling. Worry had planted a seed in me and taken root. And though I struggled against it, it pressed on my mind, growing and stretching and making my head ache.

As the pain spiked, I suddenly realized this wasn't just a guilty conscience. *Something* had started to run rampant through my mind, beyond my control. My head felt heavy and full as a melon. My vision fuzzed. I stumbled forward a few steps, then lost my balance, scraping my hands as I fell to the rough stones of the bridge. Wild thoughts raced through my head. Had I channeled too much quintessence? It felt as if the agony couldn't possibly grow. My senses faded before it. Panic rose in my chest, and my breaths came quick and shallow. I thought I would faint.

My mind split open.

Colors and lights flashed around me. I spun around and around, disoriented. Only as my turning slowed did I see that I floated apart from my body.

I was now in a different Oedija.

I tried gathering my wits as I looked wildly around. The Pyrthae appeared the same desert as it had before; only now, it had gained a new feature. In the center of it, a huge, black chasm yawned open, leaking motes of light and shifting waves of iridescent colors. I stared at it with dread and a slow understanding. The worry had not left my mind, but swelled further by the second. It grew and grew until it became a drive I'd neglected, a desire I'd never fulfilled, a thirst I'd never slaked. To my horror, I found myself drifting closer to the pit, the hunger that roared inside me directing all of its attention toward it, as if I might be satiated by whatever lay within. A horrible suspicion seized me. I knew what this was.

Then he emerged.

His head came into view first, as large as a dozen palaces stacked on top of one another. His black, pitted eye seemed to see everything and nothing at once. His maw, gaping impossibly wide, showed long, sharp teeth nearly as dark as his eyes. His body came slithering out after, covered in dark, great scales oscillating between the deep purple of thunderclouds and the scarlet of blood. Two pairs of powerful legs were attached to the lithe, snake-like body, bowed like a lizard's and ending in wickedly curved claws. His long form stretched nearly the length of the ruined Oedija below as his tail emerged, sparking with lightning and fire.

The dragon's sinuous body curled and undulated across the sky. From his dance, Famine seemed to enjoy his newfound freedom. I drifted ever closer, unable to help myself. The hunger had wholly seized me. I felt nothing but the desire to lose myself in the daemon god. To be consumed.

Take me! I flung toward the dragon. *Come take me! I offer myself to you!*

He didn't even turn his head toward me, but froze. Like a predator suddenly smelling prey, Famine jerked his head to the side and stared east.

I didn't care what he looked at. *Here!* I thought desperately, then launched myself up at him.

But the Quintyr had his sights set on something greater. His yearning suddenly poured out from him so that I nearly drowned in it. His serpentine body writhed and began to slither through the air with impossible speed. I stared in despair after him as he faded into the distance, finally drifting to a halt. The hunger inside me ached, then suddenly abated.

With it returned reason and horror. Only with the desire's release did I understand what I'd witnessed. I would have collapsed had I been in the real world.

Vusu had already failed. Famine had returned. And there was no one to save us from him now.

No one, if Vusu was to be believed, but Linos and me.

I drifted through the desolate, mirrored world, staring after the daemon god. For several long moments, I could do nothing but watch, expecting at any moment for him to rush back and seize me in his jaws. But he was gone. For now, there was no sign of his return.

I drifted back down to myself. Though the bridge was broken in this version of Oedija, I knew my body waited just below. And if the end of the world had come, I couldn't lie in the middle of the bridge and wait for it. For what little good it would do, I had work to attend to.

And no time for even a night of reprieve.

I descended into my bruised body and, as pain washed

over me afresh, rose shakily to my feet. I almost turned toward the Conclave grounds and Talan waiting at the Silvencrest. But I imagined the disappointment on his face when I told him all that could not be. And in this moment, I couldn't bear it.

Despair sapping my strength, I turned and walked heavily back the way I had come.

EPILOGUE

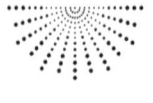

EAZAL

E azal stared at the endless expanse laid out before him.
Perched atop a dune, the desert stretched for miles in every direction. The world had been leeched of color. Gray dominated the landscape, the strange sands of the Wumofu seeming the ashes from a great conflagration that had long ago swept over the land. Nothing but twisted trees survived here now. Neither men nor spirits walked this place, the sand and air undisturbed by the passage of even the wind.

His were the only footprints on the still dunes as he pushed ever further into the wasteland's heart.

As if sensing his mood, Azhi spoke into his mind. *I am with you. Do not fear. I have walked this path before, long ago. Would you like me to tell you of it?*

Eazal bowed his head. Being comforted by a child — was this what he'd come to? "I'm fine, lad," he responded aloud. "But I would hear that tale still. I should know what is to come."

Despite his words, as the boy spirit began to speak and Eazal continued his long walk, he barely listened. The loneliness of the desert pressed in around him, no matter his constant companion. Azhi, the spirit who had first brought Valem's curse of magic to him, had been with him ever since his hasty departure from Oedija. When he'd failed the Valemish and was most at risk, the boy had appeared to him through a whisper finch and led him safely from their grasp. And after, when he'd begun wandering as he had in the years before his return to Oedija, Azhi appeared again, this time to give him purpose. Eazal had listened, though he hadn't believed him. The words the boy had spoken were impossible. Taozu the Corrupted — or Famine, as Oedija knew the God of Hunger — was not only real, but reborn. Even coming from a spirit, it was too far beyond his experience to comprehend. What did he know of gods and the higher and lower realms? He'd failed to retain the religion of his ancestors. How could he now believe the gods not only existed, but that one had awoken to bring chaos and ruin to the world?

But Azhi hadn't given up. How he'd convinced him in the end, Eazal couldn't explain. He'd ignored the boy's first urgent warnings, dwelling on his own losses. His wife and daughter had slipped fully from his grasp. It had been one thing to be pursued by the Finch girl, Airene, and her companions. It was another to stand against the whole of the Valemish. Despair had made the days of walking meld into one another, numbing him to any sense of purpose.

Yet all the while, Azhi stayed by him. At night, he watched over him while he slept, and had saved Eazal's life from beasts and highwaymen by waking him with a sharp peck. Eazal had come to trust the boy, and with trust came a listening ear.

Slowly, the emptiness of his life filled with the spirit's unwavering resolve, and he'd taken Azhi's task as his own.

Only when he'd accepted the call had Azhi given him the visions. He showed him the things he'd seen of Taozu's past comings: the great rent in the earth south of Avvad's provinces; the lake that had once been filled with blood in the Bali highlands; the vast, wasted empire of the Wumofu Desert. All, Azhi had claimed, had the Corrupted to thank for their destruction. And the same ancient spirit who would inevitably claim the whole of the world — unless something was done to stop him.

Then he'd told Eazal what he meant to do, and how he needed Eazal to do it.

And so Eazal had traveled northeast to the far reaches of the Four Realms, where the Qao Fu cavern-cities marked the edge of civilization. Then they'd pushed past even that boundary, out into the Wumofu Desert, despite all the warnings they'd received. *Only the Yusishu could walk the path,* they'd told him, *before the last went and never returned.* Eazal had his own misgivings looking at the forbidding desert. But Azhi had told him not to fear. He'd walked this path before and would lead Eazal true. Trusting him as he'd trusted him many times before on their sojourn, Eazal had packed water and supplies for five days, then walked into the desert with only the spirit to guide him through it.

All was calm and quiet around him as he walked. But Azhi spoke of a different time in his mind. *The wind never ceased,* he was saying. *Only by wearing veils woven by a lost art could one travel the desert. An endless storm, deep at the heart of the old empire, drove those gales howling through the rest of the Wumofu.*

Eazal listened as he walked without replying. The spirit's voice had grown stronger as they continued their journey. When they'd reached the Qao Fu caverns, he had spoken to Eazal directly for the first time rather than through the whisper finch. Why he could suddenly speak into his mind, the boy didn't have an answer. Yet they had been through much together. To doubt him now would be folly. He had to trust that the spirit would bring him through this task alive, as he had done through the rest of this journey.

This hidden road was called the Ancestor's Path in those times, Azhi was saying. *The spirits of our dead kin would sing the path to the one who walked it, if they had ears to hear. I kept my mind open to their calls for days as I walked, for to shut out the ancestors would be to lose your way, and to become lost meant certain death.*

Azhi went quiet for a moment. Eazal wished he had found another point in his tale to cease speaking. The reminder of death was the last thing he needed in this forsaken place. He sighed and rolled his aching shoulders. He was far too old to be plodding up dune after dune, taking two steps where one would have served on firmer ground. He wondered what he was even doing here, traveling this desolation. Why had he let the boy convince him this was necessary?

Look, the boy said suddenly. *Look to the horizon ahead, and tell me what you see.*

Eazal obliged, though without interest. As he'd expected, he saw nothing. The air was hazy with heat. Mirages were commonplace; he'd seen enough false watering holes now to know that much. Perhaps even a spirit's eyes could be fooled.

He began to tell Azhi as much when the words died on his lips. At the top of his vision, something projected from the blue sky. It was faint with haze, but it didn't disappear as Eazal blinked. The mirages had always been near the desert floor where the heat's movement was greatest. And this was no watering hole. It looked like a multitude of pale fingers scratching against the sky.

"What is that?" he asked, his dry tongue moving thickly around his mouth.

Our destination. The place where we will recover what was lost long ago. And, by it, we will seal Famine away once more.

≈

It took all the rest of that day to reach it. Eazal had watched with unceasing awe as what looked like an impossibly gargantuan tree emerged from the sky. Its bark was gray, though Azhi claimed it had once been white as fresh-fallen snow.

My ancestors bound Famine in this place. For a thousand years, the one named the Yusishu would walk the Ancestor's Path to here, the Chains, and sacrifice themselves in order for him to remain bound. The Yusishu were lauded and praised, so much so that it was an honor every child dreamed of attaining themselves. Children cannot comprehend the end of their lives. They only saw the glory in it, the offerings left to them before their journey, and the statues carved of them afterward. They didn't understand what the sacrifice truly meant.

Eazal listened, thinking it strange that the boy spoke as if he were not himself a child. But then again, the spirit had no doubt existed for years. He was likely older than Eazal, though he'd not said so one way or another. The way he spoke of events in a distant past betrayed his age. By now, Azhi was much less a child than Eazal himself, no matter the youthfulness of the voice in his head.

Finally, their long walk came to an end. Reaching the base of the Chains, Eazal stared at it. The trunk was as thick around as the Ten-Tiered Bazaar, the greatest of Oedija's markets. Its bark, if it were truly bark, was as smooth as stone and as textureless as still water. For some reason, Eazal was loathe to come nearer to it. Something about the structure seemed strange and malevolent. This was as much a product of magic as anything he'd seen. Surely, only the gods themselves could grow such a tree.

Suddenly, a wind whipped up from the ground next to him, swirling the sand into a small squall. Eazal flinched and stepped away. There'd been no wind in all the desert; why would a gust rise now? The wind didn't die away, but seemed to lazily float through the air, resolving into a strangely human form. Lips formed of gray sand smiled at Eazal. A chill ran down his spine as he stared at the desert spirit.

"Hello, Eazal," a familiar boy's voice said. It had a strange echo to it, but Eazal couldn't mistake its owner.

"Azhi?"

The figure twisted his sand-shaped head to look at the great tree. "Our worlds are closer here. The Chains anchors them together. Here, I can almost be as I was in life." The spirit looked back to him with swirling gray eyes. "I admit, sometimes, I miss it."

Eazal couldn't explain the fear that stirred in his stomach. He wished they could be away from this strange tree. "This place makes me uneasy. Where is this thing we must retrieve?"

Azhi didn't respond for a long moment. Then he turned and floated over the gray to the base of the mammoth tree. "It is somewhere here, buried under the sands. But if the storm died after Famine departed, it shouldn't be buried deep. Stand back and cover your eyes."

Eazal obeyed, putting both hands over his face. A moment later, sediment whipped against him, the force of it stinging the exposed skin on the back of his hands.

"Here," Azhi said softly. "Come see it."

He dropped his hands and reluctantly walked up to stand next to the sand spirit. At the bottom of a small pit, the smooth, white shaft of a scepter was exposed. It looked like the femur of a long-dead creature. Though it didn't appear notable to his eyes, it was apparently the object of their quest.

Still, Eazal hesitated to reach for it. "That is the Binding Ruyi?"

"Yes. The scepter that once kept Famine sealed away for a millennium, and may do so once again. Will you take it, Eazal? Will you do what I, a spirit with no mortal hands, cannot? Will you help stop Taozu from consuming the rest of the world?"

Eazal sighed out heavily. He'd trusted Azhi this far. No matter his discomfort, he had to see this through. And why else had he come here? He hadn't walked a thousand miles to turn aside from his duty.

Or from his redemption.

"I'll do what I can," he spoke, almost to himself.

He eased his aching body down into the pit, sliding along it and barely avoiding stepping on the scepter at the bottom. Clinging to the eroding walls around him, he reached out and gripped the scepter, then pulled. It came free easily, as if the sand wished to be rid of it. Eazal lifted it before his eyes. The haft was smooth, and all of it was as white as bone. The end curved into the head of a threatening snake, its mouth open wide to strike, four long fangs protruding forth. As eerie as it had seemed above, it now seemed a small, delicate thing for such a large task. Could this elegant scepter possibly do what Azhi claimed?

"I have it," he said. "I'm bringing it back out."

He turned back to climb out of the pit. He didn't see Azhi standing above and wondered where he'd gone as he studied his escape. The walls eroded before his touch, but the pit wasn't very deep. If he scrambled quickly, he could ascend it. He set his exhausted limbs to the task, taking care not to crush the scepter as he climbed.

It struck his mind, quick and deadly as a viper.

Agony as he'd never known burst through him. For a moment, he lost hold of his senses. He couldn't tell if he screamed or if his limbs writhed. All his mind was filled with it. Desperately, he sought an end, but wave after wave washed over him.

Why? he cried out. *Why must I suffer more?*

As abruptly as it had come, the pain eased. Eazal slowly came back to his senses. But something felt wrong. Though he could feel the rough touch of the sand against his face, the breath rattling in his lungs, the exhaustion in his limbs, something felt broken.

For no matter how he commanded his body, he couldn't even twitch his eyelid.

Then his body moved of its own power, rising onto one elbow. "This body is heavier than I would have thought," Eazal's own lips muttered as he awkwardly pulled at the sand. His body moved as if for the first time. As if it had forgotten how.

The truth struck him as hard and sudden as the pain had. He tried to scream, but he couldn't form the words. He felt the muscles of his face tighten, but it wasn't his words that came out.

"I am sorry," his mouth spoke. He felt the other presence move his tongue even as he heard the words. "I did not wish to do this, Eazal. You must believe me. But time is too short to hesitate."

Every part of him roared against this intrusion. His own body, taken and controlled against his will! Like an animal in a cage, he battered what was left of himself against the invisible walls that penned him in— or tried to. But as he sought his boundaries, he found he couldn't understand his prison. There seemed nothing binding him, yet no way free. His anger melded into horror as he ceased to struggle.

A daemon possessed him. Azhi, whose purpose he had taken as his own, whom he'd trusted with his life, had seized his body.

Eazal's lips again spoke unbidden words. "Once, long ago, another spirit sought to do to me what I have done to you. She failed, and in doing so, allowed Famine to break free." His head bowed forward against the sand. "No. That is denying my part in it. I let her whispers of glory manipulate me into believing I was something I knew I was not. I let myself believe that I had a greater part to play in the world, one only I could perform. In a way, she was right. I did have a part to play, great and terrible. For it was I who let Famine loose. And in doing so, it was I who doomed the Lower and Higher Planes both.

"So it must be I who rectifies this, Eazal. And to do so, I must have a body. I hope you will come to understand. I won't harm you, nor your body, as much as I can prevent it. And when the task is complete, I will give it back to you so that you may live out your days in peace. Trust me as you have trusted me this whole journey. I did not lie when I spoke of the importance of this task. The danger to both of our worlds is the same. Taozu, Famine — he has come again, and will consume everything if he is not stopped. I ask no more sacrifice of you than I have given myself."

Eazal had ceased to struggle. It was futile. The daemon had an iron hold on him now. He could do nothing but listen to the boy's lies, trapped in his own flesh.

"I can feel him, Eazal. Can you? He has broken free of the Yusishu who yoked him. Vusumuzi, a man of more strength than I have ever seen before, has finally succumbed to his struggle. And in doing so, he has fed the Dragon enough so that he can once again hunt. His presence cuts across the Higher Plane as he seeks worthy prey. It will not be long before he grows powerful enough to break free into your world. And when he does, I fear it will be for the final time."

Eazal's arm raised the Binding Ruyi before his eyes. His gaze traveled up its length. "We must find the Corrupted before that happens," Azhi spoke through him softly. "We must seal him away, forever if we can. I hope we will do it together, Eazal."

Eazal didn't try to reply. If he was trapped, he wouldn't assuage the daemon's conscience, if one could exist in such a creature. He tucked himself small into the dark corners of his body where he remained. He'd watch and wait for his moment.

Then he'd take back what was his, no matter the cost.

Azhi made him sigh. "Brace yourself, my friend. I have shown you much. But now you will see all."

Eazal had channeled before, when Valem's curse first manifested in him. He had felt the power of the Molten God run through his veins to burn at the single toe that showed his mark. But what he had felt then was but a fraction of the power that filled him now. As energy carved its way into him, he thought he would burn away before it.

Azhi raised Eazal's arm with the scepter in it, then cut it sharply down in front of him. A tear appeared in the air before them. Eazal stared at it, numb with fear, wondering at what he witnessed.

The daemon hauled his body up, reaching for the tear in the world. It swirled with shifting colors and light like a pool formed of pyrkin. He extended Eazal's hand toward it.

It was too much. Eazal threw himself at his cage again, begging Azhi not to touch it. He knew such magic must destroy him.

As his finger brushed the substance of the other realm, it seized him. Eazal felt himself pull away, then leave the world behind.

GLOSSARY

Avvad, or the Avvadin Imperium - The ever-expanding empire that lies to the south of Oedija.

Bali - The people who reside among the plateaus to the east of Oedija.

The Four Realms - Considered the last bastions of civilization in a backwards world, four nations are united in peace by a concordance. These nations are: Oedija, the Bali ishakas, the Qao Fu jaitin, and the Avvadin Imperium.

Honors - The lowest caste of Oedijan society. They are not permitted to own property, including money, nor choose their own employment, and are often housed and work within the estates of patricians. Honors are the descendants of the Kalthuae, the native inhabitants of the lands Oedija now claims, before settlers sailed from the west to found the nation.

Ishakas - The tribal kingdoms of the Bali people.

Jaitin - The matriarchal groups of the Qao Fu people; grouped by the caves in which they reside.

Oedija - The "Pearl of the Four Realms"; the primary location of the story. A republican society undergoing significant turmoil, with threats from within and without.

Qao Fu - The people who reside among the desert caves to the northeast of Oedija.

Tefra - Priests of Avvad who use Silks, or bound spirits, to fight on their behalf.

Servants - The elected leaders of Oedija, with semi-proportional representation from across Oedija's ten demes. They number one-hundred and twenty-one, minus those Servants who are elected to the Demos Council. They are responsible for legislative actions.

The People's Conclave - The legislative body of Oedija. Within their parameters lies the making and governance of laws, the taxing and determination of the treasury, the governance of commerce, and the defense of the nation.

Demotism - A system of democratic republicanism in which representative officials are elected by citizens, or landowners, into a legislative ruling body.

Demos Council - The ruling council within the People's Conclave. Traditionally, it numbers eleven Low Consuls, with the Archon acting as a moderator, though often, the eleventh seat is disputed. Their responsibilities largely lie in determining the agenda within the larger Conclave. In times of strife, however, they are granted powers of military action and broad budgetary powers.

Low Consuls - The members of the Demos Council. Low Consuls are elected from the Conclave, requiring the support of ten of their fellow Servants to gain a seat.

Archon - The representative of the Despot or Despoina within the People's Conclave and Demos Council. Their powers are primarily limited to moderation, except when a member is missing on the Demos Council or a tie vote must be broken.

Demes - Districts of the city of Oedija.

Prefectures - Areas of governance across Oedija's countryside.

The Peninsula - A rural area of Oedija to the north of the city of Oedija.

Finches (as a title) - Hunters and peddlers of secrets. While in purpose, their mission is to expose wrongdoing and uncover hidden truths, in practice they often perform small jobs recovering and threatening others with incriminating information for those who will pay.

Order of Verifiers - A branch of Oedija government tasked with routing out corruption. It was disbanded a few years after its founding, and a century before Airene of Port fashions herself after them.

Verifiers, or Verifiers of Truth - Members of the Order of Verifiers, who were tasked with routing out corruption in Oedija's government, and were met with often violent resistance.

The Underguild - A semi-legitimized criminal organization. Overseen by five Guildmasters, the Underguild has a great hold over criminal activity in Oedija, and is largely responsible for its relatively low crime.

Guilders - People who work on behalf of the Underguild.

The Despot/Despoina - The Ruling Wreath; a symbolic ruler who acts as a figurehead for Oedija. Small powers as the official emissary of Oedija and the nominal leader of Oedija's militia (when marshaled).

The Wreaths - The royal family of Oedija, formerly the true rulers of the nation when it was a monarchy.

Taxoi (s. taxos) - The militia of Oedija. As Oedija has no standing army, the taxoi are organized and financed by patrician households whenever the need arises.

Stratechons - The five permanent military leaders of Oedija. Responsible for the city guard and the taxoi (when they are gathered).

Valemism / The Valemish - Worshippers of the volcanic god Valem, the religion of Valemism began in Avvad. It is considered a strict religion with a heavy emphasis on subjugation and obedience to authority, and the punishments for disobedience.

Wardens - People who are attuned to the Pyrthae and are able to manipulate forms of energy as magic. Across the Four Realms, they are forced into hiding, killed, lauded, and enslaved, depending on the nation. In Oedija, they are feared and kept to specific roles, such as Acadians or Shepherds, that suppresses their freedom and use of their abilities.

Energetic elements - The forms of energy present in the Pyrthae. Three energetic elements are commonly known: radiance, or heat and light; kinesis, or force; and magnesis, or the fields of magnetism. Other energetic elements are believed to exist, but are unconfirmed.

Hilarion - The jester to the Despot or Despoina. Hilarion is always chosen from among Oedija's male wardens. Traditionally, he wears a crown of wheat, sackcloth clothes, and sandals bound with rope. Hilarion's nominal purpose is to entertain at the whim of the Ruling Wreath, but his true purpose is understood to be to diminish fear that people hold for wardens by making him an object of laughter and ridicule.

First Laurel - The leader of the laurel guard, the soldiers defending the Laurel Palace and other Wreath properties.

The Confessionary Tribunal - The judicial branch of Oedija's government, they are responsible for enforcing the rule of law, including the containment and punishment of rogue wardens. They are not elected, but are recruited by their own.

Tribunes - Members of the Confessionary Tribunal, they act as arbiters of Oedija's justice.

Shepherds - Members of the Confessionary Tribunal, they act under the guidance of a Tribune to contain or punish any rogue warden.

The Acadium - Nominally, the center of learning and education within Oedija. The Acadium serves a dual purpose, however: the reeducation and containment of wardens.

Acadians - The scholarly residents of the Acadium; often, they are wardens. While not all Acadians are wardens, any warden caught are forced to become an Acadian, or face the penalty of death.

Eidola - The gods of the Eidolan religion.

Eidolanism - The religion of the original settlers of Oedija, in Airene's time, it is a fading religion, with many of its beliefs considered antiquated.

The Pyrthae - The plane of spirits, which is said to run parallel to the material plane, Telae.

Telae - The material plane; or, the world as it is known, including The Four Realms.

Pyrkin - A moss-like substance that is considered somewhere between plant and animal, it is supposed to have a connection to the Pyrthae, on account of its bioluminescence.

Pyr - Spirits who are considered either benevolent or innocuous.

Daemons - Spirits who are considered evil or mean-spirited; also a derogatory term for wardens.

OEDIJAN SOCIETY

SOCIAL HIERARCHY

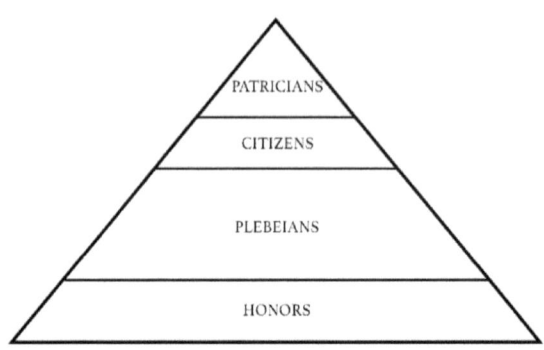

POLITICAL ORGANIZATION

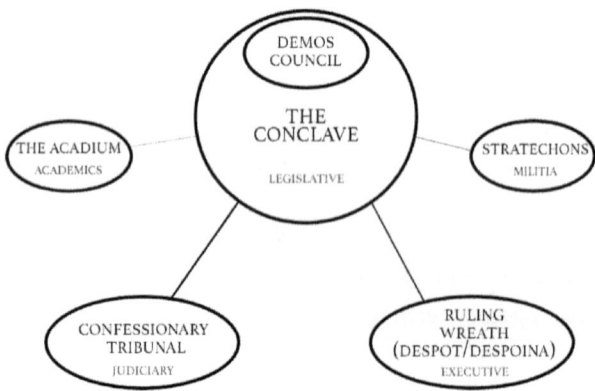

ACKNOWLEDGMENTS

A brief, but no less heartfelt, thank you to…
Kaitlyn — my partner, first reader, and voice of reason.
René Aigner — for his fantastic cover illustration.
Friends and family — for your constant support.
And, of course, you, dear reader.

BOOKS BY J.D.L. ROSELL

Sign up for future releases at jdlrosell.com.

THE FAMINE CYCLE

1. Whispers of Ruin

2. Echoes of Chaos

3. Requiem of Silence

Secret Seller *(Prequel)*

The Phantom Heist *(Novella)*

LEGEND OF TAL

1. A King's Bargain

2. A Queen's Command

3. An Emperor's Gamble

4. A God's Plea

THE RUNEWAR SAGA

1. The Throne of Ice & Ash

2. The Crown of Fire & Fury

3. The Stone of Iron & Omen

GODSLAYER RISING

1. Catalyst

ABOUT THE AUTHOR

J.D.L. Rosell is the author of the Legend of Tal series, The Runewar Saga, The Famine Cycle series, and the Godslayer Rising trilogy. He has earned an MA in creative writing and has previously written as a ghostwriter.

Always drawn to the outdoors, he ventures out into nature whenever he can to indulge in his hobbies of hiking and photography. Most of the time, he can be found curled up with a good book at home with his wife and two cats, Zelda and Abenthy.

Follow along with his occasional author updates and serializations at www.jdlrosell.com or contact him at authorjdlrosell@gmail.com.